PAMELA TAYLOR

THE REST OF HIS DAYS

Black Rose Writing | Texas

This is a work of fiction. Names, characters, businesses, places, events, and incidents are either the products of the author's imagination or used in a fictitious manner. Any resemblance to actual persons, living or dead, or actual events is purely coincidental.

ISBN: 978-1-68513-395-5
LIBRARY OF CONGRESS CONTROL NUMBER: 2023948140
PUBLISHED BY BLACK ROSE WRITING
www.blackrosewriting.com

Printed in the United States of America
Suggested Retail Price (SRP) $22.95

The Rest of His Days is printed in Garamond Premier Pro

*As a planet-friendly publisher, Black Rose Writing does its best to eliminate unnecessary waste to reduce paper usage and energy costs, while never compromising the reading experience. As a result, the final word count vs. page count may not meet common expectations.

To Gregory

You may not be a reader, but you help me believe I'm a writer.

*It is recorded that in the year of Our Lord MCCCXXVII on the 21st day of
September, Edward of Caernarfon, until earlier in that year, king of
England, was murdered at Berkeley Castle in Gloucestershire. He was buried
in Gloucester Cathedral on the 20th day of December.*

*For five hundred fifty years, this was the undisputed history
of the fate of Edward II of England.*

*Then, in 1878, a letter was discovered that claimed otherwise.
It was found in a cartulary belonging to the bishop of Maguelonne in France.
A letter to Edward III from Manuele Fieschi, a priest and papal notary.
The authenticity of this letter is not in question. Nor is the fact that it is
contemporaneous with the events described. Its veracity, however,
remains a matter of debate among historians.*

What if the Fieschi letter is true?

Capet Family Tree (France)

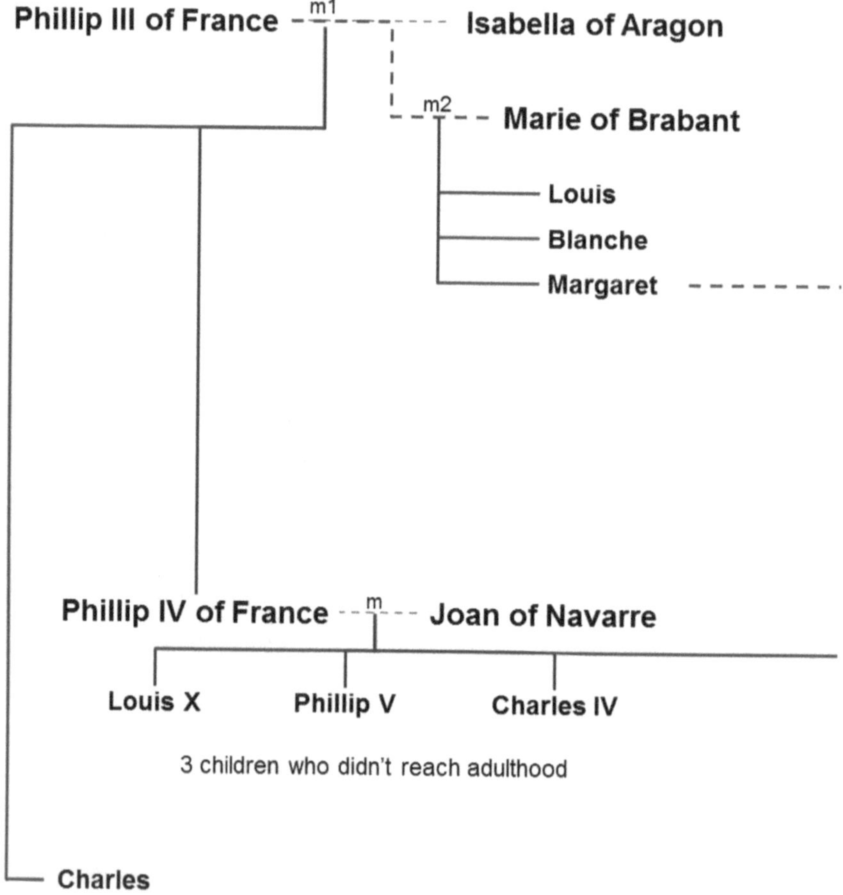

Plantagenet Family Tree (France)

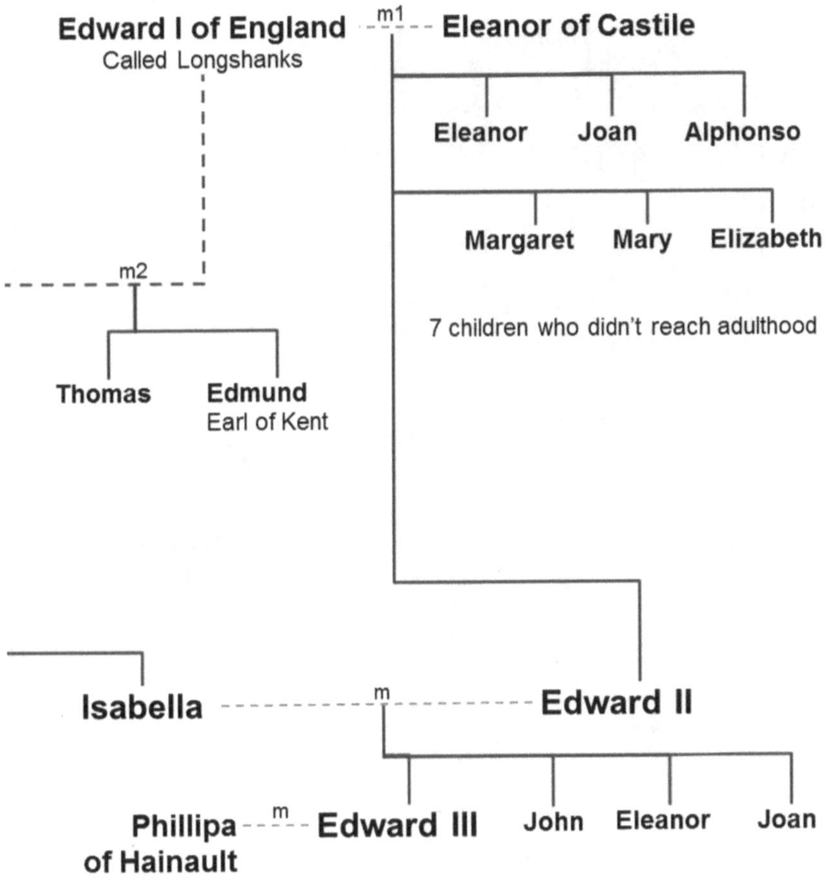

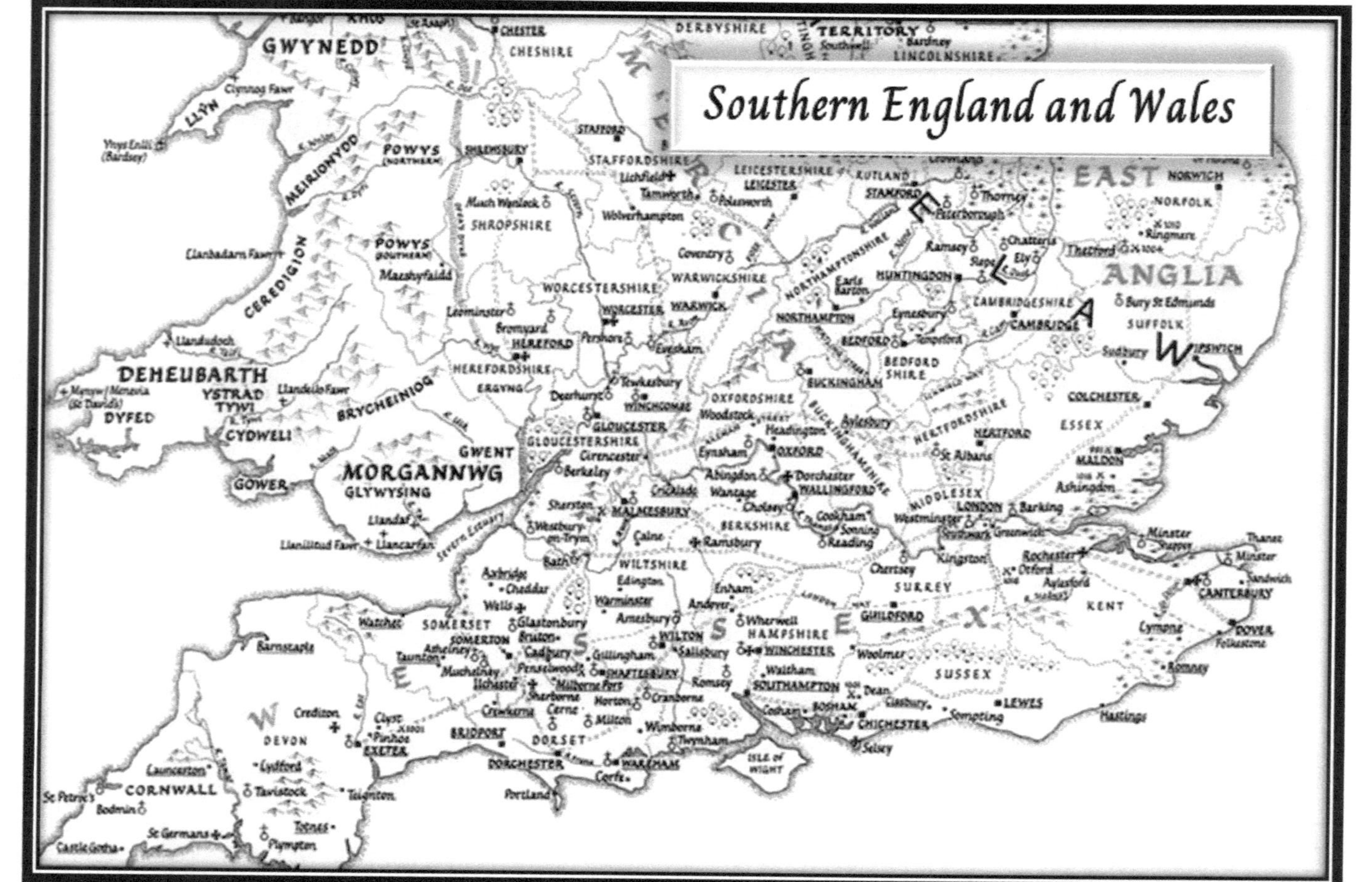

Southern England and Wales
GWYNEDD
POWYS (NORTHERN)
POWYS (SOUTHERN)
MEIRIONYDD
CEREDIGION
DEHEUBARTH
YSTRAD TYWI
DYFED
CYDWELI
BRYCHEINIOG
GWENT
MORGANNWG
GLYWYSING
GOWER
CORNWALL
DEVON
SOMERSET
DORSET
WILTSHIRE
HAMPSHIRE
BERKSHIRE
OXFORDSHIRE
GLOUCESTERSHIRE
HEREFORDSHIRE
WORCESTERSHIRE
SHROPSHIRE
CHESHIRE
STAFFORDSHIRE
DERBYSHIRE
LEICESTERSHIRE
WARWICKSHIRE
NORTHAMPTONSHIRE
BEDFORDSHIRE
BUCKINGHAMSHIRE
HERTFORDSHIRE
MIDDLESEX
SURREY
KENT
SUSSEX
ESSEX
CAMBRIDGESHIRE
SUFFOLK
NORFOLK
RUTLAND
LINCOLNSHIRE
MERCIA
WESSEX
ESSEX
EAST ANGLIA
TERRITORY

THE
REST
OF HIS
DAYS

Chapter One

April 1327

"What now?" Sir Guy muttered as he strode up the slight rise from the stables. The servant who'd brought the message had been no help. "All I know is m'lord the earl wants to see you. And he said I'd best make haste to find you."

Sir Guy was a big man. Tall – when he stood beside his sixteen-hands destrier, the top of his head rose above the horse's withers – tall and well-muscled. In full armor and with his heaume in place, he was an imposing figure even before he cradled his lance and began the charge toward his opponent. Gossip among the squires said more than one opponent had veered away at the last minute to avoid a direct hit on the shield arm or the breastplate. Better to be unhorsed by a glancing blow and live to joust another day than to lose everything in the lists. Or so the gossip said.

Making his way past the keep, Guy entered the leftmost of the two new buildings in the castle compound. New being relative, of course. They were built when King John added the outer wall and expanded the mere, making Kenilworth well nigh impregnable. It was said that Henry III had undertaken some refurbishments when he took the castle back from Simon de Montfort after the siege in 1266, but it was Thomas – the present earl's predecessor – who was responsible for its current luxurious furnishings. And it was into the earl's own presence chamber that Sir Guy was shown.

"Ah, Bickerstaffe. They found you quickly, I see." Seated at his writing table, the earl acknowledged his visitor then rummaged among the papers in front of him, finally finding the right one and proffering it to Guy. "Read that."

> *My dear Lancaster,*
>
> *Our hopes have been dashed that the difficulties attendant on an attempted assault on Kenilworth would be sufficient to discourage those who might seek to free the personage we gave into your charge. Though we are grateful for your success in repelling the efforts of the Dominican and his brother, it now seems prudent to remove your charge to a different location.*
>
> *Two days before Palm Sunday, you may expect the arrival of our well-beloved Lord Berkeley and his companion, Sir John Maltravers. They are under orders to take custody of the aforementioned personage and convey him to his new permanent lodgings at Berkeley Castle. The men-at-arms who serve you as his guards are hereby ordered to render that service to Berkeley and Maltravers for as long as those two shall deem necessary.*
>
> *As from Palm Sunday, your stipend for the care and comfort of said personage is revoked, but you retain all other rights heretofore granted you by the Crown.*
>
> *Isabella R*

Affixed to the message was the king's privy seal. Finished reading, Sir Guy handed back the page without comment. "It seems I'm to be relieved of responsibility for the prisoner," said Lancaster. "Not a moment too soon for my liking. Let Berkeley have him." The earl folded the page and stowed it in a drawer of his table. "And all the problems that come with being both host and gaoler." He rose from his chair and began pacing to and fro in front of the hearth. "Comfortable captivity," he snorted. "*He's* comfortable, but I'm the one who feels like a captive."

"But at least, sir, you're free to come—" Sir Guy ventured to offer reassurance, but Lancaster cut him off.

"Free to come and go as I please? Spare me the platitude, Bickerstaffe. I daren't leave here lest some band of plotters steal him away in my absence."

"But isn't it *my* job to prevent that?"

"Your job, but my responsibility. God's bodkin, man, who do you think they'd throw in the Tower if their precious prisoner be stolen away? And what am I to do if a parliament is summoned? Stay here and lose my voice in matters of state? Or attend and risk losing a lot more than my voice?" His rant apparently exhausted, the earl returned to his seat behind the writing table. "Let Berkeley have him, I say. I'd rather live without the constant worry of who's hatching the next plot or what new wind's going to blow from Mortimer's arse. Berkeley should be immune from *that*, at least – or maybe accustomed to it," Lancaster allowed himself a chuckle at the idea, "given that he's Mortimer's son-in-law." Guy kept his expression neutral and his thoughts to himself.

"Looks like you aren't so lucky, Bickerstaffe. Tomorrow's Friday. God knows when they'll arrive, so you don't have much time to get your men organized. Best get to it then. I'll inform our guest." The earl waved his hand in dismissal, Guy's cue to leave.

Once outdoors and headed across the open lawn toward the old Norman keep where he and his men lodged, Sir Guy's frustration got the better of him. "***God's teeth***!" he exclaimed to no one in particular. *Why me? What dastardly sin did I commit that's landed me in this Purgatory on earth? Did I covet this knighthood so overly much that the moment I received it, I'm given the worst job in all of England?*

No sooner had the queen lifted the sword from his shoulder and said "Rise, Sir Guy" than she'd added, "Now, the first service I require from you is that you assemble a cadre of men-at-arms and proceed with all due haste to join the Earl of Lancaster and put yourself and your men at his disposal. The earl is even now making his way to Neath in Wales."

The only reply available to Sir Guy was a bow and a simple, "Yes, Your Grace." In the normal course of things, a newly minted knight didn't question the wishes of he – or she – who'd just elevated his rank in society. God knew that was the only ordinary thing about this whole situation.

That it was the queen who'd knighted him wasn't the first bizarre turn in this particular drama. That it was the queen who'd invaded her own kingdom was what had started it all. It had been – what? – over two and a half centuries since the last invasion, when William of Normandy put paid to the last Anglo-Saxon king and took the throne and the kingdom for himself. But a queen invading her own kingdom not to oust an occupier but in opposition to her own husband? That was passing strange indeed.

Nevertheless, London quickly rose up in support of Isabella. They'd had their fill of the Despensers, the king's current favorites and the objects of Isabella's fury. The Despensers were widely hated because of their theft of lands and extortion of merchants and nobles alike, general corruption, theft from the Treasury, and even – in the case of Hugh the Younger – piracy in the English Channel – none of which Edward made any effort to curtail. The Earl of Lancaster also threw his support to the queen the moment her forces landed on English soil.

Guy considered himself an upright and righteous man. Reverence for his God and loyalty to his king – in that order – formed the core of his beliefs and guided his every action. So the extraordinary turn of events was more than a little unsettling. But that was nothing compared to what happened once he caught up with Lancaster at Llanylted on the banks of the River Neath.

He was brought straight to the earl, who was poring over some sort of diagram with two other men. Guy cleared his throat, making his presence known, and the earl looked up. "Sir Guy Bickerstaffe, my lord, here at the behest of the queen with my men-at-arms."

To the other two, the earl said, "That'll be all for now. Just be sure your men are ready in the morning." Then he turned his attention to Guy and surveyed him from head to toe. "Bickerstaffe, you say?"

"Aye, my lord."

"How many men-at-arms?"

"Twenty, my lord."

"Good. And just in time." The earl snapped his fingers, and the last two men in the tent – presumably servants – scurried out, leaving Guy and Lancaster alone. "Sit," said the earl, pointing to a stool beside the small camp table. It was more an order than an invitation. He took the only chair for himself. "Do you know why you're here?"

"All I know is that I'm to put myself and my men at your disposal, sir."

"Very well. On the morrow, we take the king into custody. My information is that he's ready to put an end to the madness and come quietly. But I'm taking no chances. Even if *he's* ready, God knows what those around him think. That's why I have enough men here to suppress anything the force still inside Neath Castle might take it into their heads to do." He paused to take a sizable swallow of whatever was in the mug on the table.

"And we're to join with your men?" Guy felt a need to fill the silence.

"Quite the contrary. You're to stay out of the fray, if there is one. When we have the king's person secured, you're to take charge of him and get him safely to Monmouth. I'll stay here to deal with whoever's left, and then I have to go give evidence in the younger Despenser's trial, though the outcome of that is a foregone conclusion. For now, if word gets out that the king has surrendered, his supporters are going to assume he's with me, so they'll pay little or no attention to your small band headed east. Your route will, of necessity, put you in the vicinity of Abergavenny Castle. You should have nothing to fear from them – the baron is married to one of Mortimer's daughters – but avoid drawing attention to yourselves anyway."

"And once we reach Monmouth, sir?"

"Wait there for me. Keep the king under guard. Choose a couple of servants to tend to his needs and provide food. But, Bickerstaffe, the queen's orders are that he's *not* to be harmed – only to be confined to the premises with no access to anyone I haven't personally approved. And so far, I haven't approved anyone but you."

In the end, the journey was uneventful, but that didn't mean Sir Guy wasn't on edge for the entire two and a half days. What surprised him was just how compliant the king was. Subdued even. And later, at Monmouth – after Lancaster had joined them – when the queen sent her envoy to fetch the king's privy seal so she could rule in his name, Edward handed it over willingly. Yet another peculiarity in this drama of the bizarre.

Guy had asked Lancaster about it. "He's trying to win her back," said the earl. "Doing his best to convince her that he's put the Despensers behind him and wants them to rule together as king and queen. Though if you ask me, I don't think there's much chance of that now that she's with Mortimer."

Whether it was Mortimer's influence or Isabella's own reluctance to take another chance – after all, Edward had behaved himself for a time after Piers Gaveston's execution until the Despensers came on the scene – Lancaster's prediction was prescient. Parliament, sitting at Wallingford, deposed the king in favor of his fourteen-year-old son, who was crowned Edward III, with his mother as regent. That same Parliament acceded to Isabella's insistence that her husband come to no harm and declared that he should live "in comfortable captivity" for the rest of his natural life.

England had never deposed a king before – kings died of disease or in battle – and no one knew quite what to do with him. But Kenilworth was generally reckoned one of the most unassailable places in the kingdom, so Lancaster wound up with the short end of the staff. And Sir Guy wound up in the unenviable position of showing loyalty to his new king by serving as prison warden to the old one.

Finding no one on the ground floor of the keep, Sir Guy dashed up the steps to the first floor where a few of his men not on duty were tending to their weapons. "New orders, men," he announced. "We're moving the prisoner again. Tomorrow. Jump to it and get the troop ready for the journey."

"Not *again*," Aldwin, the senior man-at-arms, complained. "Don't they know every minute on the road is a chance for someone to grab him?"

"Ours not to reason why, Aldwin."

"Where to this time?"

"Berkeley Castle. Lord Berkeley's arriving sometime tomorrow. Our orders are to put ourselves at his disposal."

"Why Berkeley? It's no safer than here."

"Mortimer's doing, I suspect. Lancaster is Isabella's man . . . and Edward's first cousin. Mortimer probably wants his own man in charge." Sir Guy paused and looked around the room. "Where's Will?"

Aldwin shrugged. "Haven't seen him since we came off duty at midday. I'd wager he's off drinking in the village."

"Aye," chimed in a man in the far corner of the room. "Taken quite a fancy to that new barmaid, he has."

Guy tried not to grimace. "Alright, Aldwin. Send someone to fetch him back."

"Begging your pardon, sir, but if you really want him back, you'd best fetch him yourself. He'd just tell any of us to go take a leap into the mere. And he's *your* cousin, after all."

"Second cousin," Guy growled. "Alright, I'll go. But I want to see everything ready when I get back." He spun on his heel and stormed down the stairs. "***God's bollocks***, what else could go wrong today?" he raged at the empty courtyard. *That's going to cost me more than a couple of Hail Marys,* Guy thought. *At least no one heard me. Maybe I don't have to confess to the priest exactly how I took the Lord's name in vain. Of course, I wouldn't put it past him to ask.*

But Aldwin was right. Will Makepeace went his own way and didn't give much of a damn what anyone else thought. *Will Maketrouble, more like,* thought Guy. *What in God's name were his parents thinking when they named him William? Didn't they know people would call him Will?*

And what was I thinking when I made him part of this troop? About your promise to his mother, Guy reminded himself. *You swore on her deathbed you'd look after him. If only I'd known what I was signing up for.*

CHAPTER TWO

It wasn't the barmaid Will had come to see today, though he was at pains to ensure that's what everyone believed, giving her backside a pat when she served them and eyeing her up and down whenever she passed by. No, it was the man across the table draining the last drop of ale from his mug who was the reason for Will's presence.

Will had known Simon since they were boyhood friends in London, where Will's father, a master mason, was involved in the New Work – the eastward extension – at St. Paul's Cathedral. Simon's father was a man-at-arms in Edward Longshanks's service. Shortly after Will's eleventh birthday, his father was invited to come work on raising the tower and spire at Salisbury Cathedral. It was exceedingly dangerous work, but the wages were an astonishing six pennies a day. So the family immediately packed up and moved west.

The lads' paths didn't cross again until Will wandered into the bar at the inn not long after his arrival at Kenilworth and noticed what seemed like a vaguely familiar face drinking alone at a table by the small window on the far side of the room. While he waited for the landlord to pour his mug of ale, Will inclined his head toward the window and asked, "Who's that man over there?"

"Been staying here the last couple of nights. Says he's from Gloucester but he's pretty close-mouthed about his business. Keeps to himself and doesn't cause any trouble . . . pays his room and board every day. That's all I care about."

Will put half a farthing on the bar, picked up his mug, and wandered across the room. "Care to join me?" the man asked when Will approached. "Best spot in the place. I come early to claim it before the others get here."

Setting his mug on the table, Will asked, "Do I know you?"

"I hope you do . . . because for certes I know you. You haven't changed a bit. Well . . . become a man and all . . . but I'd know that face anywhere, Will Makepeace." He rose from the table and spread his arms wide. "It's me. Simon. Simon Forster." The open arms became a bear-hug as Simon went on with his exuberant greeting. A bit over-exuberant to Will's way of thinking, but Simon had always been the more gregarious of the two. Releasing his friend at last, Simon added, "Sit, sit."

Will took a big swallow from his mug. "Well, this is certainly unexpected."

"Indeed," said Simon. "When we said farewell in London, I was sure I'd never see you again. What have you been doing with yourself?"

"Threads and thrums. Never had Pa's talent with the stones, so I just picked up whatever bits of work I could find until my cousin came along and took me on as a man-at-arms. That was last autumn, not long after Ma died. We're in service to the Earl of Lancaster. What about you? You look rather prosperous."

"Wasn't long after you left that my father got assigned to Edmund of Woodstock's household. Edmund was complaining about not having a companion his own age, so Father put me forward. The prince took to me straightaway. Even made up a title for me – Companion of the Privy Chamber. And that's what I've been ever since. We get on well enough, so I'm content with the arrangement. When his brother created him Earl of Kent, he was granted Gloucester Castle and that's where we spend a lot of time now. I'm just passing through on the earl's business."

Over the next two hours, they'd reestablished their acquaintance and made plans to meet again two weeks later when Simon said he'd once again be passing through. That turned out to be a very different sort of meeting.

They exchanged the usual pleasantries over the first mug of ale, but when the barmaid left after pouring their refills, Simon hunched over the table and lowered his voice. "There's something I want to ask you, Will, but it's best not overheard. That's another reason I like this table, see. Here in this nook by the window, it's far enough away from the rest to make eavesdropping difficult. Anyway . . ." He paused as Will put his forearms on the table and leaned forward. "Edmund knows his half-brother Edward is at Kenilworth. Hell, everyone of any importance knows that. What he doesn't know is how his brother fares . . . if the comfortable captivity ordered by Parliament is being observed. And he'd like to hear about his brother from time to time. Mortimer and the queen – Mortimer, in particular – are suspicious of anyone who shows too much interest in the former king. So Edmund dare not make his own interest known."

"So how does this concern me?" asked Will.

"You're part of Sir Guy's troop, right?"

Will hesitated then nodded his head. How did Simon know this?

"So that probably means you come into Edward's presence from time to time."

"As a guard, but hardly to have a chat."

"Ah, but you know the servants who wait on him, I presume."

Will was growing suspicious. Where was this going? He took a long draught of ale.

"All Edmund wants is a way to get news of his brother from time to time without running afoul of Lancaster or Mortimer," Simon supplied the answer.

"So you're asking me to take that risk instead?"

"No risk to you, as I see it. You have a couple of mugs of ale with a childhood friend whenever he's passing through. How could anyone be suspicious? Especially since the landlord witnessed our joyful reunion a couple of weeks back."

Now the pieces were falling in place for Will. That reunion was no serendipity at all. Simon had carefully contrived it. And his exuberance was less for Will's benefit than for the landlord and everyone else in the bar that evening.

What if I agree? Will wondered. *Is this just the harmless first step down a path toward treason? I don't owe Simon anything. And I most certainly don't owe the Earl of Kent anything. On the other hand, Simon and I were inseparable as lads. Surely he wouldn't go out of his way to put me in jeopardy. But he could have changed over the years. Companion to a prince of the realm – that almost certainly changes a man's ideas of who his friends are.*

Noticing both mugs were empty, Will picked them up and walked to the bar. A chance for some more soul searching. Despite what everyone said, Will felt rather sorry for Edward of Caernarfon, as the former king was now known. He'd never been a remarkable king. Some said he never wanted to rule. And he hadn't been strong enough to recognize when other men were using him for their personal benefit. But Will liked the man. He was kind to his servants, tolerant of his guards, pious enough.

Will left a farthing on the bar, picked up the now-full mugs, and started back toward the table. *If you say yes, Will Makepeace,* he told himself, *then you have to be prepared to say no if this turns in a direction you dare not go. Even if that costs you Simon's friendship.* He placed the mugs on the table, perched on his stool, and took a long draught.

"You may tell your companion," Will spoke almost in a whisper, "that his brother is quite comfortable. He dines well, he walks about in the courtyard for exercise when the weather is fair, he attends chapel . . . all his wants are provided for."

"That is exceeding good news. Thank you, Will. And should you find yourself in a position to speak to Edward circumspectly, perhaps you might mention that his half-brother inquired after his health."

That had been almost four months ago. In the weeks since, Simon had brought news of growing support for Edward in various parts of England but was always adamant that the Earl of Kent was *not* involved in any plots. On one recent visit, though, he mentioned that Kent was coming to regret his earlier support for the queen and Mortimer. "In truth, not so much the queen," he added. "The Despensers had to go. But Mortimer's starting to take too much on himself – almost as if he believes *he's* the regent instead of the queen. Isabella reins him in from time to time, but how long will it be before she can no longer control him?"

Somewhere along the way, Will had realized that his best protection lay in being seen regularly in the bar, whether Simon was there or not. It was costing him far more of his wages than he really wanted to spend, but a man can't afford to count the cost of keeping his head firmly on his shoulders and his entrails safely inside his belly. It was also costing him Guy's goodwill. But the former king seemed to take comfort in the fact that one man among his guards actually took an interest in his welfare.

Now, Simon raised his empty mug in the air and waved it about to get the barmaid's attention. She wasted no time bringing the pitcher to pour him a refill. Will reached out his hand, intending to give her backside a squeeze, and she swatted it away. "You keep your hands to yourself, Will Makepeace. I've had quite enough of that for one day." Then she turned to him with an impish smile. "Unless you have something more in mind." She held out her hand. "You got a penny you're itching to spend?"

"Not if I have to keep buying drinks for this cheap bastard." Will laughed and dropped half a farthing in her hand for Simon's ale.

The impish smile turned to a broad grin. "About what I thought." She winked at Will then walked back to the bar with an exaggerated swing of her hips, obviously intended to arouse him – and every other man in the bar, for that matter.

"By God, she knows how to get under a man's skin," said Simon.

They both quaffed a rather large swallow of ale in an effort to shake off the distraction.

"As I was saying," Simon returned to the conversation they'd begun earlier, "after the failed attack on Kenilworth, the Dunheveds and their gang managed to avoid being caught. According to my sources, Friar Thomas is holed up in a Dominican priory somewhere and Stephen's gone to ground – no one has much of an idea where he might be. That doesn't mean they've given up. Just biding their time. You can be certain they'll try again."

No sooner had Simon finished the sentence than the room was bathed in a swath of sunlight as the door opened. Sir Guy stood there a moment, looking around the room, then shut the door behind him and strode directly to Will's table. "Come on, Will," he said. "It's time to go."

"At least let me finish my ale. I've already paid for it."

"Then down it quickly. I've got things for you to do." Guy stood with his arms crossed over his chest, his feet spread apart – the stance Will thought of as the stern father pose.

Normally, that would be enough for Will to do anything to avoid complying. It wasn't that he particularly liked provoking his cousin. It was just that, now and then, Guy could be so pompous and sanctimonious that Will couldn't help himself. But now was not the time. The last thing he needed was for his cousin to start asking questions about the man across the table. So he emptied his mug in two enormous gulps, rose from his stool, and started toward the door, calling "Good journey, my good fellow" over his shoulder as Guy fell into step with him.

Once they were outside and on the road to the castle, Will asked, "So what did you think of the barmaid?"

"What barmaid?"

"Oh, come on, Guy. You can't play coy with me. I saw you eye her from head to toe as we walked out of the bar. Pretty nice, eh? Enough to make any man's trousers bulge – even yours."

"Great God in heaven, I absolutely *despair* of you sometimes, Will Makepeace." It was obvious Guy was in no mood for humor. "And of late, you seem to be getting worse. Not a week goes by I don't get some report of you being off at the inn – sometimes twice in a week. Drinking and dallying with barmaids? What would your mother think?"

"And what's wrong with drinking and barmaids? I've got nothing else to spend my wages on. Besides, the ale at that inn's a far sight better than what they brew at the castle."

"Then I'll just have to pray that the ale where we're going is better and that there's a village bylaw that keeps locals out of the inn."

"If there is, I'm sure there'll be a tavern for the locals." As Guy's words finally registered, Will stopped in his tracks. "Wait a minute. What do you mean 'where we're going'?"

"That's why I came to fetch you. We're to move the former king again. Tomorrow. So you have to do your part to get ready."

"Tomorrow?" Will's tone was incredulous. "Where?"

"Berkeley Castle. It's a damn sight safer to keep him here, but the queen and her paramour seem to have other ideas. So move him we must."

They walked in silence the rest of the way to the castle, with Will contemplating that his offhand farewell to Simon was another parting that might be forever. Even worse, he had no way to let his friend know what was afoot.

***

It wasn't the barmaid Guy had turned back to look at but the man who'd been sitting across from Will. *Not someone from the village but from elsewhere*, Guy mused. *What was it Will had said? "Good journey, my good fellow?" What's Will doing consorting with strangers? The barmaid, for certes – at least that's what all the men say. Drinking with the locals – men he knows from the village. Hardly a worthwhile way for a man to spend his time or his money. But strangers?*

Utterly unable to comprehend Will's good-natured affability, Guy felt compelled to attribute purpose to everything his cousin did. After all, that's how he lived his own life – every thought, every deed, every spoken word chosen to preserve his honor and advance his position in life. So, what was Will up to?

Why would a stranger passing through have any interest in Will? Guy wondered. *Unless he knows Will's in my troop. And Will's so damn naïve he'd never recognize when someone was plying him for information that would be useful to the plotters.*

And then something else dawned on him. What if Will was actually in league with the plotters? Another reason to try to constrain his cousin's behavior. Maybe this move to Berkeley was a good thing after all.

***

Will needn't have worried about Simon learning about the move. As the procession passed by Gloucester Castle on Sunday, two men watched from the parapet. "It appears our informant was right," said Edmund. He and his companion watched in silence for another moment before he added, "Which leads me to wonder why your friend didn't mention this."

"The same thought occurred to me. And yet, on reflection, I don't think he knew. His conversation on Thursday was as forthcoming as always, and he seemed in no hurry to leave. It was Sir Guy who came to fetch him. Rather peculiar in and of itself. But the abrupt way he practically dragged Will out of the inn, speaking of duties to attend to, does lead one to think those at Kenilworth had only just learned of the move."

"Perhaps we shouldn't be surprised at that, Simon. Keeping the plan a closely held secret certainly reduces the chance of the wrong people getting wind of it."

They watched in silence as the carriage and its twenty armed escorts slowed as it approached the turn onto the Bristol road. "Isn't that Lord Berkeley's livery the coachmen are wearing?" asked Simon.

"Well spotted, my friend. So *that's* where they're taking him. An interesting choice. Something of an out corner of the realm. But is that safer? Or might it be even better suited to the scheming of those who would see him freed and returned to the throne?"

Uncertain if the earl really wanted to debate the question or if he was simply musing aloud, Simon held his tongue. And then a smile spread across Edmund's face. "You know, Simon, it may happen that I'll have business in Bristol sometime in the coming months."

CHAPTER THREE

Thanks to Edward's insistence on attending Palm Sunday mass, the travelers' departure from Gloucester had been delayed until almost midday. Sir Guy had breathed a huge sigh of relief when Lord Berkeley stood firm against going to the cathedral, where Edward would certainly be recognized and it would be impossible to keep him separated from the throngs. Even at the small church just inside the town walls, Guy noted that at least one of the worshippers appeared to have an inkling of the identity of the stranger in their midst. Fortunately, the solemnity of the service and a quick exit out a side door meant they were well on their way before anyone could start asking questions.

The late departure meant it would be impossible to reach their destination before sundown, but Guy decided this suited his purposes well. He'd been anxious about the arrival at Berkeley Castle – one could never know with any certainty exactly who or what might be lying in wait at any new destination. Now, though, he had an opportunity for more control over the situation.

They camped in an open field just south of the River Cam. When Guy judged that those in the big tent would have finished their evening meal, he presented himself at the open tent flap and waited patiently until there was a break in the lively conversation. Finally, Maltravers took notice. "Ah, Bickerstaffe. Don't just stand there – come in. Is something amiss?"

"Not at all, sir. I just need a private word with Lord Berkeley, if I may."

"No sooner said than done," Maltravers rose from his stool. "Come on, Caernarfon. Let's have a walk about the camp."

Berkeley intervened. "Better you two stay here, John. Sir Guy and I will do the walking."

He rose and strode through the tent flap as Guy stepped quickly aside to make way. Once they were out of earshot of anyone in the camp, Berkeley said, "Very well, Bickerstaffe, what's on your mind?"

"It's the arrival at your castle, sir. We've no idea what we'll find there, and I don't fancy the prospect we might have to fight our way in."

"Not sure that's likely. This has all been done quickly and quietly. I rather doubt the Dunheveds could have gotten wind of it in time."

"Be that as it may, sir, we haven't moved him successfully twice before this without taking all the possibilities into consideration."

"I presume you have a plan?"

"I do. Tomorrow, the prisoner should ride among my men, dressed as they are. I have his clothing from when we moved him previously. One of my men will ride in your carriage in his place. Anyone watching will still count only twenty men-at-arms – no change from the past three days. When we come to the turning to your castle, your carriage will veer off and go home. The rest of us will ride on toward Bristol, as if you've dismissed us and we're headed for a new posting. We'll go as far as Thornbury. Once the situation is known, my man in the carriage can ride to meet us with the news. If all's well, we'll have the prisoner safely inside your walls by midafternoon. If there's any reason we shouldn't return straightaway, you can send your instructions with my man."

"Well thought out, Bickerstaffe. But do you really think you can avoid having someone grab Caernarfon on your own any better than you could at my castle?"

"We've moved him twice before, sir. We know what we're doing – and so does he. I really think this is the safest choice."

Berkeley stroked his chin in thought and took a few steps forward so that his back was to Sir Guy. When he finally turned around, he strode purposefully back toward the camp and motioned for Guy to follow. "Alright, Bickerstaffe, we'll do it your way. But take care you don't lose him.

There'd be the devil and all to pay, and both our heads would be on the block. And make sure whoever you put in my carriage can be relied on to keep his ears shut during the journey and his mouth shut afterward."

"Aye, sir. The man who'll travel with you is my second cousin. He knows I'd have his hide for any indiscretion." Not to mention, he's the only one, besides myself, who's tall enough that having Edward replace him wouldn't stand forth.

In the event, Sir Guy's precautions, while prudent, were unnecessary. "Everything's quiet around the castle," Will reported when he caught up with them in the village of Rockhampton, where Edward had asked for a chance to pray at the Church of St. Oswald.

"Maybe when you arrived, but what about after?" Guy asked.

"I spent some time looking around. Even had a mug of ale at the village tavern." Will struggled mightily to suppress his amusement at his cousin's failed attempt to suppress his rage.

"*Christ on horseback*, Will. Can't I trust you to do **anything** but that you're not off drinking and carousing? What must Berkeley have thought?"

Will finally let his smile break through. "Come on, Guy. Where better to get a good feel for what's going on in a village than to listen to the talk in a tavern?"

"Alright," Guy conceded. "You've made your point. Apparently what you learned wasn't disturbing, else you wouldn't have caught up with us so quickly."

"Seems I was the first stranger anyone had seen thereabouts in months. Those who live there mostly serve the needs of the castle, and once they learned I was newly in service to the baron, they seemed to accept me as one of their own. Since folks traveling the Bristol Road rarely divert to the village unless they have business with Lord Berkeley, people there don't often get news from the outside world, so they were eager to ply me with questions." Will hesitated briefly but decided he couldn't resist tugging on Guy's strings. "I only got away after one mug of ale by promising to come back soon to drink with them again."

Guy gritted his teeth and held his exasperation in check. He wasn't ready to admit that Will's dissolute habits might actually prove useful, but this time, at least, they'd garnered the information he needed. "Very well, gather the men. As soon as our charge finishes praying, we mount up and head for our new home."

They rode into the inner ward of Berkeley Castle well before sundown. While the guards dismounted and headed to the stable and Sir Guy went in search of the baron, Edward remained in the saddle, surveying his surroundings. "So this, now, is where I'm to spend the rest of my days?" he asked of no one in particular.

Will approached, leading his mount. "I'll take your horse, sir." It's *my* horse, after all, he refrained from adding aloud. As Edward climbed down, Will added. "I'm sure Lord Berkeley will be here momentarily to show you to your quarters." *Not my idea of the proper way to greet either a guest or a prisoner*, he thought to himself, *but then who am I to question my betters*?

"You're a good man, Will Makepeace," said Edward, handing over the reins.

The two men stood in silence, alone in the middle of the courtyard, for what seemed to Will like an inordinately long time. At one point, he found himself thinking, *What if this portends the future? What if he and I are somehow inextricably bound together in God's plan?* But then he dismissed the thought out of hand. What could possibly link captive and guard, a highborn personage and a common man of little means and no real skill, one pious and educated, the other barely literate?

When Berkeley and Maltravers finally appeared, descending the steps from the keep, Will bowed his head briefly to Caernarfon and slowly led his horse away.

CHAPTER FOUR

As Whitsuntide approached, life at Berkeley Castle had settled into a routine. Will frequented the local tavern twice, sometimes three times a week. It wasn't because the barmaid was pretty. She might have been once, but what was almost certainly thirty summers had taken their toll. "She may not be much of a looker nowadays," one of the villagers had told Will, "but if ye've got a spare penny, by God she knows what a man needs." Will hadn't yet been tempted to find out for himself. The saucy little kitchen maid at the castle was more to his liking, though he hadn't yet convinced her to succumb to his charms. But that was only a matter of time, he was certain.

It wasn't the barmaid that brought Will to the tavern so often. Nor was it the ale, though what they served was more than passable. "We buy from the white monks at Kingswood Abbey," the landlord replied when Will asked if he had his own brewhouse. "Why trouble meself with the guilds and the sheriff when the monks' ale is good enough and their price is fair?"

No, what brought Will to the tavern was less the brewing of ale than any hint of the brewing of trouble. Even though he'd taunted Guy that his tavern habit was actually a good thing, Will had recognized long before becoming a man-at-arms that locals who frequented the taverns knew everything that was happening in the vicinity and that drink could lead any man to indiscretion.

Lately, it seemed as if Guy had come around to Will's way of thinking. He'd chide his cousin from time to time for dissolute habits, but the admonishments now seemed more for the benefit of the other men than for

Will himself. They still included enough oaths and shouting to leave no one in doubt of Guy's opinion of his cousin's behavior. That didn't keep the others from their own visits to the tavern now and again. But as Will observed, *their* goals were strictly to relieve the boredom of guard duty and to satisfy their carnal needs.

Not long after the feast day of Saint Pancras, Will was surprised to see a stranger sitting by the hearth. "No stranger to us," the landlord replied to Will's question. "That's Simple Dickon. Not right in the head, if you know what I mean. Wanders around the area. Shows up here from time to time."

"Does he have a home somewhere?" Will asked.

"Oh, he lives at the priory – least that's where he's supposed to live."

"Priory?"

"The black monks over at Leonard Stanley. But he says he gets tired of all the rules, so he just wanders away to be on his own for a bit. Goes to one village or farm or another. Then when he gets tired of doing for himself, he goes back to the priory 'til the rules get too much again. Haven't seen him here in . . . must've been a year or more. Didn't know if he was even still alive 'til he showed up yesterday."

"Any idea how he lives when he's out wandering?"

"Only what he does when he comes here. Helps in the stable, mucking out and such. Sleeps in the hay loft. I give him a bit of potage and some small ale of an evening. Sometimes he just sits for long spells in front of the last house at the edge of the village – like maybe he's looking for someone there. Mistress Maud says he goes away if she steps out the door. All passing strange, if you ask me. But then he's not right in the head."

"Does Mistress Maud know him?"

"Not that she'll say. She's the only wise woman hereabouts. Maybe when he was a young'un, his ma took him there looking to get his head straightened out."

"Seems kind of sad."

"Aye. That's why I give him a bit to eat. He never stays here long, mind you. Mark my word – he'll be gone afore Whitsunday."

Will had sampled his ale while he chatted with the landlord, and now, he picked up his mug and walked over to the table where Simple Dickon sat alone. "Alright if I sit here?" he asked. Dickon looked up from his bowl of potage and nodded. "The landlord tells me your name's Dickon." Another nod and then he returned his attention to the bowl. "Mine's Will."

It seemed like the conversation would end there, but Dickon eventually looked up again and studied Will's face. "Will."

"Aye. I'm a guard at the castle. See?" Will patted the dagger on his belt.

Dickon held out his hand, apparently wanting to examine the dagger. Uncertain if it was really a good idea – he had no idea if this man had a penchant for violence – Will nevertheless drew the dagger and laid it on the table between them. "Be careful. It's very sharp."

Dickon eyed the weapon closely, then grasped it by the grip and held it vertically. Touching the tip with the forefinger of his other hand, he smiled. "Sharp. Could kill a rabbit."

"That you could," said Will.

"Could kill a man."

Will wasn't sure he liked where this conversation was going, but he saw no malice in Dickon's eyes – only curiosity. "Aye. That's why guards have them. But I've never done that."

Dickon slowly returned the dagger to the table – like a jewel he didn't want to part with – placing it in exactly the same spot and the same position as Will had laid it. "Better to use for rabbit."

Smiling, Will returned the dagger to its sheath. "Yes, Dickon. Much better to use for a rabbit. After all, a man can eat a rabbit."

Dickon grinned. "I like rabbit. I like you, Will."

They sat in silence for a bit, Dickon finishing his potage and Will sipping his ale. When the bowl was empty, Dickon wiped his mouth on his sleeve and downed what was left in his mug. Pushing the empty vessels aside, he said, "You live in the castle?"

"Yes," Will replied.

"I sit and watch the castle sometimes. Guards on towers. You go to the top of towers?"

"Now and then." Will didn't have regular sentry duty, but he'd ventured up to the towers once or twice to admire the view. On a clear day, you could see across the Severn to Wales.

"I think someday I maybe see inside castle."

"Perhaps you will, Dickon."

Will took his empty mug to the bar and paid for a fresh mug of small ale. Taking it back to the table, he offered it to Dickon, who accepted greedily. "Maybe I'll see you here again sometime, Dickon," Will said then turned and made his way to the door, no longer in the mood for a lively evening.

***

Sir Guy took his time getting out of bed the following morning, his attention drawn to a conversation between two of his men in the far corner of the room as they prepared for duty. Speaking in low tones to avoid waking those who still slept, Will seemed to be describing his previous night's adventures to one of his fellow men-at-arms. Guy couldn't hear everything, but he perked up at the word "stranger." And again at "here now and then."

All right, Will Makepeace, let's see if you tell me about this person who's suddenly shown up in the village.

When a week passed and Will had made no further mention – especially not directly to his captain – of a person who came to the village from time to time, Guy's suspicions began to harden.

***

The landlord was right. Simple Dickon vanished from the scene two days before Whitsunday. Where he went and when he'd return – even *if* he'd return – was anyone's guess. But Will's wager – based on the young man's fascination with the castle and the dagger – was that it wouldn't be long before he wandered back.

***

The Wednesday following Whitsunday, Will was assigned to walk the ramparts, scanning the countryside for anything that might be a threat. Boring duty – but no less boring, really, than any other assignment.

Certainly no less boring than Guy's almost daily exhortations to all and sundry that constant vigilance was their duty to the king – by which he meant the regent, of course, since the young king wasn't really issuing any orders himself. Will had only made one circuit when he heard Guy bellowing from the inner courtyard. "Makepeace, get your arse down here."

What have I done now? Will wondered as he retraced his steps toward the nearest tower where he could descend to ground level. Before he even reached the tower door, Guy's voice came again. "Right anon, Makepeace. Don't keep me waiting."

Making his way down the spiral stair, Will met his replacement going in the opposite direction. "Any idea what he wants, Aldwin?"

"Not a clue. He just ordered me to take your place. But he's in a mood, so watch yourself."

Will picked up his pace – a bit – but he wasn't going to give his cousin the satisfaction of showing up breathless from running the entire way. If he was about to be chastised for something, he was in no hurry to find out what it was.

"Took you long enough," Guy fumed when Will arrived.

"I'm here now. What's this about?"

"Caernarfon wants to see you."

"Me? Why?"

"Christ's donkey has a better idea what he wants than I do. All I know is he wants to see you, Berkeley thinks it's harmless, and I'm to comply. So see him you will. There's a servant waiting inside to show you the way."

Will was careful to keep his aspect calm and disinterested, but his curiosity was piqued. *Could this have something to do with the Earl of Kent? I have no news without Simon to bring it. But what else could it possibly be? I have no other connection to the man.* By the time he took his first two steps toward the entrance to the living quarters, an entire swarm of butterflies had taken up residence in his gut.

"Will!" Guy's voice reclaimed his attention, and he turned to face his cousin again. "Do *not* do anything stupid. You're his guard – not some conspirator helping him plot his escape. This whole thing seems like a singularly bad idea to me, and if it goes wrong, Berkeley won't remember *he* was the one who authorized it. Don't bring disgrace on both of us, Will."

The butterflies rose up in unison, but Will put on a big grin just to provoke Guy. "Don't have an apoplexy, cousin. I'll wager all he wants is for me to bring him some ale from the tavern instead of the pissy-tasting stuff we've had here of late. That, or maybe a barmaid." Will winked and set off quickly toward the entrance, leaving Guy fuming.

"I'll have your bollocks if you dare suggest that, Will Makepeace," Guy shouted at Will's back, eliciting a roar of laughter from his cousin that annoyed him even further.

The servant led Will through a sequence of corridors to an open door, where he said "Wait 'til he summons you" and then promptly disappeared around the next corner. Inside, Caernarfon was gazing out the window, which, if Will had his bearings right, overlooked the outer ward of the castle. Cap in hand, Will cleared his throat to announce his presence.

Caernarfon turned and broke into a smile the moment he recognized his visitor. "Will Makepeace. At last. I was beginning to think Berkeley had had second thoughts and was going to deny me your company. Do come in." Will stepped tentatively through the doorway and reached for the doorknob. "Let's leave it open for now, shall we?" said Caernarfon. "I'm quite certain Berkeley and Maltravers and even Sir Guy are so curious they'll all dispatch someone to lurk in the corridor and eavesdrop, so let's not spoil their little game."

Will's anxiety was quickly giving way to confusion. Taking another tentative step into the room, he asked, "How may I be of service, sir?"

"First, by setting aside your reluctance and joining me here." Caernarfon gestured to a seating area near the fireplace, which was spotlessly clean and free of ash for the summer.

The room was anything but a prison. Luxuriously appointed – if not fit for a king, then at least fit for an earl. A large canopy bed with rich draperies and coverings stood on one wall, the fireplace with its sitting area on an adjacent one. An ornately carved chest for clothes and personal belongs adorned the wall opposite the hearth. Candelabras sat anywhere one might want light of an evening. Also in the sitting area was a table flanked by two chairs with a game board in its center. The playing pieces were elaborately carved and arranged in neat rows on opposite sides of the board, one set painted white with red and gold decoration, the other made of dark wood with silver appointments.

"Do you play chess, Makepeace?" Caernarfon asked then continued before Will could reply. "Thomas – Lord Berkeley, that is – claims he has no time for such diversion. I can't imagine what keeps him so busy even in the evenings, but I'm hardly in a position to question him. And Maltravers is so inept I can best him in a dozen moves or less, which quickly gets boring."

Will stepped over to the table and looked carefully at the game board then back at his host. "I'm sorry, sir, but I don't know how to play."

Caernarfon's pleasant expression vanished and he didn't speak for several long moments, during which a few of Will's butterflies once again took wing. Eventually, he said, "You studied the board, Makepeace. Tell me what you saw."

"It looks like two armies facing each other across a battlefield. Or at least, what I imagine that would look like. I've never been in battle myself."

The smile returned. "Quite astute, young Will. That's precisely what you saw. The foot soldiers here in the front," he gestured to the pawns, "with the knights and others arrayed behind. And the objective is to capture your opponent's king." Unable to think of anything remotely intelligent to say, Will simply gazed back at the game board. "Perhaps I could teach you the game," Caernarfon continued. "I have a feeling you might be rather good at it."

"But I don't know anything, really, about battles, sir."

"Then if I teach you, you'll learn the *right* way to outwit your opponent. Though I'm told you're rather good already at outwitting Sir Guy." Caernarfon chuckled and Will couldn't suppress a smile. "Please . . . sit here and play the white pieces. I'll be the defender." He took the chair on the side of the board with the dark pieces. "It's easier to learn by beginning on offense."

Will slowly eased himself into the chair as Caernarfon began. "Now these are your pawns – your foot soldiers. They move straight ahead, one square at a time, until they're in position to capture an opponent's piece, when they can move diagonally left or right to effect the capture." He demonstrated by moving one of his own pawns forward four squares and then capturing one of Will's pawns. Then he reset the board.

By the end of the afternoon, Will's head was spinning, but he'd at least memorized the basic moves for each of the playing pieces. They tried one game and Caernarfon beat him handily but still offered encouragement. "Not bad at all, Will. Most novices lose in four or five moves on their first try. You survived for eight. Quite commendable indeed." He rose from his chair and Will followed suit. "I know you have obligations to Sir Guy, but perhaps we can resume your tutelage two days hence? I'll arrange it with Berkeley."

They made their way to the still-open door, and Caernarfon scanned the corridor right and left. "It seems our eavesdroppers have gotten bored and gone on their way," he chuckled. "It has been a very pleasant afternoon, Will, and it occurs to me that I've been rather high-handed in presuming you would want to continue. A habit of royalty, I fear."

"If it pleases you, sir, I'm quite agreeable," Will replied. As he made his way along the corridor, he began to wonder why he'd agreed without even a second thought. *It's bound to be less boring than walking the ramparts. And there's no doubt it will get under Guy's skin like nothing else I've ever done.* He grinned to himself. And then he came to an important realization. This afternoon's encounter had only served to increase his liking for the former king. If he could bring some small pleasure into the life of a man who once ruled everyone and now couldn't even rule his own fate, then that was a service worth rendering.

***

"Chess?" The incredulity in Guy's voice was unlike anything Will had ever heard. "He wants to teach you *chess*?"

Will couldn't suppress a grin. "He thinks I might be good at it."

"What in the name of God's best breeches would make him think that?"

"Maybe the way I manage to circumvent you and get away to the tavern whenever I want to?" Will watched his cousin's face turn an angry red and worried he might have gone one step too far.

But then Guy let out a deep sigh as the color subsided from his cheeks. "This is without a doubt the strangest thing I have *ever* heard of. But at least if he's teaching you chess, I have a guard in his presence more often than I would otherwise. And you, Will Makepeace," he poked Will's chest with his forefinger, "won't be wasting time and money in the tavern."

CHAPTER FIVE

Over the course of the next three weeks, Will strove diligently to improve his skill. At times, it was frustrating. Caernarfon always sat utterly relaxed in his chair and moved his pieces almost nonchalantly. Whereas Will carefully studied each move and often held his hand on the playing piece for several moments before finally committing to the move. From time to time, Caernarfon would raise an eyebrow at Will's choice or suggest he think twice about what he was about to do. Will sometimes thought the former king already knew how the game would play out.

And then one day, recognition dawned. Caernarfon was explaining what would happen next if Will left his knight in the position he'd chosen. *God's bones*, Will thought to himself. *He really does know exactly which move will follow which and how to win.* In that moment, Will also understood that his role was to try to disrupt what his opponent expected him to do. *This might just be far more interesting than I thought.*

As Will began to apply his new understanding, their games started taking longer – and Caernarfon began paying more attention – or at least, so it seemed to Will. One afternoon, when Will confidently moved one of his knights to a position where it was completely unprotected from capture by the opposing bishop, Caernarfon sat up straighter in his chair and propped his chin on steepled fingers while studying the board. "Have I done something wrong?" Will ventured.

Caernarfon didn't answer straightaway, his attention still focused on the disposition of the playing pieces. At long last he made a seemingly innocuous choice, moving his king's pawn one square forward then leaning back in his chair. "Quite the contrary, Will," he finally answered the question. "In fact, this reminds me of when my son was learning the game. Now and again, he would do something so totally unexpected that it required a complete change of tactics on my part. That's precisely what you just did." He paused a moment before adding, "And I applaud you for it. Putting one's opponent off balance is a skill much to be valued. You're learning quickly, Will Makepeace. As I had hoped you would."

Will smiled, basking in the approval from his tutor. But he was also learning just how much more there was to learn. When to tempt your opponent into making a mistake, when to temporize and force your opponent to take the initiative, when to sacrifice a piece to achieve a better position. This was certainly the most intellectually challenging thing he'd ever done – and perhaps one of the most enjoyable.

Each time Will arrived at the door to Caernarfon's chamber, he found the former king looking out the window, surveying the outer ward. One day early in July, instead of returning his attention immediately indoors and to the game table, Edward beckoned Will to the window. "Look down there," he directed Will's gaze. "See that small garden?"

"Aye, sir. I've seen it up close. It's actually rather sad. All the plants are droopy all the time – like they're not getting the right tending."

"They're not, Will. I can tell that even from here. And I can tell you precisely why they're suffering."

"Sir?"

"The soil is too wet. The drainage is all wrong. The plants are sitting with their roots in water all the time, and that's not good for them. If I could have just one week with them, I'd have them all on the road to recovery and the cooks would actually be able to harvest some vegetables before the summer's out."

"You, sir?"

"Of course. There's nothing I enjoy more than working in the soil, clearing drainage ditches, helping nature to produce her bounty. It's exhilarating, Will. People laughed at me for doing such things when I was king. Said it was completely unfitting for my position to toil alongside ordinary laborers. Perhaps they'd no longer laugh now that I'm no longer king." He paused, returning his gaze to the little plot of land. "Oh, how I'd love to get my hands on that garden and coax it to life!"

Will studied the garden, avoiding catching Caernarfon's eye. He was almost certain what was coming next . . . and he wasn't to be disappointed.

Finally turning away from the window, Edward ventured, "Is there any chance, do you think, Will, that I might be allowed to do so?"

"I've no idea, sir. It's not my place to make those decisions." They sat in awkward silence until Will was overwhelmed by a need to fill the void. "In any event, sir, your attire doesn't seem suited to gardening."

"You're as observant as always, young Will. But perhaps we can strike a bargain. If I can persuade Berkeley to allow me some time tending the garden, then perhaps you can find me some servants' clothing that's more suited to the purpose."

"I can certainly try, sir."

"And I can certainly try to secure Thomas's permission."

***

Making his usual rounds to check in with Berkeley's sentries and his own guards on the ramparts, Sir Guy was surprised to see Will crossing the inner ward carrying his spare clothing. *What's he up to now?* Guy wondered as he scampered down the stairs of the nearest tower and hurried across the courtyard. "Will!" he called out to get his cousin's attention before he reached the door to the main living quarters. Catching up, Guy pointed to the clothes Will carried. "What's this?"

"Caernarfon needs some gardening clothes. None of the servants are anywhere near his height, so I'm letting him use mine. He'd be terribly conspicuous in ill-fitting clothing, and we think it's better that he have the appearance of an ordinary gardener."

"*We?* Holy Mother of God, Will. Didn't I warn you not to get too friendly with the man? Not to conspire with him?"

"There's no conspiracy, Guy. He just wants to tend the vegetables in that little garden in the outer ward. An alternative to walking about this courtyard for exercise. Only difference is, his fine clothes aren't suitable for gardening."

Guy couldn't disguise his exasperation. "Don't you see, Will? Think about it. He's come up with an excuse to get his hands on some peasant clothing. So he can blend in. So one day he can just wander out with the servants when they go to market."

"That seems pretty unlikely if I'm with him while he's weeding and hoeing. Besides, not once since we took him into custody last November has he been anything but completely compliant."

"You're too trusting, Will. That's why guards shouldn't get familiar with their captives. It's one thing to play chess with him in his quarters . . . though I *still* don't like that. Quite another to become part of his entourage. I'm putting a stop to this right now. You stay right here until I get back." Guy stabbed a finger toward the ground beneath Will's feet. "Understood? You don't move one step from where you're standing."

"Can I at least sit on that bench over there?" Will gestured to the stone bench under the nearest window. Guy might want him to wait, but there was no reason he had to stand the whole time.

"Oh, alright. But I'd better find you there when I get back . . . and with those clothes still in your possession." Will took his seat, and Guy stormed off in search of Lord Berkeley.

He found the baron in his study surrounded by papers and shelves filled with scrolls and folios and more papers. If there was any sort of order to it all, it wasn't apparent to the casual observer. "What is it, Bickerstaffe?" asked Berkeley without looking up from the page he was studying.

"It's this business with the prisoner tending the garden in the outer ward, sir. Do you know about it?"

"Of course I do." The baron scribbled something on the page then finally looked up at Guy. "He asked my permission. I gave it. It's as simple as that."

"With respect, sir, do you really think it's a wise idea?"

"Not all that different from when he exercises in the inner ward. He'll still be inside the castle walls. If it makes him happy and keeps him out of my hair, then I'd be a fool to say no. Besides, your man Makewood—"

"Makepeace, sir," Guy interrupted.

"Makepeace then. Anyway, he'll be with Edward the entire time. If it makes you feel better, you can post all your guards on the ramparts of the outer ward and leave the rest to my sentries. Besides, this is probably just a whim, and he'll tire of it after a week or two."

"Very well, sir." Though he was seething inside, Guy recognized he'd get nowhere with Berkeley by continuing to object.

"One thing, though, Bickerstaffe. See that Edward has proper gardening attire. I don't want him mucking in the mud in his finery. I get a stipend from the Crown for his upkeep, but it's not nearly enough to buy him new clothing every week."

"Yes, sir."

"Now, if there's nothing else, Sir Guy? My steward's due here any minute to go over the household accounts. The man's fixated on buying ale from one of the priories – says we need the extra for all the extra men here now – but I'm having none of it. We have a brewhouse. If he needs more ale, then all he has to do is brew more."

Acknowledging the dismissal, Guy bowed slightly before turning on his heel to leave the room. He could have saved himself the effort. Berkeley had already returned his attention to his papers.

First chess, now gardening, Guy fumed to himself as he retraced his steps back to the bench where he'd left his cousin. *What's it to be next? Horseback rides around the countryside? Outings to wherever he takes it into his head he wants to pray? And how much longer will I have to be responsible for overseeing the twists and turns of comfortable captivity? I swear by God and all the saints, Will Makepeace, if I ever find out you were behind this, my promise to your mother is an oath I'll break without a second thought. You'll be lucky if I just throw you out and don't throw you in Berkeley's dungeon.*

***

Fully aware that Caernarfon's little enterprise already had Berkeley's approval, Will knew Guy's mood would be in no way improved when he returned, so he'd resisted the temptation to hide his extra clothing inside his shirt. But he couldn't resist the small provocation of moving to the opposite end of the bench from where Guy had left him.

If Guy noticed at all, he ignored it. Waving a dismissive hand in Will's direction, he announced, "Alright, get to it. But if anything goes wrong, it'll be *you* that suffers the consequences. Don't expect me to come to your defense." With that, he marched back across the courtyard and into the tower from which he'd originally come.

Will watched his cousin's retreating back. *Guy is changing,* he mused. *He's always been a bit rigid and sometimes rather pompous, but now he seems . . . I don't know . . . put upon? Is his job weighing too heavily on him? God knows he takes it all terribly seriously. He certainly hasn't taken any respite from duty for all these months.*

Rising slowly from the bench and approaching the door to the living quarters, Will smiled to himself, confident he'd hit on the true source of his cousin's malaise. And certain he knew the cure. *All he needs is a visit to the tavern now and again . . . maybe an evening with the barmaid. But how on earth do I ever get him there?*

CHAPTER SIX

July 1327

Will could scarcely credit the transformation in the former king when he stepped into the garden plot. No longer did he seem somewhat detached from the world around him. No longer the subtle ennui with his circumstances. No longer the sad wistfulness for what had been taken from him.

"Just as I thought, Will," said Caernarfon as he walked among the plants. "Mud everywhere. And yet we haven't had rain all week. Hand me that shovel." Will retrieved the implement from the wheelbarrow they'd used to bring tools from the gardener's storage room. Edward sank it into the wet earth, turned over a little mound, and shook his head in dismay. "Look how compacted the soil is. It's been like this for a long time." He gestured toward two rows of rather limp, feathery green foliage. "Those carrots and parsnips will never form properly in these conditions."

He jammed the shovel into the dirt and it stood on its own, not even the slightest hint of falling over. Caernarfon shook his head again then turned to Will with a smile on his face. "But we can fix this, Will. And then those sad little plants will give us a harvest no one's expecting." In his tone was an excitement Will had never heard from him before.

Caernarfon yanked the shovel from the ground and began walking the perimeter of the plot. "There must have been better drainage here sometime in the past." Suddenly, he stopped. "Will, grab that hoe and come here. I think I've found it."

They spent the rest of the afternoon clearing what was once a small drainage ditch at the low end of the plot that had become clogged with dead leaves, mud, acorns, small pieces of stone, and even a couple of rat carcasses. To Will's surprise, the former king was in no way squeamish about grabbing those two finds by what was left of their tails and tossing them into a bucket with the rest of the detritus.

"Now..." Caernarfon leaned on his shovel once the little ditch was fully restored. "What we need is a couple of bucketfuls of water to prove everything is flowing as it should. Why don't you dump those buckets of muck in the cesspit and bring them back filled with water?"

"Sorry, sir, I can't leave your presence. Sir Guy won't hear of it."

Caernarfon looked up, scanning the ramparts, and Will followed his gaze. "Seems there are enough of Sir Guy's men up there keeping watch to ensure I can't go anywhere."

"I can't dispute that, sir, but he gave me a direct order never to leave you alone."

"Sir Guy's not fond of our little enterprise, is he, Will?"

"The responsibility for your safety weighs heavily on him, sir."

"A bit too heavily, perhaps?"

Will kept his own counsel. Sharing his thoughts about how to lighten Guy's burden was probably a step too far in the direction his cousin had warned against . . . though Will was sure Caernarfon would find the diagnosis and proposed cure amusing.

Apparently sensing Will's unease, Caernarfon hoisted the two buckets. "Very well, then, put our tools back in the wheelbarrow, and we'll return everything to the gardener's storeroom. One of his lads can dispose of this." He lifted the buckets a bit higher. "And tomorrow we can bring these back full of water and test the drainage."

Within a week, the little garden was already looking healthier, but Caernarfon insisted they tend it regularly. "If I were Thomas's steward, I'd have dismissed that gardener long since," he told Will. "But I shan't look a given horse in the mouth. This is quite the most pleasant thing I've done in many months."

***

A week later, Sir Guy himself was walking the ramparts, ensuring the vigilance of his guards while the absurd tableau of two men gardening played out below, when the wagon pulled up to the outer gate. Driven by two monks clad in black, the conveyance carried two large barrels secured in place by ropes spanning the wagon bed and tied to the side rails. A pile of black canvas behind the barrels looked as if it had just been shoved aside to reveal the cargo. *So the steward won out in the end.* Guy permitted himself a little chuckle, remembering Berkeley's determination not to pay good money for someone else's ale.

Both guards stepped out of the gatehouse, one walking around the wagon to survey its load and the other addressing the driver. "State your business, Brother."

"Ale for the castle, my good man. Ordered by your steward to be delivered today."

"No one told me about any deliveries."

"Then for certes, they forgot. Perhaps they told the men on duty before you, and those men failed to pass on the instructions."

"We've been here since sunrise, Brother, and nary a word about any ale coming in. What priory do you come from?"

Guy missed the reply. His ears had picked up a different sound. Hoofbeats in the village. Moving fast. "Lower the gate!" he shouted.

The men at the gate continued their interrogation and inspection, apparently oblivious to the threat hurtling toward them. Guy cupped his hands around his mouth and shouted again, "Lower the gate!" just as dozens of horsemen rounded the turn from the village high street into the lane leading to the castle. At a full gallop, swinging flails and battle axes, they charged the gate.

The man inspecting the wagon was cut down straightaway by a flail to the back of his skull. His companion, suddenly aware of the danger, tried to scamper back into the gatehouse, only to be felled by the blow of a battle axe between his shoulders.

Guy watched in dismay as three more men dressed as monks scrambled from beneath the canvas and, joined by one of the drivers, made straight for the garden plot.

***

Will's ears perked up when he heard Guy's first shout. The sound of pounding hooves that followed sent a chill down his spine. And the sight of four monks running across the courtyard told him it was up to him to protect the former king.

Monks in black. Dominicans, most likely. The Dunheveds. It all went through his mind in a flash as he grabbed a shovel and shouted over his shoulder to Caernarfon, "Leave this to me! Stay back!"

Will moved forward, swinging the shovel rapidly from side to side in front him in an effort to keep the advancing intruders as far away as he could, desperate to buy time until help could arrive. The monks slowed their pace, all four watching Will carefully, and Will held his ground.

Out of the corner of his eye, he saw Caernarfon grab a hoe from the wheelbarrow and press forward. *For God's sake, man, can't you listen?* But then a lesson from all those games of chess popped into his head. *Maybe he has the right idea. Confuse your opponent. Make it hard for them to decide which of us to capture. Or even if we're their targets at all.*

Maybe this would work. Caernarfon now stood to Will's left and a few steps back, brandishing his hoe. The monks stopped just out of reach of the garden tools. "Which one is it?" asked the one on the right.

"They said the tall one," replied the man next to him.

"They're the same height," said the first man.

The monk on the opposite end asked, "Are you sure they're not just gardeners? Look at their clothes."

No one spoke. Time seemed suspended. As if someone had forgotten to invert the hour glass and all was frozen in place until the grains of sand flowed once more. And then suddenly, from the monk who hadn't spoken before, "Take them both . . . *now*!"

The monks charged. Will and Caernarfon brandished their tools to fight off the two directly in front of them. In an instant, both were grabbed from behind, their arms pinned to their sides. As the monks wrenched the shovel and hoe away, Will struggled against his captor, trying desperately to break free and reach for the dagger he'd stowed in his boot. To no avail. The man holding him merely squeezed his chest tighter, leaving Will gasping for breath.

He looked to his left. Caernarfon had given up the struggle and was submitting to having his wrists bound together with a cord one of the monks had taken from the waist of his habit. At that moment, it dawned on Will that their strategy of confusing their captors would fail unless their behaviors matched. So he let his body go slack and bowed his head in conciliation as another monk pulled the cord from around his waist and bound Will's wrists.

"Come on, let's go," said the monk who appeared to be in charge. "We've been too long at this already."

***

Guy watched in horror as Will and Caernarfon were half dragged, half shoved to the gate and thrown into the wagon. And still the horsemen kept coming. Now that there was no risk of hitting Caernarfon, two of his men had taken up their crossbows and brought down as many horses. But as soon as the riders realized what was happening, a group of them clustered in the outer courtyard and began slinging battle axes toward the defenders. With no cornels on the inside of the parapet, the guards had nowhere to shelter.

"Leave them to it," Guy shouted, "and come with me."

They ran full-tilt for the inner gatehouse tower and practically stumbled over each other trying to get inside. As he started down the stairs, Guy heard an ominous clang. Gritting his teeth, he hurried his pace and emerged at the bottom to find the gate closed. "You idiot sons of Satan's whore," he raged at the sentries, "why did you close the gate?"

"Your . . . your order, sir," the nearest sentry stammered out while the other one tried to fade into the shadows.

"That was for the outer gate, imbecile! Now you've trapped the invaders in here to wreak God knows what kind of damage. And worse yet, you've trapped *us* so we can't give chase. Now *get that gate raised*!"

He beckoned the men from the ramparts, and they stepped into the inner courtyard, into utter chaos. Horsemen everywhere, breaking windows with their flails, assaulting doors with their axes. A few had fallen victim to the crossbowmen on the ramparts, but there were still dozens storming about wreaking havoc. "Ignore them," Guy admonished his men. "They were just sent to distract us. Now get to the stable and get all our horses saddled and ready."

He watched his guards dodge among the rampaging horsemen and make it safely inside the double doors of the stable then ran to the nearest tower and up the stairs to the ramparts. "Aldwin," he shouted from the tower door, "everyone to the stable. Now!" He waited only long enough to be sure they were coming before tearing back down and weaving his own way among the horsemen, pausing only to glance over his shoulder toward the gate. *Halfway up. They'd better have it full up by the time we come charging through.*

Inside the stable was a different kind of chaos. Half their horses were saddled and waiting while the stable boys rushed about trying to get the rest ready to ride. Once all his men were mounted, Guy gave his orders. "Full battle charge out of here, men. Ignore the invaders. Their job is just to slow us down. Once they realize we're chasing the kidnappers, they'll follow. But their mounts are already tired. So if we stay at the gallop as long as the horses can hold out, we should be able to leave their pursuit behind. We'll regroup on Berkeley Heath. Aldwin, you stop in the village and find out what direction that wagon went then catch us up on the heath."

"Wagon, sir?"

"Carrying a couple of ale barrels, driven by monks, several men in the wagon behind the barrels. They were probably moving fast."

"Aye, sir."

"Alright, men, ready?" He didn't wait for a reply. "The outer gate is open. The inner one should be by the time we get there, but if it's still low, just lie on your horse's neck and get through." He signaled to a couple of stable boys, who flung the doors wide, then turned in his saddle. "At the gallop, men . . . *now*!"

CHAPTER SEVEN

The wagon careened through the village and seemed in danger of overturning as the driver turned east at full speed. The monks had seated Will and Caernarfon shoulder-to-shoulder by one of the barrels then covered them with the canvas. From the sounds that followed, Will guessed the four of them took their own seats at the back of the wagon. With their wrists bound together and no way to brace themselves, Will and Caernarfon toppled sideways during the reckless turn but managed to right themselves.

"Why did you stop fighting, Will?" Caernarfon asked in a whisper. "Why come with me?"

"To keep them confused for as long as we could."

"Ah, so you recognized my little ploy then."

Will could imagine the former king's approving smile, though it was too dark under the canvas to actually see it. "I also thought maybe I could help you."

They continued in the softest of whispers, hoping the canvas would muffle the sound. "I'll be recognized, of course," said Caernarfon, "once they bring us to someone who's seen me."

Will wasn't sure how to reply, so he changed the subject. "What's troubling me at the moment is how Guy is going to figure out where they've taken us. He'll be hell-bent on getting you back and rounding up the perpetrators."

"I suspect your cousin is resourceful. It didn't escape my notice that our captors are Black Friars. I doubt it escaped his either."

"If they're even monks at all."

"Ah, Will, don't underestimate the Dunheveds. Friar Thomas sees it as his holy mission, ordained by God, to restore me to the throne. He'd have no qualms about recruiting his brethren to the cause. The horsemen, I suspect, were Stephen's contribution. Nothing more than a bit of mayhem to divert attention from the main objective."

They sat in silence, listening to the muffled sounds of the horses' hooves and the creaking of the wagon. But Will's mind was in turmoil, trying to think of any way at all he could leave a trail for Guy to follow.

***

On fresh mounts, Guy's men left their pursuers behind well before they reached the heath. Now, as they waited for Aldwin, they walked the horses around slowly to let them cool down. They hadn't long to wait.

"They came this way," Aldwin reported. "Folks in the village said the wagon was moving fast and headed for the Bristol Road. Four monks in the wagon, one driving, but they didn't see any other men. Just the barrels and a black canvas slung haphazard-like over them. The landlord at the tavern wagered as how they were probably black monks from the priory at Leonard Stanley."

"Benedictines?" Guy asked.

"Aye."

Guy shook his head. "My wager's on Dominicans. And I'd better be right, since it's my job in the balance."

One of the other men called out, "Sir Guy, look!"

Sir Guy turned in his saddle to see a column of horsemen coming down the road two abreast. "Alright, men, form up on me. If they want trouble, we flee. Scatter so they have to break up their formation to chase us down. Then make your way back to the castle. Understood? Our job is to find Caernarfon and get him back, not to engage when we're so badly outnumbered."

As the column neared their position, Guy's feet in the stirrups were held away from his horse's sides, ready to urge the animal to action at the slightest sign of aggression from the road. The horses sensed the tension of their riders, some pawing the ground, others shaking their heads, one or two nickering as if asking "Do we go now?"

Whoever was in charge of the column called for a trot, and the horsemen picked up the pace. The lead riders came even with where Guy's troop waited on a little rise twenty yards or so back from the road . . . and kept on going. Not a single head turned to glance in the troop's direction.

"That was passing strange," said Aldwin once they were watching the backs of the last pair of riders.

"Just confirms my notion that their only purpose was to distract us and slow us down."

"What now?" asked Aldwin.

"We follow them. I want to see which way they go when they reach the Bristol road. But stay on the heath. No need to alarm them with the sound of hooves coming up behind them."

When they reached the Bristol road, Guy couldn't suppress an oath. *"God's beard!* They're no help at all." The column was turning both right and left, the right man of each pair headed south, his companion pointing his horse's nose north. When the last pair had gone their separate ways, Guy looked up to the sky. "Great God in heaven, can't I get just one simple break today?"

"What now?" asked Aldwin.

Thoroughly frustrated, Guy took it out on his senior man-at-arms. "Is that all you can say? Don't you have anything useful to contribute?" Aldwin lowered his head and mumbled something unintelligible. "What was that, Aldwin?"

"Nothing, sir. Nothing at all."

"Good. Alright, we're going with my gut. The nearest Dominican priory is in Gloucester, and so is the Earl of Kent. That's most likely where they've taken him, so we look there first."

"If I may, sir?" Aldwin's tone was tentative, conciliatory.

"If you have something useful to say." Guy's was still gruff.

"If they've gone south, we'll have wasted valuable time searching in Gloucester. What if a few of us scout south? Look for any signs the wagon might have gone that way." His temper just a heartbeat from exploding, Guy glared at his second-in-command. Aldwin didn't back down. "It was just a suggestion, sir."

And actually a rather good one, Guy admitted to himself. *Get a grip on yourself, Bickerstaffe. It's not Aldwin's fault this day is your worst nightmare come to life. You'll never find them by raging around the countryside like a madman.* He lowered his gaze to the ground then returned it to Aldwin, hoping he'd transformed his expression from rage to resolve. "On reflection, Aldwin, quite a useful one. Take two men with you. But don't go more than a couple of miles south. I still think Gloucester's our best bet, so I'll take the rest of the troop north. If you find something, send one man back to fetch us. If not, rejoin us as soon as you can." Without further comment, Aldwin gestured to the two men nearest him and they set off at a canter.

Barely a mile north, they found the wagon abandoned in the corner formed by the main road and a small lane that turned left to who-knew-where. Guy dismounted and walked completely around the conveyance. The horses had been unhitched, but there was no sign of them anywhere about, so they must have been put to some other purpose. *Doesn't make sense they'd put their captives on horseback. Good riders could easily gallop away and have to be chased down. Not a risk I'd want to take.*

He climbed up into the back of the wagon. The barrels remained where they'd always been, the black canvas tossed in a heap against one of the side rails. Guy walked to the front of the wagon and pushed against the top of one barrel. It leaned precariously sideways then slammed back down to the wagon bed when Guy released his hand. "Just as I thought," he announced to no one in particular.

Not expecting a response, he was startled when a voice came from the direction of a dense grove of trees just west of the wagon's position. "Aye. They be empty. I tried – thought I might get some free ale."

"Whoever you are, show yourself," Guy ordered. He watched as a shadowy figure moved among the tree trunks and stopped at the edge of the grove, apparently unwilling to come any closer to a group of mounted and armed men. Jumping down from the wagon, he started toward the man, who began to retreat into the trees. "Wait! I mean you no harm. I'm just curious if you know anything about this wagon."

The figure stopped but stayed in the trees. Guy couldn't tell much about him other than that he was a bit taller than average and his clothes didn't seem to be ragged or torn. "Please," Guy tried to sound reassuring. "My cousin was in that wagon, and I'm trying to find him."

"Black monks. I hid. Didn't want black monks to see me."

"Do you know something about the black monks?"

"I live with them." A long pause. "Sometimes."

"Where?"

"At the priory."

Guy could barely make out the man pointing vaguely northeast. *Probably Leonard Stanley. Wrong black monks.* "Then what did you do?"

"Sat in the woods and watched. I sit and watch a lot. The blacksmith. The wise woman's house. The market. The castle."

Guy could feel his impatience rising. How long was it going to take to get the story from this creature? "So what did you watch today?" he prompted.

"A carriage there."

The shadows and light among the trees were playing havoc with Guy's attempts to see where the man was pointing. "Where?" he asked.

"Beside the road. Across the lane."

"And the wagon?"

"The wagon came. More black monks and two men tied up."

Do I have to pull every detail out of this village idiot bit by bit? Guy railed to himself. But he knew he'd never get the whole story if he frightened the man. "So what happened then?"

"Put the two men in the carriage. Some monks got in with them. Then drove away."

"How many monks in the carriage?"

"Three."

"And which way did they go?"

"Up the road."

Up? Does that mean north? It was Guy's turn to point. "That way?"

"Aye."

"And what was this carriage like?"

"Brown."

"Was it fancy? Like a rich man's carriage?" *Maybe sent by the Earl of Kent?*

"No. Old."

"What about the horses that pulled the wagon? Where are they?"

"I don't know."

"Someone obviously unhitched them."

"Black monks. Rode off on them. Don't know where they are now."

Despite what it had taken to draw the story out of this man, Guy was grateful for the details since the wagon itself had yielded no clues beyond the fact that it was abandoned. "What's your name, my good man? Who is it I must thank?"

Silence from the grove of trees. Whoever it was, was already gone . . . or perhaps simply finished talking.

Mounting back up, Guy told the men, "We'll wait here for Aldwin, now that we know they won't find anything to the south. Then it's on to Gloucester. I want to be there before nightfall."

CHAPTER EIGHT

"Come on, get out." The voice was one Will hadn't heard before, a deeper pitch, a hint of impatience. Hands that presumably belonged to the voice reached into the carriage and took his arm, tugging him out of his seat and toward the open door. "Now step down."

Once both feet were securely on the ground, Will assessed the situation as best he could without the help of his eyes. He and Caernarfon had been blindfolded as soon as they were transferred from the wagon to the carriage. His nose didn't tell him much, but his ears picked up the clang of metal on metal – perhaps from a smithy nearby. He felt, rather than observed, the presence of other men in close proximity. The monks who had been in the carriage? Other men who'd been waiting for them here? Wherever "here" was. Without hearing more voices, it was impossible to tell how many men there were. But they all remained stubbornly silent except for the occasional sound of footsteps.

"You next." The deep voice again. Presumably pulling Caernarfon out of the carriage. "Watch your head." Then what sounded like a bit of a scuffle followed by, "Watch how you go, you clumsy oaf. I've got this one coming down from the carriage."

Someone took Will's bound wrists by the bindings and tugged. "This way." Same voice. Was this the person in charge? Will was surprised how much concentration was required to avoid tripping on the uneven ground without the advantage of seeing where he was putting his feet. A few yards onward, he who was apparently the only one allowed to speak announced, "Alright, four steps up."

They hadn't gone much farther when Will heard what sounded like a door groaning on its hinges. Was Caernarfon still with him? No way to know until, "Alright, take them down."

The steps were wide enough a man could get his whole boot on them without turning his foot sideways. For some reason, Will started counting the steps as they descended. And as he counted, his nose finally made a contribution. A musty smell. Where were they being taken? An undercroft or cellar? Certainly not a cellar used for brewing – there was none of the aroma of grain fermenting. It was also noticeably cooler here than outside.

He knew he'd reached the bottom when someone shoved him from behind, forcing him into some fancy footwork to regain his balance. *Why is it so hard to stay upright when you can't see a thing?* he wondered.

Once again, someone took his wrist bindings and led him forward. When they stopped, he was manhandled rather awkwardly into a sitting position, apparently on the floor given that his legs stretched out in front of him while his back rested against a stone wall. The cold stone sent a shiver up his spine.

At long last, the blindfold was removed and Will could take stock of his surroundings. Two monks making their way up the stairs, still not having uttered a word. *Why? We saw them in the wagon and heard them in the castle courtyard? Or are these different men?*

They were in a cellar of sorts, surrounded by stone tombs, the only light coming from a few dirty windows at the top of the walls. "The crypt of a church?" he asked Caernarfon, who sat beside him.

"Or the mausoleum of a wealthy family. Perhaps the names carved on these burial boxes will provide a clue."

They both scrambled to their feet – another ordinary action made awkward by having one's wrists bound together – and began to tour their prison chamber. Though all the stone boxes were decorated with carvings, only one had an effigy of the person inside. "Presumably, the most recent burial here," Caernarfon remarked. Of the others, some, but not all, had the name of the occupant carved on the side or the lid. Caernarfon read them aloud. "It appears," he concluded as they completed the circuit of the room, "that all these men were priests. So your first notion, Will, must be correct. This is indeed a church crypt."

"Gloucester Cathedral?" Will wondered aloud and then answered his own question. "No, not likely. We weren't on the road long enough to have reached Gloucester."

"Nor is this crypt large enough to be part of a great cathedral. Perhaps it's part of a priory church. And yet, I know of no Dominican priory closer to Berkeley than Gloucester or Bristol." Caernarfon surveyed their surroundings yet again. "I suppose there's nothing for it but to return to the discomfort of these cold flagstones." He sat back down and leaned against the wall. When Will didn't move, he added, "Unless, of course, you fancy standing upright all night."

"Not really. I was just thinking. Look over there . . . between the second and third windows. Something's boarded up. Maybe a broken window? The spacing's right when you look at the other four."

"And how might that do us any good down here?"

"If I could just get up there somehow . . ."

"And do what?"

Will leaned over, reached into his boot, and retrieved the dagger he'd stowed there. No one had thought to search either of them. "We're not without resources, sir." He slipped the dagger back into its hiding place. "If I could get up there, I could pry those boards loose and see what's possible. For that matter . . ." He reached into his boot once again. "Why don't I get us free of these bindings?"

"Patience, Will. If they return and find us free of our bonds, they'll almost certainly adopt harsher measures to restrain us. We're already most fortunate that our hands aren't behind our backs."

"Very well." Will reluctantly stowed the dagger away.

"What you're suggesting is an escape, yes?"

"Aye."

"Do you think that's wise? We've no idea where we are, so how would we know where to go? We'd be on foot. They have horses. I doubt we'd succeed in the end."

"But we have to try, sir. Guy's almost certainly come to the conclusion that I've been in league with our captors. Which means he'll brand me a traitor. As I see it, that leaves me only two choices – escape here by myself and flee to France or the Low Countries, leaving you to your fate, or find a way to get us both back to Berkeley unharmed."

"Both rather daunting." Caernarfon inclined his head toward the floor beside him. "You might as well sit. It's pointless trying to make plans until we observe what their routine is and if there's something in it we can exploit."

"Nor can we wait too long, sir. What if they move us again? Right now, we can't be too far from home. It was no time at all before the carriage turned off the Bristol road. So we're somewhere to the east, but no more than an hour's ride. Wherever they might take us would certainly be farther away – harder to get back."

"A fair point, young Will. But remember your lessons from chess. Lure your opponent into a level of comfort. Now sit. The light is beginning to fade, so I suspect they'll be bringing our supper soon. We should try to get them to speak."

"I hope they bring blankets too. It's going to be a cold night if they don't."

***

After two days of searching in Gloucester, Sir Guy was weary and increasingly despondent. No one had seen a carriage, old or new, enter the priory grounds. No one recalled a carriage, brown or otherwise, approaching the gates of Gloucester Castle. Most folks seemed to think the Earl of Kent was at his other seat in Arundel, though the sentries wouldn't confirm it. "If you truly have business with Lord Edmund," Guy was told when he led his troop up to the gates, "then you know when and where to find him. We've not been told to expect armed men. Now be on your way." Guy contemplated rushing the gate, but he knew his men would be easy targets for archers on the ramparts once they were inside the castle walls.

The prior didn't even try to disguise his disdain when Sir Guy told him they were looking for Dominican monks who'd kidnapped a king's prisoner. "Surely you know, Sir Guy, there are more than fifty houses in Britain. Who's to say the men you seek aren't from, say, Canterbury or York or even Edinburgh?"

Guy refused to be intimidated. "And who's to say they aren't in hiding here? After all, yours is the closest priory to where the incident occurred. It would be easy enough for them to blend into your community."

"But that supposes I would give them sanctuary, does it not? Are you suggesting it's my practice to harbor thieves and kidnappers? We're an order of preachers, Sir Guy, not an order of outlaws."

"Well, there's one among your order who would take issue with that. Friar Thomas Dunheved. Perhaps you know him?"

The prior shook his head slowly, a sad half-smile on his face, as if admonishing a child. "My dear Sir Guy . . . you think that among the hundreds upon hundreds of my brethren scattered all across this realm I would somehow know this man of whom you speak?"

"Very well. If you're so confident they're not here, then you won't object to my men searching the place."

"That I cannot allow. This is a place of scholarship and worship and contemplation, and I will never permit its tranquility to be disrupted by men-at-arms charging about unconstrained. I think you must accept, Sir Guy, that you've no choice but to look elsewhere for those you seek. You will not find them here. And so I bid you good day and ask God's blessing on you." And with that, the prior left the room, leaving Guy no better informed than when he'd walked in.

So for two days, they'd combed the town looking for even the smallest clue to where the two captives might be. Even posted men to keep watch at the priory overnight in case the monks should try to smuggle anyone out. And with each passing hour, Guy felt the executioner's breath on his neck grow closer and warmer.

Thinking back on the encounter with the prior merely added to his frustration. *He was hiding something. The monks involved? The captives? Maybe both. And his choice of words – 'you will not find them here.' Not 'they aren't here' or 'no one has come here.' 'You will not find them here.'* Not if you *won't let me look, I won't.* The more he thought about it, the more convinced he became that what he sought was within the priory walls. *But how can we get inside?*

His entire future depended on recapturing Caernarfon. Of that, he was under no delusion. He couldn't return to Berkeley without the former king in his custody. Or at the very least, without certain knowledge of where the man was and a plan to engage Berkeley's help to recover their charge.

And what of Will? Was he part of the plot? All that carousing in taverns – is that how they got messages back and forth? Why else would they take him other than to prevent him from revealing what he knows about the plotters? By the Blessed Virgin, if I get my hands on him . . .

To add to Guy's mounting woes, Aldwin had disappeared this evening, and no one knew quite where or why.

It was nearing midnight when Aldwin came into the room where Guy was sleeping and shook him awake. "Where in *hell* have you been?" Guy whispered to avoid waking the others in the room, though he'd much rather have shouted his displeasure.

"In some of the taverns."

"Holy Mother of God, Aldwin, not you too."

"I've got news. Come outside and I'll tell you."

Guy didn't bother to hide his irritation as he climbed out of bed and followed Aldwin into the corridor, down the stairs, and out into the cool night. "Couldn't you just have told me inside?" he chided his second-in-command.

"Didn't want to risk being overheard."

"Alright, out with it."

"Since we weren't having much luck, I thought I'd try Will's idea. You know – find out what the locals might let slip after they've had a drink or two. Nary a word about anything out of the ordinary at the priory. But then I happened to stop in the bar at that big inn just off the Bristol Road. Got to talking to a man who said he'd traveled up from Bath. Spent last night in Dursley."

"So?"

"So, according to this traveler, the talk in the tavern in Dursley was about the Black Friars who'd arrived a week before. The locals said they were living in the bell tower at St. James the Great. The rest of the church has been demolished for rebuilding – but the tower's still standing. Speculation was the friars had arrived to oversee the work on the new church."

"So how does this help us?"

"Think, Sir Guy. Dominicans. Only just arrived. As fast as we rode to Gloucester, wouldn't you think we'd have caught up with a decrepit old carriage? And we didn't. So what if they turned off the main road? They could easily guess we'd be focused on a Dominican house, so a different hiding place would be harder to discover."

"Hmmm . . ." Guy mused, interested now. "Hiding their captives close by while we chase off to Gloucester or Bristol following their horsemen. They knew if we headed north, we'd find the abandoned wagon. But that might have been an intentional clue to make us think we were on the right track. And it worked, Aldwin. Those bastards tricked us. And we've wasted two days here. Two days they could have moved their captives somewhere else."

"Maybe not, sir. My traveler said the monks were still in Dursley last night. Maybe their plan is to lie low while we raise the hue and cry for searches far and wide. And only when that yields nothing do they take the former king to wherever they've planned to take him."

"Alright. Let me sleep on it."

Guy turned to go back inside, but Aldwin grabbed his arm – a rare familiarity. "Think about it now, Guy. That traveler thought nothing of telling a total stranger what he'd seen and heard. It's a safe wager he'll tell anybody else who cares to listen. And if we don't get there first . . ." Aldwin let the thought hang in the air. "If we don't find them there, then we're no worse off than we are right now." He paused, knowing he was pressing harder than he'd ever done. Perhaps a bit of conciliation was in order. "Unless you've thought of a way to get inside the priory."

"Not yet."

"Only thing I could figure is to keep up the watch for anyone being moved. But I suspect they'd just wait us out."

His brow furrowed, Guy started pacing to and fro, six steps away from Aldwin, six steps back. *Aldwin knows the stakes,* he thought. *But wagering everything on the word of one traveler who might have had too much to drink in Dursley and didn't get his facts right? Everything else Aldwin says makes sense though. And it's the one thing we know that that sanctimonious prior isn't aware we know, so he can't get word to the captors. Unless he had a spy in that tavern.*

That final thought spurred Guy to a decision. "Very well, Aldwin. We ride at dawn. As soon as there's even a hint of light. We *have* to get there first."

CHAPTER NINE

They wasted little time on the way, leaving the Bristol Road just south of Cambridge on a country lane that made directly for Dursley, nestled in a notch at the southern end of the Cotswold Hills. As they drew within sight of the hills rising on both sides of the little valley, Guy called a halt. "Let's not alarm them by riding in all at once. Aldwin, take two men with you and ride slowly, as if you're just passing through. Find the bell tower and keep your eyes open for any activity . . . and anything that might prove useful to us. Then circle back a different way. The rest of us will take the next woodland track up the hill and wait for you there."

The heavily wooded hills provided good cover for the men and a narrow stream for the horses to drink. To Guy, the wait seemed interminable. He tied his horse to a small tree and made his way to a large stone outcropping, hoping for a glimpse of the village. Hoping in vain, as it turned out. All he could see was more forest and another trail that seemed to head downhill, though for how far it was impossible to tell. Returning to his horse, he checked all four hooves for stones, even though he already knew what he'd find since the animal had shown no hint of lameness. Waiting patiently was not one of Guy's virtues . . . and right now, it felt like the devil's own curse. *Give them time,* he told himself. *Aldwin knows what to look for. And you have no idea what route they'll have to take to get back. It's only just midday. There's still time.*

The other men had all taken this opportunity to get food from their packs and sat in a group on some rocks and fallen logs in the little clearing.

The sight of dried meat and bread whetted Guy's appetite, but as he reached into his pack, he was struck by another thought. *There's still time. That means there's still time for a messenger from that sanctimonious prior to reach the village. If he does, all our efforts may come to nought.*

"Diggory," he called to one of the men. "I need a watchman. Get yourself back down the trail to the edge of the forest. Stay hidden in the trees, but keep an eye out for anyone headed into Dursley. If you see anyone, come get me straightaway. And if who you see is a monk, grab him and bring him here."

"A black monk, sir?"

"I don't give a sard what color," Guy growled. "If it's a monk, bring him. Otherwise, don't leave your post until I send someone to relieve you."

Still, time dragged. By the time Aldwin and his men returned more than an hour later, Guy was on the verge of sending a search party to look for them, but he held his impatience in check while they dismounted and gave their horses a drink.

"We had a meal in the tavern," Aldwin began.

"You *what*?"

"Well, isn't that what travelers do when they reach a town or village at midday?"

"Sorry, Aldwin. I've just been anxious for news."

"Anyway, we asked how far it was to Tetbury and kept to ourselves while we ate. The tavern was across from the market and the bell tower, so it was the perfect spot to watch comings and goings from either. There's definitely something afoot in the tower, sir. We saw one monk headed back there from the market with what looked like more food than a few monks could possibly eat. Then later, a monk left the tower and went to the baker's shop just past the tavern then retraced his steps carrying three large loaves of bread.

"The landlord was more than helpful. Not that we asked questions. But he brought our meals just as that monk was passing with the bread. He was eager to tell us how the whole village is excited about the church being rebuilt. They're expecting masons to arrive and walls to start going up any day now. Seems when they demolished the old church, they left the floor and the crypt intact so they wouldn't have to dig new foundations."

It took all of Guy's self-control not to shout for joy. An old crypt in a place no one could go to worship. What an exquisite hiding place for captives you didn't want found! Instead, he asked calmly, "Did you see Diggory on your way up?"

"Aye. He said you told him to stay until you sent a replacement."

"Send someone to replace him, Aldwin. Diggory can pass on my orders. You and I have plans to make. When you've dispatched your man, join me on that stone outcrop over there."

Aldwin had barely sat down when Guy began. "I've been thinking. Where's the access to the crypt? Sometimes it's from the transept, sometimes from the apse. But either of those would require the monks to leave the bell tower and cross the ruined floor to get to the captives. Has anyone mentioned seeing that? Either your traveler last night or the landlord today?"

"No." Aldwin shook his head. "All the talk is about them coming and going from the tower."

"Then there must be an entrance to the crypt from inside that tower. That makes things both easier and harder for us."

"Sir?"

"Easier because we know how to get to the captives. Harder because we have to immobilize all the monks before we can get on with the rescue. And we can't be sure how many of them there are or if they're armed. No chance to scout for another entrance – that would be noticed and would give the game away." Guy paused. "No, I think a full-on assault is our only option. The question is when. Seems to me monks have some kind of prayers going on at all hours of the day and night."

"There's a gap, sir, between Compline and Vigil. The only time everyone can sleep."

"How do you know this, Aldwin?"

"My brothers and I lived in a monastery for a couple of years after Ma died, 'til Pa took a new wife and brought us back home."

"So the best way to catch them unawares would be between dark and midnight."

"The closer to midnight, the better, sir, if you want them sleeping soundly."

"If we're right about the captives being in the crypt, then my guess is they have someone on watch even during those hours. But it's probably only one man. Even still, I doubt we can avoid a confrontation."

"But the moon's in our favor, sir. Waning quarter – won't rise until midnight, so we have the cover of darkness going in and a bit of light for our escape."

"Light that would help pursuers as well. Which means we need to leave all the monks tied up or incapacitated. Tell me, Aldwin, how far are we from town?"

"Less than a quarter of an hour, even at a walk."

"So if we leave a little before midnight – while it's still dark, we'll be at the tower long before they ring the bell for Vigil."

"If they ring it at all. Remember, this is a village church, not a monastery."

"Then we know what to do. Prepare the men. Maintain the watch for any arriving monks only until time for Compline. Even if someone arrived after that, it would be too late to interfere with our plans. We've no extra horses, so two people will have to ride double. Put our best horsemen on the two strongest horses and make sure they know their job is to get the captives back to Berkeley Castle no matter what else may happen.

"And Aldwin?"

"Yes, sir?"

"When we get back to the castle, Makepeace goes straight to the dungeon."

Aldwin couldn't disguise his dismay. "To the dungeon, sir?"

"To the dungeon. And that's an order, Aldwin. Understood?"

Aldwin's shoulders slumped in resignation as he replied, "Aye, sir."

***

"Did you hear that?" Will asked his companion. The monks had just left after bringing supper – the familiar bowl of thin potage, a chunk of bread, and a mug of small ale. They'd been talkative this evening, speaking among themselves but not addressing their captives. No one could have mistaken, however, that the conversation was intended for the captives' ears.

"Aye. The arrival tomorrow of Friar Thomas, who'll know which of us is the former king. Thomas Dunheved himself, I'd wager."

"Which means if we're going to do anything at all," said Will, "it has to be tonight."

"I've been thinking, Will. If you were to stand on my shoulders, you could almost certainly reach those boards and see if it is indeed a broken window."

"I'd have to cut our wrist bindings. You could never hold me up without having your hands free. And I'll need both hands to pry the boards loose."

"Aye. So we wait until they collect our bowls. We'll still have a bit of light, but it will fade fast."

"Unless there's a full moon."

"Something I rather doubt. These past two nights have been quite dark once the sun has set." They sat in silence for several moments before Caernarfon spoke again. "Will, if you find an open window, you must make your escape. Whoever has taken us has hopes of restoring me to the throne, so they'll do me no harm. The same cannot be said of you if anyone believes you were part of the plot." He paused before adding, "Or if the plotters want you out of the way."

"I couldn't leave you behind, sir."

"Indeed you could. And you must. You've been a fine companion, Will Makepeace, but you mustn't sacrifice yourself on my behalf."

The hinges creaked on the door at the top of the stairs, and two black-robed figures descended. They said nothing as they collected the empty bowls and mugs and retreated back up the stairs, but the hinges did not creak shut. Someone was listening for sounds of anything out of the ordinary in the crypt. Caernarfon put his finger to his lips, and Will nodded. At long last, the listener gave up and the door clanged shut.

They waited several long moments to be sure no one was returning. They never had before, but neither had they ever before delayed closing the door. At last, Will got to his feet and retrieved his dagger. "We'd best get started," he whispered, "while we still have some light." Caernarfon rose and held out his hands. The dagger was sharp and the cord a little frayed, so Will made quick work of freeing his companion. Then he handed the dagger to Caernarfon to return the favor.

They spent a few minutes shaking out their hands, flexing their fingers, and working the kinks out of the muscles in their arms then made straight for the wall with the windows. It took a couple of tries before they managed it successfully, but eventually Will stood upright on Caernarfon's shoulders. "Can you move a couple of steps closer to the wall?"

Caernarfon grabbed each of Will's ankles to steady the weight and carefully approached the wall. "I believe that's as close as I can get."

"It's fine."

Will soon realized trying to pry a board loose from the side wasn't going to work. The boards were thin – rather like shingles – but they were nailed firmly in place. He needed better leverage against the nail at the top of the board, so he slid the dagger vertically behind the board all the way to the hilt and began prying from the top. At one point, he put so much effort into it that he was in danger of toppling over backward, but Caernarfon quickly recognized what was happening and took a couple of steps back, allowing Will to recover his balance. *That was close. But the nail finally budged, so the rest should be easier.* When the top of the board was free, he gave it a sharp tug and it splintered around the bottom nail, revealing that it had started to rot from the bottom up. He balanced it in the opening and began to work on the next board.

By the time he had three boards off, it was obvious there had once been a window here but nothing was left of it save the wooden frame. "We were right, sir," Will called down in a loud whisper. "It's open to the outside. Should we rest for a bit?"

"No, Will, finish. We'll rest while we wait for darkness to settle in."

I can scarce believe the man's strength, Will thought. *Holding me up all this time and shifting sideways for each new board. And he's doing all this for me – not to save himself.* In that moment, the former king solidified his place in Will's affection. *How will I ever repay him?*

With the last board free, they had to work out how to get Will back down on the ground. There was still too much light for him to make good an escape. Caernarfon grasped Will's right ankle tighter, then reached up with his left arm. "Balance your weight with one hand on the window frame, then lean down and hand me the dagger." Ever so slowly, Will stretched his left arm down, holding the dagger by its tip. He finally exhaled when he felt Caernarfon grasp the hilt and tuck the dagger back into his boot.

"Now, pull yourself upright again, then walk your hands down the wall like you did getting up." When Will was bent almost horizontal from the waist, Caernarfon let go of the left ankle. "Now slide that leg down my chest … slowly … keep bending the other knee … that's right. Now I'm going to let go of the other ankle." In a rather awkward position now, Will held onto the rough stones for dear life. Caernarfon reached up his left hand. "Take my hand and keep your weight shifted to the left." Then he reached up his right hand and settled it firmly under Will's right buttock. "Now, free your right foot and let go of the wall. I'll lower you to my shoulders." As soon as Will settled, Caernarfon crouched down and lowered him to the ground then stood upright and flexed his shoulders.

"Wait here, Will," said the former king, "while I fetch the blankets. It seems prudent for me to sleep here tonight rather than trying to navigate this sea of sarcophagi in the dark. I can return to my usual spot at first light."

He returned with both blankets and they sat on the floor to wait.

***

"Time to wake the men," Sir Guy nudged Aldwin from his own nap. "The Summer Triangle's nearing its zenith. Time for us to move."

Aldwin stretched and got to his feet. "You know, sir, I was thinking earlier. Maybe it's a good idea if we go into the village in small groups. It'll be less noisy – less likely to wake folks. We can regroup in the cover of the market building and leave our horses tethered there while we grab the captives."

"Makes sense. You take the first group since you know the layout. I'll ride with the last. Now let's get underway."

By the time Vega was directly overhead, they were in position to execute their plan, horses loosely tied, men assembled just inside the arches of the market. All except for two men who remained mounted, ready to gallop away as soon as the captives were aboard. Guy left Aldwin in charge and tiptoed across to the churchyard to scout the target. Staying in the grass where his footsteps would be muffled, he made a partial circuit of the bell tower, never venturing far from the building lest someone inside catch a glimpse of him. His reconnaissance complete, he walked south for several yards then crossed the street to return to the market.

"It's quiet," he reported to Aldwin. "No sound of movement. No evidence of candlelight, but there's no way to tell what might be deep inside on one of the upper levels. Are we ready?"

"Aye, sir."

"Remember . . . subdue the monks first, then search for the captives."

***

He must have dozed, though he hadn't meant to. But Caernarfon was shaking his shoulder. "Wake up, Will," he whispered. "I judge it to be almost midnight. Time for you to go."

"I suppose so, sir. You can still change your mind though. I'll stay if you ask me to."

"No, Will. I shall be fine. There's no reason for you to be persecuted on my account. Now here . . . take your blanket."

"You keep it, sir. It's cold down here."

"You'll needed it, Will, if you have to sleep in the open." Will reluctantly took the blanket from Caernarfon's outstretched hand. "Now let's get you back up to that window."

Knowing what to do this time, they managed the maneuver on the first try. As he reached for the window frame with one hand, Will looked down. "I shall miss you, sir. I think perhaps there was much more about the game of chess that you could have taught me."

Caernarfon smiled up at his companion. "It would have been a pleasure. I shall miss your company as well. And I'll offer prayers for your safety. Now, on your way." Will turned and started pulling himself up into the window, his feet scrambling up the rough stones. As he made his exit, he heard a voice from below. "Godspeed, Will Makepeace."

The bottom of the window frame was mere inches from the grass of the churchyard. Will had to drag himself forward on his belly until his feet cleared the window before he could rise to his knees and assess his surroundings. It appeared he was on the opposite side of the ruined church from where they'd stopped the carriage. But he needed to get to the road and make his way out of town as fast as he could.

Rising to his feet, he darted to the side of the bell tower and crouched low, hugging the wall to avoid being seen by anyone looking out the windows. As he came to the corner, he peered around, all his hopes pinned on there being no one posted at the door to watch for strangers. Just as he was about to celebrate his luck at finding no one, something in his peripheral vision caught his attention. Shadows in the market building across the road. Someone or something moving about. Whatever or whoever it might be, it meant danger for Will. He pulled his head back and sat down in the grass to think.

Go the other way. Past the demolished church. Sneak around in the alleys and lanes until I'm clear of the town. I don't think they spotted me. Should be able to escape . . . maybe find some woodlands to hide. Wait and watch to see if they come this way.

Then another thought struck him. *What if they're after Caernarfon? He was so sure no one would harm him, but was that just wishful thinking? Is there some place I can hide here in town and watch what happens? Should I go back? Sneak back in the same way I got out? At least I have a dagger and could offer him some kind of protection.*

What are you thinking, Will? he chided himself. *There's only one of you. You'd be horribly outnumbered. You're on your own now. If you don't get out of here, you're going to get caught up in something you might not survive. That's why Caernarfon sent you away, isn't it?*

***

While Will wallowed in indecision, Guy's men began to cross the road, swords already drawn, and formed up for a direct assault on the bell tower door. Guy raised his hand, and every man's sword rose to the attack position.

From his place beside the door, Aldwin tried the latch and it yielded. But as he gave it a shove to open wider, the screech of the rusty hinges told every man in the troop that their presence was no longer a secret.

Guy stepped inside, scanning his surroundings, and beckoned for the first group to join him. No sooner had he given the signal than a monk emerged from the dark recesses. Guy held the man at sword-point and hissed, "Not a sound if you value your life." The monk began singing the sort of chant Guy had only heard in church. Guy ran him through.

Noises from above said others were scrambling about on the next level. Guy waved his men up the stairs. "Capture them if you can; kill them if you must," he ordered. "We need someone alive to lead us to the captives."

***

Hearing the door screech open, Will hovered for a moment between terror and curiosity. Then he heard the chant that was suddenly silenced and curiosity plus concern for Caernarfon won out. He ventured to peer around the corner of the tower once again . . . and gasped audibly as he recognized familiar faces. Aldwin standing at the door, his head scanning right and left, obviously on lookout. His head snapped in Will's direction at the sound of the gasp. Then he pointed at two men and waved in the direction of the corner of the building.

Knowing nothing good could come of Guy's men capturing him lurking about, Will jumped to his feet, dashed around the corner of the tower, and made straight for Aldwin. "Aldwin, thank God!" He didn't even try to keep his voice down. "I thought you were new kidnappers. Where's Guy?"

***

It took Aldwin a minute to realize what was happening, and then, "Holy Mother of God! Will? Is that you?"

"Aye, Aldwin. You men are a sight for sore eyes. Where's Guy?"

"Inside with half the men, rounding up the monks. The rest of us are waiting for his signal to begin searching for the captives. But I warn you, Will, he's *not* going to be pleased to see you."

"That doesn't matter. I know where Caernarfon is – how to get to him. Come with me."

"Will, this is *lunacy*! You know what Guy's like if his orders aren't obeyed."

As Will stepped through the door, he called back to Aldwin, "I don't care. I'm not taking any chances they don't find all the monks and someone knows another way to get to Caernarfon before we do."

Guy froze in his tracks, his jaw dropped open, when Will came through the door.

Will didn't hesitate. "Come on, Guy. Follow me. Let's get Caernarfon out of here."

That was all it took for Guy to snap back to reality. "You're not going anywhere, Will Makepeace." Then he shouted, "Aldwin, get in here. Take this man into custody."

"Come on, Guy," Will persisted. "I know where he is. What I don't know is exactly how many monks there are here, so there's no way to know if you've rounded them all up. And I also don't know if there's another way into the crypt that a monk on the loose could get to Caernarfon first." *I do know there's another way in if anyone got away and found the unboarded window, but I don't know if there's another way out.*

Aldwin took a couple of tentative steps toward Will, who evaded him and hurried to the only other door in the room. "This'll be locked. Have someone search the monks for the keys. Somebody find a candle." Then he caught sight of something in the shadows. A hook holding a large ring on which was a single key. "Never mind." Will grabbed the ring and quickly unlocked the door.

A flicker of light on the wall announced the arrival of the lit candle. Will grabbed it and started down the stairs, Guy, Aldwin, and five other guards hot on his heels. Holding the candle high, Will signaled for the others to wait then made his way among the tombs to where he'd left Caernarfon. No one was there. Not even the blanket. Will's spirits sank.

He raised the candle higher and started turning in a slow circle, hoping to spy a shadow where one shouldn't be – any indication of where Caernarfon might be hiding . . . if he was still here at all. In the calmest voice he could muster, he said, "Lord Caernarfon, it's Will. I'm back. And those with me are friends. The monks are in custody. Please . . . if you're still here, it's safe to show yourself."

As Will completed his circle, a figure slowly rose from behind the tomb with the carved effigy. His voice as calm as Will had ever heard, Caernarfon said, "I heard all the commotion above. Thinking it might be more of our foes, I deemed it best to hide and let them think I too had escaped through the window."

Guy rushed forward. "Lord Caernarfon, you're safe now. We'll have you back in Berkeley Castle before daybreak. And those who dared kidnap you . . ." He then looked directly at Will. ". . . and those who dared help them will receive the king's justice." He gestured toward the stairs. "Let's go home."

As he passed Aldwin, Guy hesitated only a moment to say, "Take Makepeace into custody. You have my orders."

Aldwin hung his head sadly, then stepped to Will's side. "Come on, Will." But he made no rush to follow Guy up the stairs. When Guy and Caernarfon passed through the door, Aldwin took Will's elbow. "He's in no mood to argue with right now, Will. Last two days, he's been certain he'd be hauled up on charges of dereliction. Once we're all back home and Berkeley praises him for recapturing the old king, he'll come to his senses. Then he'll realize what you just did and that you're not to blame for any of this."

"I hope you're right, Aldwin. But Guy's not always an easy man."

CHAPTER TEN

The high windows on the walls of his cell reminded Will of the crypt. But that was the only similarity. At least in the crypt, he had someone to talk to and the hope of escape. He wasn't quite sure how many days he'd been here – he hadn't bothered to count. The final total was almost certainly going to be all the days of the rest of his life, so there was little point, really, in counting.

Aldwin had visited twice but didn't stay long either time. The first time, he was full of enthusiasm. "Lord Berkeley was eager to celebrate the fact we'd gotten the old king back. Gave Guy a commendation in front of all of us and sent us food from his own table. That was some fine eating, I don't mind saying. Wish I could have figured out how to smuggle some in for you.

"Berkeley's still grumpy about all the damage those horsemen caused, so Guy's set us the task of helping with the cleanup when we're not on watch. For now, we're boarding up the broken windows until the glazier can make new ones. And if you ask me, a few of the doors are going to have to be replaced too. Some of the axe marks are really deep – like it wouldn't have taken much more for the attackers to break through."

Will didn't really have any useful contribution to make to the conversation, but the company was welcome and Aldwin's volubility cheered him up, if only for a few moments.

"Anyway," Aldwin said, "I can't stay long. Guy wants to inspect all our weapons later this afternoon, and I need to make sure nobody's slacking off on their cleaning and sharpening." He made his way to the door and raised his hand to bang for the guard's attention but stopped short and turned back to Will. "I haven't forgotten, Will. Guy's still a little short-tempered, but in a couple of days, I'll try to get him to see sense." Then he rapped hard on the door. The little window at the top slid open and a pair of eyes peered inside. Apparently satisfied, the owner of the eyes turned the key in the lock and Aldwin made his exit, leaving Will with only the sound of the key being turned in the opposite direction.

On the second visit, Will could tell from Aldwin's expression there'd be no enthusiasm in his words. "I tried, Will," he said. "Truly I did. To the point where I almost sent him into a rage. He's having none of it. Told me to mind my own business or I'd be joining you down here.

"He's changed, Will. Used to be his gruffness was mostly show and bluster. Now he means every word. The men are learning to stay out of his way. Hiding out in the kitchens when they're not on duty, spending more time exercising their horses than usual. I try to keep their spirits up, but it's not much use." Aldwin hung his head. With a final, "Try not to despair, Will," he rapped on the door and made his exit.

Will felt sorry for Aldwin . . . almost as sorry as he did for himself. *Why didn't you run the other way when you had the chance?* he asked himself. *You could have been long gone – free as a bird on the wing instead of locked up in this cell. Yes, that would have sealed Guy's conviction that you were one of the plotters, but maybe that conviction was a foregone conclusion anyway. Helping with the rescue did nothing to help your cause.*

But deep in his soul, Will understood that his real motivation had been helping Caernarfon. Guy was so fond of challenging Will's behavior by asking what his mother would think. Will knew. He could hear her voice in his head. "Because you're a kind and gentle man, my William. The sort that God smiles on."

Apparently not the sort that Guy smiles on. Certainly not the sort that Guy deigns to visit in this cell.

***

The servant who brought the message didn't utter a word – merely held out the folded paper and walked away when Guy took it. Now, reading the note for the second time, he wondered why the servant couldn't just have told him what he was to do.

> *Bickerstaffe,*
> *Join me in Caernarfon's quarters an hour hence.*
> *Berkeley*

The formality of the invitation. The meeting place. It all had an ominous feeling. A feeling that weighed on Guy for every moment of the hour he had to wait. So his senses were all on high alert and his posture stiff and formal when he stood in the open doorway of Caernarfon's chamber at the appointed time.

Berkeley and Caernarfon sat at a small table, a chess board between them, apparently in the middle of a game, as none of the pieces were in their starting positions. There was a third chair at the side of the table.

"Ah, Bickerstaffe, join us," Berkeley's greeting was affable enough . . . but not enough to allay Guy's apprehension. "Do sit. Do you play chess?"

Perching on the chair, his spine still rigid, Guy replied, "I learned a bit as a lad, but I've had no time for diversions in many months."

"Then have a look at this board. I fear Edward's got me cornered. Do you see a way out of it?"

Guy studied the arrangement of the pieces for a few moments then shook his head. "I was never very good at the game, sir. Any suggestion I might offer could all too easily lead to your defeat."

"If I move my queen to protect the king, he takes her in two moves and the king on the third." Caernarfon smiled. Berkeley stroked his chin in thought. "Now perhaps if I move the bishop?"

"Makepeace would know what to do," Caernarfon said quietly.

"Then why isn't he sitting here instead of me?"

"That, Thomas, is a question for which I have no answer."

So that's what this is all about. They're going to try to get me to release Will. Well, they can try, but I'm not going to have a traitor to the king in my troop.

Both men turned to look at Guy. Neither spoke.

"With respect, sirs, I believe the disposition of my men is my own responsibility."

"True. And yet," said Berkeley, "that leads me to wonder what offense Makepeace has committed that he remains all this time in my dungeon rather than standing watch or helping repair the damage to my home."

"I have sufficient reason to believe he was in league with those who *caused* the damage, sir."

"On what evidence?"

"Too much time spent in the tavern, where messages could easily be exchanged. Failing to prevent Lord Caernarfon's capture. Letting himself be taken captive as well – going with his compatriots, if you will, sir. And then, when we found him lurking in the darkness, pretending to help us as a way to disguise the fact that he was one of the plotters."

Berkeley turned toward Caernarfon. "Edward?"

"And yet, Sir Guy, your reading of the situation in no way matches my own observations. You were watching from the ramparts on the day of the raid. I trust you saw Will leap to my defense using whatever he had to hand. In fact, we both tried to fight off the kidnappers. But we were outnumbered, and garden tools are inferior weapons in the face of flails and battle axes. Throughout our ordeal, Will kept up the pretense that we were both merely gardeners . . . that, in their zeal, the monks had taken the wrong men. He helped keep our captors sufficiently confused that they had to send for Thomas Dunheved to sort things out. That's how we know it was the Dunheveds behind the whole business."

"And yet," said Guy, "we found him lurking about the bell tower, obviously having deserted you. Caught in the act of escaping, he thought to deceive me by leading us to you. I am *not* so easily deceived."

"I'll grant you have the right assessment of Will's original purpose that night, but equally you have the wrong reason. Will was indeed escaping from the crypt. At my insistence. Not only had he revealed to me his fear that you would find him somehow culpable, but I also knew that once Dunheved identified me, they'd want Will silenced forever since he had seen too much. I sent him away, Sir Guy, to save his life. And I'm grateful to him for intervening to preserve mine."

Guy didn't reply straightaway. Could it be he had things the wrong way round? *Unlikely. These men don't know Will like I do. They haven't seen how he follows his own whims just to aggravate me . . . how he wastes time and money in the taverns carousing with who knows what kind of schemers who might be there . . . how he's too naïve to avoid revealing things he shouldn't.*

Deciding he had to stand his ground, Guy looked Caernarfon straight in the eye. "And why should I believe you, sir? You have everything to gain by spinning me a tale of Makepeace as an unselfish participant in these events. But I have everything to lose by failing to act on what I believe to be true."

"Come, come, Bickerstaffe," Berkeley stepped in. "Isn't it just possible that your fear of being thought culpable for not preventing the kidnapping is coloring your judgment? My God, man, I gave you a public expression of gratitude for returning our . . . guest. What more do you need?"

"With respect, sir, keeping Lord Caernarfon safe from intruders and plotters is a heavy responsibility."

"And it's *my* responsibility. I've heard two very different views of Makepeace's . . . well, not so much his behavior as his motivation. And no irrefutable proof of either. I think we should give the man the benefit of the doubt. "

Guy opened his mouth to object, but Berkeley raised his hand to forestall any comment. "Let him take my seat here with the white pieces so I can get on with my business. We'll know in due course if he's consorting with plotters. Just keep an eye on him."

"That, sir, would require my diverting men to the tavern. Makepeace is overly fond of spending time there."

"And what's wrong with time in the tavern? Most of my own people spend time there. Are you suggesting my household is filled with conspirators?"

"Not at all, sir."

"Then why assume your own man is one?"

For that, Guy had no answer. Berkeley turned his attention back to the game board. "Alright, Edward, show me what move Makepeace would choose."

Caernarfon picked up the white king and captured the black knight on the next square. "Then if you follow through on that correctly, Thomas, you'll have my king in five moves."

Guy had no idea if that was correct or not, but he didn't miss the meaning of taking a knight out of play. This was a skirmish he was *not* destined to win. "Very well, my lord, I'll release Makepeace for regular duty, and he'll be allowed to resume his tutelage in the finer points of chess."

"And assist me with the gardening as well, I hope," said Edward.

"No gardening," Guy blurted out. "That's how all this got started in the first place."

"For God's sake, man," Berkeley slammed a hand down on the table, causing the game pieces to dance around. "You're strung tighter than a bowstring. What's the harm in a bit of gardening? I, for one, am looking forward to the harvest from that garden appearing on my plate in the coming weeks. So you will free Makepeace from his cell and assign him his former duties, which by my reckoning, include rendering companionship to Edward for chess, gardening, or anything else I might approve."

Guy wasn't stupid. He recognized an order when he heard one, so he nodded his head smartly and replied, "Yes, sir. As you wish."

"Alright, Bickerstaffe, you can be on your way. I should get back to the business of losing this game." Caernarfon smiled. "Again," Berkeley sounded resigned. Then turning his back on Sir Guy, he added, "So, Edward, five moves you say? Damned if I know what they are."

***

Defeat stung. And this was defeat at Caernarfon's hands, so it stung that much more. Fuming as he strode toward the dungeon, Guy thought to himself, *They didn't say anything about how much watch duty I assign him. You may no longer be a prisoner, Will Makepeace, but I can for certes make sure you have so much duty you're too exhausted to go carousing in the tavern. Let this be a lesson to you.*

CHAPTER ELEVEN

September 1327

Some years earlier, he had observed that when business was being conducted in his father's privy chamber, everyone's focus was intent on the matter at hand – the documents, each other, the debate – perhaps occasionally the doorway to the chamber if someone new was announced. But no attention was given to anyone or anything not directly involved in the conversation. Curious by nature – and keenly aware that he would one day be king – Edward had hit on what he thought of as a clever ruse to eavesdrop on matters of state. One day, armed with some pages of Latin his tutor expected him to translate, he wandered in as the adults were gathering and perched himself in the window ledge in the corner of the room, pretending to study. No one paid him any mind. After all, what would a lad his age possibly understand about the business of running the kingdom? So he began to make it a habit, particularly at Westminster Palace, where the window ledges were wide and he could sit for hours, if necessary, in reasonable comfort.

His father had asked him once why he was doing this. "The light's better there than in any room in the palace," he replied. "Makes it easier to read the cramped writing on these pages." To his surprise, his father took the explanation at face value. And in that instant, it dawned on him he'd need to study in that spot regularly, even when no business was being conducted, if his excuse was to remain unquestioned. That wasn't too much of a hardship though – what he'd said about the light in those south-facing windows was absolutely true, regardless of the season and especially if it was cloudy or raining.

Now that he was fourteen and taller, the ledge felt more cramped, but that didn't dissuade him from folding his growing frame into the space and keeping his ears tuned to the conversation while his eyes remained assiduously focused on his purported studies.

This afternoon, his mother and Roger Mortimer, apparently in the throes of a heated debate, had stormed into the room not long after Edward climbed into his perch. "I tell you, Isabella, we have to *do* something." Mortimer sounded angry.

"Come now, Roger," Isabella's tone was the sweet voice Edward knew she used when trying to calm someone down, even if she wasn't backing down herself. "If I recall, it was you who reassured me he'd be safe in Berkeley's care."

"That was before the Dunheveds' raid."

"And didn't Berkeley find him and return him to the castle? Besides, we have Thomas Dunheved imprisoned at Pontefract."

"And you think that's the end of the plotting?" Mortimer refused to be placated. "Now there's *this*." He waved two pages angrily in the air. "William Shalford writes there's a Welsh plot brewing to free him," he continued, thrusting the pages toward Isabella. "Read for yourself."

Isabella took the letter but set it aside on a nearby table. "It seems to me the first thing to do is to inform Berkeley so he's ready to thwart the plotters."

"Don't you see, Isabella?" Mortimer wouldn't be swayed. "These are just the plots we know about. God knows how many other people are out there plotting to free him . . . maybe even to try to restore him to the throne. And I'm not sure even God knows what the Earl of Kent is up to. He makes great show of staying far removed from his brother's supporters, but that doesn't mean he's not secretly in league with them. It's up to us to make sure a restoration isn't possible."

Edward was well aware that if Parliament could depose the father in favor of the son, a different Parliament could reverse that action. That presented a direct threat to the pre-eminence Mortimer now enjoyed.

"You're forgetting, Roger." Isabella's tone now bordered on stern. "It's *not* up to us. Parliament decreed he should live out the rest of his days in captivity. You're also forgetting it was never my intent that he should be harmed – only that he should no longer have the power to let others wreak harm in his name."

"A pox on Parliament! What do they know?"

Edward watched his mother clench her fists at her side and then relax them – twice. A sure sign, he knew from experience, that she was trying to control her anger. This time it didn't work. "A pox on Parliament?" she raised her voice. "A pox on me as well, Roger? Is *that* what you mean?"

"God's beard, Isabella. Why can't we ever discuss the man without ending up in an argument? Now, I have to go. I'm expected in Lincoln, and then I have business in Abergavenny." He strode across the room but paused with his hand on the door handle. "Read Shalford's letter. Then open your eyes, woman. Your precious son isn't safe on his throne as long as that man's still alive." With that, Mortimer stormed out and slammed the door in his wake.

Isabella watched him leave then clenched her fists, stamped her foot, and shouted "Bastard!" at his retreating footsteps. Her anger apparently dispelled, she turned back to the table and retrieved the letter she'd set aside.

Edward slid down from his perch and approached her. "A word, Mother?" he asked quietly.

Startled, Isabella spun around, her expression an odd mixture of fear and fury that turned quizzical the moment she saw who was there. "Edward . . . you gave me such a start. Where did you come from?"

"Just there." Edward pointed to the window. "I was studying my mathematics."

"Studying?"

He handed her the pages covered with arithmetic problems.

"But . . . you haven't written any answers."

"I like to practice doing them in my head. So I can know the answer well before anyone who has to fetch quill and paper to figure it out. My tutor says that could prove quite advantageous for a king." She handed back the papers. "But that's not what I want to talk with you about." He paused for a moment, girding his thoughts in anticipation of what he was about to say. "Mother, you're not going to let Mortimer get away with it, are you?"

"Get away with what?"

"Don't feign innocence with me, Mother. I heard his words. He's proposing to have my father executed. That's not something to take lightly."

"I don't take it lightly, Son. But neither do I take these plots lightly."

"Then round up the leaders of the plots and imprison them – just as you've done with Thomas Dunheved."

"Cut off one head of the hydra at a time? Is that what you're saying? I seem to recall that's a losing proposition."

"What I'm saying, Mother, is that you mustn't let Mortimer run roughshod over your authority – and mine. He may be your lover, but he's not your consort. He's Baron Mortimer of Wigmore – nothing more. And if you let him get away with what he's proposing, you'll be taking the first steps toward the mistake Father made."

"And what mistake was that?"

"Allowing your favorite to assume far more influence and authority than his position entitles him to."

"Don't be impertinent, Edward." Isabella's tone was stern.

"You only say that because you know I speak the truth."

"I think you need to find a different place to study. Eavesdropping on matters of state is unbecoming in a future king."

"In point of fact, I'm *already* king. I'll be fifteen in less than three months, so it's high time I was present at discussions about what's to be done in my name."

"I'm not sure if—"

Edward cut her off. "If Mortimer would agree? The only one who needs to agree is *you*, Mother. Everything that's happened has been at your instigation."

"Very well, I'll think about it."

"What you need to think about even more urgently is how to prevent any harm coming to my father."

"And you, Edward, need to realize that you're far too inexperienced to understand matters of state. Now be on your way . . . to your tutor . . . or wherever it is you're supposed to be. Leave these things to me."

Edward offered a slight nod of the head to his mother then turned on his heel and left the room, even more troubled than he'd been earlier. His mother's final words told him with absolute clarity that Mortimer was right about one thing. She was already far down the path of relishing power, and he – her son, the actual crowned king – was but a pawn in her game – the guarantee that power wouldn't be stripped from her. *At least not until I come of age*, he reminded himself. She had been astute enough to recognize the abuse being wrought by the Despensers and to do something about it, but she was blind to where that success was leading her. *Would that have happened if she hadn't come under Mortimer's influence?* he asked himself. *No way to know, really. But of Mortimer's greed for power there can be no doubt – it's on display for anyone who cares to look.*

Mulling these things over as he made his way to his bedchamber, Edward came to another realization. His mother was not going to protect his father if there was even the slightest possible cost to her. It would be up to him. And it would depend on there being someone he could trust absolutely.

Once inside his bedchamber with the door firmly closed, he threw himself on the bed without bothering to remove his boots. "Who *can* I trust?" he wondered aloud. Until today, the answer might have included any of his mother's retainers. But no longer. He knew there was only one – William Montagu.

From the moment he'd arrived at court as a ward of the king some seven years ago, Montagu had taken an interest in the eight-year-old prince, and they'd remained fast friends ever since. The twelve-year difference in their ages seemed never to matter. Even when William became Baron Montagu three years later and married not long after that, he still made a point of spending time with Edward, the two of them sharing their most personal thoughts. They were both present at the defeat of the English army by the Scots at Stanhope Park, and both laid that humiliation squarely at the feet of Roger Mortimer.

Now, staring at the tester above his bed, Edward was coming to grips with the reality that no one else – not even his mother – had his interests at heart. He also knew time was not on his side.

But apparently Mother Nature was. The following morning dawned sunny and pleasant, and Edward presented himself early at Montagu's Westminster lodgings. The baron was still in his nightshirt and robe when summoned by a servant to greet the early-morning guest. "Your Grace . . . my friend . . ." Montagu was expansive. "We weren't expecting you."

"And certainly not so early," Edward finished the thought for him, sparing his friend the embarrassment of being unprepared. "But it seems I've achieved my ends to be the first to lay claim to your time today."

Montagu grinned. "That you have, Edward. That you have. Please . . . take a seat." Edward chose a chair and Montagu sat opposite him. "Now, what is it I can do for you?"

"It's a lovely day. Fancy a ride up to the Manor of Hampstead? Maybe a gallop around the heath?"

"You needn't ask twice. But I'm hardly dressed for riding." They both chuckled. "I shan't be long. Shall I have a servant bring you food or drink while you wait?"

"That won't be necessary. I've quenched my morning thirst already."

Montagu rose and made for the door. "Then I'll just order two horses saddled and be back with as little delay as I can muster."

The young king knew William's quick acquiescence meant he understood their conversation must be held in complete privacy. Edward had lain awake much of the night thinking about how to frame his dilemma. In the end, he decided that trust required he be free-hearted and plain-spoken. Nevertheless, he didn't broach the topic as they rode north.

After a good gallop across the heath, he reined his mount to a halt in a spot with unobstructed views for at least fifty yards in every direction. No one could come within eavesdropping distance without being seen. He loosened the reins to let his horse graze and William followed suit. "Something's troubling you, Edward, and yet you seem reluctant to talk about it."

"Troubled, yes. Reluctant, no. I'm just not sure where to begin."

"Then begin with what troubles you most deeply."

"Mortimer's of a mind that it's necessary to end my father's life, and I'm convinced Mother will do nothing to stop him." He went on to describe the scene in the privy chamber and how his mother had dismissed him out of hand.

"And you think this is a sign that your mother is losing control." William paused. "We've always spoken truth between us, Edward."

"Your truth is what I need right now," Edward answered the unasked question.

"From what I've observed, Isabella seems increasingly under Mortimer's thrall. I think your fears are justified."

"Then I'm the only one who can get word to my father that he's in danger."

"That may be."

The horses continued methodically cropping the grass in front of them and to one side, now and again taking a step forward to reach new grazing. Each time the horses stepped forward, their riders paused to scan all around, making sure they were still alone.

"I agonized over this all yesterday afternoon and evening, William. What if Mortimer's right? My first reaction was that he's merely trying to protect his own position of power. But what if *my* position – even my person – is at risk while my father lives?"

"I've heard nothing of plots against you. Of course, any attempt to restore your father to the throne would automatically depose you. Still, I rather doubt the plotters have anything in mind other than restoring what they think of as the natural order – that your father should rule until he dies in battle or of natural causes and that only then would it be the proper time for you to succeed him."

"That may be," Edward mused, "but can we have any confidence in that?"

"There's no way to be sure."

"Aye. And with that, you've hit on the core of what's troubling me – what kept me awake long into the night – and the truth I have to contend with every day until I rule in my own right. I'm isolated . . . alone. In all the world, William, you're the only one of my ken who I can trust."

"Never doubt that, Edward."

Their horses took another step forward, and they paused to scan the heath once more.

"So what am I to do about Mortimer's threat to my father's life?"

"Is Roger still here where your mother can wear him down?"

"No. He left for Lincoln yesterday afternoon and said he had other business in Abergavenny."

Montagu furrowed his brow. "That truly does *not* bode well. Abergavenny would be the perfect place for him to join with Shalford to round up the Welsh plotters. Which would no doubt fuel his determination to eliminate your father. Not to mention that if he gave that order while so far away, your mother couldn't possibly learn what he'd done in time to put a stop to it."

"Then what am I to do, William? I'm the only one who can warn my father, but it could never be known that I did so. So must I just let things play out as God wills? I don't know if my conscience will let me sit idly by, knowing he's probably in danger."

Montagu reached across and laid a comforting hand on his young friend's shoulder. "Unfortunately, Edward, this is one of those lessons of rule and of power. Lessons you've been learning all your life. But this is the most difficult one you've yet faced. And if you can take any comfort from my words, know that I think the way you're grappling with it shows a maturity beyond your years."

"Of course I take comfort from your words, but I still have no answer."

"Ah, but you do. You had the answer when you knocked on my door as the cock crowed this morning. Entrust this problem to me, and return to the palace with a demeanor as if you had no greater care in the world than those of the day before yesterday. Though I suspect you *will* have to give up your habit of eavesdropping on royal business."

Finally, something Edward could smile about. It was good to have a friend – especially one who could lighten your heart. And even more especially if he was your only true friend amid a sea of false ones.

CHAPTER TWELVE

Two mornings later, William Montagu kissed his wife goodbye in her sitting room, where she was preparing to entertain some ladies of the court later in the day. Ordinarily, he'd have dismissed the servants who were bustling about so he could say a private farewell, but this morning it suited his purposes to be overheard. "How long will you be gone?" Catherine asked.

"Two weeks . . . maybe a bit more. Depends on what I discover at our lands in the West Country. But don't fret, my dear. The days will pass quickly, and my boots will be back at the foot of your bed in no time."

He spent the first night at an inn in Bredeford, going out of his way to make sure he was seen by as many people as possible. When he departed the next morning, he gave the innkeeper six pennies more than the bill. *Remember I was here, my good man, if anyone should ask.* The next night, in Andover, he once again made his presence known, but settled his bill with the innkeeper before going to bed. "If I'm to make Cheping Blandford by nightfall tomorrow, I'll have to be away at dawn," he told the innkeeper. "And I've no wish to disturb you before the cock crows." Once again, the extra six pennies. *Remember I was here and where I said I was going.*

Before sunrise, he'd collected his horse and was on his way. At the fork in the road where he'd normally go left toward his family's West Country holdings, he checked to make sure no one was around then reined his horse right, headed for Gloucester. He pressed his horse as much as he dared and almost managed to reach Cirencester by day's end, but he and the animal both needed rest, so he camped beside a bridge over a little stream that offered plenty of grazing and water for the horse.

He was grateful for a short journey the following day, since what was coming next would require him to have all his wits about him. Arriving in Gloucester at midafternoon, he found a better-than-average inn not far from the castle. As he was arranging lodgings for the night, he casually asked the innkeeper, "Do you know if the earl is in residence?"

"Aye. Been back for a couple of weeks."

"Then perhaps I might trouble you for some paper, ink, and a quill . . . to be added to my bill, of course. Courtesy demands that I should make the earl aware of my arrival in the town and offer to call upon him."

The innkeeper disappeared into a back room and returned shortly with a mostly smooth sheet of paper, a quill badly in need of sharpening, and a small bottle with very little ink in the bottom. "That'll be a shilling if ye want to take it upstairs," he said. Seeing Montagu struggle to control his reaction to the outrageous fee, the innkeeper added, "On account of whatever goes upstairs always disappears and I have to buy new."

"And if I write my message standing here?"

"Ye can use the quill and ink ye signed in with and pay me a penny for the paper."

Montagu produced the penny, took the paper, and began composing his message.

> *My dear Kent,*
>
> *It is with great pleasure that I find myself in your fair town. A greater pleasure still to learn that you are in residence. The greatest pleasure of all would be the opportunity to call on you and bring greetings from our king, by whom, for many years, I have been fortunate enough to be considered a friend.*
>
> *The business that brought me here will be concluded by midday, so I am free of obligations in the afternoon. I should be honored if you would consent to receive me and will present myself at the time of your choosing.*
>
> *William, Baron Montagu*

Montagu folded the page and wrote "To the Earl of Kent" on the outside. Ordinarily, he'd seal it, but he was pretty sure the innkeeper would want a king's ransom for a bit of wax. And, in truth, it didn't matter so much. The messenger would undoubtedly be illiterate, and by the end of the day tomorrow, it would be known by more than a few people that he'd paid a visit to the earl. *A risk that has to be taken,* he told himself yet again, *if I'm to find a way to convey Edward's concern to his father.*

"And now, my good man, have you a messenger who could deliver this to the castle for me? A penny now to deliver it, another penny when he returns with the reply."

The innkeeper stepped into the street and let out a shrill whistle. "You there, boy," he shouted. "Come here." He stepped back inside accompanied by a skinny lad in clothes that were a bit too big for him and shoes run down at the heel. "This gentleman has an errand for ye. Now ye do as he says or I'll see ye don't get any supper tonight."

The boy took the penny and the message, and Montagu went upstairs to sit on his bed and hope for the best. The sun was lowering in the western sky and his anxiety was mounting when the boy finally reappeared. He held out both hands, one with a message and the other palm-up for his reward. Montagu unfolded the page and glanced at it briefly to be sure he wasn't getting his own note back, then produced the promised penny and the boy darted off without ever having uttered a single word. Montagu sat down to read.

> *My dear baron,*
> *I shall have a quarter hour available to exchange greetings*
> *tomorrow afternoon at precisely two hours past noon. It would*
> *be my pleasure to receive you at that time.*
> *Kent*

Terse, thought Montagu. *But then I suppose he's wary of anything and anyone associated with the court. Can't say that I blame him. The queen and her lover would throw him in the Tower at the least sign he might be part of a conspiracy to free his brother.*

Not wishing to draw attention to himself here, William had his meal at the inn but didn't linger in the bar. The next morning, he left the inn early and wandered aimlessly around the town to kill the hours before he could make his way to the castle. The smell of baking bread drew him to what turned out to be a shopping street of sorts. He bought a warm roll from the baker and ate it as he walked up one side of the street then turned to come back down the other. A display of lace in the window of a dressmaker's shop caught his eye, and he stepped inside. "Only just arrived from Flanders," the proprietress told him. "Perhaps the finest I've ever seen. You have exquisite taste, sir." He left with a length of what the woman declared to be her favorite – a gift for Catherine.

At the appointed time, Montagu presented himself at the main gate of the castle and was quickly shown into the earl's presence chamber where two men sat in front of the hearth. "Baron Montagu, my lord," the servant announced then left, closing the doors behind him.

"Montagu, do join us," said Edmund. "I don't know if you know Simon Forster, my Companion of the Privy Chamber. Neither my father nor my brother would give him a proper title, so it was left to me to create one myself."

"Your lordship." Montagu offered a slight bow to the earl. "Forster." A nod of the head toward his companion. "Indeed, I've not had the pleasure, though I've certainly heard you are an honored member of this household." Forster nodded in acknowledgment.

"Then you'll most certainly have also heard," Edmund continued, "that he's privy to all my conversations. Now, your message said you bring greetings from the king. I hope my nephew is in robust health."

"He is, indeed, sir, though he does suffer from some anxiety for the health and safety of his father. He was most relieved when his father was rescued from the Dunheveds. But he has no regular news, so he would, I'm sure, be grateful if you have any to impart."

Edmund bristled. "I am most certainly *not* in communication with my half-brother. Anyone who says otherwise or who supposes I had anything to do with those plotters is completely misguided."

"I beg you not to misunderstand, sir. The king himself is confident of your loyalty, unlike some who see traitors behind every shrub. And I daresay he'll be sad to learn that you get as little news as he does." Edmund visibly relaxed.

"What troubles the king in particular at this moment is that we have news of yet another scheme being hatched, this time in Wales. One that might put his father's life in danger."

"It troubles me as well to hear of such a thing. But as I said, I have no communication with my brother. Perhaps it's Lord Berkeley to whom the king should address his concerns." He paused. "But no, Berkeley is Mortimer's man. That would never do."

"I agree it would be unwise."

"Very well, if there's nothing else?"

"Nothing at all, sir. I shall take my leave. And thank you for receiving me."

Montagu left without further ceremony. And without any better idea of how to get Edward's message to his father than when he'd arrived. *I suppose it was futile to think he'd be any more forthcoming. Probably thinks young Edward is under Mortimer's thumb. So now what? He's right about Berkeley. Maltravers? I know little about the man – certainly not enough to know if he can be trusted.*

He was deep in thought, halfway back to the inn, when he heard someone call his name. He looked around but saw no one. "In the alley to your right, my lord." He turned to see Simon Forster a few steps off the street, beckoning.

As Montagu stepped into the alley, Simon said, "This way. We shouldn't be seen together." They set off down the alley. "You'll have to forgive Edmund, sir," Simon wasted no time with pleasantries. "He's under constant suspicion. But there *is* someone you can trust. A man-at-arms – one of Sir Guy Bickerstaffe's men – Caernarfon's guards. Will Makepeace. He'll be found drinking in a local tavern two or three nights a week. You can tell him I trust you. But remember . . . only Will. Not Bickerstaffe. Nor anyone else."

They'd reached a point where another alley veered off to the left. "My turning," said Simon. "Your lodgings are back the way we came. Good luck to you." And with that he was gone.

CHAPTER THIRTEEN

Once again, Montagu left at first light. With no idea how many days he'd have to loiter around the village before finding a chance to speak to this Makepeace fellow, he felt urgency rising. It had already been a week since he'd spoken with Edward. Pray God he wasn't already too late.

On the way, he worked out his ruse for being there, so when he reached Berkeley Heath, he led his horse into the woods and dismounted. Dagger in hand, he lifted the horse's left forefoot and began prying on the shoe. Loosening it was harder than he'd expected. "The one time in my life I wish my blacksmith wasn't so damnably good at his trade," he grumbled to himself. When he finally got two nails loose, the rest came free easily and he tossed the shoe as far away as he could throw it.

Next, he scoured the area for a suitable stone. Pocketing it, he returned to his horse and stroked his cheek and muzzle. "Sorry about this, old boy. I'll make it up to you with some nice rest in a stable." Then he lifted the shoeless foot once again and jammed the stone into the groove of the frog, pushing hard so it wouldn't be easily dislodged. The horse whinnied and jerked his foot away. "Don't blame you, old boy." He took the reins and led the animal back to the road.

By the time they reached the village, the poor beast was limping severely, and Montagu asked the first person he encountered for directions to the blacksmith. By now, it was nearing sundown, so he was confident this ruse would play out to his purpose. "What have ye there?" the big, bearded man asked as they walked up. "Looks right lame to me."

"We were on our way to Bristol. He threw a shoe just before the turning to the village, so I thought I'd get him reshod here. But he's gotten lamer and lamer as we walked here."

"I've shut down the forge for the night, so it'll be tomorrow afore I can make him a new shoe, but let's have a look at that leg." The blacksmith patted the horse on the left shoulder then crouched down and felt all along the leg from the shoulder to the hoof. "No heat. And nothing feels broke." Then he lifted the hoof. "There be your problem, sir. Whopping great stone in his foot." He released the hoof, but the horse refused to put any weight on it.

Making his way to a bench at the back of the shed, the blacksmith returned with a tool, lifted the hoof once again, and removed the stone. "That foot's gonna be sore for a couple of days. Hope your business in Bristol be not urgent, on account of it be smart to let him rest," he patted the horse's shoulder again, "afore ye ride him much at all."

Montagu tried for his best chagrined expression. "I guess I don't have much choice. I'm pretty far from home and he's my only way back. Don't need him coming up even lamer, that's for certes. Besides, he's the best horse I ever had, so I don't want to have to sell him . . . or put him down."

"Alright," said the blacksmith, "let's take him to the stable and get him settled. I'll shoe him in the morning so's he's not standing hard on that sore spot, then we'll have a look him the next day and see when he be fit enough to be on the road again."

When they had the horse in a stall with hay and water for the night and Montagu had paid for two nights' board, he asked the stable master, "I trust there's an inn in this village?"

"Aye. Couple of doors up the high street. Opposite side from the church."

As soon as he was out of earshot of the stable, Montagu let out a big sigh. *So far, so good. At least I have two nights here guaranteed. Not sure what I'll do if it takes longer. Guess I'd best pray it doesn't come to that.*

The innkeeper was welcoming. "We don't get strangers here often, sir. Sorry to hear about your horse. But you can rest assured he's in good hands with Big Rob. Best blacksmith I ever did see. Knows everything there is to know about horses' feet. And you're in luck here on account of my only private room isn't occupied. It'll be a penny more a night, but a gentleman such as yourself..."

"Would be quite grateful for the privacy. Do you require payment in advance?"

"From the ordinary riff-raff, aye. But a gentleman such as yourself would never fail to honor his debts."

"That I would not, my good man. And here's six pennies in advance to show my good faith. You can deduct it from my final bill."

"The room's on the left at the top of the stairs. No lock, but you can keep the door closed."

"And do you offer food?"

"I might be able to scrape up some supper, but you'll like what they have at the tavern better. Just down at the crossroads. Food or drink whenever you need to quench your thirst or fill your belly."

The room was surprisingly clean with what appeared to be fresh sheets on the bed. It also had a window that looked out over the high street, so it might be noisy in the evenings, but Montagu planned to spend his evenings in the tavern anyway. He'd had far worse at inns in the big towns. But that didn't mean he wouldn't sleep with his purse and his dagger under his pillow.

He spent most of the evening in the tavern, sitting at a back corner table where he wouldn't be the center of attention but could still watch all the comings and goings and hear most of what was being said. But luck wasn't with him. After three mugs of ale and no hint of anyone being the man he sought, he wandered slowly back to the inn and his bed.

CHAPTER FOURTEEN

Will had recognized straightaway what Guy was up to with all the extra duty, especially when he was assigned the night watch. He went along with it for a while, thinking that the best way to allay his cousin's distrust. But by the second week in August, he'd had enough. *I'm as loyal as any man in this troop, and if Guy can't see that, then he's not the man of honor he imagines himself to be. From now on, I go to the tavern when I please.*

He'd told Caernarfon what he was planning. "Just so you'll know what's happened if I'm not here tomorrow afternoon."

"You've done your penance, young Will. Though neither Lord Berkeley nor I ever believed you've been anything but loyal." Caernarfon moved his queen's pawn forward two squares. He was playing white that day, teaching Will the finer points of defense. Will moved his own queen's pawn so the two sat directly opposite each other. "It's the right move at the right time, Will. If Guy continues in his stubborn belief that you're in league with plotters, he'll be forced to send another man to the tavern to observe you. Then one of two things happens. He realizes he's wasting manpower and gives up his nonsense. Or you start inviting men to join you, and he gets so many reports of you being up to nothing at all that he has to admit his mistake. Though he'll never admit it to anyone but himself, and even *that* will be a struggle."

Will chuckled. He really liked this man, who finally seemed in his element, living comfortably but unburdened by the expectations of others.

Caernarfon proved right. For the first week, whenever Will left for the tavern, Guy made no attempt to stop him – just sent a minder following right behind. Both men knew the minder's role. Both pretended they didn't. And neither spent any time in the company of the other.

Until it was time to depart. Then Will would approach his fellow man-at-arms and say, "Come on, Tom." Or Alf or whoever had been sent that evening, for it was never the same person. "Time to go home." And they'd walk back to the castle together. Will knew this would just make his cousin even more suspicious of what he might be up to, but he couldn't resist the provocation.

The following week, he decided to turn the tables on Guy and asked Aldwin to accompany him. Reluctant at first . . . "Not sure I want Guy suspicious of me too," he'd told Will . . . it didn't take much for Will to convince him that an evening's entertainment would do him good.

Guy was waiting with the sentries at the gate when they returned. "I was told he'd dragged you off into mischief, Aldwin. What have you two been up to?"

"Just getting to know the villagers," Aldwin replied. "You should try it, sir. They're really quite pleasant, and it's a nice change from duty."

"I'd rather have a clear head in case there's another raid."

"You know, it occurred to me the villagers might be quite helpful if there *was* another raid."

"Or they could be even more help to the raiders. You let *me* worry about such things. You and Makepeace are part of the morning watch. Be sure you're not late." And with that, Guy turned on his heel and strode away.

Will and Aldwin made a pact and relieved the night watch early. When Guy learned of that, he was furious . . . so the gossip said. And the gossip was all it took for a new pattern to develop among the men-at-arms. Those who didn't have night duty would find their way to the tavern with increasing frequency, sometimes on their own, sometimes in groups of two or three. But every last man made it a point to be early for the following day's assignment, so it could never be called a mutiny. Will called it a triumph of sanity over sanctimony.

***

Tonight, Will arrived at the tavern first, knowing others from the troop would likely be there in due course. There was no longer any need for the ploy of going together to thwart Guy's suspicions. Surprised to see an unfamiliar face at a table in the back corner of the room, he asked the landlord, "Stranger in town?"

"Aye. Horse came up lame on the way to Bristol. Biding his time here 'til the blacksmith declares the animal sound again."

Although his natural inclination would be to engage the traveler and find out what was happening in the wider world, Will knew that would seal his fate with Guy. *Let others do that. We'll all find out soon enough.* He joined Milo, the baker, at a table on the opposite side of the room. He knew this was the smart move, but it still grated that he had to humor his cousin.

When Tom and Alf arrived, they made straight for the stranger's table and struck up a conversation, but Will was too far away to eavesdrop. When he stepped up to the bar for a refill, Alf called to him, "Hey, Makepeace! Where've you been? Come join us. Nick here is down from Coventry. Got lots of news. Seems the king's men caught one of the Dunheveds."

Will was sorely tempted. After all, he'd just be responding to a friendly invitation from one of his mates, right? But then he heard Caernarfon's voice in his head. *Don't be lured into a mistaken move, Will. If your opponent is truly clever, there might be no way to recover from it.* So, reluctantly, he replied, "In a bit, Alf. I want to hear the rest of Milo's story about when his father met Longshanks during the Scottish campaign." Will had no doubt Milo had told the tale many times, but he was a lively storyteller and those gathered at the table encouraged him with rapt attention and prompting questions. When he rejoined them, Will took pains to be equally enthusiastic, but now and then, he stole a glance at the three men in the far corner of the room.

The stranger left first. Quietly. No one else seemed to take any notice of his departure. Milo had launched into another tale, this one about his one and only visit to the baker's guild in Bristol. Tom and Alf stopped by the table. "We're heading home, Will," said Tom. "Coming with us?"

Will glanced at the contents of his mug. "Can't down this in one gulp. I'll stay 'til Milo finishes this story. Tell the sentries I'll be along shortly."

"See you on the morning watch then."

"Early as always, my friends." Will raised his mug in a mock toast.

***

What Will really wanted was a chance to be alone with his thoughts, so he was grateful no one offered to walk with him when he finished his ale and bade them goodnight. *What was this stranger really doing here? A lame horse. Perhaps it was no more than that. The blacksmith would certainly know if the man was dissembling and the horse was perfectly sound. But it's not all that difficult to induce lameness in a mount. Run him too long. Press him for too fast a pace over rocky ground. Ignore a missing shoe too long and the foot gets sore. It's a good trick, though, to have the animal come up lame at precisely the place you want him to, so maybe the man's motives aren't nefarious after all.*

But a horse not truly lame – maybe just a slightly sore foot that needs only a new shoe and a day of rest . . . Perfect chance to study the lay of the land, the castle defenses, how to make a quick escape. Make friends with the villagers so they're not suspicious if they see you again. Pretty crafty reconnaissance, if you ask me.

Utterly engrossed in his thoughts as he approached the churchyard, Will was startled to hear his name called from the shadows. Not called, exactly. More of a loud whisper hissed in his direction. "Will Makepeace." He peered in the direction of the sound, but saw nothing, so kept on walking. Three steps later, there it was again. The hissed whisper, a little louder this time. "Will Makepeace." And then. "Over here. Among the gravestones."

Will looked around to make sure no one else was in the street, watching, then took a few cautious steps into the churchyard. Once his eyes adjusted to the shadows under the big oaks, he could make out a figure crouched beside the nearest tree, beckoning to him. "Over here." The whisper was quieter this time.

As Will moved closer, the figure moved away from the tree and behind a large gravestone, ensuring that he couldn't be seen from the street or from any of the buildings on the opposite side. Will found him there, sitting on the ground. "Sit with me, Will Makepeace. We mustn't be seen together."

It was then Will realized this was the stranger from the tavern. He froze. *Holy Mother of God*, he thought. *What kind of trap have I walked into?* His head swiveled in all directions, looking for watchers. His first inclination was to run – to get back to the castle and send someone to capture this man. What better proof of Will's loyalty – to Guy or to anyone else who doubted him.

But for some reason he couldn't explain, a strange sense of calm overtook him. His initial panic turned to rational thought. *The stranger's right – I can't be seen here. But how does he know my name? My full name. Alf only called me 'Makepeace' in the tavern. Did Alf or Tom say more when I didn't join them? Or has someone else told him who I am?* Slowly, he sank to the ground beside the stranger.

"Thank you for trusting me, Will," the stranger whispered.

"It isn't trust – more a wish to save my own skin by avoiding being seen here."

"That's understandable. I have a message for Edward of Caernarfon from his son, the king. It's vital that Caernarfon receive the message, so it is I who must trust you."

Will's skepticism came through in his tone, even in a whisper. "Why should I believe a man traveling from Coventry to Bristol bears a message from the king? Is the king not in Westminster?"

"You're wise to be cautious. And you're well informed for someone in such an out corner of the realm. The king is indeed at Westminster, along with his mother, the regent."

"Who are you that you could possibly have a message from the king?"

"Who I am doesn't matter. In truth, it's safer for us both that you do not know. But know that Simon Forster trusts me. That it was from him I knew to look for you."

"And how am I to know Simon didn't give my name under duress?"

"Alas, I have no proof to offer. I can only tell you that Simon was well when I saw him at Gloucester Castle in the company of the Earl of Kent."

So if Simon is still with the earl, then he's not a prisoner being tortured for information. But dare I trust any of this? Will sat in silence, uncertain how to proceed. The stranger seemed to understand Will's dilemma and didn't press. At long last, Will reached a decision. *If I learn the message, then I can decide in my own time whether to reveal it to anyone or not. If I don't know what the message is, than I've no way to know how to act – even if I should reveal to anyone that this man approached me.*

"Very well." Will hoped his acceptance of the situation came through in the tone of his whisper. "What's the message?"

"The king believes his father's life is in danger. Not from those who might plot to free him but from those sworn to protect him. The king further believes that the danger is imminent. He wants his father to know that if strangers arrive – particularly if they claim to have instructions from Baron Mortimer – his father and those who protect him must be exceedingly wary. The king is most desirous that no harm should befall his father."

"And how might Lord Caernarfon have assurance that this message is truly from his son?"

"A most wise precaution, Will. I have seen this night why Simon was so keen to recommend you to me. As to your question, you may tell Lord Caernarfon that his son would have him know that he has found it necessary to abandon the window."

"A curious message indeed."

"Perhaps. But one that the king's father will recognize and will grasp all the meaning of."

"Is there anything further? I shouldn't delay my return to the castle any longer."

"Only this. In all probability, we will never meet again. But know that you have my everlasting gratitude and that of your king. Now go. I'll wait here for a long while so no suspicion can be attached to either of our movements."

***

Will lay awake, listening to the snores of his fellow men-at-arms, interrupted occasionally by the loud snort of someone waking enough to turn in his bed. What to do with the message he'd been given?

If it's truly from the king, then I'm honor-bound to convey it to Caernarfon. Am I duty-bound to tell Guy as well?

But what about that obscure sign of proof? And especially the stranger's peculiar turn of phrase – 'all the meaning.' Is that merely some sort of code between father and son?

Or what if something entirely different is at play? The stranger met Simon in the company of the Earl of Kent. Kent has always claimed no affiliation with any of the plotters. But what if he's changed his mind? Is the so-called proof something long ago agreed between brothers – well, half-brothers – as a signal of some sort? Is this whole business merely a charade to let Caernarfon know a more serious plot is in the works and to warn him to take care for his safety when the raid occurs?

If that's the case and I fail to tell Guy, then that seals my fate as being in league with the plotters.

There's only one way for me to win – and no way to know what it is.

He tossed and turned in his bed, unable to find any position where he could drift off to sleep. Then, for the second time that night, he heard Caernarfon's voice in his head. *When your opponent's strategy is full murk, young Will, then it's often wise to bide your time. The more moves you see, the more manifest his intent.*

CHAPTER FIFTEEN

The problem with temporizing to discover your opponent's strategy is timing. Wait too long, and your seemingly safe moves may box you into a corner you can't escape from. Move too soon and you may make a potentially disastrous mistake. Will decided to wait four days before making a decision.

On the day following Will's encounter in the churchyard, Lord Berkeley and his entire family decamped for Bradley, in Hampshire. Their departure was something of a spectacle, with all the baggage perhaps an indication that they planned to be away for quite some time and with the inclusion of nursery maids and wet nurses for the youngest boys, all under the age of three.

A move, yes, but enough to resolve Will's dilemma? He thought not. It could be no more than a long-planned journey. For all Will knew, it could be an annual event in the lives of the Berkeley family. But he couldn't entirely rule it out as a signal that something was afoot that Lord Berkeley had no wish to be associated with. Why else undertake such a long trip with such young children, one of them just an infant? The balance tipped ever so slightly toward the message being authentic, but Will wasn't yet ready to act.

***

Simple Dickon was back. When he saw Will walk into the tavern, his face broke into an enormous grin and he waved frantically for Will to come join him. An invitation Will couldn't resist, though he did take the time to buy a mug of ale before making his way to the table, where Dickon's grin had widened even further, if that was possible.

"You got away," the young man said before Will had even fully sat down.

"Got away?"

"From the monks. I saw them, you know. Putting you and the other one into the carriage."

Will took a long swallow of ale. "Ah, yes. We're safe home now."

"I told the man what I saw."

"Which man?"

"The angry one. With all the horsemen. I thought maybe they wanted to take me and lock me up somewhere, so I didn't come out where they could see me good. But he asked about the wagon, so I told him what I saw."

"That must have been Sir Guy. He's not a bad man. If he seemed angry, it was just because he was anxious to find us."

"He didn't ask me about the monks."

"What about the monks?"

"They weren't ours. I know all our monks. There's Brother Jacob and Brother Odo and Brother Walter and the old one we have to call Father and Brother Joseph and . . . and lots more. But the monks that took you – I never saw any of them before and I didn't know their names."

"You did a really good thing telling Sir Guy what you saw, Dickon. I'm sure it helped him find us."

Dickon beamed with pride at the praise being heaped on him. "Those monks didn't come back for their wagon."

"Really?"

"No. It was still there when I went by this morning. So I told the stable master, and he said he might go fetch it."

***

Day three and Will was still no closer to knowing whether to trust the churchyard messenger or not. He played chess with Caernarfon and actually won a game. The fact that Caernarfon let him win as a way to teach a series of moves in no way dampened Will's joy at his triumph. He left their session with a smile on his face almost as broad as Dickon's grin.

It had been tempting to reveal what he'd been told to the former king. If it was a legitimate message from his son, who was Will to withhold it? If Caernarfon knew what that peculiar bit about the window was all about, maybe everything would become clear. *No,* he told himself. *You gave yourself four days. Stay with the plan.*

Guy was increasingly grumpy or morose or generally out of sorts, depending, apparently, on nothing in particular. Will and Aldwin were of like mind that he needed a respite from the weight of guarding the most valuable prisoner in the kingdom. But they were of equally like mind that trying to talk to him about it would only end in grief for the messenger. So Aldwin did his best to shield the men from Guy's gruffness, and Will did his part by making sure they went to the tavern now and again.

CHAPTER SIXTEEN

21 September 1327

Sunset was approaching when Will came off duty on the rampart and emerged from the tower into the inner courtyard. He knew it would be a sleepless night. Tomorrow, he had to act. And he had no more information to go on than when he'd left the churchyard four nights ago.

You're a good man, my Will. He could hear his mother's voice in his head. *You have good instincts, and if you follow them, they'll not steer you wrong.* And not just his mother. Of late, he'd heard it from Caernarfon as well. Though Will had become more skilled at chess, he would often move a piece tentatively but not commit to the move until he'd studied it at length. When he'd sit there too long with his fingers still on the piece, Caernarfon would chide him gently, "Sometimes it's useful to trust your instincts, young Will."

Why don't you listen to them? he asked himself. *Has Guy intimidated you so much that everything you do is colored by fear of his reaction? Or have you been learning a different kind of wisdom from the guard and the guarded? Maybe the answer lies in giving your instincts equal weight with logic.*

He'd resolved to do just that when his musings were interrupted by the sound of horseshoes on paving stones. Six horsemen had ridden into the inner courtyard, presumably with no ill intent as they'd been passed through by the sentries at the outer and inner gates and they rode at a slow walk. "You there," called the one in front, his tone that of one who expects to be obeyed. "Come here."

Will complied, but at his own pace, reaching the horsemen just as they stopped beside the steps to the keep.

"Who's in charge here?" asked the same man.

It took Will a moment to realize that, with Berkeley away and no one having any idea where Maltravers was, that dubious honor fell on his cousin. "Sir Guy Bickerstaffe, at the moment. Shall I fetch him?"

"No need for fetching." Will hadn't heard Guy approach from behind. "I'm here. To whom do I have the honor of speaking?"

"William Ockley, Sir Guy. In the king's service. I have a message for Lord Berkeley."

"The baron isn't here. You can find him in Hampshire – at Bradley Manor."

"The message won't do him much good there," said Ockley. "Give us lodgings for the night and then we'll be on our way."

Since Guy's arrival, Will had been walking toward the entrance to the family living quarters – slowly so as to remain within earshot. What he heard almost stopped him in his tracks, but somehow he had the presence of mind to keep walking, as if he'd taken no notice at all. In that moment, though, his instincts came alive. Neither the snort of a stag nor the slap of a beaver's tail could signal danger more urgently than Ockley's words.

Will picked up his pace – not so much that anyone would take note, but enough to reach the entrance by the time he heard men dismount and begin to lead their horses toward the stable. Once inside, he showed no such caution. He knew now what he had to do – and that he had to do it quickly. He dashed to the room where he and the others slept and stopped outside before sauntering in and casually picking up his satchel and a tinderbox. The only two there were sound asleep, so no one would be asking inconvenient questions. Fortunately, since he'd just come off duty, he was already wearing his sword. Back in the corridor he made straight for Caernarfon's chamber, entered without waiting for permission, and closed the door.

Caernarfon turned away from the window at the sound. "Will! I wasn't expecting you today – and especially so late. Come. Have a look at the lovely sunset." Then, apparently noticing Will's agitation, he added, "Are you alright? Is something wrong?"

"There's no time to explain right now, sir. Just get into your gardening clothes as quickly as you can. Please, just do as I ask."

As Caernarfon shed his finery, Will folded each piece and stowed it in the clothes chest. "You needn't do that, Will. The servants will take care of it."

"Sir, the last thing we need is for someone to think you've changed your clothing. Your life may depend on it. Please, sir, hurry. And put anything of value – any money or jewels you might have – in this satchel. But take nothing that someone would notice missing from the room. It has to look like you've just gone for a stroll."

Will went to the window while Caernarfon finished. It would be twilight by the time they got outside. There was no unusual activity in the outer courtyard. Apparently, the recent arrivals hadn't raised enough concern for Guy to post additional guards. He turned back to Caernarfon.

"I'm ready, young Will, though for what, I don't know."

Will peeked out into the corridor. There was no one about and no sound of anyone approaching. "Put the satchel over your shoulder and come with me, sir." Caernarfon cocked his head to one side, questioning. "I'll tell you what this about once we're both safe. For now, I have to ask you to trust me."

"Very well, I'll do as you say." Caernarfon joined Will in the corridor and they left the chamber door open, as it always was unless its occupant was sleeping.

Whispering, Will gave his instructions. "We're going down through the kitchens and then out of the castle. But everything depends on your not being recognized. Hunch over, like an old man, so you don't look as tall as me. Limp, as if you've hurt your ankle. And don't say a word. Let me do all the talking."

No one in the kitchens paid them any mind, and Will kept his head down, hoping no one would remember later that he'd been there. Once they were outside, Will stood as tall as he could, hoping to give the appearance of towering over his companion. At the gate between the courtyards, one of the sentries called "Evening, Will" and waved, but asked no questions. Will waved back.

At the outer gate, they weren't so lucky. Alf, always gregarious, was on duty. "Evening, Will. Off to the tavern?"

"Aye."

"Who's that with you?"

"One of the kitchen helpers. Twisted his ankle on the stairs. I said I'd see him home on my way for a mug of ale."

Caernarfon played his role to perfection. He put some weight on the foot he'd been limping on, then feigned serious pain and almost falling over. Will ducked under his arm to support him, saying, "Let's get you home so your wife can tend that ankle."

As the two made their way out the gate, Alf called after them, "Have a mug for me, Will. I'm stuck here tonight."

"You can count on it, Alf."

They kept up the ruse of the injury until they turned onto the high street, where luck was with them once again. The people who were out and about were all at the other end of the village, past the crossroads. Whispering "You can walk normally now," Will led the way into the churchyard and to a small door on the side of the church. It opened onto a tiny vestibule where steps went down to the left and another door was straight in front of them. "Entrance to the vestry," Will whispered. "We go down."

The steps led to the crypt. "Are we repeating our last adventure, Will?" Caernarfon asked quietly.

"Only for as long as it takes me to move my pieces into position." He led the former king to the far corner where a stone tomb stood a couple of feet away from the wall. "It's a bit of a squeeze, but if you hide there, I don't think anyone will find you. It's unlikely someone would be down here anyway, but we can't take chances."

As Caernarfon wedged himself into the space and sat down so he couldn't be seen over the tomb, Will removed his sword belt. "Take this." He handed over the sword. "If you're found, at least you can defend yourself."

"What about you?"

"I never wear it for an evening of drinking, and things need to look as ordinary as possible. So keep it here for me. I'll be back as soon as I can."

***

Letting his instincts shape his actions, Will made his way to the far edge of the churchyard, where he had a pretty good view of the crossroads. It was full dark by now, and a few people had started to drift into the tavern, but Will's attention was on the road from the stable. It wasn't long before he spied a lone figure coming up the road.

Luck was still with him, and he passed through the crossroads without being recognized then headed toward the person coming his way, reaching him well before the tavern. "Evening, Dickon. I was just coming to see you."

"Here I am."

"Do you remember, Dickon, that night when you held my dagger?"

Dickon grinned. "Aye. Sharp. Could kill a rabbit."

"I remember you told me you'd like to see inside the castle one day."

"Aye."

"What about now?"

Dickon practically danced with excitement. "Could I, Will? Could I really?"

"Come with me. But remember, you mustn't say anything to the guards. Just let me do the talking, and don't say a word. Can you do that?"

"I can, Will."

"Promise?"

"I promise."

"Alright, let's go."

As they approached the first gate, both sentries stepped out to block the passage. Then, recognizing Will, Alf waved his companion away. "Back so soon, Will? That's not like you."

"Well, the kitchen helper didn't want to lose any wages, so he sent his son to do the job." Will clapped Dickon on the shoulder. "Lad's never been here before and his father begged me to show him where he needed to go. Poor man was in such pain, I couldn't refuse."

"Soft-hearted, that's what you are, Will Makepeace." Alf chuckled. "Get on with you then. I'll see you later."

They weren't challenged at the gate to the inner courtyard, so as they rounded the steps of the keep, Will led the way, not to the kitchens, but toward the entrance to the family living quarters. Dickon was slow to keep up, gazing in awe at his surroundings. "Hard to see much at night, isn't it?" Will remarked.

"Aye. But bigger than I thought."

Opening the door and letting Dickon precede him inside, Will resumed his instructions. "Now, there won't be many servants about because the family is away. But we should still be quiet."

Dickon tiptoed as they made their way through the corridors, pausing now and then to look inside a room. "Pretty," he whispered when Will showed him the great hall. "And big."

Upstairs, they made their way to Caernarfon's chamber, and Will shut the door. Dickon walked around, touching things gingerly as if afraid he might break something. Then he went to the bed and stroked the bed coverings. "Soft." His hand went to the hangings. "Pretty. I wish I could sleep in a bed like this someday."

"How about tonight? This is a guest room. Would you like to be the guest?"

Dickon's face lit up. "Could I?"

"For just this one night, Dickon, you will live like a nobleman. And then when you leave in the morning, it will be daylight and you can see the courtyards better. But we mustn't tell anyone."

"I promise."

"Very well, the first thing a noble lord would do in the evening would be to have some wine." Will poured two glasses from the pitcher that was always kept filled on the sideboard. "Ever had wine, Dickon?"

The young man took the glass and sipped, scrunched his nose a bit, than took a long swallow. "Different from small ale. Good." He emptied the glass and held it out. "Would a lord have more?"

Will smiled. "Indeed he would." Refilling the glass, he added, "Sometimes he might drink an entire pitcher in one night."

Dickon emptied half the glass in one gulp and wandered over to the table where the chess board was set for a new game. "What's this?"

"A game that some lords play."

"I like games. Can I play?"

"Well, it takes two people . . . and since I don't know how and you don't know how . . ." *It's a harmless lie,* Will thought. *And anyway, he wouldn't be able to learn all the moves.* Then, overtaken by a momentary pang of emotion, he thought, *I'm going to miss that chess board and our games. God knows when we'll ever play again.*

Emptying his glass once again, Dickon held it out for another refill. "I like wine." Will was happy to accommodate. What he needed now was for Dickon to drink enough to get sleepy. But even when the pitcher was empty, there were no signs that would happen. Time for a different tactic.

Will finished off his wine and went to the sideboard, opening one of the lower doors. His luck hadn't deserted him. Inside were two glass bottles mostly full of golden-brown liquid. He retrieved one and beckoned to Dickon. "Now this is something quite special that noble lords drink just before they retire for the night." He poured a double-portion into Dickon's glass and a mere taste into his own.

Dickon took a rather large swallow, no doubt expecting it to be similar to wine, then scrunched up his face and shook his head. "What is that?"

"It's called brandy. It's very expensive and only the finest manors and castles can afford it. But for your special night as a guest in this castle, you should have only the best. Try it again. This time not such a big swallow." Will emptied his own glass.

"It's funny," said Dickon. "Tastes good but burns."

"After you drink a bit, you don't notice the burn any more – just the taste."

Will went back to the sideboard and returned the brandy bottle – along with his empty glass – to its hiding place. When he turned back to Dickon, the young man's eyelids were beginning to droop. "Sleepy, Dickon?"

"Aye. Worked hard today."

"Very well, let's get you in bed." Will turned back the bed covers. Dickon started to climb into the bed, but Will stopped him. "A noble lord removes his boots before retiring." Showing signs of inebriation, Dickon struggled with his left boot. "And sometimes his servant helps him." Will removed both boots. "I'll just put them here, under the bed, where you can find them in the morning."

By now Dickon was in the bed, his head resting on two pillows. "Soft," he murmured.

Will pulled up the covers and Dickon squirmed down into them. "Sleep well, Lord Dickon. I'll be back for you in the morning." That lie was the hardest part. *But he'll be fine. Once Ockley's men discover the man in the bed isn't who they expected, that'll put an end to their nefarious plans. Guy will question Dickon unrelentingly, but even Guy will soon be able to see the lad is ignorant and harmless and let him go. Sleep well, Dickon. It's what you deserve for giving me time to get away.*

He pulled the bed hangings closed. Everything must look like Edward of Caernarfon had retired for the night.

***

The next bit was the trickiest. Will had to leave the castle without anyone knowing. And there was only one way to do that. A tunnel led from the back of the brewhouse to a cesspit where they threw the spent mash, emptied the chamber pots, disposed of the offal from butchering, and tossed in any dead vermin found on the premises. A ghastly place, so Will had heard, with a stench that would linger in a man's nose for days. The tricky part – aside from controlling his gag reflex as he circumnavigated the pit – was getting to the brewhouse unseen. It was vital that Alf remember he'd come back from the village and never left again.

Time for his own bit of play-acting. Ducking into a nearby bedchamber, he grabbed the chamber pot and pissed and emptied his bowels into it. Then he pulled his cap low over his eyes, hunched his shoulders, picked up the pot, and started down the corridor. His pace too quick at first, he almost sloshed the contents out onto his hands. *How in God's name do the servants do this day after day?*

Despite encountering half a dozen servants along the way, he made it to the brewhouse unrecognized. *Apparently, it's assumed no one but another servant would be carrying a chamber pot.* He chuckled to himself.

The brewhouse was unoccupied at this time of night, so he set the chamber pot on the floor right beside the door and began fumbling around in the dark looking for a candle. It took every ounce of self-control he possessed not to shout an epithet when he jammed his toe against the mash tun, but at least that gave him a sense of where he was in the room and where the nearest table might be. Groping about on the top of the table, his hands finally identified a candle holder. Sparks from the flint and steel in his tinderbox soon had the candle aflame, and Will could finally make out his surroundings.

The candle was only about two inches high, but that would be enough. He retrieved the chamber pot and set it just inside the entrance to the tunnel then picked up his candle and began walking toward the tunnel exit. Rather a longer walk than he'd expected, and the farther he went, the more stale the air smelled. As he drew nearer to the exit, his thoughts grew increasingly anxious. *What if the exit's locked? What if there's no way out? Everything I've done so far will have been for naught if I have to be seen leaving through the gate again. But I have to get back to Caernarfon no matter what. I have to honor his son's warning and the man who brought the message and Simon, who sent him.*

The tunnel suddenly took a sharp right turn. Rounding it, Will found himself face to face with a door barricaded by a large iron bar. It took all his strength to lift the bar out of the brackets mounted in stone on either side of the door. *How on earth do the women servants manage this?* he wondered. *Maybe it's only the men who come down here. And I'd wager there's always two of them to manhandle that bar.*

Having no idea where he was relative to other parts of the castle, Will took great care laying the bar down on the floor of the tunnel so as not to raise an alarm over some unexpected sound. Then, holding his breath, he reached for the knob . . . and exhaled when it turned smoothly. A gentle nudge and the door opened slightly. Now his prayer was that the hinges were well oiled and wouldn't scream of his presence when he pushed it further open. *Have I ever heard such a noise when I was walking the ramparts?* He simply couldn't remember. For a brief moment, he considered fetching the chamber pot and hiding it here at the tunnel exit, then rejected the idea. He needed all the time he could muster to be well away from the castle by daybreak. Besides, he'd managed to get that pot as far as he had without spilling the contents all over himself. *Don't tempt fate. It'll take them a while to find it in any event.*

The candle guttered. It was time to go. He blew out the flame, set the candle holder on the floor, and leaned into the door.

CHAPTER SEVENTEEN

Will glanced at the sky as he made his way to the churchyard. Plenty of stars, but no moon in sight. He'd been so preoccupied lately with questions about the mysterious messenger that he'd paid no attention at all to what phase the moon was in. Not that he'd had any reason to care until now. But since it hadn't already risen, that boded well for waning. *I just hope it's last quarter. A bit of light in the small hours wouldn't go amiss.*

A bit of light in the crypt wouldn't have gone amiss either, but he hadn't thought to bring the candle. As he tried to find his way through what, in the dark, felt like a complicated maze of tombs, he called out in a loud whisper, "Lord Caernarfon? It's me . . . Will."

"Over here."

Will turned left toward the sound and soon encountered the large tomb in the corner.

"Give me your hand, Will," said Caernarfon, "so I can climb out of here. One gets rather stiff sitting in one position for so long, unable to move around." With Will's help, he was soon upright again. "Here. You'll want to strap this on." He handed over Will's sword belt. "Fortunately, I had no need of it." As soon as Will had buckled on the belt, Caernarfon continued. "Now, take my hand again and I'll lead you to the exit. My eyes have had longer to adjust to the darkness."

When they emerged at the stop of the stairs, Will put a finger to his lips then listened at the door to the vestry before sticking his head out the opposite door to look around. Once he was satisfied all was quiet, he beckoned to Caernarfon and they stepped out into the churchyard. Without uttering a single word, they fell into step side by side. They stayed in the shadows of the big oaks around the church for as long as possible, then crossed the high street and took the first little lane to the right. As soon as he was confident they were out of sight of anyone on the castle ramparts, Will took to the fields and turned south.

Though there was as yet no moon, the starlight in a clear sky proved surprisingly helpful to avoid obstacles in their path. The Little Avon River was quite narrow at the point they encountered it, so they simply waded across. Whenever a lane or trail went in the right direction, they used it for easy walking, but as soon as it changed to any heading other than south, it was back into the fields. Before they reached Thornbury, they turned east, crossed the Bristol road, and eventually found themselves at the village of Warre Wyke. By then, the waning crescent moon had risen, giving them enough light to identify what appeared to be a vast woodland just to the east. Skirting the village, they made their way into the woods and turned south yet again.

They'd gone about half a mile when Will called a halt. "Listen," he whispered. "Do you hear that?"

"Water?"

"That's what I thought."

They resumed their walk, pausing every few steps to be sure they were still heading toward the sound of the water. What they found was a rocky stream flowing down a hillside – sweet, fresh water that a man could drink without fear of getting dysentery. When they'd satisfied their thirst, Will looked around for someplace secluded where they could hide and get some rest. He finally found a copse of hawthorn with some young holly on one side that served rather like a hedge. It would do.

As they settled on the ground, Caernarfon said, "Now, young Will, it's time for you to tell me what this is all about."

"Four nights ago, on my way home from the tavern, I was waylaid by a man claiming to have a message from your son. According to the messenger, you son wanted you to know that your life was likely in danger, not from the people who want to free you from captivity but from those who are supposed to be upholding Parliament's edict. He also claimed he'd visited the Earl of Kent and that it was Kent's companion who'd sent him to me.

"Of course, I'd never seen this man before, so I had no way to judge if any of it was true. Could all just as easily have been a ruse to trick me into joining forces with the wrong people. But just in case, I asked him for a sign that would prove to you that the message really *did* come from the king."

"And how did he answer?"

"He said, 'You may tell Lord Caernarfon that his son would have him know that he has found it necessary to abandon the window.' He also said something about how you would understand all the meanings."

To Will's surprise, Caernarfon chuckled. "The message is almost certainly from my son. When young Edward was about ten or eleven – especially when the court was at Westminster – he took to sitting on the window ledge in my presence chamber to prepare the lessons his tutors had given him. His excuse was that the light was better there, but I quickly realized he had stumbled on quite a clever solution to one of my own problems. I knew the lad needed to be in the room to observe how business of the kingdom is conducted – after all, he *would* be king in due course. But there were many among my entourage who would have objected strenuously if I'd done such a thing. So I simply ignored his presence, everyone else followed suit, and he learned the lessons I needed to teach."

"So why has he abandoned the practice now?"

"Several possibilities come to mind. He might simply have grown too tall or too mature to comfortably spend hours on that ledge. But it seems more plausible to me that either his mother – or more likely, that bastard Mortimer – finally took notice of what he was doing and forbade him to continue. That's undoubtedly what was meant by 'all the meanings'." Caernarfon paused for a moment. "Tell me about the messenger, Will. Was he perhaps a man who might have seen more than twenty summers? Not so tall as you or me. Clean-shaven. Well-spoken."

"I'm a poor judge of a man's age, sir, but I'd guess him to be just a bit older than me. As for his height, I only ever saw him sitting down – first in the tavern and then crouching in the shadows of the churchyard. I think perhaps he's normally clean-shaven and the bit of facial hair was either from traveling or to avoid being recognized. He was very well-spoken. In other circumstances, I'd have taken him to be a gentleman. Do you know who he might have been, sir?"

"Perhaps. But it's safest for everyone – not least for my son – if I keep my own counsel. But tell me, Will, what made you decide to act today?"

"My gut. Six strangers arrived at the castle. The man in charge said he had a message for Lord Berkeley. But when Guy told him where he could find the baron, he said something about his message being useless in Hampshire. And then they asked to stay the night. It seemed like the sign I'd been waiting for to tell me whether I should believe that you were in danger."

"Then I'm grateful to your gut, Will. But what do we do next? Do you have a plan?"

Now that the furious excitement of getting away and putting some distance between themselves and Berkeley was subsiding, Will was suddenly overwhelmed by exhaustion. "No, sir, I don't have a plan. Everything had to be done so quickly, there was no time to think. In the moment, I somehow knew we should go south – that once they discovered your absence, the searchers would look first to Gloucester, thinking you might have sought refuge with your brother, and then they'd look west, thinking we must be headed toward London and the corridors of power. But beyond that . . ."

The fact that Will could barely hold his head up and keep his eyes open wasn't lost on Caernarfon. "This seems a safe enough place for now, young Will. I suggest we get some sleep. Then when daylight comes, we'll make a plan."

CHAPTER EIGHTEEN

Sir Guy tossed and turned, unable to drift off to sleep. His mind kept coming back to William Ockley and the men with him. Something about them wasn't quite right. *If they indeed had a message for Berkeley, why didn't they leave straightaway when I told them where to find him? Why did they insist on staying here for the night? Admittedly, it was almost sundown, but men who bear urgent messages like to get ever closer to their destination before bedding down for the night, even if that means camping.*

And why does it take six men to deliver a message? They didn't mention carrying anything of value – and, in truth, they seemed to have only the bare necessities with them – so it's unlikely their numbers were for defense against brigands.

Then there was Ockley himself. Something about the man set Guy on edge, though he couldn't quite put his finger on what it was. Sure of himself, yes – a bit cocky even. But Guy had dealt with that type before. This was something else. Not evil, as Guy understood it, but . . . menacing, perhaps?

Guy had offered them suitable accommodations, but Ockley said they preferred to sleep in the hall. When offered an evening meal in the dining hall, Ockley refused, saying they'd make their own arrangements with the cook. In every way and at every opportunity, Ockley made it clear that Guy was a superfluity, utterly without any authority over them or whatever it was they were about.

All of which raised the hackles on Guy's neck. *I wonder who they do answer to – whose orders are they acting on? Berkeley? Unlikely. Maltravers?*

Perhaps. But if they're his men, why isn't he with them? Another, far more clever ploy to abduct Caernarfon? The Dunheved gang has been decapitated, but there've been rumors of late from Wales and from the North and even about the Earl of Kent.

He thought back to Lancaster's admonishment about protecting the prisoner. "Your *job*, Bickerstaffe, but *my* responsibility." How he wished now that someone with real authority was here to take on the responsibility. But that was not to be.

His eyes were finally getting heavy when an unexpected sound startled him bolt upright in his bed – horseshoes on paving stones. He quickly pulled on his boots and grabbed his sword then made for the courtyard at a run. By the time he was outdoors, the sound was receding in the distance. He rounded the corner of the keep in time to see two horses' rumps passing through the outer gate.

The anxiety he'd felt all evening turned into a terrible sense of foreboding. Still running, he reached the outer gate as the two rumps turned right on the high street, headed toward the crossroads. "Sir Guy, sir," Alf greeted him. "What ye be doing out?"

"Who just left, Alf?"

"Those six men what arrived earlier."

"Just the six?"

"Aye, sir. Same six that rode in just before sunset. Seems passing strange they'd ride away on a moonless night, but that Ockley fellow said there was naught else for them to do here so they'd just as soon be on their way."

"Naught else to do here? Are you sure that's what he said, Alf?"

"His exact words. Hasn't been so long since he said them that I'd have forgotten."

Guy paced back and forth in front of the sentry tower door, his mind racing.

"Should we mount up and go after them, sir?" Alf asked.

"No, Alf. By the time we could rouse some men, saddle the horses, and give chase they'd be long gone and with us having no idea what direction. We'd never find them on a dark night. For that matter, they might be lying in wait to ambush us. For now, close the gate. And raise the alarm if anyone wants to come in. Anyone at all – even if it's Lord Berkeley coming home.

I'm going to make the rounds to be sure nothing's amiss." *And God help us all if it is.*

Filled with trepidation, Guy headed back to the inner courtyard as Alf and the other sentry began lowering the gate. Caernarfon's quarters first. Only six men left and Alf seemed sure they were the same six who'd arrived, but could he really be certain in the dark? If they'd taken Caernarfon, then they'd left a man behind. Where might he be now? What mischief might he be plotting?

Guy slowed his pace and tried to control his breathing as he walked down the corridor toward Caernarfon's chamber. If the former king hadn't yet retired, Guy didn't want to greet him in a state of anxiety. When he reached the door, it was closed – the usual sign that the man inside was sleeping. Guy tapped gently on the door. When there was no reply, he knocked louder. Still nothing, so he turned the knob and pushed the door open. Everything was completely still. The hangings were drawn around the bed. Proof that all was normal? Or an attempt to lull him into thinking just that?

He had no choice. He tiptoed to the bed and drew back the hangings on one side. There was a man in the bed, apparently asleep. Still, something nagged at Guy. Something wasn't quite right. He took the candle holder from the table beside the bed, went to the hearth, and managed to coax the candle alight from the last embers of the evening's fire. Setting the holder back on the bedside table, he opened the hangings all the way. The sleeping figure hadn't moved. *Could a man really sleep that soundly with someone moving around in the room?*

There was nothing for it. Guy reached out to shake the man's shoulder to awaken him. The figure rolled flat onto his back, and Guy gasped. "Holy Mother of . . ."

The face was one he had never seen before. And the man was very, very dead.

***

What had earlier been merely anxiety over Ockley's arrival and his demeanor was now a full-blown disaster crashing down on Guy like a building collapsing. For several long moments, he stood looking at the corpse, wave after wave of panic washing over him. *Who is this man and how did he get here? And where's Caernarfon? Whatever has happened, the blame will fall on me. Maybe I should just saddle my horse and ride away from here . . . leave someone else to sort things out. Go to ground somewhere so no one can find me. Go to Scotland. Go to France. Go anywhere that no one knows me.*

The guttering candle jarred him out of his trance. Making his way quickly to the sideboard, he grabbed a new candle and managed to light it from the first before that flame extinguished itself in a pool of melted wax. Shoving the fresh candle into the holder, he held it aloft to take stock of the room. Except for the dead man in the bed, everything was much as it always was. The wine pitcher on the sideboard was empty, a used glass beside it with a few drops left in the bottom. The chess board set in preparation for starting a new game. A pair of boots under the edge of the bed. Nothing lying about as if it had been casually tossed aside for the servants to deal with.

Alright, Bickerstaffe, he told himself, *your only hope to come out of this with your life and your honor intact is to figure out what's happened and who should bear the blame. And you need to do it without causing an uproar among your men or Berkeley's servants. Once the gossip begins, there'll be no way to get to the truth.*

His wits somewhat restored, Guy tried to think methodically. He pulled the bed hangings closed once again. Then he grabbed the candle, put a couple of spares in his pocket, and left the room, closing the door behind him. Now to search the castle – every chamber, every nook and cranny – to see if Caernarfon was in hiding somewhere. *Best do that before anyone's up and about to ask what I'm looking for.* He started with Berkeley's bed chamber, thinking that might be the most likely place for the former king to seek refuge if he felt threatened. Nothing. On to the rest of the family quarters and the nursery. Nothing. He saved the kitchens and the brewhouse for last, and by the time he got there, he'd already decided that the search was futile – that Caernarfon was no longer inside the castle walls. The only thing he found in the kitchens were the banked cook fires and two large buckets of water sitting ready to start cooking the next day's potage. The brewhouse was cool compared to the kitchen. A couple of mice scurried across the floor and into the tunnel when he stepped inside with his lit candle. *Mice wouldn't be out foraging if someone was in here,* he reasoned and retreated the way he had come.

Nothing. Not Caernarfon. Not one of Ockley's men left behind if the former king was among the six who left. Nothing. *Did one of Ockley's men go into the village before nightfall and they collected him when they rode away? Or maybe he stayed in the village to observe what we do here? One thing's certain – the villagers will take notice of a stranger.*

Glancing at the sky, Guy saw the crescent moon climbing toward its zenith and realized dawn wasn't far away. If he wanted things to proceed as usual until he could sort out this catastrophe, he needed to be seen in his bed when the guards rose to relieve the night watch.

CHAPTER NINETEEN

Will awoke to the sounds of birdsong in the still-leafy canopy above. It had been such a long time since he'd slept in the woods that he'd forgotten how the variety of calls were like a choir welcoming the new day. He stood and stretched muscles that weren't used to sleeping on hard ground then brushed the leaves off his clothing.

Caernarfon had already risen and was sitting on a fallen log a few yards away. "Good morning, young Will. Not far along that way," he pointed toward the end of the holly-hedge, "is a decent place to relieve yourself."

When Will returned, he sat on the ground facing Caernarfon. "I suppose we should make our plan."

"I've been thinking about that. Your instinct to go south was a good one. If we make our way to the coast, we'll be well positioned to flee the kingdom if our pursuers learn of our whereabouts. So we should continue in that direction. But I think we must avoid the large towns."

"But surely, sir, the towns would be so crowded that no one would even notice two men passing through. And we'll need to buy food and drink if we're to survive to reach the coast."

"You make a good argument, Will, but consider this. It's not out of the question that I might be recognized in, say, Bath, for instance. Should that happen, all our efforts to mislead would have been for nought."

"Very well, but we'll still need to find food."

Caernarfon smiled. "Indeed we will." He paused. "It occurs to me that we could reach the safety of the coast much sooner on horseback than on foot."

"No doubt. But I don't have enough money to buy horses. We'll need what little I have for food. Maybe I shouldn't have spent so much of my wages in the tavern."

"Don't chide yourself, Will. You couldn't have known what was to come. And if you hadn't been in the tavern . . ." He let the thought hang in the air, rose from the log, and retrieved the satchel that he had used last night for a pillow. "Perhaps I have a solution to our problem of money." He withdrew a small leather pouch from the depths of the satchel and poured its contents into one hand. "Somehow no one ever thought to take these rings from me while they were taking all the money I had in my possession."

Will gazed at the two rings. Both with elaborate gold bands. One set with a large red stone, the other with a somewhat smaller blue stone surrounded by what looked to Will like small diamonds. "No doubt those are very valuable, sir, but we could never sell them in a village – no one would have that much money. And besides, might not someone recognize them as yours?"

"Of course we must be careful where we attempt to sell them."

"Better still, let's save them for an emergency. If we should have to flee by sea, it might be we'd have to bribe a ship captain to give us passage." Caernarfon put the rings back into the pouch, pulled the drawstring shut, and stowed the pouch back at the bottom of the satchel. "Then we shall walk for now."

"I've been wondering where we should go," said Will. "Sutton might be best. Far away from the corridors of power and from the plots so far. Easy to get passage on a ship."

"But quite a far distance to walk. I think perhaps I have a better idea. Sir John Pecche is constable of Corfe Castle. Pecche can be a bit of a scoundrel at times, but unless he's turned his coat quite recently, he isn't Mortimer's man. It shouldn't be difficult to persuade him to give us shelter and safety until we see which way the wind is blowing."

Will furrowed his brow. "Are you sure that's a wise move, sir?"

"Sure? No. Of a mind that the risk is small and worth taking? Yes. Pecche knows he owes his current preferment to me. And he's always been loyal to whoever advances his career, so if we convince him he's doing my son a favor, he'll most likely see that as a path to even more royal patronage."

"Then Corfe Castle it is." They both rose and Caernarfon slung the satchel over his shoulder. "But first," Will added, "let's go back to that stream. We don't know when we'll find another one that's safe to drink."

***

Feigning sleep was the best Guy could do, but by the time he heard the first men getting up, he had a rough plan for what to do next. Yawning and stretching, as if coming out of a deep sleep, Guy took his time donning a clean shirt and pulling on his boots. Others were beginning to stir, and the more who noticed him leaving his bed, the better.

First stop, the steward. "Lord Caernarfon gave me instructions last night that he's not to be disturbed before midday. He wants to spend the morning in prayer."

In point of fact, that was the only person he needed to tell, as it was the steward's job to inform the rest of the staff. But Guy had no intention of letting anything go awry, so he sought out the head house-maid and left her in no doubt of how much trouble she'd be in if anyone disturbed the former king's devotions. In the kitchens, he made sure both the cook and the kitchen maids knew they were supposed to wait until Caernarfon requested a meal before taking food or drink to his chamber.

Then he went in search of Will. Not finding him in any of the usual places, he went back to the room where his men slept to see if his cousin might be malingering when he should be on duty. *Wouldn't put it past him to have gotten so drunk in the tavern last night that he's still sleeping it off.* Aldwin emerged from the room just as Guy arrived. "Makepeace in there?" Guy asked.

"No. I thought he was on duty already."

"Can't find him. Any idea what he got up to last night?"

"Not really."

"You didn't go to the tavern?"

"Not last night. With those strangers here, seemed like we'd need all our wits about us if they tried to make trouble."

Guy clapped his second-in-command on the shoulder. "You're a good man, Aldwin. I can always count on you. Any idea if Will went?"

"You'd have to ask the sentries. They're in there," Aldwin gestured with his thumb over his shoulder, "but they've only just gone to sleep. Ask them later."

Not wanting to pique Aldwin's curiosity, Guy assented, and they parted ways, going in opposite directions. But the minute Guy could no longer hear bootsteps, he doubled back to the sleeping room, found Alf's bed, and shook him awake. "Just one question, Alf. Did Makepeace go out last night?"

"Huh?" Alf shook his head in an effort to wake up.

"Makepeace. Did he go out last night?"

"Aye. Took that injured servant home. But then he came back and didn't go out again."

"You're sure?"

"Yes, sir. Ask Tom. He'll tell you the same thing."

"I believe you, Alf. Just because I can't find him doesn't mean he's not in the castle somewhere. Go back to sleep."

"For certes this time?" Alf seemed dubious.

"For certes. I won't disturb you again."

Guy left the room and headed for the courtyard. *Where the devil could Will be? He could take care of what I need next with no fuss. Now I have to figure it out for myself. Why in the name of God's left ear can't I find him when I need his special talents?*

Still fuming, Guy crossed the courtyard and passed through the inner gate. As soon as he was within shouting distance, he called out to the next pair of sentries, "Raise the gate!" A head popped out of the gatehouse to see who'd given the order, then slowly, the heavy gate began to rise. By the time Guy arrived, it was high enough a man could duck under it. Once on the other side, he turned and gave more orders. "Leave it open for now. But don't let anyone in without my explicit permission. Understood? No one."

"But, sir, how do we get your permission if you're not here?"

"You don't. Keep them waiting until I get back. I won't be long."

Now what? Will would go to the tavern. But no one will be there this early. Turning onto the high street, he momentarily considered talking to the priest. *Who'd be more concerned about last rites and the dead man's soul than my current predicament.* Few people were out and about this early in the morning. No one was stirring at the inn, but then he had an idea. *The blacksmith will be getting his fires ready so they're hot enough to work metal by the time he needs to start on the day's work.* He made his way to the crossroads and turned left.

"How fare ye this morning?" the blacksmith called out as Guy approached. "Ye come from the castle, right? Am I needed there?"

"It's not your services I need, my good man, but I hope you can tell me where to find someone who *can* help me. You see, one of my men has fallen terribly ill, and I fear he may die if he doesn't get the right medicine. Is there a wise woman in the village? Or someone who knows herbs and potions?"

"Ye need Mistress Maud."

"And where might I find her?"

"Go back to the crossroads and turn left. Her house is at the end of the street – the last one before the meadows."

"I shall seek her out straightaway."

"Aye. Go thy way, good sir."

When he reached the crossroads, it suddenly occurred to Guy he'd forgotten to ask which side of the street the house was on, but he didn't want to waste time, so he turned left and hurried his pace. It turned out he needn't have worried. There were three more dwellings on the left side of the street than on the right, so he marched up to the door of the last one and knocked. No one came straightaway. His impatience getting the better of him, he rapped on the door again, this time louder and longer.

From inside came a woman's voice. "Bide your time. I'll only be a moment longer."

When the door finally opened, there stood a woman of indeterminate age with a large satchel slung over her shoulder. She might have been quite pretty in her youth, but time had etched its passage on her face and leached much of the color from her hair. Time had not, however, dimmed the sparkle in her eyes or – as Guy would soon discover – the spring in her step.

"Mistress Maud?" Guy asked.

"That's what I'm called, good sir. And where am I needed this fine morning?"

"How did you know—?"

"Men don't knock on my door to pass the time of day, good sir. May I know your name?" She pulled the door closed and started down the short path to the street with Guy hurrying to catch up.

"Sir Guy Bickerstaffe, Mistress."

"Then you must be from the castle. Let's not tarry." She stepped out briskly. "A man in need of my ministrations must not be kept waiting."

Back at the castle, Guy led her past the sentries without commentary and straight to the living quarters and Caernarfon's chamber. Only a thin sliver of light came through the joining of the draperies across the window, but it was enough to avoid stumbling around as he crossed to open the curtains and let in the light. He turned to find Mistress Maud setting her satchel beside the bed and reaching for the hangings.

"Before you attend the patient, Mistress, I have a confession to make." She dropped her hand from the bed hanging and turned to face him. "The man in the bed," he continued, "is already dead. But I don't know how he came to die here, so it's vital no one know about this until I can discover the answer. What I need is for you to prepare his body – to embalm and shroud him so that he may be preserved here until we learn to whom and where we should present him for burial."

Maud studied his face for a long time in silence. Guy could only hope that his plea wouldn't fall on deaf ears. At long last, she addressed him. "Who's in charge here?"

"At the moment, I am. Lord Berkeley is away and we've not been told when he might return."

"Very well. I shall do as you ask. But you must be diligent, Sir Guy, in pursuing your answers. Every man deserves a proper Christian burial." She pulled back the bed hangings and studied the corpse then said, "Help me remove his clothes."

As they removed the clothing, Maud carefully took note of everything about the man. Finally, she had Guy lay the man on his back at the side of the bed so she could easily reach to conduct her ministrations. While Guy gathered up the clothing and retrieved the boots from under the bed, Maud opened her satchel and took out several bottles, some instruments Guy had no idea the purpose of, and a huge roll of white fabric. "I think I can answer one of your questions even now," she remarked.

"Oh?" Guy stood with his arms full of clothing.

"I'm fairly certain I know how this man died. He has no injuries. No signs that he's been ill. In fact, it appears he was in quite robust health. All that, plus the appearance of these pillows, points to the fact that someone smothered him to death."

"What? Wouldn't he have tried to fight off an assailant? Shouldn't there be signs of a struggle?"

"There might be. But if he was in that deep, deep sleep of a man who'd imbibed far too much, he might not have come to his senses sufficiently to offer much resistance."

"Even so . . ."

"Look at all the pillows. All smashed flat – the feathers all compressed. Unless he slept on every one of them in sequence, one or two would still be fluffed up from when the bed was made yesterday morning. And sleeping on a pillow tends to leave an impression of one's head – rarely does it flatten the pillow so completely."

Guy placed the clothing on a chair and walked over to examine the pillows. Maud was right. They were all thoroughly flattened.

"Had he been ill," Maud went on as she withdrew a canister of something from her satchel, "I'd have you burn his clothes and even his bedding to be sure the illness didn't spread. But since that won't be necessary, perhaps you'll give them to me. From time to time, it's useful to have extra on hand if a patient has soiled the only clothing they have while ill, and I'm able to restore them to health."

"Of course."

"Now, I need two basins and a pitcher of hot water. And then you must leave me to do my work. Return when the church bells toll midday. I should have finished by then."

***

Will and Caernarfon were determined to put as much distance between themselves and Berkeley Castle as possible before nightfall, so they were grateful to find the country lanes in the area mostly led in their preferred direction. Threading their way between Bristol and Bath, they crossed the River Avon just before Keynsham then followed the River Chew, arriving at the small village of Compton Dando about an hour past midday. Tired, hungry, and thirsty, they decided it was worth the risk to try to find sustenance in the village.

Once they crossed the Chew at a low-water ford, their progress was hindered by a heavily laden hay wain moving slowly down the lane. Taking to the verge to go around, they startled the driver, who reined his horse to a quick halt. "Ye could scare a man out of his wits coming up alongside like that," he shouted down from his perch. "Don't ye know any better than sneaking up on a man?"

"Our apologies, my good man," Caernarfon took the lead. "We meant no harm."

"Well, ye best be glad no harm be done. Now get on with ye."

"Aye, we will. Is there anywhere here a man might find a bit to eat and drink?"

The driver laughed. "Ye think there be taverns in a little village? Ye must come from a big market town." He chuckled again, apparently quite amused by the ignorance of strangers. "But mayhap if ye be extra nice to Mistress Hannah and help her with the washing, mayhap she feed ye a morsel or two."

"And where would we find Mistress Hannah?"

"She be the washerwoman and today be washing day. She be with her wash pot and a fire in the square. Ye'd have to be blind not to see her. Now go thy way so I can get on with my business."

The wain driver was right. A couple hundred yards on, they came to the main part of the village where a robust, red-faced woman was busily scrubbing all manner of clothing and bedding and hanging things to dry on makeshift racks. Will and Caernarfon circled around to approach her from the front rather than risk startling her as they had the wain driver. "Are you Mistress Hannah?" Will asked.

"I might be. But I don't do washing for strangers."

"It's not washing we need, Mistress, but a bit of food. We've been walking a long way and ate the last of ours two days ago. The man driving the hay wain said you might spare us a bit if we did some work for you."

She stopped what she was doing and appraised both men from head to toe. "Ye don't look like ye be starving."

"Nay, not yet, but even a bit of bread would be welcome if you have any to spare."

She put her hands on her ample hips. "How is it ye come to be walking so far?"

Caernarfon replied. "We're farmers, Mistress. Brothers. Evicted from our lands. Now we're looking for a new place to grow things."

"There be nothing hereabouts, so ye needn't bother asking. All these farms have tenants now. Best ye try farther south."

"We'll take your advice," Caernarfon nodded his head in a small gesture of respect. "But about the bread?"

Hannah hesitated, then grabbed a large wooden fork and lifted what looked like a bedsheet out of the wash pot, holding it up to let the excess water drip out and then dropping it unceremoniously on an empty rack. "Ye take this pot down to the river and empty it for me, then bring it back full of fresh water and set it on the fire. Ye can use that little cart over there. When ye get back, mayhap I'll have found you a scrap or two of something."

Will and Caernarfon struggled to manhandle the heavy pot full of water onto the cart, which had a rope at the front to pull it by. Caernarfon pulled and Will pushed from behind. Water sloshed everywhere. "What I wonder," said Will, "is how we're going to get this thing back without losing all the water on the way."

"Very slowly," Caernarfon replied. "What I wonder is how in the name of all that's holy she does this by herself."

When they returned, with the pot mostly full, Mistress Hannah emerged from one of the small houses by the square carrying a small parcel and two mugs. "Small ale," she handed a mug to each man. "Hauling water be a thirsty business." While they drank, she inspected the wash pot. "Well, at least ye didn't spill it all on the way back." She held out the parcel, which Caernarfon stowed in his satchel. "Half a loaf of horsebread and a bit of cheese. Don't eat it all in one meal. Now go thy way, and God lead ye to a good farm."

The two men drained every last drop of liquid from the mugs before returning them to Hannah then bade her farewell and resumed their trek south. Past Compton Dando, the terrain became much hillier, with fewer smooth lanes to follow, so the going was more difficult. They carried on until sunset when they reached Wellow Brook, just outside Midsomer Norton. Tempted as they were to push on into the town and find a soft bed and a decent meal at the inn, caution prevailed. A little rocky stream just east of the bridge across Wellow Brook seemed to be clear enough to drink from, so they made a meal of horsebread, cheese, and water and were sound asleep by the time the first stars appeared in the sky.

***

When Guy returned to Caernarfon's chamber, he found Mistress Maud sitting primly in a chair by the hearth, her satchel at her feet. The bed hangings were drawn closed on the sides, left half open at the foot so one might glimpse the corpse. The unknown man lay in the center of the bed, the covers drawn up under his arms, which lay straight by his sides, the hands palm-down. He wore a tunic of blue and a supertunic of scarlet. The hands were wrapped in cloth, as was much of the face, but the forehead, hair, and eyes were uncovered.

"I dressed him from that clothes chest," Maud pointed across the room. "Whoever's room this may be was possessed of fine garments. It seemed fitting to lay him out properly." Guy wasn't so sure about that but chose to keep his thoughts to himself. "The aromatic herbs and oils beneath the wrappings will slow the corruption of the body and will mask the weffe for a time even after, allowing for the arrangement of a proper burial."

"I'm grateful, Mistress. And now there's just the matter of your fee."

"Since you've allowed me to keep the clothing he was wearing, six pennies will suffice."

Guy opened his purse, retrieved two groats, and placed them in her hand. She looked at him quizzically, as if wondering whether he didn't know the value of the coins he'd given her. "I think, Mistress, your kindness and care with the corpse are worthy of some generosity." He hoped he'd struck the right balance between securing her discretion and piquing her curiosity.

"Your kindness will be remembered, Sir Guy. Now, it's time for me to return home."

Guy escorted her to the inner gate and bade her farewell. He was watching her pass through the outer gate when a huge commotion in the courtyard drew his attention. The brewster and the head house-maid were screaming at one another with the cook alternately chiming in with one or the other of the adversaries while the brewster threatened first one and then the other of the women with some kind of paddle. *Can't these people solve their differences without coming to blows?* Guy wondered as he hurried toward what seemed about to become a brawl.

"What in the name of Beelzebub is going on here?" Guy's shout quieted the cacophony only long enough for the participants to realize there was someone new they could make their complaints to.

"This slattern won't admit she left a full chamber pot in my brewhouse. But she did, and its foul humors have spoiled the wort so I've had to pour it all out and start afresh. Wasted a whole two days of brewing, she has, and she refuses to admit it."

"Never would I do such a thing, nor any of my maids either. There be nary a reason to set down a chamber pot so close to where ye be going to pour the shit out. And besides . . . who was it left the exit door of the tunnel open? 'Tweren't me. *He,*" she stabbed a finger at the brewster, "he be the one what closes up the brewhouse at the end of the day. 'Twas the foulness of the cesspit that spoiled the wort."

Fury still painted on his face, the brewster raised his paddle again, leaving no doubt what he thought about the suggestion he might be in the wrong.

"Sir Guy," came the shout from the inner gate. "Sir Guy, come quick!"

Now what? Guy groused to himself. *Can't anyone around here do anything for themselves?* Aloud, he called out, "In a minute."

"You're needed at the outer gate now, sir. There's a horseman demanding entry, and he's getting impatient the sentries won't let him in."

"You – brewster," Guy barked. "Get back to the brewhouse and start a new batch so you don't waste yet another day. You – madam," he addressed the head house-maid, "tend to your cleaning. And you," he stabbed a finger at the cook, "make ready my midday meal." Then he turned on his heel and strode toward the outer gate, where a lone horseman was being held at bay by the two sentries.

"Who wishes to enter?" Guy asked.

"He won't say, sir," replied one of the sentries. "Only that he has orders."

"Well, he'll have to tell *me*," Guy addressed the horseman, "or he'll not pass through this gate."

"And who might you be, to have such audacity?" asked the horseman.

"The man who's inside the gate and demands to know what business you have here." Guy refused to give the new arrival the upper hand.

"Business with Lord Berkeley, of course."

"The baron is away. If you have business with him, then seek him in Hampshire – at Bradley."

"My business involves these premises."

"Then you'd do well to tell me your name and your business. Lord Berkeley left me in charge during his absence."

"My name is Beaukaire, sergeant-at-arms in the royal service. My business involves the former king."

The hairs on the back of Guy's neck prickled. *What did this man know about Caernarfon? Was he somehow connected to Ockley and his men?* Regardless, Guy had no choice. To maintain the illusion that Caernarfon was still in his bedchamber, Guy had to admit the stranger. "Then you'd best enter." He signaled to the sentries to step aside. "But first, dismount, if you please, and lead your horse. I'll not have anyone riding me down – nor would you enjoy the response of my men should you attempt such a thing."

Beaukaire gazed down at Guy, the expression on his face a mix of annoyance and contempt. At long last, he slowly dismounted and led his horse through the gate. "Perhaps now, you'll identify yourself to *me*." Beaukaire's tone matched his expression.

"Sir Guy Bickerstaffe. Commander of the guards for the prisoner and left in charge of these premises by Lord Berkeley."

They walked in silence through the inner gate and into the courtyard, where Guy beckoned to a passing servant. "Take Sergeant Beaukaire's horse to the stable and see that he's properly settled."

"Have him unsaddled, brushed down, and fed," Beaukaire added, handing the reins to the servant. "I won't be leaving anytime soon."

Arrogant bastard, thought Guy.

"Now, Sir Guy, you will show me to the former king's chamber."

"Not without some explanation." Guy planted his feet and crossed his arms over his chest. Beaukaire met Guy's gaze squarely, but refused to reply. "I'll not be intimidated," Guy said. "There've been too many plots surrounding the man. I won't be responsible for letting yet another one succeed."

"Very well, I'll find the room myself." Beaukaire turned and started toward the stairs to the keep.

"Not that way, you won't." Beaukaire stopped in his tracks and turned back to face Guy. "Just tell me your business. If you're not a plotter, there's no reason not to."

Beaukaire exhaled deeply and returned to where Guy waited, his stance unchanged. "Perhaps you weren't listening when I said I'm in the royal service. My orders are to guard the body of the former king until arrangements are made for the burial. Now will you please show me to the chamber?"

Guy's mind reeled as he struggled to keep confusion from showing on his face. But the last thing he needed right now was for a servant or one of his men to overhear Beaukaire's words. "Follow me." He strode toward the entrance to the family living quarters and led the way inside, determinedly staying several steps ahead of Beaukaire before finally stopping outside Caernarfon's door.

"Open the door," Beaukaire demanded. Guy complied. Inside, Beaukaire went to the gap in the hangings at the foot of the bed and glanced in. "Good. The body's been prepared. One less thing to concern me." He picked up a chair from beside the hearth and took it into the corridor then beckoned Guy to follow him, closed the door, placed the chair in front of it, and sat down. "Now, you'll give orders that my meals are to be brought to me here, then you may be on your way."

"I'll tell the servants, but I'm not going anywhere. I'm in charge here until Lord Berkeley returns."

"I have my orders, Sir Guy. Your presence is no longer required."

"I take my orders from Lord Berkeley, not from you."

"And my orders are from a much higher authority. I'm in charge here now and the services of you and your men are no longer required. You're to be gone by sundown."

Guy was about to object when realization dawned. *This is my way out. My key to escaping responsibility for whatever it is that's happened here these last two days. My path to avoiding the gallows – or worse. But is it dishonorable? Hardly as dishonorable as being associated with whatever foul plotting is at play. And if I'm a free man, I at least have a chance to vindicate myself against any culpability for Caernarfon's disappearance or the death of whoever lies in that bed. For God's sake, Beaukaire didn't even look carefully to see if the corpse was truly that of the former king. Something terrible is going on, and I want no part of it. Nor do I want my men being drawn into it either.*

His mind made up, he gave Beaukaire one last hard stare before saying, "I'll gather my men and leave. Ordering your meals is your responsibility. No doubt a servant will come up sometime this afternoon to check the chamber."

Guy made straight for the ramparts to find Aldwin and order him to assemble the men in the courtyard with all their belongings, ready for departure. "But, sir—" Aldwin started to object, but Guy cut him off.

"I only want to explain this once, Aldwin. Just get the men assembled and tell them all their questions will be answered."

Guy remained on the ramparts, surveying the landscape that had become so familiar over these past five months. What would he do now? Returning to Isabella for a new assignment wasn't an option since he couldn't know exactly where this Beaukaire fellow's orders came from. Best, perhaps, to disappear until all this could blow over – or events revealed what it was all about. But that would mean he couldn't return home . . . or show his face at tournaments . . . or even earn his way in the world for a time. Just as well, then, that he'd saved every penny he'd been paid by Berkeley, and Lancaster before him. Well, every penny except what he'd paid to Mistress Maud.

The sound of voices in the courtyard drew his attention and he turned to see his men-at-arms forming ranks. *Best get this over and done with.* Making his way to the nearest tower, he descended to the courtyard, marched to where the men had gathered, and surveyed the faces. One was missing. *Where in Satan's whorehouse was Will?* "Anyone seen Makepeace?" he asked aloud.

Only a few nays and shaking of heads among the men.

"Very well. He'll find out soon enough. We've been dismissed. Our assignment finished. You're all free to go home."

A chorus of mumbling ensued within the group. Finally, Alf asked, "What about our wages, sir?"

"There are none, I'm sorry to say. I haven't been paid, so I've nothing to pay you with. If I'd had any say in the matter, it wouldn't end like this. The only thing I have to give is my thanks. You have that in abundance. You've served our masters well, and for that you can be proud. Now you're free to go home to your loved ones. Our orders are to be gone from here before the sun sets, so I recommend you make straight for the stables, collect your horses, and be on your way."

Guy and Aldwin watched as the men slowly dispersed and waited until the last one rode out the gate before retrieving their own mounts. They rode together as far as the Bristol Road. "I'm coming with you, Guy," said Aldwin. "Don't know much else except soldiering, so I want to be around when you get your next orders."

"I've no idea when that will be, Aldwin. Or, for that matter, where I'm even going. You should go to your family for now. If and when I get a new commission, I'll come and find you."

"Somehow it doesn't feel right, sir. But if you promise . . ."

"You can count on it, Aldwin."

"Very well, sir." Aldwin turned his horse to the right. He'd be home in Somerset before the sun set again.

Before he'd gone a dozen steps, Guy called out to him. He reined in his horse and turned in the saddle. "Do you have any idea at all what's become of Will?" Guy asked.

"None at all, sir. I just hope no harm's come to him."

Guy turned his horse's head north and rode away. *Hope all you want, Aldwin. But if I ever get a single clue – even the slightest whiff – that he was complicit in this madness and the harm it's done to my career, then I will hunt him down to the ends of the earth and inflict harm beyond anything you can imagine. Even if it takes the rest of my days.*

CHAPTER TWENTY

23 September 1327

Parliament had adjourned at midday, so many of the magnates started their homeward journey straightaway, leaving Lincoln's innkeepers and tavern landlords to count not only their coins but also the days until the next such gathering would bring their next windfall. But this Parliament had left Edward with a growing sense of unease. Despite the humiliating defeat at Stanhope Park in August, his mother and Mortimer seemed determined to fight the Scots. A war that was increasingly expensive, turning every summons of Parliament into a demand for more money.

"It may be expensive," his mother told him when he'd questioned the wisdom of continuing to pursue the Scots, "but what might be the cost of losing control of those warlike hordes on our northern border?"

Edward knew that wasn't an entirely illegitimate concern. But he also suspected that the immediate cost his mother and her paramour were worried about was to the legitimacy of their rule if they failed to keep their response to the Scottish threat uppermost in people's minds. So far, though, they had little to show for all the money – unless one counted the Scots' night raid to collapse the royal tent, trapping the king and everyone who slept there beneath it. Edward shuddered every time he recalled the fear – panic, if he was truthful with himself – of trying to claw his way out with no idea who or what was waiting on the outside.

He was glad Montagu had stayed behind to return to Westminster with the court. It would be a chance to get his friend's private opinion on these latest developments. Tonight, though, he was relieved that the departure of the magnates meant there were no elaborate entertainments lasting into the middle of the night so he could seek his bed at a reasonable hour. *Expensive entertainments*, he thought to himself as he made his way from the dining hall to his bedchamber. *What is Mother thinking? Trying to distract the barons from all the money she's asked for to prosecute the Scottish campaigns? She wasn't always so profligate. Another step down the dangerous path Mortimer's set her on?* Something else he wanted to discuss with Montagu.

With the last candle doused and the manservant settled into his pallet on the floor beside the king's bed, Edward was alone with his thoughts for the first time in days. And those thoughts inevitably turned to his father. Was Mortimer going to act on his threat? Or was it just a fit of rage to intimidate Isabella? Either way, the fact that he'd voiced the words meant they were now present in his mind – which meant the danger was real.

Edward had just dozed off when loud banging on the bedchamber door startled him back to wakefulness. The manservant was on his feet in an instant and had barely opened the door when a guard carrying a torch pushed his way inside. "Begging your pardon, Your Grace." He bowed toward Edward, who was still sitting in his bed. "A messenger's arrived. Says it's of utmost urgency he speak with Your Grace and the queen straightaway."

"And what's been my mother's response to this late-night summons?"

"I couldn't say, Sire. A different guard was sent to waken her."

"Very well." Edward climbed out of the bed while the manservant scurried about fetching a robe for his master to don over his nightshirt. "Where am I to go?"

"Come with me, Sire."

"Just tell me where to go. I have another errand for you." His robe now belted closed, Edward reached for a candle and lit it from the guard's torch. "Go fetch Lord Montagu and have him join us."

"As you wish, Your Grace. The messenger is waiting in the great hall."

Edward made his way to the great hall but waited outside the door for his friend, who arrived looking rather disheveled. "Any idea what's afoot, Edward?"

"None at all. But it must be of some import to warrant such a late arrival. No matter what it is, Mother's not going to be pleased."

"Oh, now I understand." William grinned. "I'm here to shield you from her wrath." He clapped Edward on the shoulder. "Let's go in and find out."

They found the messenger standing at the far end of the hall, looking out the window, though what he might be watching in the darkness beyond was a mystery. Studying the sentries' positions? Plotting an escape? He didn't turn at the sound of their footsteps, so Edward and William took positions by the hearth, where there was still a bit of warmth from the fire that had been banked, and waited in silence. And waited. And waited.

Until at last Isabella stormed through the door, fully dressed and obviously in high dudgeon. "You, there," she called to the messenger, who turned and walked toward the hearth. "Who do you think you are, barging in and demanding that your queen be roused from her bed and dressed to receive you?" Glancing to her side, she added, "And my son as well."

When is she going to stop treating me like a child? Edward fumed to himself.

Then, finally taking in the entire scene, Isabella turned and pointed an accusing finger at Montagu. "What's *he* doing here?"

"I sent for him, Mother, should there be any need for protection." *From your willful misinterpretation of whatever the message might be,* Edward completed the sentence in his mind.

Only barely mollified, but at least no longer pointing the accusatory finger, Isabella turned back to the messenger. "Very well, say what you have to say."

"Your Grace." The messenger bowed deeply to Edward then offered a rather more perfunctory bow to Isabella. "My Lady."

Edward fought the temptation to look at William, knowing neither of them would be able to suppress their amusement at the messenger's strict observance of protocol in the face of Isabella's ire. Better not to stoke that flame.

"I'm Sir Thomas Gurney, and it's my sad duty to bring news of the death of our former king – your father, Sire – your husband, Madam."

Edward's heart skipped a beat. Had Mortimer made good on his threat?

Isabella, on the other hand, had different questions. "How could this be, Sir Thomas? I was not aware he was in anything but his usual robust good health. And when?"

"He was found expired in his bed at Berkeley Castle this Monday just past. That's all I know about his demise, but one would naturally assume, from the circumstances, that it was some natural cause. Perhaps God simply decided it was time to call his servant home."

"Monday?" Isabella asked. "How is it you come to be here so quickly? Might it not have been the Monday a week past?"

"I make no mistake, Madam. Knowing the king would want the news urgently, I rode as fast as I could, exhausting several horses along the way and changing to a fresh one every couple of hours. That's also why I dared to 'barge in,' as you put it, so late in the evening. My devotion to duty, even such a duty as this, would brook no delay."

"Is there anything further you can tell me, Sir Thomas?"

It may have been his imagination, but Edward thought Gurney suddenly seemed on edge, hesitating, however briefly, before answering the question. "No, Madam. Anything else that may be known would have been discovered after I began my journey."

"In which case," Isabella said, "you've done your duty. Leave us now to contemplate our loss."

Gurney repeated his formal bow to Edward, bowed his head to Isabella, then took three steps backward before turning to walk through the door. And now, Isabella seemed subdued. "I can barely take it in, Edward. Your father was never prone to illness. Nor was he old and decrepit."

Tempting as it was to remind her of Mortimer's threat, Edward held his tongue. Something wasn't right – he could feel it in his bones – but his mother was no longer a confidante, if she ever really had been. "It's late, Mother. We should return to our beds and cope with our private grief. Tomorrow will be soon enough to begin thinking of how to honor him."

Isabella walked to his side, and he leaned down for her to kiss him on the cheek. In just the last year, he'd grown taller than her. "Sometimes your wisdom surprises me, my son. I'm glad we both still bear some love for him in our hearts." She swept from the room, unable to suppress her air of superiority even in what she claimed was grief, but at least the irascibility was gone.

When she was out of earshot, Edward beckoned to William. "Come with me."

Montagu followed his young friend out into the courtyard and around the perimeter at the pace of a forced march. When they finally reached a point at the farthest distance from the sentry tower, he grabbed Edward's arm to stop him. Edward turned, looking as if he might lash out at the restraint. "Edward, stop," William said, his tone hushed. "I know you've just had a shock, but I can tell there's more that's troubling you."

"God's beard, William!" Edward made no effort to muffle his voice as he jerked his arm loose.

"Sound carries great distances on a clear night like this, my friend." Montagu looked up into the starlit, moonless sky. "This is the best place to talk and not be overheard. But keep your voice low."

Edward relaxed his shoulders . . . but only a little. "This is Mortimer's doing, William. I know it is. And I wasn't able to warn my father." Edward's entire posture slumped in despair. "I wasn't able to prevent his death."

Montagu didn't reply straightaway. And when at last he did, his words were hardly what Edward expected. "What makes you so sure your father is really dead?"

The young king perked up. "What are you saying, William?"

"Think about it. From Berkeley to Lincoln in a mere two days? That's a four-day journey . . . more likely five at this time of year, with the days growing shorter. If he rode at a gallop most of the way, that would mean changing horses far more frequently than he said. There's no moon these past few days until close to dawn, so he couldn't ride at night . . . and even if he kept at it a bit after sunset, he'd have been forced to a much slower pace. Two days?"

"So you're suggesting he lied about when my father died?"

"I'm suggesting that either Gurney was dispatched from somewhere much closer to Lincoln or several days earlier than Monday."

"Which means someone told him when Father died . . . or would die."

"If he died at all."

"Which also explains why Gurney couldn't say how he died."

"If he died at all."

By now, Montagu had Edward's full attention. "Which means there's almost certainly a plot of some sort afoot."

"Now you're thinking like a king. Just as you did when you sent Isabella back to her bed so you wouldn't have to discuss this with her tonight."

"I'll have to discuss it with her eventually."

"Perhaps. Perhaps not. But we don't know enough yet."

"Agreed. Surely Mortimer's involved. Is Mother as well? Has she come around to his way of thinking? But how are we to get to the bottom of it?"

"Patience, my young friend. For now, go along with whatever your mother suggests. Watch how events unfold. Listen, not just to her words, but to what she doesn't say. Notice what she doesn't do. Present your very best impression of bearing up as a king should under the grief of losing a father. And in the morning, I'll have a friendly conversation with Sir Thomas Gurney to see what slip of the tongue I can lure him into."

"Thank you, William. Now I think I'll take my own advice and seek my bed. So should you."

Back inside, they parted ways with Edward in a more thoughtful frame of mind. But the following morning, Sir Thomas Gurney was nowhere to be found.

CHAPTER TWENTY-ONE

As they'd drawn nearer to Wareham, Will couldn't help but notice that Caernarfon grew increasingly pensive – distracted, even. Their comfortable conversation lapsed, Caernarfon's responses mere acquiescences to whatever remark Will might have made. Will couldn't work out what had changed . . . or why. Was the former king regretting putting himself in the hands of a simple commoner? Had he changed his mind about their choice of destination? Worse yet, did he think some of the many plotters should have already rescued him from his current predicament? Will needed answers. Before they arrived at Corfe Castle.

They'd reached Wareham just at midday. Will was ready for something to eat after the long morning's walk, but Caernarfon seemed bent on nurturing his soul rather than his body. When they came upon St. Martin's-on-the-walls, he announced, "We should go inside to pray, my friend." Knowing the former king's piety, Will was under no illusion that his companion could be dissuaded, so now it was *his* turn to simply acquiesce. But then he realized this might be the perfect opportunity to get answers to his questions. The demands of his stomach would just have to wait.

Two people were at prayer before the main altar, but a chapel-like alcove on the left side was unoccupied. Caernarfon made his way there, Will following at a respectful distance. He waited, head bowed, while the former king knelt at the tiny altar. Will had never been particularly diligent in his devotions – certainly not during the past year in Sir Guy's service. He believed that an omniscient God would see his efforts to live a good life, regardless of how often he attended to the formal rituals. But his mother had been devout so, to honor her, he respected anyone who followed that path.

When at last Caernarfon made the sign of the cross and rose to his feet, Will stepped forward to join him. "Something's been troubling you over the past day, sir. Have your prayers put your mind at rest?" A more personal question than Will would ever have ventured in other circumstances, but if they were to continue their journey together, he needed to understand.

Caernarfon looked into the nave of the church. The two penitents had left. "Sit with me, young Will." He gestured to a bench facing the tiny altar of the alcove. Once they were seated, he continued. "You're right. In fact, I've been quite anxious now that our destination is so near. Plagued with questions about what could go wrong. What if Sir John Pecche isn't in residence? What if I'm wrong and he's switched loyalties? What if he's no longer constable and the castle is now in the hands of someone who might be under the same orders as those men we escaped at Berkeley? I'll have led you to your death, young Will, for helping me in the first place. Perhaps this is where we should part ways, and you should leave me to my fate."

Will's relief escaped as an enormous sigh that was louder in the small space than he'd intended. "Forgive me, Will, if I've caused you distress," said Caernarfon.

"It's not for you to apologize to me, sir. And there's nothing to forgive. It's only that I was concerned you'd changed your mind about casting your lot with me."

"Quite the contrary. I'm grateful for your help."

"I've been thinking about our arrival at the castle too. We need to scout the situation first."

"So what do you propose?"

Will rose and checked the nave once again to be sure they were still alone. When he returned to the bench, he said, "What can you tell me about the castle and its surroundings?"

"It stands on a quite prominent hill with unobstructed views in every direction. It was built by the Conqueror to guard the route inland from the Isle of Purbeck, and even today, the constable of Corfe is charged with that duty. There's a village at the base of the hill, of course. You know, Will, conventional wisdom is that the villagers can retreat to the castle for safety should there be an attack. But I've often wondered if perhaps the truth is quite the opposite – that those who first built these fortifications considered the village and the people who live there to be one more obstacle an enemy would have to subdue before there was any threat to those manning the fortress."

"That's a pretty grim assessment, sir."

"Alas, defending a kingdom can be a pretty grim business. But that's not why you asked your question."

"Any idea how far it is from here to the castle?"

"Not precisely. Only that we're quite close."

"Very well." Will glanced toward the nave then squared his shoulders as if he'd made a decision. "Here's what I think. We'd get the best information from the people in the castle village, but it seems to me that showing our faces there too soon would leave our king exposed, vulnerable to all manner of countermoves."

"You're proposing to deny the king the chance to participate in his own defense?"

"I'm proposing that the king might be wise to bide his time until we at least know the lay of the land."

"And how to you propose we acquire that knowledge?"

"I suspect the people here in Wareham know quite a lot about what goes on at the castle. Some of the merchants and tradesmen probably make deliveries there from time to time. If we stay here for a couple of days, we should be able to pick up in the taverns enough gossip about the castle folk to sort out how to make our approach."

"Something I'm given to understand you're quite good at. But I rather doubt I have your skill."

"You've told me how much you used to enjoy working the fields, clearing ditches, mingling with those who do that sort of work. These are the same people, sir – just in a different setting. You'll be fine." Caernarfon's little chuckle pleased Will – the former king was himself once again.

"Where do you propose staying?" Caernarfon asked.

"Now we're far enough away from Berkeley, I think we can risk staying at the inn. The odds they'd be looking for us here seem small. And if we *are* recognized, I still have enough money we could hire a fishing boat to take us away quickly."

They sat quietly for a long moment, Caernarfon finally breaking the silence. "You know, Will, the priests tell us God doesn't always answer our prayers in the way we want him to, yet we must pray nevertheless. When I knelt before that altar," he pointed toward the tiny one in the alcove, "I was seeking a way to convince you to leave me for your own safety and the strength to face my fate alone. Instead, he's shown me there's a way I can continue in your companionship and comfort and protection."

"My mother always said God rewards those who think of others as much as of themselves. Maybe he thinks neither one of us can do this alone."

Caernarfon smiled and clapped Will on the shoulder. "Then let's go find ourselves an inn. And hope God delivers us to one where we won't have to share a bed with complete strangers."

***

Three sharp raps on the door jarred Edward from a deep sleep. He'd tossed and turned most of the night thinking about his conversation with Montagu. William seemed dogged in his conviction that the report of Edward of Caernarfon's death was suspect at best – perhaps even an outright falsehood. But whose lie? And for what audience?

Increasingly, Edward felt as if he was living in the midst of a strange tableau. A crowned king, a deposed king, and a man who fancied himself king all on stage at the same time. And the queen who'd put things in motion – was she now losing control of her most volatile actor? Or was she still writing the script? And if so, where was it leading and who would be in the next scene?

He was sure he'd only just fallen asleep, but then came the knocking and the hurried footsteps of the manservant. Surely just a dream, a reliving of last night. But no, there was sunlight peeking around the edges of the draperies that covered the windows. And when he at last opened his eyes, there stood his mother's private secretary in the doorway looking thoroughly annoyed. Edward raised himself on one elbow, rubbing the sleep from his eyes with his other hand. "What is it, Griffin?" Even his sleep-clouded mind knew the man wouldn't speak to his king without an invitation to do so. But he wouldn't be standing there unless he had a message to deliver.

"Your mother the Queen Regent requests your presence in the privy chamber straightaway, Your Grace."

By now, Edward had roused himself to a sitting position in the middle of his bed. "Tell her I'll be there in due course."

"She did say straightaway, Sire, and it's my experience that when she says—"

Edward cut him off. "Are you suggesting, Griffin, that I should answer this summons in my nightshirt?"

"N-n-no, Your Grace, I just . . ." Griffin looked quite uncomfortable as he stumbled over the words.

Bumbling fool, Edward thought. *Best I put him out of his misery.* "You can tell my mother that I'll join her as soon as I'm suitably dressed for the day." *And have taken enough time with dressing to shake off the stupor from lack of sleep so I'm ready to match wits with her*, he added to himself.

"Very well, Your Grace." Griffin bowed then turned on his heel and left, his footsteps resounding in the corridor.

Marching smugly back to his mistress while lesser mortals scurry out of his path, Edward thought, the image finally bringing a smile to his face.

Two hours later – bathed, dressed, and in a better frame of mind – he found Isabella seated at the writing table, quill to paper, with a small stack of letters to one side. She finished her letter then folded and sealed it and added it to the stack before acknowledging her son's presence.

Why must she continue to play these games? I made her wait so she must do the same to me? Looks like she had plenty to occupy her time while she was waiting. Or is she just falling back on her habit of treating me like a child?

"Do have a seat, Edward, now that you're here." The sarcasm dripped from her words. She couldn't quite look down her nose at him while she was seated and he standing, but Edward had no doubt she was contemplating attempting the feat.

"I didn't sleep well last night, Mother, so I hadn't risen when Griffin knocked on the door." He took a chair on the opposite side of the table facing her. "I'm sure he told you as much."

"Be that as it may, dear, there's much to be done. I've ordered that the magnates still here be informed of your father's death and have written personally to those who already left. Now it remains for you to write to our closest family."

"But, Mother—"

"It's your duty, Edward," Isabella cut him off. "As king, you're head of the family."

"Hear me out, Mother." Isabella didn't look inclined to do so. "Please."

"Oh, very well." Her tone was somewhat testy. "What is it now?"

"Before we start bruiting it about that Father is dead, shouldn't we make some effort to be certain that's the case? After all, we have only the word of one man. One I've never seen before in my life." Seeing irritation start to creep into his mother's countenance, he rushed to add, "Though I certainly can't speak for you. But regardless, this Sir Thomas is not a man we know well – not someone who's often at court – not even someone who regularly tilts in the lists. And he brought no written message. Wouldn't it have been more seemly for Lord Berkeley – or even Maltravers – to have written to us of the death of such an important personage who'd been given into their charge? Might we not be well advised to take steps to confirm what Gurney said?"

Isabella hesitated for the briefest moment before replying. An instant so fleeting that it may have been missed by someone not as alert to her every nuance as Edward was that morning. *Almost like that hesitation I witnessed from Gurney last night*, he thought, *when Mother asked him if there was anything else to tell. Is she reluctant to admit I'm right? Or does she – do they both – know something they don't want revealed?*

"Your father's body would have been attended to by someone from the village – a wise woman, most likely. If it will put your mind at rest, when we get back to Westminster, I'll send for her and question her about the corpse. Now . . ." She rose from her chair. "Sit here and write your letters. Put them in the pile with mine, and Griffin will see that they're all dispatched."

Edward was not at all satisfied, but, remembering Montagu's words, he dutifully moved to the opposite side of the writing table, sat down in the chair Isabella had vacated, and picked up her quill. She leaned over his shoulder and drew a piece of paper toward him. "There. I've made you a list of everyone you must notify. It shouldn't take long. Then you can join me for the midday meal." She kissed the back of his head, and then she was gone.

A quick glance at the list revealed that it included none of his father's siblings, and rummaging through the pile of letters revealed his mother had already written those letters. *I guess she thinks I'm only head of the junior branches of the family*, he groused to himself. Feeling rather queasy about telling people his father was dead when that was far from certain, he allowed himself the perverse pleasure of starting at the bottom of the list.

> *By the grace of God and given this day under my privy seal, to John de Bohun, Earl of Hereford I send Greetings*
>
> *It is my sad duty to inform you, dearest cousin, that our one-time king, known since my accession as Lord Edward of Caernarfon, my father, your uncle has been commanded to God. The news has reached us only in the past day that he was discovered no longer alive in his bed at Berkeley Castle. Thus it is that there has not been sufficient time for consideration of when or how he is to be interred. Be assured, my dear cousin, that such news shall reach your ears in due course.*
>
> *Edward R*
>
> *At Lincoln, 24 September 1327*

When the last missive was added to the pile, he pushed back from the table as if the table itself were just as distasteful as the task he'd just completed. There was no way he could avoid dining with Isabella, though he dreaded where her conversation might lead. *Go along for now, Edward*, he reminded himself. Tomorrow, they'd begin the journey back to Westminster. He'd already decided to eschew the comfort of the carriage and the company of his mother. On horseback, he'd have time to think.

***

Two days later, William and Caernarfon had their answer. They were sitting in a quiet corner of the tavern, watching and listening as the locals crowded around a newly arrived traveler at a large table nearby. "Funny, don't you think?" Will chuckled softly to the former king. "Just two days ago, we were the new faces in town and commanded all the attention."

Caernarfon smiled and took a sip of ale. "Men's infallible and apparently insatiable curiosity about the latest new thing has always intrigued me. It's what makes an unexpected move so irresistible and why most men walk, eyes wide open, straight into the trap that's been set. Only a thoughtful opponent pauses to consider what might be lurking behind that move."

The traveler, it seemed, was on his way to Corfe Castle. "Message for Sir John Pecche."

"Well, ye won't find him there," said the landlord, who'd wandered over to the noisy table to refill mugs. "Pecche's been away most of the year."

"Aye," chimed in a burly man they'd learned was the local butcher. "Left when? March, was it?"

"Something like that," replied the landlord.

"Then where am I to find him?" asked the traveler.

"Mayhap the castellan will know," said the butcher.

"Then I suppose I'll have to go to the castle tomorrow and inquire. And who is the castellan?"

"Oh, ye needn't trouble yourself to go there," said the landlord. "Lord Thomas attends mass every Sunday at Lady St. Mary's right here in Wareham. Rain or shine. Only thing that keeps him away is if the road's so iced up he can't get down off that hill. Just look for him at the church tomorrow. Always sits at the very front – folks save that space for him."

"Lord Thomas?" asked the traveler.

"Lord Thomas Faintree."

"Come, Will." Caernarfon spoke softly and rose from his stool. "I feel like a walk." Will downed the last of his ale and followed his companion outside.

They walked slowly up the street that ran through the village, glancing back occasionally to be sure no one from the tavern had decided to leave and come their way. "It seems, young Will, that God has provided yet another interesting answer to my prayers."

"In what way, sir?"

"Thomas Faintree. He knows me. He'll recognize me. And he's long been a quiet but ardent foe of Roger Mortimer. The sort that stays out of Mortimer's way rather than overtly challenging him. He'll have no qualms about doing anything to thwart Mortimer so long as the risk to himself and his family is minimal. But the question remains, how can we approach him? We can hardly walk up to the sentries as two peasants and ask for an audience."

"Seems to me the landlord gave us the answer to that, sir. If this Lord Faintree will be here for mass tomorrow, then that's where we make our approach."

"Knowing you, Will, I suspect you have some scheme taking shape in your mind." Caernarfon laughed softly.

"Well, coming from Corfe, he'll almost certainly arrive in a carriage. And probably the finest one we'll see in these parts. So we wait outside Lady St. Mary's – on the other side of the street – until we see him arrive. Then we make our way quickly inside and watch who sits at the very front, to make sure we've got the right man."

"That won't be necessary. I'll recognize him when he descends from the carriage."

"Then at least we'll know we've got the right carriage. So we sit at the back where no one will pay us any attention, and, after the blessing of the Eucharist – when folks go up to receive communion – we leave quietly to wait outside."

"Should we not take communion? After all, God has blessed us most generously this week."

"It's the best time for us to leave, sir. If we're not already outside, he could easily make his exit and get into his carriage before we could get through the crowd leaving the church. People will be moving about while communion is being served. No one will take notice of what we do. And I suspect God won't take offense."

Caernarfon smiled. "I think God must have a particular fondness for you, Will. He certainly seems to smile on your endeavors, despite your rather sporadic attention to the rituals of our faith."

"Then we watch and wait and blend in as best we can. When Faintree is about to step into his carriage – that's when we make our approach."

Having reached the last house in the village, they turned to retrace their steps back to the inn. "It's not clear your scheme will succeed, young Will. But as I have no better idea, then it's the one we must try. And if we fail, we'll simply have to think of something different."

The next day, they sat on the low stone wall near the gate to the churchyard as the bells began to ring signaling the end of the service. Faintree's carriage waited just across the lane. Throngs of villagers emerged first, with Lord Thomas bringing up the rear. He paused to greet the priests, then started toward his carriage. That was the cue for Will and his companion to leave their perch.

A footman was holding the carriage door open for his master when the pair approached. "A word, Lord Thomas?" Caernarfon asked. "If you'd be so kind."

Faintree turned. "Yes?"

"I need your help, Thomas."

Faintree's expression turned harsh. "Have you no manners, man?"

"Look at me, Thomas. Look carefully. You know me." Caernarfon stood patiently, looking Faintree straight in the eye. As recognition slowly dawned, a half smile appeared Faintree's face. Caernarfon put a finger to his lips.

"Perhaps I do at that," said Faintree, speaking more quietly now. "Fetch your horse and follow my carriage."

"We have no horses, I'm afraid."

"Then my carriage will wait for you just outside the village. No need to give the folk here something to gossip about."

"As you wish, my lord." Caernarfon removed his cap and bowed his head for the benefit of anyone who might be watching.

Will had paid their bill at the inn earlier that morning, so there was no reason for them to return. They killed some time by walking toward the quay, hoping anyone who saw them would think they were leaving by boat. Then they quickly zigzagged through the alleys back to the main road where they found Faintree's carriage waiting with the door open. As soon as they were inside, the carriage moved out at a lively clip, slowing only when it began to climb the hill.

No one said a word until they passed through the gates and Faintree led them inside and dismissed the servants. "Now, Lord Edward," he said, "how may I be of service?"

For the first time in a week, Will heaved a huge sigh of relief. They were safe. For the moment, anyway.

CHAPTER TWENTY-TWO

Mortimer was already there when the king's party arrived in Westminster. Isabella waited until the three of them – she, Mortimer, and Edward – were alone to announce the news of the former king's death. Edward kept his eyes on Mortimer while his mother described Gurney's arrival and what he'd revealed.

Holy mother of God! Did the bastard just smile? He knew about this all along. Edward wasn't sure whether to be incensed at the man's audacity or smug in his own assessment of what may or may not have happened at Berkeley Castle. Of one thing he no longer had any doubt. His friend was right. Biding his time and playing along was the right path to discovering the truth. Of course, that didn't mean that he and William might not do a bit of investigating on their own. He'd already decided that, when the time was right, he would insist on having some neutral parties – clerics, most likely – view the body and confirm its identity. Or expose the lie. They just had to decide who they could trust.

Isabella made good on her promise to send for the woman who'd embalmed the body. Toward the middle of October, a small coach pulled to a stop in the courtyard. The queen's envoy descended followed by a much older woman dressed plainly, her mostly grey hair tucked under a generous hat and pulled into a bun at the nape of her neck. Once out of the carriage, she stood stock still, surveying the grandeur of her surroundings, her expression a curious mix of awe and utter puzzlement as to why she'd been summoned here.

To Edward's surprise, his mother had agreed that the two of them should receive the visitor alone. She'd also agreed that the interview might be more successful in a less intimidating setting than the king's presence chamber – or even the privy chamber. So they were waiting in a small sitting room where Isabella sometimes did needlework with the ladies of the court when the envoy showed the visitor in. "Mistress Maud, Your Grace, My Lady. From Berkeley village," he announced then offered a quick bow and left, closing the door behind him.

Maud managed an awkward curtsey – clearly, she was out of her element – then stood rooted to the spot. Isabella rose from her seat, crossed the room, and took Maud's hand, leading her toward an empty chair. "I'm Isabella, my dear." She gestured to Edward. "My son, Edward. We're grateful you accepted our invitation. Here . . ." now gesturing to the chair ". . . please sit and be comfortable."

Edward watched in amusement. This was the mother he remembered from his childhood. The one who was charming and kind. Who could put anyone at their ease. *What had happened to that version of her? Or did she always use that charm with ulterior motive, and I was just too young to understand?*

"Now, Mistress Maud," Isabella continued, "my son and I hope you can help us with a bit of a conundrum we're facing. You see, we've been informed of the death of the former king – my husband, Edward's father. But royal duties have made it impossible for us to travel to Berkeley to view the body and see the truth for ourselves. So we've brought you here to give us some piece of mind. You did embalm the body, didn't you?"

Maud sat stiffly in her chair, her hands clasped in her lap, looking suspicious about the proceedings and unready to succumb to Isabella's seduction. She stared at her hands then murmured, "Aye, m'lady."

I'd be suspicious too, thought Edward, *if I'd suddenly been summoned to the king's presence.* "There's no reason to be afraid, Mistress Maud," he said aloud. "You're not in any trouble. No harm's going to come to you."

Maud looked into his eyes and seemed to relax ever so slightly. "Thank you, Your Grace. It's just that the man what came for me said I was ordered to come, and it didn't seem to me any good could come from an old peasant woman being ordered to the king's presence."

Edward smiled. "Well, I give you my word. Nothing bad's going to come from your visit here." Since he seemed to be getting through to her better than his mother had, he continued. "Why don't you tell us how you came to be the one who embalmed the body?"

"It's just that I'm the one who does that in Berkeley Village. At the castle too. Whenever somebody goes to God, I'm the one what gets called to prepare the body so God will be pleased with the care taken of his servant. I know about herbs and such, you see. Learned it from my grandmother."

"So someone from the castle sent for you?" Isabella asked.

This time, Maud didn't seem so afraid of her. "Not exactly, m'lady. He came to fetch me. The man in charge of the guards. He came himself and when I was finished, he paid me all proper like."

The guards! Edward suddenly realized he hadn't given them any thought. *Where were they in all this? Most specifically, where was Sir Guy Bickerstaffe – the man his mother had put in charge of ensuring his father's safety? What was he doing then and where is he now? Something to discuss with William.*

"Tell me about the dead man," Isabella said.

"Well, he was in a big bed in a fine chamber. He was in his nightshirt when I arrived. But the last thing I did was dress him proper-like. There were fine garments in his clothes chest. Fit for a noble gentleman. So I dressed him in the best of them so he'd look nice for his loved ones."

"Was he my husband – our former king?"

"I couldn't say, m'lady, on account of I've never seen any king or queen before today."

"And did the man who fetched you say anything about who the dead man was?"

"Not really, m'lady. Maybe if it was the king, they wanted to keep things quiet."

*Or maybe if it **wasn't** the king, they wanted to keep **that** quiet.* Edward kept his musings to himself. *Maybe that's why Bickerstaffe hasn't presented himself here to give an accounting of events. Yet another piece of the puzzle.*

Isabella contrived to look thoughtful. "It could be as you say, Mistress. Was the man tall?"

"Taller than some, I think, m'lady. But it's hard to say when a man's not standing beside others."

"Was his hair wavy?"

"Not curly. But I suppose you could say wavy."

"Do you know how he died?" asked Edward. "Were there marks on his body? Or wounds?"

"I couldn't rightly say, Your Grace. There were no marks or wounds – of that I *am* certain. He wasn't stabbed or run through with a sword. No bruises on his skin, and I didn't detect any broken bones, so I don't think he was beaten. Mayhap we'll never know."

"Is there anything else you can tell us, Mistress Maud?" Isabella asked sweetly.

"Can't think what it might be, m'lady. I did my best for him, same as for every other poor departed soul I tend to. If he was your husband, then I hope he receives God's grace."

The three of them sat in awkward silence for several minutes, Isabella studying Maud, Edward contemplating the floor. At long last, Isabella said, "Thank you for coming, Mistress, and for answering our questions. There's nothing more we need to know. When you leave the room, you'll find the man who brought you here waiting in the corridor. He'll see to it that you get back home safely. You're free to go."

Maud rose somewhat tentatively and started making her way to the door, glancing over her shoulder once in apparent uncertainty that she was really being allowed to leave. As she reached for the doorknob, she stopped her hand in midair and turned back around. "Oh . . . I'm sorry, Your Grace." Once again, the awkward curtsey, then she hurried out of the room.

"Well, that seems to confirm what Gurney said, don't you think, Son?"

"If you think so, Mother."

"Then what we must do is decide where he's to be buried. Roger has suggested Gloucester Cathedral."

"Why not here in the Abbey church? That's where grandfather's tomb is."

"Edward, do you really think it's wise for the body to travel all that distance? It would just be a target for troublemakers. And we have enough trouble with the Scots as it is. No need to stir up yet more among our own people."

"Whatever you think best, Mother." *Go along for now.* "If there's nothing else?"

"No. You can run along."

Edward cringed. *There it is – back again – treating me like a child.* But he kept his face neutral and his steps measured as he left the room, though inwardly, he couldn't get out of there fast enough.

Mulling over what he'd just heard, he went in search of Montagu. *That was anything but convincing. Yes, there is – or was – a corpse at Berkeley castle. Said corpse wasn't brutally killed. The man had wavy hair. He might have been tall. That proves nothing, least of all that the dead man was my father. The key to everything is Bickerstaffe. It's him we need to find.*

CHAPTER TWENTY-THREE

October 1329

It had been two years since Sir Guy had ridden away from Berkeley Castle. Two long years of nursing his grudge against his cousin. Two years without turning up a single clue as to what had happened that night or where Will and the missing former king might be.

He'd spent the first night after what he thought of as the ignominious end of his career at a seedy inn in Gloucester. The last thing he needed was for someone to recognize him as the head of the guards at Berkeley and start asking questions. Luck was with him. The only other resident of the inn was the landlord's brother, who apparently showed up whenever his habit of drinking himself into oblivion cost him his job. The man could barely climb the stairs to his bed, so Guy was spared the further ignominy of having to tolerate his company. Even still, Guy spent the night lying on his back, his sword and his purse beneath him. Uncomfortable, but better than having it stolen while he slept.

The next morning, still uncertain what he was going to do – or where he was even going, for that matter – he headed east into the Cotswold Hills. By the time he reached the Manor of Northleach, he was still of two minds where to go. Back to Berkeley and start looking for clues to follow? A risky proposition in such an out corner of the realm where some villager might recognize him, but if he found the trail . . . Or on to London, where there was more likely to be news and even gossip about the former king's fate? An expensive proposition, to be sure, but an easier place to blend in and even lurk about the fringes of the court looking for clues.

He camped that night on the grounds of the manor and made his calculations. He had a bit over thirty pounds left from his wages for the past year. He hadn't really had much to spend it on since he didn't frequent the taverns or buy the services of the barmaids. *Unlike Will*, he groused to himself. He'd bought himself a fine sword when he was knighted that had cost him twelve shillings – he could have gotten one suitable to his rank for less, but he wanted something to set himself apart – something for other men to envy. And he'd spent a shilling on two sturdy pairs of boots. The captain of the former king's guards shouldn't look down at the heel. Six pennies once a month to a stable boy to keep his armor clean and free from rust. Lodgings, food, and drink were provided by his employer, along with stabling, feed, and blacksmith services for his horse.

Guy wasn't destitute. He'd left considerable funds in his brother's safekeeping when he took up the Queen Regent's commission. But the only way to get his hands on any of that money was to fetch it himself. And he had no intention of going home in his current disgrace. *God's bones!* he chastised himself. *You could have paid Aldwin to collect some of it for you. At least he's trustworthy. What were you thinking, just sending him on his way?*

The money he had was enough, Guy calculated, to live for about a year in London if he was careful. It would last longer in the countryside. But London was where the court – and particularly Lord Mortimer – spent much of its time. Still undecided, he doused the fire and lay down to sleep. When morning came, he saddled up and pointed his horse's head east.

His money had lasted longer than he expected. He had no choice but to spend the first few nights in the city at an inn, which set him back the considerable sum of three shillings for his bed, his meals, and his horse. So the first order of business had been to locate cheaper lodgings. A baker who'd recently lost his wife agreed to rent him one of the two rooms above his shop for five pennies a week. The baker had a stable master friend, and Guy bargained to board his horse for two pennies a day, year round – a bit more than usual for the summer but not the typical three-and-a-half pennies for the winter months. He could have sold the horse and added to his funds.

But then he'd have to buy another one when he picked up on Will's trail, and there was no guarantee he'd find one as good as what he had now. Besides, having a horse would allow him to follow the court when they decamped to Sheen or Greenwich or even as far as Windsor.

That settled, he began frequenting all the places where he might pick up a bit of news. Churches and markets. Inns and taverns, particularly those in proximity to the Inns of Court and Westminster Palace. He was careful to guard his meager funds – he could make one mug of ale last an entire evening as he listened to the friendly banter – and the occasional brawl – hoping for even a tiny tidbit of information. Now and then, he'd avail himself of the services of a barmaid – after all, barmaids heard everything – not so much to enjoy her favors as to ply her with questions.

He convinced himself God would forgive him if the fornication wasn't for his personal pleasure but in pursuit of his mission to put to rights what had gone so horribly wrong at Berkeley Castle. Just to be on the safe side, though, he confessed his sin each time. He'd figured out that the priests tended to leniency with a man who wasn't known to be a habitual fornicator – half a dozen Hail Marys and a penny for lighting a candle to honor the Virgin was the usual penance. And with scores upon scores of churches in the city, Guy could go months without having to make his confession in the same place.

They'd buried Edward II – or whoever the dead man was – in Gloucester Cathedral in December of 1327. Gossip had it that Isabella had commissioned a carved effigy for his tomb. People spoke only in whispers of Roger Mortimer's growing power. The young king had created him Earl of March in September 1328. Everyone knew this was Isabella's doing – a reward for her paramour – but no one said it aloud if they thought anyone in authority might be listening.

Otherwise, time passed for Guy with nothing of substance to show for his efforts. And as time wore on, he grew increasingly dispirited. This quest had reduced him to the level of Will Makepeace – spending his days and nights and his money in the taverns, consorting with barmaids, doing nothing to advance his standing. In fact, adding even more ignominy to his already tattered honor and reputation. But knowing it was Will's fault merely drove him to continue. "Even if it takes the rest of my days," he'd sworn when he rode away from Berkeley Castle nigh on two years ago – and Sir Guy Bickerstaffe didn't take his oaths lightly.

Now, though, he was growing concerned that his money might run out before he found any answers. London was expensive. Things were much cheaper across the river in Southwark, he'd heard, but he hesitated to make the move since living there would mean he'd have to pay a wherry to cross the river whenever he wanted to make the rounds in London or Westminster. Taking his horse would be too risky – it might be stolen while he spent an evening in a tavern.

He'd learned something last week, though, that he wished he'd known months ago. Men of means – even some of the highest-ranking – had no qualms about frequenting the bath houses in Southwark. And if ordinary barmaids heard everything and knew everything in the daily life of London, just think what the women who plied their trade in the bath houses might hear from men who were actually close to the seats of power.

So Guy bade farewell to the baker, collected his horse, and rode across London Bridge to reestablish himself in the Stews of Bankside. He didn't know how he was going to get access to what was spoken of in the bath houses – *God help me if I have to become a regular customer*, he thought to himself – but his gut told him that was where his answers lay.

***

Edward and Montagu weren't having much better luck than Guy in getting to the truth of the matter – and even less luck finding Sir Guy himself. "I have men on the lookout for him," William told Edward on one of their trips to Hampton Manor. The heath had become their favorite place for private conversations. "Men who knew him in the lists," William added. "Before this wretched business with your father."

"How do they know where to look?"

"They don't. All they can do is pay close attention to the men they encounter. And all we can do is hope for a godsend."

That conversation had been almost two years ago, and still they hadn't found him. God was apparently ill-disposed to getting involved.

Much to Edward's surprise, Isabella had agreed to have a delegation identify the body when it was moved to Gloucester Abbey a month after Gurney's visit. Mortimer, on the other hand, was adamant in his opposition. Edward had overheard them arguing about it the day his mother revealed her intentions. "For God's sake, woman, it's absurd! The man's dead. Bury him and be done with it."

"I know my son, Roger. He won't stop asking questions until he's sure the corpse is that of his father. This is a simple enough way to give him that assurance."

"Just tell him *you're* sure and that's that. He's still a child, after all."

"And he's also the king. He may not be of age yet, but he soon will be. And when he rules in his own right, do you want to be the man he remembers as standing between him and the truth about his father's death? I wouldn't. He's going to be much more like Longshanks than his father ever was. If you'd bother to notice, you'd see that already."

"Oh, for the love of Christ. Do what you have to do. But I'm having *no* part of it." And with that, Mortimer stormed out of Isabella's sitting room, taking no notice of Edward waiting in the corridor to speak to his mother.

Two weeks later, the delegation – which included the abbots from Bristol and Gloucester Abbeys and the mayor of Gloucester – gave their report. They had viewed the body superficially and believed it to be that of Edward of Caernarfon, God rest his soul.

"Superficially?" Edward asked Montagu when they finally had an opportunity to speak in private. "What does *that* mean?"

"In truth, I don't know. A brief glimpse maybe? Or perhaps the wrappings weren't removed from the face? Maybe the body was starting to smell and they dared not get too close? We can only guess unless you question them yourself."

"So how could they know it's my father?"

"I'm afraid I don't have an answer for you."

"Nor does Mother, but she's declared the report to be proof positive of the dead man's identity and sufficient to proceed with a proper burial. I can't think of any way to delay other than to insist on viewing the body myself. She crossed swords with Mortimer over sending the delegation, but I doubt she'd go any further. And I don't need either of them to get it in their head that I'm behaving like a petulant child." William chuckled. "What's so funny?" Edward asked.

"Oh, just a brief mental image of you throwing a tantrum in front of your mother and Mortimer and the entire court."

Edward couldn't help but smile. His friend had an extraordinary knack for putting things into perspective.

"Seriously though, Edward, you're right about having reached an impasse. All you can do . . . all you *should* do publicly for the moment . . . is to go along. But just because we've been stymied at this juncture doesn't mean we stop looking for answers."

"You *will* keep helping me then, William?"

"Of that you should have no doubt. And when we have our answers, if they fly in the face of what we're being told now, you can throw as colossal a royal tantrum as you'd like."

Their endeavors since then had produced a few tantalizing clues. Sir John Pecche had, for some reason, returned from abroad a year earlier than expected, going initially to Corfe Castle to attend to his duties as constable. Some months later, as was his wont, he managed to draw attention to himself, being accused along with others of stealing horses in Warwick. But what interested William and Edward was his association with Sir Ingelram Berenger, who was known to be in contact with the Earl of Kent.

Recently, one of Montagu's men claimed he'd almost certainly spotted Bickerstaffe going into a tavern on New Street in Holborn. But he'd been running late for dining with his wife's family and had no stomach for listening to his wife and her mother berate him at length over his disregard for social courtesies, so he hadn't gone after the man. Sadly, despite returning to the same tavern several times over the course of the following weeks, he reported no further sightings.

And now, as the chill winds of autumn evenings began to herald the coming winter, there were whispered rumors of Caernarfon's survival. No one would speak the words aloud – certainly not in the presence of anyone who might be connected with the court – but such things have a way of oozing into the atmosphere, no matter how secretive those in possession of the knowledge might strive to be.

***

Riding slowly through the lanes of Bankside, Sir Guy felt a renewed sense of purpose. At the corner of Made Lane and Rose Alley, an altercation in front of a bath house drew his attention – a woman, apparently the proprietress, alternately hurling epithets and personal belongings at a man in the street whose arms were raised to deflect the flying objects. "Take yourself and your garbage and get out of my sight, John Baskin. I've *had* it with you."

"But mistress, I just—"

The poor man tried to get a word in edge-wise as he ducked to avoid being hit in the head with a flying boot, but the woman cut him off. "No more excuses, you bastard son of a whore. I hired you to protect this house and my girls and you do nothing of the sort. When you're not drunk, you're sleeping it off." She paused to hurl a pair of trousers, which landed in the muck below an upstairs window. Guy didn't want to think about what might have been poured down from above.

"Now look what you've done," the man tried to protest, earning himself nothing more than another flying boot.

"You can't tell me you didn't let two fine gentlemen walk out last night without paying. And Bessie looks like someone slapped her around. That's the last straw, you godforsaken lout. Get yourself gone. And your muddy trousers with you."

"But, mistress, what about me wages?"

"You think I'm going to pay you for letting my money walk out the door in those men's purses? You're dumber than a sheep. I could pick any man off the street and he'd be a better protector than you."

Guy recognized his chance and knew he had to act quickly, even if he didn't know precisely what he might be getting into. "Indeed you could, madam," he said and doffed his cap to the woman.

She whirled toward the sound of his voice and planted her hands on her hips, her rage still unspent. "And who in the name of Beelzebub do you think *you* are?"

"A man off the street, madam. Guy Willoughby, at your service. It seems you're in need of a guard for your premises." He'd had to think fast. Using his real name here, where someone associated with the court might drop in at any time, probably wasn't wise. So he picked the first thing that came to mind – his mother's family name.

The woman appraised him from the top of his head to the hooves of his horse. "And what makes you think you'd do any better job than *that* cumberworld?" She jerked a thumb over her shoulder toward the object of her insult.

"Well, I trained with a knight for a bit." Best to have some logical explanation for his skills, in case he ever had to use them. "At least until my money ran out. I'm God-fearing, temperate in my drink, and in need of work."

This time, her appraisal began with the hooves, but her posture was more relaxed and her expression more curious than critical. "Any man can say as much, but that doesn't make it true. Still, I think I like the cut of your cloth. Come down off that horse. I don't do business with anyone who could ride me down."

He dismounted carefully, having no wish for her to misconstrue his intentions, then stood beside his horse's head, the reins held loosely in his hands. The woman walked completely around them, examining the saddle, lifting a hoof to inspect the shoe, then finally coming to a stop facing Guy. "Horse and saddle well cared for . . . clothes clean enough . . . neatly trimmed beard. You don't *look* like a bretheling. Tell you what. I'll give you a try. Week at a time until you prove yourself. Bed and board and you can stable your horse with mine in the back. Do your job well in the first week, then after that, your pay's a shilling a week. In return, you make sure my girls aren't harmed by the customers, you make sure the customers pay, and you keep the Bishop of Winchester's men away from my door. That agreeable to you? Willoughby, did you say?"

The pay wasn't much, but he'd have no expenses and access to whoever frequented this establishment and whatever secrets they let slip when they were alone with the women. His luck, it seemed, had just taken a turn for the better. "Quite agreeable, madam." He doffed his cap once again. "And what should I call you?"

"Everybody hereabouts knows I'm Anne Smith. Mistress Anne to you." When she opened the door and called out "Tom," an urchin who couldn't have been more than ten scurried out. "Take Master Willoughby's horse around back and settle him into that empty stall." Somewhat reluctantly, Guy handed over the reins. He'd have preferred to settle the horse himself, but apparently he didn't get a say in the matter. "Now, let's go inside and I'll show you how things work around here."

As he followed Mistress Anne through the door, Guy looked over his shoulder and caught a glimpse of Baskin, utterly forgotten, gathering up his boots and bits and walking away. The trousers were left behind.

CHAPTER TWENTY-FOUR

Guy realized quickly that fitting into Anne Smith's establishment would not be easy. Never before had he been surrounded entirely by women. There were ten in all, from little Caitrìona – a waif of a girl not more than fourteen years old — to Agnes, who must have been almost forty and knew her days in this trade were numbered. They fawned over him, which made him uncomfortable – even more uncomfortable than spending time in a tavern.

Nor had he ever even considered the possibility of taking orders from a woman. True, he'd taken his commission from the queen, but this was different. Anne Smith was no queen, at least not in the sense that Guy understood it. But he soon learned she was queen of her establishment and gave no quarter to anyone who dared challenge her.

The first thing Anne did was give him a rundown on who was trustworthy, who might try to pocket a few pennies from what the customer paid, and who might have something else going on the side. "That's why I like them to live under my roof," she explained. "But the Bishop of Winchester's code says I can't require them to. I can be fined if I don't *allow* them to, mind you, but I can't require it as part of how I do business. Does that seem right to you?" Her righteous indignation amused Guy, but he kept those thoughts to himself.

"Can't keep 'em from going to the market or the shops," she went on, "so that's when they have a chance to pick up some side business. And if they get some disease and the bishop's men find out, I can get shut down. So part of your job is to keep them on the straight and narrow when they're not here."

Guy learned Caitrìona's story his first night there. She'd been married at the tender age of twelve to a man who won her in a game of chance with a Scotsman after the battle at Stanhope Park. She'd managed to flee his household after one of his terrible beatings caused her to lose the child she was carrying. "The housekeeper tried to look after me," she told Guy, "but when he was drunk . . ." Tears welled in her eyes at the memory. "When I lost the bairn, that sweet lady helped me escape. And I never looked back. Just kept walking south until Mistress Anne took me in."

Every bit of her story offended Guy's sense of honor. It wasn't right that one so young should be reduced to this life. When he said as much to Anne, she merely smiled. "If you'd seen as much of the underbelly of the world as I have, Willoughby, you'd know what's right has very little to do with how things are."

It was Bessie, though, who became his favorite. She was every customer's favorite too. But Guy noticed straightaway that Anne made sure the best-connected gentlemen were the ones who got to enjoy her favors first of an evening . . . and for as long as they wished. What made her special to Guy was that she was a natural gossip – a trait Anne wouldn't – *couldn't* – tolerate in this profession, so part of Guy's job was see to it Bessie kept her mouth shut. It was the perfect opportunity. He made a bargain with her that she could gossip as much as she liked to him provided she didn't reveal her secrets to anyone else – an arrangement that suited them both very well. And apparently suited Anne as well, since she stopped admonishing Bessie every day to mind her tongue.

The only thing he learned of interest in the first two weeks at the bath house was that Sir John Maltravers had been appointed constable of Corfe Castle. According to Bessie, the man who told her this was close to the Earl of March and said it was the earl himself who'd insisted on the appointment. *Reward for past service?* Guy wondered. *Or was there something afoot at Corfe that Mortimer needed someone he trusted to oversee?* No way to know, so he asked Bessie to keep her ears open for any other news of Maltravers.

"Course I will," she said. "But why?"

Apparently, Guy mused, *curiosity goes hand in hand with a love of gossip.* "No particular reason. I once had a job he was in charge of, so it's interesting to know how he's rising in the world."

"You wouldn't be thinking of leaving us to go to work for him again, now, would you?" she teased.

Guy had to acknowledge her skill in coaxing people to talk. "Why would I want to go to Dorset when I've got a fine job here and the bear baiting nearby and all London has to offer just across the river? I'd be a fool to give that up."

She gave him a coy smile. "So it's the bears that keep you here, is that it?"

He leaned close and spoke in a conspiratorial whisper. "Not by half. But if Mistress Anne thought I was taking an interest in her girls, she'd chuck me out fast as she did John Baskin."

But that wasn't much to go on. He began to wonder if he'd made a grave mistake. In the stable one morning, tending to his horse with no one else around, he found himself musing aloud. "You're stuck in one place here, what with the bath house opening in the early afternoon and having to be here from then to closing. It's like you've turned the tables – instead of looking for information, you have to wait and hope it finds you. What are the odds of the right person walking into this very bath house when they have any number of places to choose from? Not good, if I'm honest with myself. Was I too quick to grab the first opportunity that came along? Too worried about my dwindling funds to remember my real purpose?"

The horse, it seemed, had no answers. Finished cleaning the animal's coat, Guy took the brush back to the bench where it was stored and returned with a hoof-pick. Lifting the horse's left foreleg, he examined the foot and removed some debris that had gotten caked on the sole. "Looks like it's time for you to be reshod, old boy. I'll wager blacksmith services don't come with the job. Maybe worrying about my money was necessary after all. Still, God only knows what I'm missing by not being able to frequent the other bath houses or spend some time in the taverns."

As he finished cleaning the third hoof, something else dawned on him. "If every other proprietress is as strict about gossip as Anne, what makes me think I'd be able to weasel anything out of a girl in some other house? God's teeth, man, you've only been here two weeks." He picked up the fourth hoof and chuckled to himself. One of the things he'd had to do to fit in here was to rein in his swearing. It felt good to loosen his tongue for a change.

"Bide your time for a bit longer," he resolved while cleaning the final hoof. "You've got ten girls here to ply for news. Then there's the gossip in the market. And you already have one new clue. Luck can't always be against you." The horse nickered in apparent agreement as Guy left the stall and closed the gate.

Business was quieter than usual during Advent. "It's like that every year," Anne told him. "But just wait until after Christmas. The men will've had as much piety as they can take – and as much of their wives' company as they can stand. Day after Christmas here is like Twelfth Night anywhere else. And by the time we get to Twelfth Night, the bawdiness hereabouts will be like nothing you've ever seen before. I make more money in a week than I do in most months the rest of the year. Course, that means you'll have to be at your sharpest. I can't afford for things to get out of hand and the bishop's men to come down on me. They'll be out in force for certes."

"You can count on me, mistress," was all he said aloud. *You can also count on me*, he added to himself, *to learn the identity of every man who darkens your door and get the girls to wheedle whatever they can out of anyone important.*

"And it won't just be Twelfth Night, Willoughby," Anne continued. "There's the coronation coming up in February, so there'll be more celebrations then." The young king had married the daughter of the Count of Hainault almost two years earlier, and now that Queen Philippa was with child, it had been decided she should be properly crowned prior to giving birth to what everyone hoped would be an heir. Guy's great hope was that the excesses of the season would loosen tongues that might otherwise be guarded.

During the lull between Twelfth Night and the coronation, Guy descended the stairs on a Wednesday evening toward the end of the month to discover the entire house in an uproar. An elegantly dressed gentleman stood in the entry hall giving his fur-trimmed cloak, his hat, and his gloves into the care of a servant. "My lord mayor." Anne's arms were extended wide. "What an honor to welcome you to our house."

"Ah, madam, here I am simply Mister Swanland. I've been told your house is as well known for its discretion as for its pleasure."

"Without a doubt, sire."

"Then I've come to the right place. I've recently received a great commission and am in the mood to treat myself to something special."

"And you shall have the best my house has to offer. Perhaps you'd like to start your evening with a bath." She waved frantically to Bessie, who responded with a measured, almost aristocratic approach from her vantage point in the parlor doorway to greet the new guest by offering her hand as a true lady would. Swanland responded with a slight bow and a polite kiss of the proffered hand.

Well done, Bessie, Guy thought. *Charm him into baring his soul to you.*

"Bessie will attend to your every need," Anne couldn't refrain from stating the obvious as Bessie led her customer away.

It took all of Guy's self-control to feign lack of interest in the mayor of London's visit – to resist the urge to rouse Bessie from her bed at first light and ply her with questions about anything the man might have said. Bessie, on the other hand, was so excited about her evening that she sought him out in the stable where he was feeding and brushing down his horse. "It was like he was bursting to tell someone what he knew, Guy," she said. "When I assured him my ability to keep secrets was why I was the most sought-after of Mistress Anne's girls, he kind of breathed a sigh of relief. 'I'm a draper, you see, by trade, and I have patrons in high places, but this may be the most important commission I've ever been given. So whatever may be your fee for the evening, I shall gladly pay.' I didn't say a word. Didn't ask him a single question. Just made sure his wine glass was never empty."

Guy knew better than to comment. Bessie was bursting to reveal everything she knew. All he had to do was to keep brushing his horse.

"His commission is from the Archbishop of York. And it's for clothing and furs, and cloth for more clothing and bed hangings and coverings, and leather for shoes and boots, and great sums of money, and all to be packaged up ordinary-like, like a tradesman delivering an order to anyone, but guess who it's going to?"

"I've no idea."

"You'll never credit this."

"Won't I?"

"It's for the late king. Except he isn't 'late.' He's still alive and hiding some place safe. And the archbishop intends to see to it that he has everything necessary to live comfortably."

Guy stopped brushing. Even though he already knew Edward of Caernarfon was almost certainly still alive, Bessie would be expecting some sort of reaction. "Are you sure you heard right?"

"Never more sure of anything. See, I only barely sipped my wine. It's a trick we all know to keep the customers from taking advantage of us. Doesn't mean they don't try sometimes, but as long as we're sober, we can usually keep the upper hand. Anyway, can you credit it? I'd heard some rumors but . . ."

"I've heard rumors too. But, Bessie, promise me something."

"Anything for you, Guy."

"This may be the most important secret you ever have to keep. You can talk to me if you need to, but don't breathe a word of it to anyone else. People could die if you do. Master Swanland could die. Mistress Anne. *You* could die."

She was immediately subdued. "You don't really mean that, do you, Guy?"

"I mean it as seriously as I've ever meant anything in my life. The Earl of March takes a personal interest in such matters. And anyone who crosses him never ends well."

She walked to his side, stood on tiptoe, and kissed his cheek. "We made a bargain, you and me. And you know I'll stick by it."

That we did, Bessie. And I just got the best part of the bargain.

***

The day of the queen's coronation dawned fair and mild – remarkably mild for the middle of February. People said it was God's way of showing favor to the queen and her unborn child. Those same people would almost certainly have said it was Satan's favor – not God's – that brought customers to the Stews in droves that evening. And Anne Smith's establishment boasted as many guests as any in the neighborhood. All the girls entertained three or four visitors that evening. All except little Caitrìona. Guy had discovered that, despite her opinion of the world's underbelly, Anne had a mother's heart when it came to Caitrìona and never permitted her more than one visitor a day, even if that meant turning away business. In due course though, Caitrìona would have to carry her own weight. He didn't know why he cared – except that he did.

After such a busy night, none of the girls rose early. When Bessie finally came downstairs at midday, Guy was with Anne in her office, tallying up the takings. "Best hide it all away for now," she said. "Likely to be a bit of a lull now everyone's spent all their money. We'll need this to tide us over." Guy looked at her quizzically. "Oh, the fine gentlemen will be back once all the feasting and entertainments and such at court be over but even *they* will drift back slowly. And if they have to keep paying more and more for the Scottish war, they may not come as often."

Bessie's knock at the door interrupted Anne's musings. "There you are, Guy. Can you take me to the shop? I need some new ribbons. Mine all seem to go missing."

"Taken by your callers for trophies, no doubt." Guy hoped the sarcasm he felt didn't come through in his voice.

"Taken as presents for their wives, more like," said Anne. "Soothe a guilty conscience." She paused to close and lock the little strongbox where she kept her money. No one rightly knew where it was she hid the box. "Go on with her, Willoughby. Keep her out of trouble. We're finished here." Then, reaching into her pocket, she tossed Guy a shilling. "Get some nice ribbons for all the girls. Bessie can pick them out. Might not be a bad idea for word to get around a gent can have his fun and a peace offering for the wife all for one price."

Once outside, Bessie launched straight into her gossip. "My first customer last night was terribly curious about you, Guy. Wanted to know how long you'd been here, if I knew anything about where you were before . . . odd stuff like that. Kept asking if I was sure your name was Willoughby. Said he thought maybe it was . . . What did he say now? Biggersly? No, that's not quite right . . . Bigger . . . Bicker . . . Bickerstaffe. That's it."

Guy's heart skipped a beat, but he managed to keep his face calm and his pace unchanged.

"Anyway, I told him he must be wrong. I was sure your name was Willoughby. And Mistress Anne must be too else she'd never have hired you. I was right, wasn't I, Guy? You *are* Willoughby, aren't you?"

"It's not the first time I've been mistaken for someone else. I must have a very common face."

She slipped her arm around his and pulled him closer. "Oh, your face isn't common. In fact, I quite like it. You know," she said, her voice lower, her tone conspiratorial, "I sometimes wish you could be one of my customers rather than our protector. I'm thinking we could show each other a really good time."

He patted her hand and eased away from her. "I seem to recall Mistress Anne said I was to keep you out of trouble, but if you keep talking like that …"

Bessie laughed. "I like you, Guy Willoughby. Never had anybody I could talk to like you. Can I tell you a secret?"

"Of course."

"I'm going to keep the prettiest ribbons for myself."

Guy couldn't help laughing. "Why doesn't that surprise me in the least?"

When they'd made their purchases and started back to the bath house, Guy listened to Bessie's plotting and planning of who'd get which ribbons with only half an ear. The rest of his mind was on his dilemma. He'd been discovered. But by who? He tried to remember the faces from last night. There'd been quite a lot of them. No noblemen – they'd all have been at the formal celebrations in Westminster. Try as he might, he couldn't recall having ever seen a single one before. In truth, there wouldn't be that many people in London who knew him. Could it be someone he'd tilted with in the lists? Someone who'd come to the city for the occasion of the coronation? If it was someone he'd jousted with, they certainly hadn't made a lasting impression. If he could work out who, he might be able work out if he was really at risk.

But that path was taking him nowhere, so he had to turn his mind to what to do. He'd survived two years in London and Southwark without being recognized. God curse all the fates that, now he was finally close to knowing where to look for his quarry, someone should expose him and he'd be called to account for his deeds before he could even begin to rectify what had gone so badly wrong that day. How much longer could he stay here collecting Bessie's tidbits before he had to move on for his own safety? Could he just move to another bath house? Anne would never forgive him – she'd probably even turn him in to the bishop's men or lead Mortimer's men straight to him. And even if she didn't, he knew Mortimer's men would turn the Stews inside out if they were set the task of finding him.

Tonight would be a sleepless one. He had to decide what to do. Perhaps all he really had to decide was when to leave – and how. But decide he must.

He wouldn't get the chance – at least not in the way he expected.

Chapter Twenty-Five

They arrived at the bath house to find young Tom out front keeping watch over a rather fine horse tethered to the post beside the front door. "Mistress be waiting fer ye," he announced as Guy reached for the door latch and stepped back to let Bessie precede him inside.

"Bessie, there you are." Anne's voice oozed charm. "You see, sir, I told you she'd be back straightaway." She took Bessie's cloak and parcel, adding, "It seems you were recommended to him specifically, my dear."

The customer offered Bessie his arm and she led him upstairs.

Anne beckoned Guy into the parlor. "The finest gentleman who's ever darkened my door." Her glee was palpable. One minute she'd perch on a chair, then she'd get up and walk around the room, only to perch again for a moment, before finally going to the sideboard and pouring herself a glass of wine. Guy would have been amused if he hadn't been so distracted by Bessie's revelation.

In less than fifteen minutes, Bessie was back downstairs, not a hair out of place, her clothing not the least bit mussed. "He wants to see *you*, Guy," she announced.

Anne sprang out of the chair she'd finally settled in. "Now you listen here, Guy Willoughby, I'll have none of that kind of business in this house. If word got out, it would be the cucking stool for me, and if I somehow managed to survive that, God knows what else the bishop's men might have in store. All my girls would be turned out in the street. I won't have it, Guy.

If that's what he wants, you chuck him out straightaway. Do you understand me?"

"I do, Mistress." Guy offered her a small bow as he rose from the chair, but it was obvious she was in no way mollified.

"I think all he wants to do is *talk*," said Bessie, wrinkling her nose.

"Just leave it with me, ladies," said Guy as he made for the door. "Whatever it is, I'll take care of it and then we can get back to life as usual."

"Well, don't you go messing up my room," Bessie admonished. "Everything's just how I like it, so it better be that way when I go back upstairs."

He paused at the top of the stairs before walking down the corridor to Bessie's room and pushing open the door, which she'd left ajar. The man he'd seen downstairs stood by the window, appraising him from across the room. "Do come in, Sir Guy." He paused. "It *is* Sir Guy, isn't it?" Then without waiting for a reply, he added, "And close the door behind you if you would. What we need to discuss is not for others' ears."

Guy knew there was nothing for it but to brazen this out. The less he said the better.

"Would you care to sit? There's only the one chair, but I'm content with the windowsill." Guy hesitated, not wanting to put himself at a disadvantage. But when the stranger half-sat on the narrow sill and leaned against the window frame, Guy took the chair – stiffly, though, ready to spring into action at the slightest hint of trouble.

The stranger continued. "We've been looking for you. For quite some time. Over two years now, to be precise." Warning bells rang in Guy's ears. "You are Sir Guy Bickerstaffe, are you not? Captain of the guard assigned to the detention and protection of Lord Edward of Caernarfon."

Guy offered no reply.

"Very well," said the stranger. "I understand your reticence. All we want to know is what happened that day at Berkeley Castle. We believe you saw and heard things that haven't yet come to light."

The stranger said no more. Eventually, the silence in the room became so uncomfortable, Guy was sorely tempted to fidget. *Stay in control,* he reminded himself. *Don't reveal anything. The man seems affable enough . . . he's relaxed . . . appears to be no threat. But who is he?*

When it became clear the stranger was willing to wait until the end of time for Guy's response, he rose from his chair. "I'm not in the habit of discussing my business with men I've never met, particularly when such men might be close to those in power. Now, either tell me who you are and what your business is, or I'm throwing you out into the street."

The hint of a smile danced across the stranger's face. "It's a wise man who keeps his own counsel. A wiser one still who chooses not to link his fate to a power he doesn't understand. For myself, I stay at arm's length from those who take power unto themselves. My loyalty is to the power anointed by God."

*Holy mother of God! Is he talking about Mortimer and the king? Who in the name of God's best breeches **is** this man?* Aloud, he said, "If I am who you say I am, then you must know that my fealty would be sworn to the power anointed by God."

Even under the stranger's intense scrutiny, Guy didn't flinch. Nor did he speak. At long last, the stranger broke the silence. "Please . . . sit back down. Perhaps it's time for some plain speaking. My name is Montagu. Baron Montagu. What passes between us next must never be spoken of outside this room. I must have your word of honor on that, Sir Guy."

With this revelation, Guy's curiosity overtook his trepidation. *What could this man – known to be a confidant of the young king – want from me? Assuming, of course, that he is indeed who he claims.* "With all due respect, my lord, how am I to know you speak truth? Never in my life have I met Baron Montagu, so I cannot be expected to know him on sight."

The hint of a smile returned. "A cautious man as well as a wise one. Qualities I respect in a man in whom I intend to place great trust. You have my word of honor that I speak the truth. And that of God's anointed if it gives you greater comfort."

Did he just speak for the king? Audacity indeed unless he truly is Lord Montagu. Is this the luck I've been waiting for? Or an elaborate trap? There was no time to ruminate, no time to weigh the risks. There was one thing, though, he could be certain of. Hesitate too long and this opportunity would walk out the door, ride away, and be lost forever. "I am indeed Sir Guy Bickerstaffe, though none here know me by that name. And you have my word, my lord. What is it you want of me?"

"First, Sir Guy, no one expects you to answer for what happened that day. There were forces in play, things afoot, that were beyond the ability of one man to grasp or to control. But it's my belief that there was an escape from the castle that night. What I want is for you to find those who got away."

Guy couldn't believe his ears. Was he really to be given a commission to fulfill the oath he swore to himself so many months ago?

"Secondly, this is a private arrangement between you and me. Do what you must, but reveal your purpose to *no one*. Is that understood?"

"It is, my lord."

"On no account are you to report your findings to anyone but me, and most especially not to those who might seek to wheedle them out of you or to use more violent means of coercion. I cannot stress this enough, Sir Guy. Lives are at stake. Yours. Mine. Those you seek. And others best left unknown to you. Do I make myself clear?"

"Utterly, my lord. But how am I to contact you?"

"Write to me announcing the birth of your son, naming the town in which the happy event occurred. When I deem it safe, I'll find you there. Use the name under which I discovered you here in this establishment."

"When am I to begin, sir? I'll have to come up with a convincing tale to explain to Mistress Smith why I'm leaving her employ."

"You'll carry on as usual for the moment. When I'm convinced enough time has passed that no one will connect your departure with my visit here – neither the people here nor those who almost certainly watch my movements with interest – I'll send you a message that your sister is gravely ill and you're needed at your family home. A week from now . . . perhaps more. In the meantime, do you have a convincing way to explain our little conversation?"

"I do, my lord. 'Twas far busier than usual here last night. Your son came home early this morning drunk, disheveled, and reeking of women's perfume. Someone told you they'd seen him here and you came to discover the truth. Not a topic you felt comfortable discussing with a lady. Or I could just throw you out."

Montagu smiled broadly. "You seem quite resourceful, Sir Guy. I think perhaps I'm making a good choice where to place my trust." He stepped away from the window to collect his cloak, which lay across Bessie's bed. From inside the cloak he retrieved a leather pouch and handed it to Guy. "Fifty pounds. Use it wisely. There'll be no way I can send you more."

"Just one more thing, Lord Montagu. Any thoughts on where to begin my search?"

"For some reason, Dorset comes to mind, though I'm really not sure why."

Chapter Twenty-Six

March 1330

It wasn't supposed to be this way. Despite Simon's best efforts to advise caution, Edmund had gotten careless. From the moment Sir Ingelram Berenger first revealed what he'd learned from Sir John Pecche, Edmund's resolve to set right the falsehood of his brother's untimely death strengthened day by day, week by week.

The problem with men like Berenger and Pecche, Simon knew, was that their zeal often exceeded their discretion. He'd urged Edmund to keep them at arm's length – to dissociate himself with any plots – to look out for his own hide first and foremost. But there was only so much he could do. Edmund was an earl, a scion of the royal family. Simon, a mere companion.

And, in the end, Edmund made a fatal error. A week after the queen's coronation – when they were back at Arundel Castle – he'd asked Simon to join him for brandy in his private study after the evening meal. "There's something I want to show you," he said. Once they were comfortably seated, glasses in hand, before a warming fire, Edmund reached into his supertunic and produced a folded page that he passed to Simon. "Read it."

Worships and reverence, with a brother's liegeance and subjection. Sir knight, worshipful and dear brother! If it please you, I pray heartily that you be of good comfort, for I shall so ordain for you that soon you shall come out of prison, and be delivered of that disease that you be in. And understand of

> *your great lordship that I have unto me assenting almost all the great lords of England, with all their apparel, that is to say, with armour, with treasure without number, for to maintain and help your quarrel so that you shall be king again as you were before; and that they all have sworn to me upon a book, and as well prelates as earls and barons.*

Simon was dismayed but managed to keep his expression neutral as he refolded the page and passed it back to his friend. Edmund's excitement, on the other hand, was not to be denied. "I had Margaret write it out for me, so if it should come into possession of the wrong people, I can easily prove it's a forgery as it bears no resemblance whatsoever to my own hand. But have no fear, Simon, it will be carried by Sir Ingelram's most trusted man who carries messages for him to William la Zouche and John Gymmynges."

"Surely you're not asking me *not* to have concern for your safety, my friend," Simon ventured.

"Quite the contrary, my friend. I mean to assure you that your fears are ill-founded. And yet they persist. We always speak plainly between us. This should be no exception. Tell me what troubles you."

Simon didn't answer straightaway, keenly aware that both their friendship and Edmund's life hung in the balance. "It's an enormous risk, sir, as you obviously know else you wouldn't have taken such pains with either the writing or the delivery. But if you wish me to say what's in my heart ..."

"I do."

"My fear is that this missive might forge your death warrant. And that's something I can't bear to contemplate."

Edmund was instantly subdued. "Nor can I, my friend. And I'm grateful for your care. Margaret, also, has counseled me against this course of action. But I must also consider whether I could live with myself if I didn't at least make an effort to come to my brother's aid. Is that not what brothers – what men of honor – would do? Much as you now offer such brotherly advice and affection."

Simon recognized that pressing any further would only drive a wedge between them. All he could do now was to hope Lady Margaret would prevail, unlikely as that seemed. He swirled the brandy in his glass and took a sip. "As remarkable as always. I suspect even the king would be envious of your cellar." If Simon knew anything, it was how effective a bit of flattery could be with Edmund if there were signs of tension developing between the two of them.

"My brother certainly was." Edmund smiled broadly. "But then, he taught me everything I know." And that put paid to the debate. A half-brother who, in some respects, was much like a father could not be denied.

***

They got news of the first arrests on a Wednesday. It was the 14th of March. Simon never forgot that date. It was the day his baby sister was born. And the day, a year later, when she succumbed to the coughing sickness. He remembered holding her in his arms, trying to comfort her as the coughing wracked her tiny body and she struggled to breathe. He'd prayed more fervently that day than any time before or since that God would spare her. And when she was finally quiet, no longer in need of breath, he sat rocking her, his tears unquenchable, singing the lullaby she loved so much. His mother had tried to comfort him. "She's at peace now, Simon. God will take care of her." But no amount of comfort was sufficient to the depth of his pain. Though he was only ten years old, that day changed him and his view of God forever. The pain had dulled somewhat with time, but the memory hadn't, and he always faced the date with a heavy heart. Now, it seemed, fate was determined to add to that burden.

"They'll come for me next, Simon," Edmund had said when the messenger left.

There was nothing Simon could say in response. Edmund was right, of course, but an affirmation wasn't what he was seeking. And, in truth, Simon had no idea how he could help.

"It's inevitable," Edmund added. "Now, come." Simon followed him through the corridors to his study, where he retrieved a strongbox from a small niche in the stone wall behind a huge tapestry. Unlocking it, he took out a large leather pouch and gave it to Simon, who almost dropped it, surprised by the weight. "I want you to leave straightaway, my friend. I'll not have you caught up in whatever is about to happen. There's enough money there to provide for your needs for quite some time."

"I can't take your money, sir. Nor can I leave. That's not what a man of honor does when he's been fortunate enough to be named companion to one of your rank. You'll need me by your side for what's to come."

"I'm grateful for your sentiment, Simon, but I can't put your life at risk. As for the money, you'll need it. And when all this is over – when I'm once again restored to my proper place in the kingdom – then I hope most fondly that you'll come back and reclaim your own position. But for now, I want you to go. Get as far away from here as quickly as you can. And don't even think of returning until I send for you."

An hour later, with as many of his belongings as he could fit into a pack and the pouch of money hidden at the bottom, Simon rode away from Arundel with a heavy heart but determined to do what he knew only *he* could do.

***

Three days later, having pushed his horse as much as he dared, he paused at the base of the road up to Corfe Castle. This was the most uncertain part of his mission, and he'd been thinking about it all day. He'd only get one chance and had finally decided that bravado coupled with the constable's name was his best option. Girding his loins, he squeezed his horse's ribs and began the climb.

Typically, the sentry who waylaid him at the gate was officious. "State your business or be on your way."

"My business is with the castellan."

"So you say. What business is that?"

"None of yours."

By now another guard had sauntered out of the gatehouse. "If you won't tell us, sir…" The word "sir" dripped sarcasm. "…then there's no way you'll pass this gate."

"And if you don't take me to the castellan straightaway…" Simon put as much menace into his tone as he could muster. "…I'm sure Baron Maltravers will be all too happy to relieve you of your duties when I tell him of my experience."

Simon held his breath while the two sentries exchanged a quick glance. "This time of day," said the one who had first demanded to know his business, "the lord will be in his private study. The porter will show you the way."

"I'm not going to have this same conversation with the porter. Which of *you* is going to show me the way?"

Another exchange of glances and five minutes later, he was being ushered into Lord Thomas's study. "That will be all, sergeant. Back to your duties." Faintree said nothing further until the guard's bootsteps no longer echoed in the corridor. "I presume you have instructions from the constable," he finally addressed Simon. "It's his usual way to communicate."

"Actually, my lord, I'm here on my own account. I simply knew of no other way to come into your presence."

Faintree's posture stiffened. "Then you'd better make a good accounting of yourself, else I'll see you thrown out."

"There's no need for alarm, sir. Until three days ago, I was in Arundel."

Simon's declaration had the desired effect. "In that case, you'd better take a seat and tell me what this is about."

"My name is Simon Forster, and I've spent many years as Companion of the Privy Chamber in the earl's household. He sent me away on the day we learned that three men with links to him were arrested on Mortimer's orders. By now, it's quite likely the earl himself has been arrested. Which means that your guest is in imminent danger."

Faintree stroked his chin in obvious contemplation. At long last, he asked, "And why do you presume I have a guest?"

"Sir John Pecche may have been less than discreet. The Archbishop of York as well."

Faintree rose from his chair. "Come with me." Simon followed the castellan down a long corridor, up a staircase, and through a series of shorter corridors on the floor above, stopping in front of an arched door. Faintree knocked twice. Receiving no response, he knocked again – five quick raps on the wood – and announced "I come alone with news from afar. You may open the door."

The faint sound of footsteps from inside preceded the noise of a lock being turned. The door opened barely enough for two eyes to peer out. "It's alright, Will," said Faintree. "Let us in." The door opened just enough for one man to slip through, and Simon followed Faintree inside while the owner of the eyes locked the door behind them then crossed the room to stand beside another man seated near the hearth.

Simon couldn't suppress a gasp. "Will?" he asked incredulously. "Will Makepeace? Is it really you?"

Equally stunned, Will abandoned all self-control and rushed to embrace his friend. Then, remembering himself, he turned toward the seated man and said, "Lord Edward, this is the friend I've told you about – Simon Forster – your brother Edmund's companion."

Faintree watched the reunion in wide-eyed disbelief.

"How fares my brother?" asked Caernarfon. "The news you have must be important for him to have sent you in person." Simon's shoulders slumped, the joy of finding Will here overcome by the grim news he bore. Caernarfon noticed. "Come . . . sit with us." He gestured to a chair near his own. "You must be tired after the journey from Arundel."

"Thank you, sir." Simon sat down. "May I ask, sir, have you received a letter from your brother?"

"None in all this time. Even back to the days at Kenilworth."

"That's what I feared." He turned to Faintree. "Wouldn't a letter for your guest have been delivered to you, Lord Thomas?"

It was the castellan's turn for slumped shoulders. "I wish I could say yes, Forster, because I would have given it straightaway to Lord Edward. But things have been different since Baron Maltravers was made constable last autumn."

"In what way, sir? Has the baron been here himself?"

"No. He's only sent a letter and two men. That was just after the New Year."

"Who were the men?" asked Simon.

"Sir Bogo Bayouse and a man called John Deveril. Maltravers's letter enjoined me to put Bayouse in charge of the guards here, with Deveril as his deputy. I knew nothing of Deveril, but it's generally known that Bayouse is Lord Mortimer's man. Since I had no choice about their duties, we set about changing the arrangements here. Will and Lord Edward moved to this room, far enough away from where guards would normally have any reason to be."

"I changed my appearance," Caernarfon chimed in, "hoping to be less recognizable." He stroked his clean-shaven face and then the back of his neck. "Though I must admit the absence of my beard and this short hair still feel exceedingly strange."

"They've stayed indoors," Faintree resumed. "Mostly confined to this room, though Will fetches their meals from the kitchens."

"It hasn't been a terrible hardship so far," said Caernarfon.

That brought a smile to Lord Thomas's face. "Give these two a chess board and they seem never to notice the passage of time." He chuckled. "But I've been quite worried that something else would have to be done eventually, though I've yet to come up with any useful ideas. Bayouse is the problem, of course. I'm completely at a loss for how to circumvent him. Mortimer's intent, no doubt. And there's equally no doubt I'm not the only one harboring his spies, unwittingly or unwillingly."

"You've just confirmed my worst fears, sir. Let me tell you all I know." He recounted everything, ending with, "If Edmund sent that letter – which I rather think he must have – then it almost certainly was intercepted by this . . . What did you say his name was, Lord Thomas?"

"Bayouse. Bogo Bayouse."

"By this Bayouse character and sent directly to Mortimer. Which means the Earl of Kent has almost certainly been arrested by now."

A pall descended on the room. Caernarfon finally broke the silence. "May God help my dear brother. If only he had listened to your advice, Simon."

"It also means . . ." Simon spoke softly now. ". . . they may come here for you soon, my lord. And I owe it to Edmund to see that they don't succeed."

"But how can you stop them?" asked Caernarfon.

"You and Will escaped from Berkeley. It's my task now to get you both to safety, and I know just the place. I have a cousin in Ireland who'll give us refuge. We just have to find a way out of *here*."

"That's something I can help with," said Faintree. "Tomorrow, I'll go, as I do every Sunday, to mass in Wareham. You three can hide on the floor of my coach until we're clear of the village at the bottom of the hill. We'll drop you off at the edge of Wareham, at a spot that's but a quick walk to the quay. Even on a Sunday, I'm sure there'll be boatmen glad to take your money for passage."

"That's an idea, sir," said Simon, "but I don't want to depart from Wareham. When Mortimer's men discover we're no longer here, if they think we might have set sail, Wareham's the first place they'd look – even before Poole or Bournemouth. I want to sail from Weymouth, but that means we need horses to get there. Walking would be too slow. Pursuers could overtake us easily. That's the part of the escape I haven't fully worked out. I could buy two horses in Wareham, but people would remember."

For a moment, Simon saw nothing but puzzled faces, but then Faintree broke into a big grin. "I've got just the solution. You and Will leave here this evening riding your own horses and taking a pack horse with you. Well, we'll make it look like a pack horse, but it'll have a good saddle and you can hide the bridle among your belongings, Simon. Camp tonight short of Wareham – Will knows a good spot where you can meet my carriage. Caernarfon comes with me in the morning in the carriage, hiding until we're clear of the sentries. You can be on your way the moment he alights from the carriage."

"I think it would work, sir," Will ventured. "I'm not overjoyed to be leaving Lord Edward behind, after all we've been through together, but it seems the best option we have."

"I'm certain Thomas will take great care for my safety, Will," said Caernarfon. "After all, he himself will be far safer once we're away."

"There's just one thing, sir," Simon addressed Faintree. "You won't get your horses back. We'll have to sell them in Weymouth."

"Don't worry, Simon. You won't be getting the best from my stables. Sound, reliable mounts, yes, but hardly my best." Finally, something that drew a smile from everyone. "Then it's agreed. Will, gather your things and meet us at the stable as soon as you're ready. Come through the kitchens – no need for you to have to answer questions for the porter or whatever curious guard may be at the front entrance."

He paused before continuing. "There's one small risk in our plan. Bayouse has likely bribed some of my staff to be his informants, so they or whoever's on sentry duty will report the departure to him. But I'm prepared to handle that. If he questions me, the constable has hired away one of my most valued manservants, much to my consternation. Simon was sent to fetch him. By the time Bayouse can check the truth of my story, you'll be long gone. And Bayouse's usefulness here will be a thing of the past."

The plan worked flawlessly, and by midday on Sunday, Will, Simon, and Caernarfon had reached Bindon Abbey. They bypassed the port at Melcombe Regis and went straight to Weymouth. As Simon had expected, most of the ships in port were wine traders, preparing to cross the channel to France. But with some persistence, he found a smaller vessel, loaded and ready to depart for Sutton. The captain was more than willing to make some extra money for adding three passengers to his cargo.

It only took one day in Sutton to find passage to Ireland. The ship was headed for Dublin, but once again, the captain had no objection to accepting an extra twelve shillings to put in briefly at Wykinglowe to discharge three passengers.

By Friday, they were safe on Irish soil. What they didn't know was that, on the day they landed at Sutton, Edmund of Woodstock, Earl of Kent, was executed at Winchester Castle.

CHAPTER TWENTY-SEVEN

Waiting was *not* Sir Guy's strong suit. He'd been waiting over two years to find a way to reclaim his honor, and he was ready to get on with it. But Montagu was still making him wait. Intellectually, Guy understood why. Viscerally, he was like a high-spirited destrier, pawing at the ground, eager for the signal to charge.

His impatience boiled over one afternoon when Anne asked him to escort two of her girls to the market. "*God's bones*, Mistress. Doesn't a man have better things to do than watch women buy baubles and lace?"

Anne planted her hands on her hips. "God's bones yourself, Guy Willoughby. What do you think I pay you for?"

Get control of yourself, Guy, he told himself as they walked away from the house. *These people have been good to you, and they haven't the least idea what's gnawing at you.* Nevertheless, his tongue was getting quite sore from the number of times he'd bitten it to avoid saying something he shouldn't.

Three days later, at the end of the first full week in March, the message arrived. Short and to the point. Signed by a priest he'd never heard of. *Probably a priest who doesn't even exist.* Guy chuckled, finally able to release the tension that had tied his guts in knots.

He made straight for Anne's office. When she looked up from her account books, he handed her the letter with no comment. She read quickly and handed it back. "You'll be leaving us then?"

"I have little choice."

"Can you stay a few days . . . until I can find a replacement?"

"You read the letter, mistress. The priest says it's dire. She might even be gone before I can get there."

Anne's eyes were kind. She was clearly affected by his plight. For the briefest of moments, he felt bad about deceiving her, but it was necessary . . . and probably kinder than the truth. "Could you at least stay tonight? It's the busiest night of the week, and I'm not sure I can handle everything alone."

With the tension inside him ebbing, Guy realized he couldn't get much farther than Windsor in what was left of the daylight and he'd probably be better served by one more good night's sleep in a comfortable bed. God knew when he'd get that again. "Very well," he capitulated. "I wouldn't get far in the few hours of daylight remaining. But I'll have to be off in the morning."

She rose from her chair and walked around the desk to embrace him. "You're a good man, Guy Willoughby. I won't be finding the likes of you again anytime soon." Breaking the embrace, she added, "Now go see that all's in order for the evening. I'll have the cook pack you plenty to eat on your journey. No need you should have to settle for whatever bulmong some innkeeper may be trying to pass off as food."

He left before daybreak, taking care to make no noise when he left the house. The last thing he wanted was women's tearful entreaties for him to take care of himself and to return to them. As he led his horse out of the stable, he caught sight of a light out of the corner of his eye. Looking up, he saw a candle in one of the first floor windows and Caitrìona's face, watching him take his leave.

***

"Do what you have to do," Montagu had said. *If Will and Caernarfon are still together,* he mused as he rode west, *I can't take them both by myself – I'll have to have help. Will is **mine**, but Montagu wants Caernarfon. For all I know, he wants both of them. Regardless, no one gets Will until I'm finished with him.* But then another thought crossed his mind. *Deliver them both if the baron wants them, but only if he agrees to restore your honor as part of the bargain.*

It took him five days to reach Shepton Mallet – a full day longer than usual – thanks to the cold rain that began late morning of the third day. He tried to push on, but by midday he was soaked to the skin and chilled to the bone and starting to lose the feeling in his fingers. Even his horse was shivering. With the rain now coming down in torrents, he finally had to concede his only choice was to put up at the next inn he came to until the weather improved. Luck was with him – a small country tavern just over the next rise had a roaring fire going in the hearth and a surprisingly dry stable in back. "We don't get many travelers," the landlady told him, "'cept in weather like this. Normally, it's just the local farmers what stop in for a mug of ale of an evening. But we've got a spare room upstairs ye can use. Ye'll have to share, though, if anyone else comes along in the same fix. Now ye settle yourself in front of that fire and try to get warm while I tend to your horse."

"If you've got some extra hay or grain to give him, ma'am, I'll pay. He needs to warm up too."

"Don't ye fret. I'll put some hay out for him now then go back later and give him some oats. Don't want him to be getting the colic on account of eating too much too fast." She stepped over to the bar and poured him a mug of ale, then pulled an oiled-wool cape over her clothes and went out into the downpour to take care of the horse.

The rain stopped shortly after dawn the next day, but it took until early afternoon for the sun to warm the air and start to dry the puddles enough for Guy to continue his journey. When he arrived in Shepton Mallet after two more long days in the saddle, it was late afternoon and he feared he'd have to spend the night at the inn and look for Aldwin the next day. But the third person he asked was able to point him to Aldwin's house. "Third lane north of the market square. Can't miss it. The only house with a little shed off to the side with a couple of horse stalls."

When Aldwin answered the door, his jaw dropped and he took a step backward. Recovering his wits, he said, "Guy Bickerstaffe? What in God's name brings you here after all this time?"

"Unfinished business," Guy replied.

"Then I guess you'd better come in. No, wait. Let's see to your horse first."

Neither of them spoke while Guy unsaddled his horse and Aldwin tossed some hay in the rack and closed the stall gate. They returned to the front door and Aldwin led the way in, still without a word passing between them. Inside was a cozy room with a warm fire and a woman sitting beside the hearth feeding gruel to a baby who looked to be still under a year of age. "Emeny," said Aldwin, "this is Sir Guy Bickerstaffe. Sir Guy, my wife Emeny and our daughter Joan."

It took Guy a moment to recover his wits. This was not at all what he had expected. Finally, he managed a rather awkward, "Hello, ma'am. I ... uh ... a very nice baby."

Emeny smiled. "She is indeed, Sir Guy. I'll just take her upstairs and nurse her a bit then she'll sleep while we have our supper. Get our guest some ale, Aldwin. I won't be long."

The conversation over supper was pleasant but inconsequential. The weather, how Guy had been forced to wait out the rain, what a nice house they had, how lucky they were that Joan was healthy – "Never sick a day in her life, thank God and all the saints," Emeny said proudly, but crossed herself for a little added protection to be sure things stayed that way.

Once the table was cleared, Emeny went upstairs and left the men to talk. "So what's this unfinished business, Guy?" Aldwin asked. "Though I'm pretty sure I can guess."

"I've finally found Will's trail, Aldwin. In fact, I'm pretty sure I know precisely where he is right at this moment. But I don't want to try to bring him to heel by myself. I need your help."

"Come on, Guy. That's all long in the past. It's been what? Two and a half years? No one holds a grudge that long. You just make the best of things and move on."

"Not if the other person ruined your life. Not if you swore an oath you'd bring him to justice to restore your honor."

Aldwin shook his head in dismay. "You always were a strait-laced one, Guy. Nothing wrong with a man having principles, but it seems to me you've become obsessed. That service back in Berkeley ... it did something to you, hardened you in a way that worried me even then."

"So you're saying you won't help me?"

"I'm saying I can't. I've made a life for myself, Guy, and it's a good one. When six months passed and you didn't come back, I decided it was time to get on with things. So I sought Emeny's favor, and we married soon after. Joan was born nine months ago. The sheriff here took me on when he needed an extra man. It's a good job and keeps a sound roof over our heads and plenty of food in the larder. And we're hoping for another baby – maybe next year sometime. So no, Guy, I won't put any of that at risk."

Guy was confounded. He'd assumed Aldwin would always be there as his second-in-command. And, truth be told, he knew no one else he could really trust. "I can pay you, Aldwin, if that's what worries you."

"The sheriff already pays me well, and I get to come home to my beautiful girls every day. That's everything I need, Guy. All that I want."

Guy decided to stay another day in Shepton Mallet, hoping that more time spent in each other's company would reawaken Aldwin's loyalties. But it was not to be. He woke on the morning he was to depart to heavy clouds and cold rain soaking everything in sight and even a thin crust of ice on the horses' water buckets. The weather dampened everyone's spirits – even baby Joan's. And Guy and Aldwin had run out of things to talk about, so when the sheriff sent for Aldwin to stand guard for a few hours over a prisoner in the town's gaol, both men seemed relieved by the distraction. A few clouds lingered the following morning, but as there was nothing falling from the sky, Guy said his farewells and pointed his horse's nose toward Dorset.

Muddy roads – some almost impassable – meant slow going, and he only made it as far as Milborne Port the first day. His sour mood was made worse by the mud and the occasional lakes still standing in the deep ruts made by heavy wagons, forcing him to take to whatever verge there might be to keep his horse from breaking a leg stepping into water that was deeper than it looked. He slept fitfully that night, awakened alternately by the snoring of the four other men sharing the room and unsettling dreams of standing over a king in his bed, ready to plunge a dagger into his heart. It didn't help that he had to sleep on the floor, since the other four had arrived before him and laid claim to the two narrow beds.

Bright sunshine the next day did its best to provide some cheer, but he was still rather glum when he put up for the night at the inn in Wareham. *How am I going to convince two men – both of them fit and keenly aware of the stakes – to come with me back into the jaws of power? Maybe I was foolish to think Aldwin and I together would be enough?* He ate slowly and splurged on a second mug of ale just to listen to the conversation in the tavern but heard nothing of interest.

So the next day, he rode on to Corfe Castle, pondering his approach. One thing was certain – it had to be surreptitious. He walked around the village a bit, surveying the fortifications at the top of the hill. He hadn't really expected to spot a way to avoid entering through the main gate, but it never hurt to look.

He also hadn't expected to find many people in the village tavern when he stopped in for a midday meal, but it was surprisingly full. Mostly ordinary village folk having a mug of ale before starting the afternoon's work, but the man sitting alone with a bowl of potage and a chunk of bread was also wearing a sword belt. A guard from the castle perhaps?

He'd have preferred to just sit quietly on his own and eavesdrop, like he had in London, but lurking around such a small village for days would only make people suspicious. And time wasn't on his side. He needed information *now*.

He'd never understood how other men could just walk up to a stranger and start up a conversation. What on earth would they have in common to talk about? Today, though, he had little choice, so he ordered his meal, grabbed his mug of ale, strode across the room, and sat down opposite the man wearing the sword – who didn't even bother to look up from his potage. *Now what?* Guy wondered. He took a swallow of ale. The man across the table continued to ignore him. *God's beard. Not even a hello?* Finally admitting conversation would be up to him, he said, "Hope the potage here is better than the last meal I had."

"Better some days than others." The man still didn't look up.

"And is today a better day?"

At that moment, the barmaid delivered Guy's own bowl of potage and chunk of bread. "Guess you'd best decide for yourself," said the swordsman.

Guy tore off a piece of bread, dipped it in the potage, and popped it in his mouth. Finished chewing, he declared, "A damn site better than the inn last night," then picked up his spoon to continue eating.

The swordsman wiped his bowl clean with his last morsel of bread, ate the bread, and washed it down with what was left of his ale. Setting the mug down rather more forcefully than necessary, he heaved a big sigh, rubbed his belly, and finally looked Guy square in the face. "So you're a traveler passing through? Headed to the quarries outside Swanage?"

Guy hadn't thought this through in advance, so he said the first thing that came to mind. "Messenger. Having trouble catching up with the men I'm supposed to deliver it to. Thinking they might be at the castle. Any idea if the castellan has any guests?"

"He did have. If you can call men who stay for months on end 'guests.'"

Guy's spirits lifted. "Months on end?"

"Aye. Two men. One older than the other. Might have been father and son for all I know."

"Sounds like they might be who I'm looking for. They still there, I hope?"

"Nay. Well, not the younger one for certes. A messenger came from Lord Maltravers and took the younger one away. Said Maltravers had another job for him. They rode off toward Wareham."

"And the older one? I could give my message to either man."

"Haven't seen him since the young one left. Come to think of it, haven't seen him since Sir Bogo arrived." The swordsman paused to try to drain a final drop from his empty mug. "Now you've got me thinking, I guess I hadn't seen the younger one either after Sir Bogo showed up – not until this past Saturday. That's when Maltravers's man took the young one away." He rose from his stool, said, "Hope you find the men you're looking for," and made for the door.

Guy pushed what was left of his potage, bread, and ale across the table and cursed his luck. There was no doubt in his mind that the two guests were Will and Caernarfon. Why else would Montagu have told him to look in Dorset? Was it really Maltravers who'd had Will taken away? *Makes no sense it would be Will and not Caernarfon when it's Caernarfon they're trying to get rid of. If they've somehow separated the two of them, how will I ever be able to fulfill my mission for Montagu?* "God's **bollocks**!" He wasn't even aware he'd said it aloud until all conversation in the tavern stopped and every man's eyes stared straight at him.

Furious with himself for drawing so much attention, he rose from his stool and strode out the door. He untied his horse and mounted up, still puzzling over his next move. In the end, though, he had no choice. He had to follow Will's trail if he was to find Caernarfon's. And that suited him just fine.

Back in Wareham, he asked everyone who would talk to him about two men who would have passed through on Saturday. No one could recall seeing anything of the sort. Had the swordsman sent him on a wild goose chase? He was almost ready to give up when he stopped ask the stable master if two men put up their horses there on Saturday night. Maybe he was asking the wrong question – maybe his quarry stopped here rather than passing through.

"Nay," the stable master replied. "Only travelers' horses I've tended to all month be yours last night." Guy couldn't help hanging his head in defeat. "But that doesn't mean 'tweren't travelers passing through. 'Twere that wagon headed to the quarries 'round about two weeks ago, then last Tuesday a man and two young boys come up from the south and kept riding north, then on Sunday, three men come up from the south and took the west road toward Wool."

Guy perked up. "Were two of them quite tall?"

"Hard to say when a man's mounted."

"Any other travelers you remember?"

"Well, not so's I saw with me own eyes, but Robbie the butcher said someone told him a couple of men camped for the night a little ways out of town in the meadow south of the river."

Guy's spirits rose again. His gut said he was back on the trail of his quarry. He thanked the stable master and made for the westbound road. He didn't know how or when Caernarfon left Corfe Castle, but he knew in his bones that he and Will were back together again. But who was the third man?

CHAPTER TWENTY-EIGHT

December 1330

When Will, Simon, and Caernarfon disembarked in Wykinglowe, it hadn't taken them long to find Simon's cousin, Fintan, who worked unloading cargo from the trading ships. His enthusiastic welcome was tempered somewhat when he learned they needed a place to live. "'S'truth ye be welcome and my Orlaith will say the same." Fintan had paused. "But Simon, we have but a wee house and seven children – barely enough room for ourselves. There's just no place to put three more souls."

"Actually, Fintan," said Simon, "we don't want to draw attention to ourselves. Best would be someplace where we can just disappear and curious outsiders would be hard-pressed to find us."

Fintan's smile returned. "I know just the place. Up in the mountains, about a day's ride west of here. It's a monastery, but it also has a large community of ordinary folk. I'll take ye there on the morrow, but tonight we sup and drink and be family again. Ye'll have to sleep on the floor, mind, but Orlaith will give ye fresh rushes and ye'll be warm and dry."

The months they spent in Glendalough were almost idyllic. Caernarfon, in particular, was in his element, with the monastery to nurture his spirit and the physical work tending gardens and animals giving him earthly joy. He'd abandoned the clean-shaven disguise straightaway and soon had the wavy beard and shoulder-length hair that had become so familiar to Will since that first afternoon at the chessboard. They'd had to create their own up here in the mountains, but one of their neighbors had a bit of skill as a wood carver and managed to shape playing pieces that more or less resembled what they were supposed to be. A bit of paint to mark the dark pieces and to designate the squares on a slab of wood they'd smoothed down for the board and they had all the entertainment they needed. Somewhat to Will's surprise, a few of their neighbors and some of the monks were sufficiently intrigued that they asked to be taught the game.

Simon went to Wykinglowe once a month to visit Fintan and get news from the wider world. On the first trip, he'd returned with news of the Earl of Kent's death. Caernarfon was distraught and took to spending all his waking hours in one or another of the seven churches. After a week, Will went looking for him and found him in the cathedral, kneeling before the altar. Will sat on the step and leaned against the column that supported the great arch separating the nave from the chancel. "A man could damage his knees beyond healing by spending so much time on them on a stone floor," he said quietly.

Caernarfon finished his prayer, crossed himself, and rose stiffly. "Is that not what I deserve, young Will?" He turned and walked toward Will, moving a bit more awkwardly than was his wont.

"Do you think that's what your brother would want?" Will rose and took Caernarfon's arm, leading him to a nearby bench where they sat together. He had never seen the former king so sad.

"So many deaths." Caernarfon sighed. "Why have so many had to die that I might live? The burden on my soul is something I fear you can't understand, Will, though I'm glad you don't have to bear it."

"Perhaps I have to bear more than you know, sir."

Caernarfon gave him a sad half-smile. "How could that be? You're young. Yes, you've lost your parents, but that's simply the normal way of our lives."

"The night we escaped from Berkeley Castle. Surely you remember, sir, the time you waited in the crypt while I moved my pieces into position."

"Of course."

"One of those pieces was a man who dreamed of living in a castle. A simple man who wasn't smart enough to suspect I'd ever mean him harm. And, in truth, sir, I didn't. I installed him in your bedchamber – told him he could spend the night there and then be on his way in the morning. I was certain the men who'd come to kill you would take one look at him, know it was the wrong man, and go searching throughout the castle to find you. The burden that's weighed on me all this time, sir, is that they may not have looked. They may have simply killed whoever they found in your bed and declared their nefarious mission completed. If that's the case, then the man buried in your tomb is an innocent whose blood is on my hands. And the even heavier burden is that there's no way I can ever know which of those scenarios is the truth."

Caernarfon put his arm around Will's shoulder. "And you have borne this alone, all this time? Without ever a hint to me of the grief you might feel."

"I came to understand, sir, that the way I could atone for putting an innocent in the path of evil was to spend the rest of my days keeping you safe from those who would take your life for no better reason than to preserve their own power."

The sad half-smile returned. "That, I'm afraid, is the way of the world, young Will. It's what cost Edmund his life." He removed his arm from Will's shoulder and gazed at the floor. "I blame Mortimer for all this, you know. Not Isabella. And most certainly not my son." He rose from the bench, genuflected stiffly toward the altar, and made the sign of the cross then turned back toward Will, much of the sadness gone from his expression. "And I think perhaps you're right, Will. Edmund would not have me drown myself in grief to the ruin of my health and the dismay of those about me. It's time to take a lesson from you and return to the world even as I keep the memory of him alive in my heart."

Summer in the mountains had been more pleasant than anywhere Will had ever lived. He worried that Simon would grow tired of such isolation, having spent most of his life in the lofty circles of wealth and privilege. His answer, when asked about it, surprised Will. "Where else would I go? All I really know is the life of a lord's companion. And now that the lord I served has been declared a traitor, I wouldn't be welcome in any other great family. So unless something changes in the halls of power, it seems all I have left is to show my gratitude to Edmund for his years of favor and friendship by serving his brother."

Simon made his December visit to Wykinglowe at the very beginning of the month. "Before it gets any colder," he'd said. With the rapidly approaching solstice and the higher mountain horizons around the little valley making for even fewer hours of daylight than on the coast, it was after dark when he returned the next day. As always, Will and Caernarfon held their curiosity in check until Simon's horse was settled in the stable and the three of them sat down to a supper of hearty potage, a loaf of fine bread from the monastery kitchens, and mugs of ale.

"The news this time is both joyous and worrisome," Simon began.

"Then best you begin with the joyful," said Caernarfon.

"A few weeks back – barely a month shy of his eighteenth birthday – the king captured the Earl of March in Nottingham and proclaimed his personal rule."

Caernarfon beamed. In fact, Will thought, if a man could actually glow with delight, that's what he was seeing before his very eyes. "And my wife?" Caernarfon asked.

"Isabella is under constant guard, forbidden to leave her apartments, but she hasn't been formally imprisoned and her servants have been allowed to remain with her."

"This is the proudest day of my life. Even prouder, I think, than the day my son was born." Caernarfon raised his mug. "A toast, my friends, to the king."

"To the king!" Will and Simon chimed in and they all drank the toast.

"Other arrests were ordered," Simon continued, "and by now, I'm sure many of Mortimer's adherents are contemplating, in their prison cells, what lies in store for them."

Will raised his own mug. "To the hope that it won't be long before we can all go home!"

Caernarfon reached for his mug, but Simon merely sighed.

"Simon?" Will asked.

"That, my friends, is where the worrisome news comes in." Will returned his mug to the table without taking a swallow. "A man arrived in

Wykinglowe the evening before I did. An Englishman. Asking questions. Seeking the whereabouts two men. Both tall. One might have a beard, the other almost certainly clean-shaven. One young, the other old enough to be his father. Both English. Both fit and in robust health. According to Fintan, the stranger said one of the men was his cousin, who'd committed an offense against a baron and dishonored a knight and had to be brought home to face justice."

The room went deathly silent. At long last, Will said, "Guy."

"That's what I think too," said Simon, "though I didn't actually get an opportunity to verify that with my own eyes. It seemed more urgent to get back here with the news, so I left early this morning."

"I'm afraid our refuge will soon be discovered," Simon added, giving voice to all their thoughts.

Will shook his head sadly. "Which means we have to leave."

"Perhaps not," said Caernarfon. "Let me speak to the abbot in the morning."

"We don't have much time," said Simon. "The fact that there were three of us will confuse things for a bit. Also, Lord Edward was still in disguise when we were there. But there was no mistaking we were English, so Bickerstaffe will soon decide he's found his quarry. We have a day my friends . . . at the most."

"I'll speak to the abbot right after Terce."

None of them slept well that night. *Why is it*, Will wondered, *that peace for us is always fleeting?* No matter how much he tossed and turned, no answer came.

***

Caernarfon joined the monks for Terce the following morning. He'd done this on a few occasions in the past, so the brothers took little notice of his presence. At the conclusion of the service, he kept his seat, knowing the abbot would be the last to leave. "Something troubling you, my son?" the abbot asked as he made for the door.

"A word if you please? A matter of some urgency."

"Come with me."

Ensconced in the abbot's study with the cleric normally in attendance dismissed and the door closed against intrusion, Caernarfon came straight to the point. "We've had news, Father, from Wykinglowe. News that places us in some danger. Someone associated with our past who has tracked us to that point. Our only choice may be to leave." He paused before going on. He'd thought carefully about how to make his request and there seemed no way better than to be completely forthcoming. "Unless, that is, you can see your way clear to offering us sanctuary here in the monastery."

The abbot rested his elbows on his desk and clasped his hands, resting his chin on them, his gaze on the surface of the desk. At long last, he raised his eyes to Edward. "I have prayed that this day wouldn't come. That Edward of Caernarfon could live out his days peacefully here in our community."

Caernarfon was sufficiently taken aback to be rendered speechless.

"You *are* Edward of Caernarfon, are you not?"

"How did you know?"

"When the rumors that you were alive persisted after your reported demise, the superior general of our order sent messages to every abbot with instructions that we were to let him know if ever we saw you alive. He was not explicit about denying you sanctuary – that would have been a step to far in the eyes of the Church – but he did say that we must surrender you to the authorities if asked to do so."

"And yet we've been here these many months . . ."

The abbot smiled. "You may not have lived a perfect life, my son, but the life you've lived among us been noble – a good, Christian life." Then he chuckled. "And no one has asked me to deliver you."

Even Edward had to smile. "Then perhaps . . ." He hesitated. "The man looking for us will most likely ask you to deliver us. In truth, he may not ask but simply barge in and take us away."

The abbot rose from his seat and crossed to the corner of the room where an illuminated Bible lay open on a lectern. He didn't turn a page or even seem to be reading the text it was open to. Simply stood there in contemplation, his back to Edward. At long last, he returned to the chair behind his desk.

"I fear, my son, that this is a time when what I *want* to do and what I *have* to do diverge. I know you would be welcome among the brethren. They understand every meaning of the word charity. But I wonder if, once the immediate danger is past, you would be happy with that life for the rest of yours.

"I've watched you with ordinary folk – working alongside them, making a contribution to the community, and – dare I say it? – taking great pleasure in the doing. It's where you thrive. And I fear you would be far less successful in a closed community like ours where our time is rigidly governed by the holy offices. In some respects it might be like being back in custody, though this time your custodian would be God.

"I could rely on my brethren to honor sanctuary. But I can't order the lay community to lie. They might wish to protect you, but they'll also have a wish to protect their immortal souls and for most, that will have the stronger pull. Which means this man looking for you will soon know the truth and ask me to give you up. I have no qualms exercising my own judgment within broad instructions from my superior, but I can't disobey an explicit order."

Caernarfon's face fell, his hopes dashed.

"But don't despair, my son. I may not be able to give you the protection you want, but there are other things I *can* do. I can give you and your friends habits so you can travel as hermits. In exchange for your horses, I'll give you donkeys – a much more convincing way of getting around for a reclusive man of God. And I'm pretty good at being evasive when people start asking questions I'd rather not answer."

"I suppose I shouldn't have hoped for more," said Caernarfon.

"A man should never lose hope, Edward of Caernarfon. God doesn't intend you to die before your time, else he would have allowed it to happen long ago. Now, you should return to your friends and lay your plans. If I were you, I'd leave Ireland. Let your pursuer shoe the goose hereabouts for as long as he likes. There are any number of harbors on the coast you can sail from, and the large ones always have plenty of ships in port." The abbot opened a drawer of his desk and retrieved a folded page that he handed across to Edward. "A map of the coast and settlements. It might be useful."

Edward tucked it into his tunic. "Thank you, Father Abbot."

"If it's any consolation, my son, know that you will be missed here."

***

When Caernarfon broke the news, Simon wasted no time taking charge – it was evident he'd given things a lot of thought. "The disguises will help enormously, but we have to leave as many false trails as possible."

Will and Caernarfon exchanged glances. So many options for the next move that it would take time to follow each through to its conclusion. Time they could use to their own advantage.

Simon spread the map on top of the table and stabbed a finger south of Wykinglowe. "Arklow's one of the busiest ports for goods transport. Sir Edward, you leave from there, disguised as a hermit."

"He doesn't go without me," said Will.

"I understand," Simon replied, looking more carefully at the map. "What looks to be about an hour and a half south of Rathdrum is a bridge over the River Avoca. Cross there and you should be able to make Arklow in one day, even riding donkeys. Find a safe place to leave the donkeys and walk into the town. Plenty of captains will give passage to a couple of hermits on foot. The donkeys would just attract unwanted attention. Get back to Sutton and wait for me. There's a church quite close to Sutton Pool, if I remember correctly. I'll find you there.

"I'm going to keep my horse, go north to Dalkey, and get passage from there. That should keep Bickerstaffe confounded here in Ireland long enough for us to make good our escape."

***

Guy had spent three days in Wykinglowe making sure he got things right this time. He'd been ever-so-close in Sutton but too eager to catch up to the fugitives. He cursed God, himself, and the devil for good measure that he hadn't had the patience to linger around the harbor for a few days in hope that the crew of a returning ship would know something to help him. As a result, he'd wasted the entire summer – and autumn, if he was honest with himself – searching in the West Country. Between the vast expanses of the moors, the hard-to-reach nooks and crannies of the Cornish coast, and the natural reticence of the people who lived there, it was a good place for a man to go to ground.

He eventually had to admit he was more likely to find fairy people than Will Makepeace in that hostile world. He had another problem too. Montagu had undoubtedly come to the conclusion by this time that he'd wagered on the wrong man and wasted his fifty pounds. Which meant that, even if the Bickerstaffe honor hadn't been impugned at Berkeley, it certainly was now. So, cursing Will with more fervor than ever before, Guy returned to Sutton – the last place he was sure they'd been seen.

There were three ships docked in Sutton Pool that hadn't been there in the spring. One was newly commissioned, awaiting its maiden voyage. The second sailed a mere quarter hour before he got to its mooring – he could still see it making its way past the headland and into the bay as he stood on the quay and cursed his luck. Whether the curses had an effect or not, he'd never know, but Fortuna decided to favor him at the third ship. The captain was more than willing for Guy to ply him with questions over a mug of ale at one of the nearby taverns – assuming, of course, that Guy was buying.

"I take passengers all the time," he said. "Best way I know to make some extra money. No horses, mind you. Takes too long to clean out the hold, and you never quite get all the stench out anyway. Who wants to buy goods that smell of horse shit, I ask you?"

"So much for thinking my luck had changed," Guy muttered to himself.

"What was that?" the captain asked.

"Oh, nothing. Just wondering, with so many passengers, if there was any chance you'd remember the men I'm looking for."

"Hard to say. How many men? I can only take so many extras on a voyage."

"Two. Both quite tall. Different ages. Might have looked like father and son."

"Happens all the time. Any way they'd stand out?"

"One might have had finer clothing than the other, but I can't be sure of that. What I *can* be sure of was that it was back in the spring. Toward the end of March." The captain downed what was left in his mug and made sure his companion noticed. "Here." Guy reached for the mug. "Let me buy you another."

When Guy returned will the full mug, the captain took a huge swallow. "That goes down well. Now, I've been thinking. Spring, you say? There was one voyage a bit out of the ordinary. But it was three men, not two. Paid me twelve shillings extra to put in at Wykinglowe so they didn't have to backtrack from Dublin. A man's got to make money wherever he can and it only cost me an hour or so to drop them off. Don't know if they were your men or not, but they're the only ones that stand out in my mind."

The captain might have been uncertain, but Guy wasn't. He'd found them. He didn't know who the third man was, but that didn't dampen his excitement in the least. Now he just had to get there. No use asking this captain – he had to find a ship that would take his horse.

Now, saddling his horse in the stable adjacent to Wykinglowe's best inn, he was confident he'd finally be able to send that long-awaited birth announcement. The townfolk here had remembered the arrival of the three Englishmen. "Fintan's cousins," they all agreed. "Didn't stay long."

"All clean-shaven though," someone had pointed out one evening in the tavern.

That didn't overly concern Guy. An easy enough disguise for a man hoping not to be recognized. "Were they tall?" he'd asked.

"Aye, two of 'em were. Taller than the other for certes." Nods all around the table.

Guy had mulled that for a bit. *These Irishmen are so short of stature, maybe their idea of tall isn't the same as mine.*

Then one of the men around the table had solved his problem. "Taller even than you."

He'd probed for where they might have gone. "Took the road toward the mountains. But one of 'em comes back now and again for a visit with Fintan. Mayhap there's more family up in the hills."

"Or mayhap they found work in the forest. Best oak for ship planks comes from around Glendalough."

"Or mayhap they were headed to the monastery to become monks," another had chimed in, earning himself a round of laughter from everyone at the table.

The following day dawned crisp and clear – not a cloud in the sky. As he rode into the hills, Guy turned his thoughts toward how he would take custody of his cousin and the former king and prevent their escape until Montagu arrived. *The worst would be if they've been given sanctuary by the monks. There'll be no way the abbot will even let me see them, much less take them away.* And then he had another thought. *Caernarfon, maybe. He's pious enough – always praying about something or other. But Will Makepeace as a monk? That's laughable! Not even **God** could accomplish **that** conversion. Not a chance I won't get **him**.*

But it's Caernarfon that Montagu wants. And whoever that third man is – well, he'll just have to share their fate.

By the time he reached the bridge over the River Inchavore, he'd made up his mind. Announce himself as the king's man, sent to bring back fugitives from the king's justice, being sure to invoke the king as often as was useful to get cooperation. Then pay half a dozen men to assist him in escorting the "prisoners" back to Wykinglowe, where he'd have the sheriff hold them in his gaol until Montagu arrived.

A couple hundred yards past the river, the road turned sharply left and Guy came face-to-face with the only other traveler he'd met. They nodded to one another as they passed, put a hand to their caps but didn't actually doff them in greeting, and each went on his way.

***

Just to be sure nothing went wrong, Simon had delayed his own departure until after Will and Sir Edward were well on their way south. They actually looked quite convincing with their habits covering their own clothes and mounted on their donkeys. The delay had also given him time to tell a couple of their neighbors that he was going to Wykinglowe to help Fintan finish making everything ready for his family's Christmas celebrations and that he'd be back in a day or two.

He rarely met anyone on the road, but today . . . He nodded to the traveler, rounded the turn, and crossed the bridge. A hundred yards on, his heart racing, he reined his mount left onto the road to Dublin and Dalkey and urged him to a canter, never slowing until the poor horse could keep up the pace no longer. Reining in, Simon crossed himself and looked skyward before allowing the horse to walk slowly onward. There was no doubt in his mind who the other traveler was. He wasn't too worried about Bickerstaffe recognizing him – they'd only seen each other once – long ago and only briefly. But he had to admit the encounter was unnerving. *What if the weather hadn't been favorable? What if something had delayed Will and Sir Edward? What if I'd dallied with my farewells?* The what ifs didn't bear contemplation. He crossed himself again, his heartbeat slowing and his breathing returning to normal in rhythm with his horse.

***

Something about the encounter troubled Guy. He had an uncanny memory for faces, and he was certain he'd seen that one somewhere before. Try as he might, though, he couldn't conjure up the name to go with it. *Where might I have seen him? If I can work out the where, maybe that will give me the who.* But it was to no avail. Still, the whole business gnawed at him.

He was close now – closer than he'd ever been – confident Will would be in his clutches before the day was over. He shook his head to clear his mind and asked his horse for a trot. *Let it go*, he told himself. *The faces you care about are the ones less than an hour up the road.*

CHAPTER TWENTY-NINE

Guy rode slowly into the village at Glendalough, expecting the villagers to take notice of a stranger and not wanting to put them on alert straightaway. At the smithy, he asked, "Is there somewhere a traveler could get a bit of bread and ale?"

"Next to the first church you come to. Not a proper tavern like in a town, but the ale is good and there'll be a bit of meat in the potage."

He found the building easily enough and tethered his horse to a post at the corner of the churchyard. Inside, the fire added light to the dim interior, there being only one window in the room. "God's good day to you, stranger," came a female voice from the dark recesses.

As Guy's eyes began to adjust to the low light, he made out a sort of bar at the back and a rather pretty woman lighting a couple of candles – tallow, by the smell of the place. "God's good day to *you*, mistress. Is it possible for a traveler to buy some food and drink?"

"Ale that the monks brew and a bowl of potage suit you?" she asked.

"That it will. Any chance for a bit of bread?"

"It'll be a farthing extra."

"And well worth it, I'm sure." He hoped that meant he wouldn't be getting horsebread.

She disappeared into a back room and returned with the potage and bread then brought two mugs of ale from the bar and sat down at the table to join him. Puzzled at first, Guy soon realized what a stroke of luck this was.

"We don't get many travelers this time of year. Pilgrims to St. Kevin's Pool for certes, but that's mostly in the summer. What brings you?"

"Looking for long-lost relatives. They left Wykinglowe some time back. Don't know where they landed up, but could be anywhere in these hills – mayhap even as far as County Kildare."

To Guy's delight, this was just the prompt she needed. "Aye, people come here from the coast when town living gets too much for them. We have a good life here – simple and godly. None of the rascals that come in on the trading ships. Not a lurdan among us. The blacksmith's apprentice – mayhap you saw him – he came up from Wykinglowe at St. Ciarán's Day. Then there were the three who came back in the spring – 'tweren't long after St. Patrick's Day. Cousins of a man down in Wykinglowe who didn't have enough room for them, and anyway, they just wanted a quiet life. Fit in here right well. One of them got some bad news not long after they came – spent day after day praying in the churches – we have seven churches, you know."

"And the people who settle here . . . do they always stay?"

"Oh, aye. And now and again, one of them will take holy orders and join the monks." Guy's stomach did a flop. This is what he'd dreaded, but maybe . . . He held out hope.

"As a matter of fact," his hostess went on, "I heard a couple of them did just that not two days ago. Two of those what came in the spring." Guy's hope crashed to the ground.

"I guess that means they're at the monastery now?" he asked. "Would the abbot let me see them to find out if they're my relatives?"

"Ye might have to wait a bit. What I heard is that he said they had to go on pilgrimage before they could be fully accepted into the order. I've often wondered about that, you know," she prattled on. "Monks come on pilgrimage here but then our monks have to go off on pilgrimage somewhere else. Wouldn't you think if both places are holy, it would be enough just to stay in the holy place where you are? Anyhow, when my husband came in for a bite of food before you got here, he said the two new monks started off this morning. But they'll be back."

"What about the third man?" Guy asked, though he thought he already knew the answer.

"Oh, he's gone down to the coast to see his cousin – you know, get Christmas things done for the wee ones and all that. Said he'd be back in a couple of days. If you want to wait for him, we have an extra room upstairs now that my wee girl be married and moved in with her husband's family. I'd have to charge you a bit for room and board, but I wouldn't be out to cheat you."

Guy took the last morsel of bread and wiped the potage bowl clean before popping the bread in his mouth and downing the last of his ale. "How much mistress?"

"Two farthings. But I could add it to your bill if you're staying."

"I think maybe I'll just go have a chat with the abbot before I decide." He put the coins on the table and pushed them across to her then rose from his stool and made for the door.

"Come back if you decide to stay," the woman called after him.

Staying was the last thing on Guy's mind as he retrieved his horse and mounted up. *God's **bollocks**! Why can't I seem to catch even the least bit of luck? If I hadn't spent that extra day in the town to be sure I got it right this time . . .* He rode slowly toward the monastery in case the woman was watching then turned left the first chance he found and meandered through some small lanes back to the main road, puzzling through his next move.

I don't believe for a moment they actually took holy orders. Not even Caernarfon. He may be pious, but he's accustomed to fine clothes and good food, not a life of deprivation. So being monks is bound to be just a disguise. If these so-called monks had traveled to Wykinglowe, I'd have met them on the road, so they haven't gone back there. But are they just going into hiding somewhere else in Ireland? No way to know. I have to follow the third man – the traveler I met on the road this morning. He'll lead me to the others.

He glanced at the sun. *If I press my horse and ride on after dark, I can make it back this evening. The moon's nearly full – that will help.* He squeezed his horse's ribs twice to ask for a canter and headed back the way he'd come.

The next morning, he found the man called Fintan on the docks – and found his luck gone from bad to worse. "Haven't seen him since the beginning of the month," Fintan replied to Guy's query. "And I remember on account of it was the first Sunday of Advent."

Guy was sorry there were other people around. He wanted to scream curses at God and every saint he could think of and Satan and Will Makepeace and his mother and Edward of Caernarfon and Lord Berkeley for leaving home and Queen Isabella for knighting him in the first place. Instead, he had to settle for one more question, hoping for a clue. "What's your cousin's name?"

"Simon," Fintan replied. "Simon Forster."

A name that was no clue at all. But his gut told him his quarry had left Ireland. *But to where?* Frustrated – almost despondent – he led his horse down the quay, stopping at each ship being loaded or preparing to depart and calling up to whoever was on deck, "Where're you bound?" When someone replied "Sutton," he knew he had to decide. *Back to the starting place yet again? Will they retrace their own tracks? I wouldn't. But maybe that's what they're counting on – that I'll follow my own instincts.*

His musings were interrupted by a shout from the ship. "If ye want passage, best get aboard now. Cap'n's ready to sail."

With no better idea and still bemoaning his luck, he led his horse up the gangway and paid the fee without haggling. No sooner was his horse properly settled in the hold than the gangplank was raised and seamen scrambled into the rigging to man the sails. He found a spot along the starboard gunwale where he could stay out of the way and contemplate what to do next as the ship pulled away from the dock and headed for the open sea.

The sudden snap of the mainsails being lowered jarred Guy to attention. And as they caught the wind and the ship picked up speed, it came to him like a flash of lightning. Two images side-by-side in his mind. The man he'd encountered on the road to Glendalough the previous day and a man he saw once, long ago, in a tavern in Kenilworth. On the day he had to drag Will back to his duties at the castle. The face he'd been struggling to remember.

Had Will been plotting to free Caernarfon then? Had he gotten wind of the plan to move the former king to Berkeley Castle and rushed to the tavern to inform his contact? It all fit. That's how the raiders knew to take both Caernarfon and Will when they abducted the former king from Berkeley.

*I was a fool to let Berkeley and Caernarfon talk me into releasing Will from the dungeon. If I'd followed my instincts then, we wouldn't **be** in this mess.* He slammed the palm of his hand down on the gunwale rail. *Will stinking Makepeace, I'll see you brought to justice if it's the last thing I ever do!*

***

"Luck's been with us so far," said Will as they stepped onto the quay in Sutton Pool. Just outside of Arklow, they'd come upon a small field with half a dozen cows munching on small piles of hay that had been left for them. Finding the gate, they turned the donkeys into the field, knowing that whoever tended the cows would be back. It had been surprisingly easy to find a ship bound for Sutton, and the captain had only one request of them – no preaching to his sailors.

"Perhaps, young Will," said Caernarfon, "God played some small part in this as well."

Posing as monks worked to their advantage in more ways than they'd expected. Pulling the hoods of their habits over their heads made it difficult for people to see their faces, and the woolen habits over their own clothes were almost as warm as a heavy cloak. The only awkward bit – for Will, at least – was his sword. When he'd first donned the habit, the problem was immediately apparent. So he'd wound up strapping the sword to his leg to prevent it protruding at strange angles. Which meant walking stiff-legged, since he couldn't easily bend his left knee. "Makes the disguise even more convincing," Simon had asserted.

"Just hope I don't have to run anywhere." Will had frowned as he walked around a bit, getting accustomed to his new gait.

"Monks do not run, my son," the abbot had admonished. "Perhaps it will be good that you have this reminder."

They found the church easily enough and the priest was only too happy to allow them to sleep and eat there while waiting for their companion's arrival. "Men of God are always welcome under this roof," he said. "Most especially pilgrims on their way to the holy shrine at Canterbury." This was the story they'd all agreed was most plausible for their journey across the south of England. They'd also agreed that staying near the coast was wise, should they find it necessary to make a quick escape yet again. What they hoped for, though, was to hear news that would let them know it was safe to simply resume their lives somewhere in the countryside, far away from the attention of anyone powerful. Caernarfon was doubtful, but willing to be hopeful, if only for the sake of those who were giving him their protection.

It took three days for Simon to arrive – days Will found himself imitating Caernarfon's prayers and devotions, grateful that at least one of them had even a fleeting notion of how to act like a monk. They almost didn't recognize their friend when he arrived in his habit, which he'd brought in a satchel and put on after leaving his ship.

They made it as far as Totnes the first day, though it wasn't easy with Will's ungainly walk. "If I have to keep on like this, I'm going to have a permanent limp," Will complained that night when they bedded down in the cell they'd been given to share at the Benedictine priory.

Simon stroked his chin in contemplation. "What if . . ." He hesitated, the idea still forming in his mind. "What if we could fashion some sort of harness so you could wear it down your back?"

"Or what if we simply dispose of it?" asked Caernarfon.

"Oh, no." Will was quick to reply. "Then I'd have no way to keep an assailant at bay for you to escape. The daggers we wear on our belts are only useful for a close-in fight."

"All we'd need," Simon was thinking out loud now, "is some strips of leather to lengthen your sword belt enough so the hilt wouldn't stick up out of your cowl."

They solved the problem the next morning, acquiring some old reins from a stable on the edge of town, and made it to Exeter by the end of the day. Another day of unseasonably nice weather got them all the way to Lyme Regis. And then the rains came. Two days of unrelenting downpour, during which they realized they had another problem. Traveling as monks, they couldn't frequent the taverns – or anywhere else, for that matter – where there'd be news of what was happening in the kingdom.

Their first idea was for one of them to discard his habit and travel a bit separately from the other two, sleeping at inns and frequenting taverns.

"There's a fundamental flaw with that plan," Caernarfon pointed out. "If Sir Guy is still on our trail, he's looking for two monks and a third person not thus disguised."

Will and Simon both sighed. Then Will suddenly burst into a huge grin. "Why don't we change the game on him? Simon and I both discard our habits, so now we're two ordinary men and a monk."

"We could even get a small cart and a horse," Simon chimed in. "Will and I could ride up front and you, sir, in the back with some hay or something, and it would look like we were just giving you a temporary respite from walking."

Caernarfon smiled. "Now you're thinking like good chess players."

"It changes our story of making a pilgrimage to Canterbury," said Simon.

"For the moment," Will replied, "but we'd keep the habits in case we need to return to that. But if we can confound Guy and get some news at the same time . . ."

They left Lyme just as they'd arrived – three monks walking. Once in the countryside with no one around, Simon and Will shed their habits, stowing one in Simon's satchel and the other under Caernarfon's habit, held in place by the rope belt, giving him a more corpulent look that added to his disguise. When they reached Chideock, Caernarfon kept on walking while Simon and Will stayed behind to purchase a horse, a cart, some hay, and a bit of black canvas. "To keep the hay dry," Simon said. "But it could also hide one or two of us should we find ourselves in imminent danger." Will's thoughts went back to the day he and Caernarfon had been kidnapped from Berkeley and the black canvas those monks had used to conceal the captives' presence as the wagon careened through the village.

They spent that night in Dorchester – Simon and Will at an inn, Caernarfon in the church – and got the first news they'd had since leaving Glendalough.

The next morning, the former king rose and left early on foot to maintain the ruse. Will was anxious every moment he was away from the man he'd come to think of as his charge, but Caernarfon was quite sanguine about it. "Where would I be safer than in a church?" he'd asked.

"They murdered Thomas à Becket at prayer in his own cathedral," Will reminded him.

"You fret too much, young Will. If we're to keep our opponents confounded, then surely we must play out the strategy we've devised." That he was right still didn't do much to calm Will's nerves.

But the new strategy paid off. Will and Simon were almost giddy when they picked Caernarfon up along the road, both talking at once so eager were they to share what they'd learned. Caernarfon finally interrupted them. "Please, my friends, take a breath. I can't take it all in at once. And we have all day for you to tell me." Simon and Will both laughed aloud. "From what little I could make out," Caernarfon continued, "I think perhaps the news is good."

"Good indeed, sir," said Will. "Your son has been quite busy. Mortimer was executed."

"Good riddance," Caernarfon declared.

"That's what most of the ordinary folk seem to think as well, sir."

"And what of Isabella?"

"She's been banished from court and not allowed any say in governing the realm. Oh, and Archbishop Melton is now treasurer of England."

"Edmund has been pardoned," said Simon. "Lady Margaret was given back her title and all her lands and goods. Little Edmund is now the Earl."

"My dear brother. Justice too late for him, but justice nonetheless. It seems my prayers for his family have been answered."

"Mine as well," said Simon.

They stayed well north of the Isle of Purbeck and crossed the River Avon at Ringwood. Caernarfon was particularly anxious about being seen in Ringwood since, as far as anyone knew, it was still in Isabella's possession, but it was the most direct route to get around the Solent. So they all resumed their monks' disguises for the day. In the first smallish town holding an open market, Simon left his companions with the cart while he purchased three sturdy farmer's cloaks, winter hats, and warm gloves. No one knew how long they would be on this journey and January would undoubtedly be colder than the unseasonable temperatures of this December.

With the expense of lodgings and food each evening and stabling for the horse and cart, Will was growing concerned about their funds running out. Even though Simon made no fuss over the cost of anything, Will felt compelled to ask. "You needn't fret," Simon replied. "Edmund gave me an enormous sum. And I think he'd be pleased with how I'm using it."

In every town they heard about more arrest orders. Bogo Bayouse, John Deveril, William Ockley, Thomas Gurney. Maltravers, it was said, had fled abroad, taking Bayouse and Gurney with him. Life in England was still unsettled as the young king rounded up Mortimer's adherents and those responsible for the deaths of his father and his uncle.

One afternoon, when Will and Simon were discussing where they might all go to ground and live a quiet life, Caernarfon seemed in a melancholy mood, contributing no ideas of his own. "So what do you think, Sir Edward?" Simon finally asked directly.

"I think perhaps it's too soon for me to stay in England. My son needs time to consolidate his position. To administer justice to those who conspired with Mortimer. To award titles and lands and to create his own court. No matter how quietly we might live, there's always the risk that someone would recognize me, and that would put my son in the extremely awkward position of having to decide what to do about it. I don't wish that for him."

Now it was Will and Simon who had nothing to say. At long last, Will asked, "Might there not be some way, sir, to mitigate the risk? Some out corner of the kingdom where news arrives slowly if at all and where people would be unlikely ever to have seen your image?"

"I'm not surprised you're reluctant to leave your homeland, young Will. Nor will I be disappointed if you choose to stay."

"Where were you thinking to go, sir?" asked Simon.

"I recall you said that one of Edmund's last duties for the Crown was a visit to the Pope in Avignon. I think I should like to retrace his steps and even request an audience with the Holy Father. It might give me some comfort to learn what they talked about and to hear what spirits my brother was in at the time."

Simon turned to Will, his eyebrows raised in the implied question. Will nodded. "Then that, Sir Edward," said Simon, "is precisely what we'll do. Dover to Calais and onward to Avignon."

***

On the outskirts of Hastings, Simon slowed the horse from a trot to a walk, his usual practice as they approached a village or town. There was a chill breeze off the sea, and all three men wore their cloaks, hats, and gloves. They hadn't seen many travelers along the way, so the sound of rapid hoofbeats approaching from behind made them instantly alert. But they'd prepared for this. Without a word spoken, Caernarfon lay down in the hay and pulled the black canvas completely over him. Simon and Will pulled their hats down low on their foreheads and the collars of their cloaks up around their ears and cheeks. Both hunched their shoulders and lowered their heads, hoping to appear older and smaller than they were. Their heads may have been low, but their eyes were fixated on the road ahead.

The hoofbeats grew louder as a horseman rode past at a full canter. Without slowing his horse, the man looked over his shoulder, a scowl on his face, then rode on. When the horseman disappeared around a bend in the road, Will heaved a deep sigh. "Christ on horseback!" He kept his voice low.

"The devil on horseback, more like," Simon said as he guided the cart to a stop on the verge.

CHAPTER THIRTY

"How in the name of all that's holy did he find us?" Will asked as Caernarfon emerged from under the canvas.

"How did who find us?" he asked.

"Sir Guy," Will sounded completely defeated.

"Is it not likely, young Will, that he has *not* in fact found us but is still looking?"

"Sir Edward makes sense, Will," said Simon. "If he had found us, why didn't he approach more slowly? And why didn't he attempt to stop us?"

"He could be waiting to pounce just around that bend in the road," said Will.

"But if he'd recognized us, wouldn't he have reined in straightaway and turned to face us?" asked Simon.

"I don't know," said Will. "All I know is that the danger is real again and it's too close for my liking."

"That I can agree with," said Caernarfon. "He's most likely picked up on bits and pieces he thinks may be clues but is still confounded by our ruses. I'd wager his intent is to search the Cinque Ports to see if we've left a trail there. And since he was most likely told in Glendalough that two monks left there on pilgrimage, he'll search in Canterbury as well."

"So what do we do now?" asked Simon.

"We thwart his plans yet again," Caernarfon replied. "It'll take him time to search all five ports, and if he's smart, he'll stop at Canterbury on his way to Sandwich. So we turn north now and make straight for Sandwich, bypassing Canterbury entirely. Ships sail every day between Sandwich and Sluis in Flanders. We take passage as three monks, then, once in Flanders, we discard the habits and travel as ordinary men. Three monks set sail from Sandwich and land in Sluis . . . and disappear, never to be seen again."

Will's smile had returned. "Just one more question, sir. What's our pretext for travel?"

"That's easy," said Simon. "A pilgrimage to Rome."

"Perhaps that's a little too grandiose," Caernarfon chuckled. "Simple is often better. We're merely going to a monastery in Flanders."

***

"Stinking farmers," Guy groused as he looked over his shoulder at the offending horse cart and its occupants. "Don't you know other people have better things to do than dawdle along behind you?" he shouted as he rounded the bend in the road. He knew full well the farmers were too far behind to have heard him, but it made him feel better.

His horse was in fine fettle and had kept up the pace for the past five miles. He'd have to slow down once they reached the town, but he'd still have plenty of time to make his inquiries at the harbor before nightfall. And if he had no luck here, then New Romney was barely a day's ride away. If the weather was good, he'd probably have time for a quick stop at Rye on the way.

He wasn't entirely certain the men he'd been pursuing were his targets, but there were too many coincidences to discount. Three men traveling all the way across the southern coast. Three monks walking in the west. Then two ordinary men in a horse cart. The remaining monk always slept in churches, but somehow he always managed to end up in the same town as the horse-cart men. In one town, three men in peasants' winter clothes staying at the same inn. Then the monk again. His gut told him he was on the right track. And with them staying so close to the coast, he was convinced they were headed to one of the Cinque Ports to go abroad. If they managed to flee his clutches on this side of the Channel, he might never be able to make good on his oath to himself and his promise to Lord Montagu. At least they didn't know how close he was to catching them up.

He'd had to start all over at Sutton after losing the third man somewhere in Ireland, but his diligence had paid off. It still made him angry that he had to stoop to Will's level, spending his evenings in taverns. Angrier still, that Will was right about taverns being the best places to get information. At least in the ports, thank God, he could get his information straight from the men who ran the docks and those who plied the seas.

In Hastings, the harbor-master could barely spare him the time of day. Guy had to follow him all over the docks as he inspected the loading and unloading of ships. "No monks been around here," he said. "*That* I'd remember."

"What about three men traveling together. Probably wearing identical cloaks."

"Just like any passenger getting on any ship this time of year. You think I'm supposed to recollect every man who walks onto the quay?"

"Two of them would have been quite tall – taller than you or even me. I really couldn't say about the third one."

The harbor-master stopped in his tracks and turned to face Guy. "Two tall men in winter cloaks with a third man you don't know what he looks like? And you think I'm supposed to have seen them and remember them just for you?" Then he shouted up at a man standing at the gunwale of the nearest ship, "Hey, Sollers, you seen any tall men hanging around the docks lately?"

"Nobody taller'n you or me."

"There you have it, then," the harbor-master told Guy. "Your men haven't been here. Now on your way and let me get back to work."

Guy spent another hour or more asking laders and sailors the same questions and getting nothing but "Nay" or a shake of the head in reply. He even gritted his teeth and stopped into a couple of quayside taverns with no better results. One of the barmaids even laughed at him. "Monks, you say?

Monks? You think monks might show up in a place like this?" In the end, there was nothing for it but to assume his quarry hadn't sailed from Hastings and move on.

Storm clouds over the Channel the next morning caused him to bypass Rye, lest the storm come ashore and prevent him from reaching New Romney that day. He glanced toward the harbor as he rode through town, then looked skyward. "Please, God, don't let this be the biggest mistake of my life." Crossing himself for good measure, he urged his horse to a canter and left Rye behind. The rain started falling just as he found an inn in New Romney.

The following morning, saying a quick prayer of thanks that the storm had passed during the night, Guy made straight for the docks. The harbor-master there was far more pleasant and willing to help, but the results were no different. Guy was certain the three men were still ahead of him – they *had* been all across the south coast – and every hour he spent making his inquiries was an hour further ahead of him that they could achieve. So he didn't linger, knowing that, even with time for a cursory check in Hythe, he could still make Dover by nightfall. And he was increasingly convinced that Dover was their destination.

Guy spent the entire next morning scouring the Dover docks, looking for any ship that might have booked passage for his quarry. If they were already aboard, he had every intention of enlisting the local sheriff to help him drag them off and lock them in his gaol. The harbor-master tried to be helpful, but Dover was such a busy port, even at this time of year, that the chances of passengers boarding a ship and escaping his scrutiny were high. As the sun approached its zenith, Guy had still found no one who'd seen any monks or two tall men, either this morning or in the previous days.

So now he faced a dilemma. *Only two more likely places they could have gone – Canterbury or Sandwich. Knowing what a pious bastard Caernarfon is, I'd wager it's Canterbury. Maybe even hoping the archbishop will give them sanctuary.*

Or maybe they're thinking I'd be convinced by those Irishmen telling me they were going on pilgrimage, and they want me to waste time in Canterbury while they're sailing off from Sandwich. God's teeth! If Aldwin had come with me, we could split up and find them, whichever choice they've made. Hell, if Aldwin had come with me straightaway, we'd have been in time to catch them as they left Corfe Castle.

Still grousing to himself, Guy retrieved his horse, took one final look in the direction of the docks, and headed north on the Canterbury Road.

By the time he reached Bewsfield, he'd changed his mind. *If I lose the trail at Sandwich, I may never catch up to them again. I can always double back to Canterbury if they haven't been seen in the port.* He took the first turning toward Sandwich and cursed Will Makepeace for putting him in this predicament in the first place.

When he reached Sandwich roughly four hours past midday, he made straight for the docks. Though the sun had set, there was still ample twilight, it being a perfectly clear day with nary a cloud in the sky. The harbor-master had gone home for the day, so Guy approached a docksman coiling ropes beside an empty berth. "Three monks? Aye. Fleeched passage on a ship returning to Sluis. Moored right here it was. Sailed with the tide barely half an hour ago."

"Any more ships sailing to Flanders today?"

"Not so I know about. Next be on the afternoon tide tomorrow. The *Duifje*. Captain'll be on deck not long after daybreak."

It was all Guy could do to control his rage. He wanted to rail at all the denizens of heaven and hell for his accursed luck. Instead, he thanked the docksman and led his horse away. He knew better than to spend the night at an inn on the docks – his horse would almost certainly be stolen – so he went back into the town and found a bed and stable for the night. Not that the bed did him much good, even though he had it to himself. He passed the night staring at the ceiling, lamenting the fact that the threesome had now gained a full day's advantage over him. At the first sign of light, he collected his horse and returned to the docks.

When he finally found the *Duifje*, the captain was at the gunwale overseeing the loading of bales of wool. "How much to transport me and my horse?" Guy called up to him.

The captain looked him over at length before replying, "Ten florins."

Guy quickly did the conversion in his head. Six pounds. Twice or more what it *should* cost. "Five," he offered.

"Eight and not a *denier* less."

Guy's funds were running low, but he didn't care. He had to get on that ship.

CHAPTER THIRTY-ONE

When they reached France, the tables were turned. It was Caernarfon, with his fluent Anglo-Norman French – his first language, after all – who made all the arrangements for lodgings and stabling of their horses, often bargaining with landlords and stable masters for a better price. They'd left Sluis on foot, still in their monks' habits, which they'd buried in a field on the outskirts of Damme. There, Simon bought horses, saddles, and bridles and oiled-wool cloaks for the three of them. "At least two more months of winter," he reasoned. "We could easily get caught out by rain or snow. And God knows we might need them for extra warmth as well."

They headed toward Bruges with a lightness of spirit that had been impossible since they left Glendalough. They'd escaped Guy's clutches for now, and Will dared to hope his cousin would give up the pursuit. *Don't let your guard down, Will,* the tiny voice in his head reminded him when he was tempted to rejoice in their escape. *He tracked you to Ireland, after all.*

"What would you say to a small change of plans?" Caernarfon asked over supper the first night.

"Might depend on what you have in mind," Will replied. They kept their voices low since they had to speak English for Will's benefit. Simon had acquired some French during his time as Edmund's companion, so when anyone was close by, he and Caernarfon reverted to French and Will kept his mouth shut.

"Our destination remains Avignon, but perhaps while we're still in the north would be an opportune time to visit the lands of my ancestors. I'd quite like to see Rouen again."

"Why do I think there's a cathedral there?" Will asked, inciting laughter from both of his companions, which in turn drew the attention of men at the nearest table.

"*Ce n'est rien,*" Caernarfon waved away their curious stares.

The three finished their meal in silence, resuming the conversation as they walked back to the inn where they'd been lucky enough to get a room to themselves. There was only one bed, but it had three mattresses, so they could put one on the floor. "Going to Rouen first would mean spending the winter in the north rather than enjoying the warmer weather of the south," said Simon.

"I can't disagree," said Caernarfon. "But we don't know what we'll be doing after seeing the Pope. If he were to intercede on my behalf . . ." He let the thought drop.

Will and Simon both knew he was hoping the Pope might have a solution for their predicament. They all also knew that was unlikely. The three of them debated the pros and cons of the diversion, but it was largely a formality. Will and Simon knew from the outset that, absent any serious risk, they would accede to Caernarfon's wish.

To avoid Calais, they stayed well south of the coast. Just crossing the main road from Calais to Paris put Will's nerves on edge. If Guy *had* pursued them, it seemed highly likely he'd start in Calais, guessing that Caernarfon might choose the Duchy of Aquitaine as a safe place to hide. *Don't dwell on it, Will,* he told himself. But he couldn't help it.

The fact that he couldn't understand a single word of what was being said around him deprived him of one of the most important arrows in his quiver – picking up on nuances of possible danger by eavesdropping on random conversations. "I might as well be stone deaf," he told his companions.

"Rest easy, young Will," Caernarfon tried to reassure him. "Simon and I will be your ears."

But will you know what to listen for? In the end, there was nothing for it. He had to trust them. And of course he did. But he missed having the visceral instincts that came from using both his eyes and his ears.

Winter weather, winter roads, short days until the equinox, a horse that came up lame and had to be rested for a week, and a bridge completely blocked by a heavily loaded wagon that broke an axle halfway across all conspired to delay their arrival in Avignon until after Easter. They took lodgings above a draper's shop in the rue des Teinturiers – much as they'd rented a room from a silk weaver in Lyon – and Caernarfon immediately dispatched a message to the Pope requesting an audience. Will was dubious they'd get a reply, much less an audience, but nothing seemed capable of dampening the former king's optimism, and Will had no desire to cast a shadow on his hopes.

***

Guy had decided, during the crossing, that his quarry hadn't chosen the Low Countries as a specific destination – they'd simply chosen the first ship that was ready to sail. His gut told him they were headed to France. What he hadn't worked out was precisely where, though he'd narrowed it to four options. So he pointed his horse's head south toward Valenciennes in Hainault and pondered his choices.

Gascony would be a safe hiding place, he reasoned. *But if that's where they're headed, surely they would have sailed straight there from Sluis. Yet people in Sluis who saw three monks disembark at the quay reported those same three monks leaving town on foot. For that matter, if Gascony was the destination, why did they even bother with the journey across England? It would have been far simpler – and certainly safer for them – to sail straight from Sutton to Bordeaux.* He relegated Gascony to his last choice.

Paris? Philip of Valois remains on reasonably good terms with Edward III, despite the latter having challenged him for the throne of France. But how would he react to the deposed English king showing up on his doorstep looking for support or sanctuary?

Hainault poses a similar question. As father of Edward's queen, the count is a staunch ally. But what if that's exactly what Caernarfon is seeking? Someone who could negotiate his safe return to England.

What if, on the other hand, Caernarfon's goal is restoration to the throne? Is that why Montagu is so intent on finding them? he wondered. *To put Caernarfon back in a prison from which he couldn't be freed – or worse? Neither Philip nor Count William would want to get embroiled in that. Only one man might be convinced to enter the fray. The Pope.*

When he reached Valenciennes, he was still undecided. No one he'd spoken to on the journey remembered any unusual travelers, but that could be just a matter of luck. But after two days in Valenciennes, when all his inquiries had produced no one who'd seen men – or monks – even remotely resembling his quarry, Guy decided to move on. This was not where he'd find them.

That left Paris and Avignon. Which to choose? Paris was closest, though where to look for them in a big city would be problematic and time was not on his side. But in all this time – all the places they'd gone – there'd been no effort to recruit a following to restore Caernarfon to the throne. So Avignon would have to wait.

In Paris, he went back to his old habits from the time in London. Frequenting taverns, following the court, wandering the small lanes and alleys, lurking in churches, roaming the quays . . . His French wasn't particularly good, but it improved quickly, necessity and obsession being strong motivations for developing one's skill. As the days and weeks led up to Palm Sunday, he realized it was time to make a decision. He'd wasted too much time in London, hoping to find elusive clues in the haystack of the city. Then, he was seeking only his own retribution. Now he had an obligation to Montagu as well. An obligation he'd been far too long fulfilling. It was time to move on.

As he rode south, he found reason to hope. He began hearing about a man called Le Galeys. Surely it wasn't coincidence that people would speak of a Welshman. Now and then, he asked about the mysterious man. Was he tall? How old might he be? Did he have a beard? Was it straight or wavy?

What about his hair? Did he have a companion? Or even two? Had anyone heard their names spoken?

By the time he reached Lyon, he was sure he was on their trail. In fact, he thought he'd spotted them entering a silk weaver's shop in La Croix Rousse, but though he waited and watched until long after the shop closed its doors, they never re-emerged. Was his new-found optimism causing his mind to play tricks on him?

Undaunted, he went on to Avignon, more certain than ever that this is where his quest would finally end. Extremely low on funds now, he found a shabby little tavern where the landlord was willing to let him sleep on one of the tables in return for throwing out the drunkards when it came time to close up. By day, he kept a vigil in one of the little orchards on the Rue des Champeaux, opposite the entrance to the Pope's palace. By night, he spent hours over a single mug of ale in one tavern or another until it was time to go throw the drunkards out and spend an uncomfortable night on a hard table. All in the hope of catching sight of or hearing mention of the man known as Le Galeys. He was sure that wherever he found Le Galeys, he would also find Will.

***

To everyone's surprise, a message from the papal palace arrived just two days later. As the only member of the group with any Latin, Caernarfon read it aloud, in translation.

> *The Holy Father would be pleased to receive you on the*
> *morrow. You will be welcome at the entrance to the palace on*
> *Rue des Champeaux when the cathedral bells toll midday.*

Folding the missive and stowing it in his tunic, Caernarfon said, "I believe this warrants a visit to L'Église des Cordeliers to thank God for his intervention. Would anyone like to come with me?" His broad smile said he knew neither of them would be willing to let him go alone.

The next morning, they wound their way through the narrow streets of the town, emerging on the Rue des Champeaux at the south end of the palace. Still dependent on nothing but his sight to sense danger, Will's eyes roved left and right, front and back, as they hurried to the entrance. Something caught his eye off to the left, but he couldn't quite make sense of it. Then, as the first bell rang and the huge doors of the palace opened, he looked back over his shoulder. "Holy mother of God!" The words escaped before his thoughts caught up with what he'd seen. As the doors closed behind them, Simon asked, "What did you see, Will?"

"Sir Guy. I'm sure of it. Among those trees just across the street."

***

It wasn't unusual for people to make their way up the little lane south of the palace to get to the *champeaux*, so Guy didn't pay them much mind at first. But when they turned toward the palace entrance rather than one of the little tracks than meandered through the *champeaux*, he sprang to attention. Three men, two taller than the third. It all happened too fast. The bell sounded. The door opened. Will stared straight at him. And before he could cover the distance to accost them, the door closed and they were safely inside.

"God curse Will Makepeace to the end of time!" he railed, shaking his fist at the heavens. People on the street gave him a wide berth, thinking him mad, no doubt. He was mad, alright, but not in the sense they thought. Simply consumed by anger. To be so close. To be the hunter who hadn't fully drawn his bow before the quarry bolted to safety.

***

Without speaking, the priest who'd granted them entrance led them to a room that opened off a long gallery, gestured for them to be seated, and left. Will had never seen such opulence. Frescoes in grisaille covered the ceiling between the ribs of the six-part vault. The ribs themselves were covered in gold, and colorful bosses punctuated the ceiling and the base of each rib.

Rich tapestries hung on the walls to the left and right of the door. Tiles painted with stylized animals, leaves, and fruits covered the floor, which was raised at the end opposite the door to support a large chair, decorated with gold and undeniably meant for the pontiff. Even the chairs for petitioners were made comfortable with soft cushions to sit on and arms for resting one's elbows and forearms. Never in his most outlandish imaginings could Will have envisioned being in such a place much less being about to come face-to-face with God's anointed representative on earth. Awe was a word insufficient to the moment, but it was the only one Will knew.

Caernarfon's voice drew Will's attention back from gaping at his surroundings. "I heard what you told Simon, young Will. Leave it in my hands. I'll find a way to let the Holy Father know that danger awaits us outside these walls. He speaks the Occitan dialect, but I understand it's similar to Anglo-Norman. We should be able to understand one another."

"How do you know these things?" Simon asked.

"Do you think I spend all my time in the confessional enumerating my sins?" Caernarfon chuckled.

When the door opened barely a quarter hour later, Pope John entered first, followed by two priests who lagged behind by half a dozen steps. The door closed quietly, managed by unseen hands in the gallery. Caernarfon rose to his feet and knelt as the pontiff approached and extended his hand for the kissing of the ring. Will and Simon imitated their companion's actions.

"*In nomine patris et filii et spiritus sancti, Amen.*" The Pope made the sign of the cross over each of them then said, "Please return to your seats, my sons. I think I shall forego the grandeur of the formal audience and join you here."

"It's why we chose the small audience chamber," said one of the priests.

"Father Manuele Fieschi," said the Pope, to which the priest nodded his head in acknowledgment. "Father Manuele is a notary whose task it is to record the audiences I grant."

"Including any petitions made and the Holy Father's response," the priest added.

The Pope then reverted from Latin to his native French. "Now tell me, my son Edward, what brings you here? Your message spoke of your half-brother and his last visit here."

"You know, of course, that Edmund ran afoul of evil not long after he left here. I never saw him again after I was deposed, so it would give me great comfort to know how he fared in that last year of his short life."

The Pope didn't answer straightaway, instead asking questions that required complex answers – "testing my French," Caernarfon told Will and Simon later – and probing for things that only the two brothers would know about each other.

Then he turned his attention to Simon. "I've seen you before, my son. I can't recall your name, but I think perhaps you were a familiar of Lord Edmund of whom we speak."

"I was his companion from childhood, Your Holiness. Simon is my name."

"And you, my son?" The pontiff addressed Will.

"I . . . I speak no French, Holy Father."

The other accompanying priest stepped forward. "Then perhaps I can be of service," he said in English with an accent Will recognized from their time in Glendalough. "I'm Father Ciarán. Raised in Ireland but did my studies at Oxford."

"Please tell His Holiness my name is Will, and I've been with Lord Caernarfon since . . . well, since he was deposed."

"As a companion?"

"First as a guard and . . . and later as a companion." They hadn't discussed this ahead of time, and Will didn't want to make a mistake by revealing too much. Father Ciarán translated for the Pope.

"Very well," the pontiff turned his attention back to Caernarfon. "Edmund told me he was certain you were still alive, and now I'm convinced he was right. You shall all stay here for now as my guests. Father Ciarán will show you to your quarters. And I would be pleased, Edward, if you would dine with me this evening. It would be nice to remember Edmund and to speak of his last visit here."

They followed Father Ciarán to the end of the long gallery, across a courtyard into another wing of the palace, and up a flight of stairs to a corridor with windows on one side looking out over the city and a series of doors opposite. Opening the first two doors, he explained, "We've made two rooms available for you but you're free to choose your own sleeping arrangements. Whatever allows you to feel safe, Lord Edward, though I can assure you no danger lurks inside these walls."

"There is a small problem, Father," said Caernarfon. "We need to settle our accounts with the landlady where we've been staying. I would send Simon or Will, but there's very real danger lurking outside these walls. A man who has pursued us for over a year now was spotted in the *champeaux* just as we were admitted to the palace. I've no idea how he found us here, but I don't question Will's recognizing him."

"Say no more, my son. Give me the address and I'll have someone settle your account and collect your things. You have horses as well, I presume? We'll fetch them, pay their board, and bring them to our stable for the duration of your visit."

"We can pay, Father, there's no need—"

The priest raised a hand to cut him off. "You're our guests, Lord Edward. It's no imposition."

***

Guy paced furiously among the apple trees in the little orchard, cursing his luck, until he finally calmed down enough to realize that, aside from those who lived there, whoever entered the papal residence must certainly come out again. He may have missed his first chance, but he would *not* miss the second.

And then reality set in. Everywhere else he'd gotten close to apprehending them, he could invoke crimes against the king to get the cooperation of a local sheriff. Here, he was a nobody. The authorities would be of no help unless he could prove his mission. And the only one who could do that was the man who'd sent him in the first place. He waited in the orchard until he had no choice but to go throw the drunkards out lest the tavern owner throw all his belongings into the street to be stolen, trodden on, or fouled by chamber pots being emptied from the first-floor windows.

When the door was shut behind the last of the drunkards and the landlord had gone upstairs to his bed, Guy lit another candle and removed the paper, ink, and quill he'd carried in his satchel all these months in anticipation of sending his message. Seated at the table that would later be his bed, he began to write.

> *My lord,*
> *It is with great pleasure that I announce the birth of my son in the town of Avignon this very morning. He is even now being blessed by the most exalted churchmen in all of Christianity. I anxiously await your arrival to help celebrate the birth.*
> *Your loyal servant, Bickerstaffe*
> *At Avignon, 11th April*

The next morning he went straight to the city center and found a place to hire a messenger, paying all but his last pound for the man to travel with all possible speed. He'd have to make that pound last until Montagu's arrival. But at least he no longer had to frequent the taverns. All his waking hours would be spent in the little apple orchard in the *champeaux*.

***

Something of a pattern developed for the papal guests. Mornings were spent with Caernarfon's devotions in a chapel in the guest wing followed by walking about in the courtyards and gardens. The main garden, reached by descending two long, steep staircases, was awakening in the warming spring air. Fruit trees were covered in buds and starting to bloom. Gardeners tended rose bushes and perennial herbs, trimming away any damage from the winter cold, and planted seeds in plots designated for vegetables or for flowers. A few bees were already humming around the blossoms on the trees. It wouldn't be long before the place was awash in color and new life would emerge from the soil. Will was hardly surprised when Caernarfon asked to help with the work.

Shortly after their midday meal, they might receive a summons from the Pope. The second day after their arrival, he insisted on giving them a personal tour of the entire palace. Will couldn't help the occasional gasp as they entered room after room, each more beautiful than the last. The third time it happened, the Pope chuckled. "I take it you find my home quite beautiful, my son."

"Forgive me, Holy Father," Will replied with Father Ciarán's assistance. "It's only that I've never seen anything quite like it."

"Then I'm most pleased," said the Pope. "We may have to live in exile from Rome for the moment, but that doesn't mean we have to live like refugees. I decided this palace should be as grand as the Lateran, and I challenge anyone to say it is not."

On the first floor, they entered a long gallery directly above the main entrance, overlooking the *champeaux*. The Pope stepped over to look out a window then beckoned his guests to join him. "See there . . ." He pointed. ". . . leaning against that tree. Is that the man whose presence you fear?"

Will instinctively pulled back from the window. "It is indeed, Holy Father," said Simon.

"I'm told he arrives just after daybreak and never leaves the spot until well after sundown." The Pope turned his back to the window. "I have an idea how we might dissuade him. On Sunday, I'll say mass at the cathedral at midday. If you walk there with me, among my entourage, I doubt he'd be bold enough to approach. And the message would be clear that you're under my protection. What do you think, Edward?" The pontiff's eyes sparkled at the idea of putting the pursuer off his game.

A broad smile crept across Caernarfon's face as he listened. "Something I would thoroughly enjoy. What say you, Will? Simon?"

They exchanged looks that couldn't be mistaken for anything but trepidation.

"Come, my sons," said the Pope. "Even if he has the audacity to try to approach, he'll never be allowed to come near us. It will be fun."

And on the day, it turned out to be more pleasurable than anything Will had experienced since he used to tug on Guy's strings now and again while they were at Berkeley. He watched Guy spring to attention the moment the palace door opened only to slump in frustration as he realized his quarry was in the company of the Pope and surrounded by prelates. A smile crept across Will's face as he imagined his cousin chiding him, *God's bones, Will Makepeace, can't you ever just do what I ask you?*

Will realized something else as he sat listening to the mass. Not since the time at Glendalough had he felt so safe . . . or so confident that Caernarfon was safe. As for the former king, his days were full. When he wasn't tending plants in the garden, he was either with the pontiff or Father Manuele – sometimes both – recounting all that had happened since they left Kenilworth. Will was grateful for this time, even as he worried about what the future might hold.

***

Guy, on the other hand, looked forward to the future. It finally dawned on him that Sunday's processions to and from the cathedral were the proof he needed that his quarry was still inside the palace and all he had to do was make sure they stayed there. It meant his days were quite boring, and, with his funds almost gone, he was reduced to a single, quite meager meal each day. But both of those problems would vanish with Montagu's arrival.

Twelve days had passed since he dispatched the message. His reward wouldn't be long in coming. The next morning, as he sat on the ground at his usual post, his back against the trunk of a tree, a man approached him, coming from the direction of the city center. *"Vous vous appelez . . ."* The man paused and studied what he held in his hand. *"Vous vous appelez . . . Bih-kehr-stahf-fuh?"*

Guy got to his feet. *"Oui."*

The man handed Guy a letter then left his hand extended, palm up. Guy had no choice. He rummaged in his pouch and came up with a *denier*. Hardly what the messenger wanted, but it was the best Guy could do. The messenger grumbled something under his breath, then stomped off back down the hill, looking over his shoulder once to shout some sort of invective that Guy didn't understand – and didn't care to.

He looked at the folded page. The wax seal was intact but there was no signet, no symbol of who might have sent it. Had the original been tampered with and replaced? With a growing sense of dread, he broke the seal and unfolded the page.

> *Sir Guy,*
> *You've done your job. Now it's time to come home. The king has other things for you to do.*
> *M*

Guy couldn't believe his eyes. He'd done his job, alright. He had them cornered. And now . . . come home? That was it? Will was to get off scot-free? Everything Guy had done was to be for nought? How could this happen?

He wandered aimlessly about the orchard wondering what he'd done – how he could have so offended God – that this was to be his fate. His spirit broken, his purse almost empty, his honor never to be restored.

At long last, he came to the realization that he had no choice. He had no resources to keep following them. And they had protection from the man nearest to God himself. There was nothing for it but to heed Montagu's instructions and go home.

Glancing up at the windows above the palace entrance, he saw a face looking out. A face he'd never forget. The face of his defeat and disgrace. He looked away and began the agonizing walk down the hill and into despair.

***

Will had taken up the habit of going to the upstairs gallery once each day to check if Guy was still keeping watch. As luck would have it, he witnessed the whole scene. He had no idea what was afoot, but he'd never seen Guy give up and walk away from something he'd made a commitment to. There must have been something in that message.

He told Simon and Caernarfon about it over their evening meal. "Perhaps he's decided we've been given sanctuary," said the former king.

The next day, the Pope summoned them to his private study in late afternoon. "It seems," he said, "that the danger you feared is no more."

"We know that Sir Guy left the *champeaux*, Holy Father," said Caernarfon, "but we've no idea what that means."

"He left Avignon yesterday on the road to Lyon. I have men following him, and one of them just returned to report that he continues on his journey north."

"With respect, Your Holiness," said Simon, "we've observed his behavior for many months, and this may be no more than a ruse to lure us into a trap he plans to spring elsewhere."

The Pope smiled warmly. "You're wise to be suspicious, my son, but I can assure you, you have nothing to fear. My men have instructions to follow him and make sure he sails for England. If he should fail to do so, they have further instructions to detain him and deliver him to the English king with my compliments." He paused to let them take it in. "So you see, my sons, you're finally free to live your lives without constantly looking over your shoulder. I've taken great pleasure in your company these past two weeks. But I believe the reason God brought you here was to put an end to your life as fugitives and restore you to comfort and safety in His grace. I'm grateful He allowed me to be His instrument to achieve that."

"Then we shall be on our way tomorrow, Your Holiness," said Caernarfon. "I've enjoyed our conversations and will miss them very much. Know that my prayers henceforth will include thanksgiving for our deliverance and blessings upon you for your generosity."

"Go with God, my son. And be happy."

Before they retired that night, the threesome discussed their plans. "It seems we could all go home," said Simon, "to that quiet country life we've talked about so often."

"As idyllic as that sounds, Simon," said Caernarfon, "I don't think that would be wise for me. My son needs time to consolidate his reign – time for the turmoil of these past few years to fade into history. No matter what far corner of the kingdom I might settle in, there's always the risk someone might recognize me, and then my son would be forced to deal directly with the situation regardless of how he should better spend his time. So I'll stay on this side of the Channel, visit some places I've long wanted to see, and eventually find one where I can live out my life."

"Then, Will," said Simon, "it looks like it'll be just the two of us returning."

Will had thought of little else since their meeting with the pontiff that afternoon. "There's nothing for me there now, Simon. Except maybe Guy looking to punish me as a way to redeem himself. If he should take it into his head to try to charge me with Lord Caernarfon's escape, there's no way that will end well for me. So I'll stay here as his companion, if you'll have me sir."

"Are you sure, young Will? I can't tell you what kind of life you might have."

"It will be a life, sir, and not the hangman's noose. Besides, I think I may finally be reaching the point where I can be a worthy chess opponent for you."

Simon's smile was tinged with sadness as he reached into his satchel and retrieved a purse still heavy with coins. "I rather suspected that's what you both might say. So I've saved out enough for my journey home." He handed the pouch to Caernarfon. "The rest is yours."

"We can't take your money, Simon. We'll manage well enough, I'm sure. And I still have the rings. We could no doubt sell them for their true value in Paris if we need to."

"Keep your rings, sir. Some day you may be glad you did. This was Edmund's money. Think of it as his gift to you. I have no doubt whatsoever that's what he would have wanted."

When they parted ways the following day, Simon said, "Write to me, Will. And let me know where you are. I want to know where to find you if you ever need my help."

"How will I know where to send the letters?"

"Send them to Countess Margaret. I made a promise to Edmund that, once this was all over, she would always know where to find me."

***

When he finally set foot on English soil, Guy had made up his mind. The king might have something for him to do, some way for him to regain his honor. But there was one thing he had to do first.

CHAPTER THIRTY-TWO

January 1338

"Leave us," said Edward, dismissing the remaining courtiers after concluding the morning's business. "All but you, Salisbury. A word if you please."

"As you wish, Sire."

When the two of them were finally alone in the chamber and the doors firmly closed, Edward reached into his super-tunic and retrieved a folded page, handing it to the earl. "Tell me what you make of this, William." Some eight months earlier, Edward had created Montagu Earl of Salisbury, a fitting promotion for the man who remained the king's closest confidant.

"Interesting," said William when he'd finished the missive and returned it to his friend. "What do we know of this Manuele Fieschi?"

"I met him briefly once. He was, at the time, what he still claims – a papal notary."

"So you believe this is genuine?"

"We've long suspected that my father was living abroad somewhere."

"Why would he be calling himself William le Galeys?"

"Well, if he didn't want to draw attention to himself, he most certainly wouldn't call himself Edward of Caernarfon."

Montagu stroked his chin. How to approach this? He knew full well that Caernarfon had been in Avignon using the title Le Galeys, but he had never told Edward. Bickerstaffe's report had been confirmed by Simon

Forster, who was now one of Montagu's trusted men. Montagu had never forgotten the man who took such great risk to help him back in 1327. So when the dowager Countess of Kent had mentioned that her late husband's lifetime companion was in need of a position, Montagu didn't hesitate. But now he had to guide Edward without revealing what he'd held back all these years. "You make a good point, Edward," he replied.

"I've had the letter for two days. Why would Fieschi send it if he wasn't sure this man is my father? He makes no request of me, so it seems he's not trying to procure favors."

"So it would seem, on the surface at least. And if there's no further correspondence with some specific request, I think that's a safe assumption."

"Do you think it would be possible, William, to find this man? For me to meet with him?"

"Such a meeting shouldn't happen here. It would stir up too many old emotions and attachments that best remain buried. But perhaps if you were abroad . . ."

"My thoughts as well. I wonder if you might undertake a plan for such a journey this year. Since Fieschi never corresponded in all this time, even though he's obviously been aware of this Le Galeys's whereabouts, my gut says there's a reason for his choice to do so now."

"It would be my pleasure, Edward. What say you to a visit to the Low Countries? Perhaps even some visits with the queen's relatives?"

"It could be quite a useful opportunity to strengthen our alliances."

"There are also those rumors about the Holy Roman Emperor softening his stance toward you – possibly even conferring some imperial honor."

"Well, that remains to be seen."

"Perhaps Fieschi's gotten wind of something and wants you to know what may be possible."

In February, Parliament agreed to support the visit, and Edward ordered the fleet be ready to leave in May. The queen would accompany him, and the Earl of Salisbury and some of his men would be among the entourage. But as events unfolded, they wouldn't actually leave England until July.

***

June 1338

> *In the name of the Lord, Amen. My dear friend. I have taken steps on your behalf which now appear as if they will bear fruit in the coming months. But it is impossible to know at this juncture precisely when the opportunity will present itself. I therefore beseech you most urgently to make your way to Cologne with some haste, there to await further communication. It is my sincere belief that if you are in the right location at the right time, one of your heart's most fervent desires may be fulfilled.*
>
> *In testimony of which I have caused my seal to be affixed for your consideration. Manuele de Fieschi, notary to the lord pope.*

Caernarfon read the letter aloud to Will. "Do you think, my friend, that such is possible?"

"That *what* is possible?"

"That my wish will be fulfilled."

"What wish?" Will was completely puzzled.

"Ah, that's right. You weren't present when I spoke of it to Father Manuele. I told him I never ceased to pray that I might see my son just one more time before leaving this earth."

"I think, sir, that as devoted as you are to God, it's entirely possible he might answer your prayers."

"Then it seems we should make preparations to go to Cologne straightaway. Are you ready for another adventure? Since it's summer, the Septimer pass will be open so we can use the trade route to shorten the journey."

Will chuckled. "Well, I certainly won't let you go alone. And it might be nice to have something besides monastery food for a change."

Caernarfon laughed out loud. "And what makes you think, young Will, that the food in taverns and inns will be any better?"

"Well, at least maybe there'll be more of it."

***

They arrived in Cologne in early July and took lodgings at an inn where they were able to secure a separate room for just the two of them. Having passed much of the last seven years in religious houses of one sort or another, they still had enough money from what Simon had left them to pay for several weeks of room, board, and stabling for their horses.

Will wrote to Simon before they left Cecima, telling him where they were headed next. "Is that really needed any longer?" Caernarfon had asked.

"Call it habit, sir. In truth, superstition, more like. I've never once failed to inform him where we were going. It seems like breaking that pattern now might break whatever it is that's been protecting us all this time."

"Have you considered, young Will, that it might be God looking out for us?"

"Most certainly. But does it hurt to have both God and Simon on the job?"

They had no idea what to expect or when . . . or even if, for that matter. July passed with no further communication from Fieschi. Will and Caernarfon spent their time walking around the city and, Caernarfon being Caernarfon, visiting the twelve large churches inside the city walls. Will had never in his life spent so much time in the presence of piety as he had in these past seven years. In the monasteries, he could go his own way and leave Caernarfon to pursue his religious devotions on his own. Here, in an unfamiliar city, he dare not let the man out of his sight, so not a day passed that he wasn't inside some church or another.

Fortunately, his companion was just as intrigued by the ongoing construction on the cathedral as by the rituals that happened inside, and that suited Will just fine. Unless the weather was foul – in which case, construction stopped anyway – they spent a part of every day watching the masons at work, talking with the stone carvers, observing the mixing of the mortar . . . Will felt as if he were back at his father's side, watching these master craftsmen turn piles of stone into sturdy walls that would last for hundreds of years. Caernarfon, for his part, was intrigued by Will's stories of the dangerous work constructing the great spire at Salisbury Cathedral. "God was truly with your father and all those men who raised that spire. The way it soars toward the heavens is unlike any other sight I've seen."

August came and went, and still there was no news. Will began to wonder if Fieschi's plan – whatever it may have been – had disintegrated, and they were wasting funds they might need later. But Caernarfon was reluctant to give up hope. "Let's wait another week. If there's been nothing by then, perhaps we should return home or find a nearby monastery." Unwilling to quash the only real hope his companion had had in all these years, Will agreed.

Three days later, as they were leaving the cathedral after their weekly visit to the Shrine of the Three Kings, Will heard his name being called from across the square. Instantly alert, he put his hand on the hilt of his sword and told Caernarfon, "Stay behind me," as he scanned the faces going about their daily business. *Blessed Mary, please don't tell me Guy has found us again after all this time.*

He took a few tentative steps forward, ready to draw his sword at the first sign of danger. And then he heard the voice again, this time from his left. "Will. Will Makepeace." He'd pivoted left and had his sword halfway out of its scabbard when he heard, "Will. Peace. It's me . . . Simon." Only when he finally recognized Simon Forster hurrying toward them did he relax and re-sheath his weapon.

When Simon released him from the embrace of a long-lost brother, Will couldn't restrain himself. "What in the name of God were you trying to do, man? Frighten me out of my wits?"

"Calm yourself, Will. I've been looking for you two since I arrived yesterday. It's a big city and having found you, I wasn't about to let you out of my sight."

Caernarfon's amusement was evident on his face. "All the time we spent together, Will, and he doesn't know to seek me first in a place of God."

"Do you have any idea, Sir Edward, how many churches there are in this city?" Simon asked.

Will roared with laughter. "Of course he does. We visit a different one every day."

Simon clapped Will on the shoulder. "Then you should be glad I'm here. I've come to take you away from all that. Both of you. How soon can you be ready to leave? We need to get to Koblenz as soon as possible. I'll fill you in on the way."

An hour later, they were riding south. "Everything changed at the last minute," Simon explained. King Edward is to be made a vicar of the Holy Roman Empire. That was to happen in Cologne, but then Emperor Ludwig insisted on Koblenz, putting everything in disarray. And as the queen is with child, the distance we can travel each day is limited.

"The investiture is to be tomorrow. We won't be in time for the ceremony, but if we can get as far as Remagen today, we should arrive soon after. The king is quite interested to meet the man known as William le Galeys, having received, not so long ago, information describing a rather remarkable journey of that individual during the past decade."

"If we're to make Remagen," said Caernarfon, "then it seems to me we should ask these beasts to cover the ground more quickly." He urged his mount to the trot and the others followed suit.

A couple of hours later, when they let the horses walk for a time to rest, Simon asked, "So, Sir Edward, where did that name William le Galeys come from?"

Caernarfon chuckled. "You remember, I'm sure, on our travel to Avignon, that men had trouble pronouncing my name, so they referred to us as Simon, Guillaume, et le Galeys."

"I do indeed."

"After you left, it was just Guillaume et le Galeys. But the 'et' went missing somewhere along the way. Will and I decided that was just as well – no need to draw attention to ourselves."

"And yet, it seems that's happened anyway," Simon chuckled. They walked on a bit before Simon spoke again. "Speaking of that time, my friends, there's something I must ask of you. There's no need to mention to anyone the part I played in your adventures. I serve the Earl of Salisbury now, but the king is quite aware I was his uncle's lifelong companion. So I go to great lengths to avoid anything that might remind the king that he was powerless to prevent Edmund's execution. He's righted the wrongs as best he can, but even a king can't restore a man to life, and that still causes him pain."

"I think, young Simon," said Caernarfon, "that there will be ample topics of conversation without wandering into such unhappy territory."

***

Simon showed his friends into a small but elaborate antechamber in the Prince Elector's castle. "You won't have to wait long," he assured them. "I need to let the Earl know we've arrived."

When the door next opened, Simon was accompanied by a richly dressed man of average height with hair trimmed short above his ears. Will was completely taken aback and couldn't suppress a gasp followed by "You!"

Caernarfon's face lit up in recognition. "William Montagu. I can't tell you how pleased I am to see you're still my son's dearest friend." Then, registering Will's reaction, he added, "Do you two know each other?"

By now, Will had his wits about him. "I saw him once outside a church. It was a long time ago and I didn't know who he was. It was just a huge surprise seeing the same man in these surroundings."

That seemed to satisfy Caernarfon, who turned his attention back to the earl. "Now tell me. You *are* still Edward's dearest friend, are you not?"

Montagu chuckled. "I fear that title 'dearest friend' has been taken over by the queen. But she's a lovely person who's actually turning out to be a rather astute advisor. I'm quite content to know he still relies on me above all others to protect his interests – and the only one besides the queen with whom he can relax and truly be himself. And, of course, he gave me this rather grand title and an income that eases my way in the world."

An awkward silence fell over the room, broken at last by the earl. "I'm afraid, Lord Caernarfon, that the friendship you value so much imposes on me a peculiar duty. That you recognized me immediately without any introduction is sufficient proof to me that you're indeed Edward's father. That, and the fact that I recognized you as well. But if Edward is to receive you, he must be in absolutely no doubt of your identity. Is there anything you can offer – a private incident from his childhood, a keepsake you may have given him – anything that would be incontrovertible proof?"

Caernarfon smiled and reached into his tunic, withdrawing the little leather pouch that never left his possession. "Show him these." He handed the pouch to Montagu. "They were given to my father by Philip IV on the occasion of Father's marriage to Phillip's sister and my betrothal to his daughter. For some reason, none of my captors ever thought to take them from me."

Montagu took the pouch, rose from his chair, and made for the door. "You might also ask him," Caernarfon called after the earl, "how long he was able to keep eavesdropping from the window ledge before Isabella got wind of what he was up to."

It was mere moments before Montagu returned. "Lord Edward, if you'd be so kind as to come with me. You too, Simon, there's something I need you to arrange." Turning to Will, he added, "I apologize for leaving you here alone for now, but please . . . pour yourself a glass of wine." He gestured to a pitcher and glasses on a sideboard. "When it's time, one of us will return for you."

Though Will understood Caernarfon's reunion with his son was a private matter, he had to admit he was just a little disappointed not to be able to witness it. He helped himself to the offered wine and settled down to wait.

Barely a quarter of an hour later, the door opened again and Montagu returned alone. He crossed the room, poured his own glass of wine, and returned to sit beside Will. "I'm grateful for your discretion, Will Makepeace."

"I should apologize, my lord. The surprise just overtook me before I could think."

Montagu chuckled. "We did a good thing, Will. Despite his youth at the time, Edward was increasingly aware of the danger Mortimer posed, not just to the former king but to the entire kingdom. Edward had little choice but to submit to Isabella's wishes in the whole business of burying the body claimed to be his father's. She still refuses to speak to anyone about what really happened in those confused times.

"In any event, there were too many things that didn't ring true in what and when Edward and Isabella were being told about his father's supposed death. That gave me hope that you'd been able to manage an escape. And while reports of Caernarfon's survival gave Edward hope, they simply stoked my sense of urgency to find you before Mortimer did. We thought Bickerstaffe was the key, since he was there on the night in question. He'd gone to ground, and no one – not his family nor any of the men who'd served him at Berkeley – had any idea where he might be. It took ages to locate him, but when we finally found him in the Bankside Stews, he didn't hesitate to accept the job I offered. What I didn't understand was his fixation on bringing you to heel – which meant, of course, that you felt the need to always stay one step ahead of him and to keep Lord Caernarfon out of his clutches.

"That was my miscalculation. I assumed he'd find you quickly so took extraordinary steps to keep my association with him secret. After all, Mortimer still had men we didn't know in places we didn't know about. Which meant that while Bickerstaffe was taking months to catch up to you, I had no reliable way to recall him. When he finally surfaced with our agreed signal, I brought him home straightaway. You have my most sincere apology, Makepeace, for those months of anxiety and distress."

"It's behind us now, sir, and it's not for a lord such as yourself to apologize to an ordinary man like me."

"On the contrary. If those of us with some measure of power can't own our mistakes and see things right, then we're no better than a Mortimer or the Despensers or others of their ilk. I owe you an enormous debt of gratitude, Will, and if there is ever anything you need – anything at all – you've only to ask." He raised his glass. "To the men we've both protected and their long-overdue reunion." Will raised his glass and they drank the toast.

"Lord Caernarfon will have a quiet supper with his family this evening," Montagu continued. "But I'd be truly honored if you would dine with

Simon and me. He's told me a bit about your friendship as youngsters in London. I suspect though, there are tales he hasn't told of the mischief that two boys got up to. Maybe you can loosen his tongue."

"That sounds nice, my lord."

"How about we dispense with the formalities for the evening? My name is William as well."

"I'm not sure I could do that, sir."

Montagu chuckled. "Then maybe I'll have to get Simon to loosen *your* tongue." They rose and started for the door. "One final thing, Will. The king wants to meet with you privately in the morning. I suspect he may want to do that early since he has other engagements during the day. So be ready by the second hour after sunrise. His manservant will fetch you when the time comes."

***

Will stood uneasily just inside the door. The manservant had announced, "Mister William Makepeace, Your Grace," before making a quick exit and closing the door behind him. The tall man who'd been staring into the empty hearth, one hand on the mantle, turned at the sound. Will could see the resemblance to his father in the younger man's face and bearing.

"Please, Makepeace," said Edward, "come and join me."

Unsure whether to bow now and then approach or wait until he was closer, Will bowed once, approached, and then bowed again for good measure. It was ever so important not to get this wrong. "Thank you, Your Grace."

Edward smiled – a kind smile, to Will's way of thinking – and gestured to a chair directly across from the one he was lowering himself into. "Please be seated."

"I . . . I never expected this, Your Grace. It's an honor you should want to speak with me. Thank you."

"It's for me to thank *you*, Makepeace. My father and I stayed up almost until the cock's crow last night talking about all that's transpired in the last ten years. Your care for his welfare has been beyond even what a son owes to the father, and yet you gave it freely."

"I came to like your father, sir, when we were at Berkeley Castle. He taught me chess and how to think like a commander in the field."

Edward chuckled. "Indeed. He told me you quickly became quite good at it and that you'd saved each other's hides on more than one occasion. I understand you also did a bit of gardening together."

It was Will's turn to chuckle. "That was a bit of a surprise, sir. I never thought, you see, of a king wanting to be digging in the dirt."

"My mother despaired of his love of digging ditches, but I always thought he seemed happier afterward." The king paused for a moment. "I wish we had longer to talk, Makepeace. But I have obligations to the emperor today – one of the duties of a new vicar of the empire. My father has decided not to return to England with us. He's convinced that, even living quietly in the country, he would be a distraction – an impediment, as he called it, to my reign. He wants to return to the monastery in Melazzo. As much as it saddens me, I know he's right, so I'll let him go even if it means I may never see him again.

"As for you, Makepeace, I offer you the chance to return home as part of my entourage. And if you so desire, I'll find you a respected position in the household of one of our noble families. I owe you no less."

Will was speechless. This was far beyond anything he could have imagined. A gentleman in a noble family's train. It would free him forever from whatever vengeance Guy still hoped to extract. And it would make his late mother proud to see from heaven that he'd found his way in the world at last. But then he thought of Caernarfon making his way back to Italy alone and knew he couldn't let that happen.

"I . . . I'm overwhelmed by your generosity, Your Grace. But I still have a duty. I'll see your father back to the monastery. He deserves no less."

Edward didn't speak for a long moment. "I was rather hoping you might say that, Makepeace. It puts my mind at ease. But when you find yourself back in England, my offer still stands." He reached into his tunic and retrieved a paper with his seal affixed. "Present this to any of my officials and request an audience. I promise to receive you and to see that you're well settled."

Will took the paper. "I . . . I don't know what to say, Your Grace."

"I'm afraid what we have to say is farewell. There'll be a knock on that door at any moment requesting my presence in the Emperor's reception hall." Edward rose and Will jumped quickly to his feet. "God go with you, Will Makepeace. I hope we meet again."

CHAPTER THIRTY-THREE

January 1339

It had been four months since the meeting in Koblenz. Concerned that an early snowfall might catch them out in the Alpine passes, they had little choice but to return to Italy through France. They followed the Moselle as far as Nancy, where they left that river's valley and headed southwest to Dijon. As they were in no hurry, the shorter days of autumn posed no problem – they simply stopped in whatever village or town they encountered once the sun began lowering in the western sky. Nor did they concern themselves with the days when pouring rain kept them in place for a day or two at a time. King Edward had been more than generous with his gifts of money, clothing, fine boots, and fur-lined cloaks, so they could stay at the finest inns and enjoy the best food without worrying about depleting their funds.

In Dijon, they boarded a river boat, disembarking in Avignon. But they didn't linger. Pope John was dead, and Pope Benedict was busy demolishing John's grand, luxurious palace and replacing it with something that looked more like a fortress. When they saw it, Caernarfon was overwhelmed.

"Are you alright, sir?" Will placed a hand on his companion's shoulder.

"There's probably nothing sadder, young Will, than seeing a man's dream demolished stone by stone." He turned and started down the hill, leaving Will to follow.

From Avignon, they made their way to Aix-en-Provence and Nice, then along the coast to Savona, before finally turning north to Melazzo and the hermitage where they'd once resided for more than two years.

Caernarfon reined in outside the gate to the monastery and sat quietly on his horse, his gaze fixed on the gate. At long last, he broke the silence. "So this is where I shall spend the rest of my days."

It reminded Will of their arrival at Berkeley Castle almost twelve years ago. Except this time, Caernarfon was a free man and had chosen this for himself.

Turning in his saddle, Caernarfon asked, "And where will you go, Will? What will you do with your life?"

"I'll stay with you, sir, if you'll have me. After all, we've come this far together."

The gentle smile that crept across Caernarfon's face was full of kindness – fatherly, even. "I think not, young Will." Will's face fell. "God could not have given me a finer companion and protector, but there's more for you to do. The game is finished and we have won. Not by capturing the king, it's true, but by capturing something even more valuable. Redemption from the trials foisted upon us. That and the love of my son. I'm content, Will. And that's all I've ever truly wanted.

"So you must go home and find your own contentment. Reconcile with your cousin if you can. Find a woman to love, as I have always and still do love Isabella." He reached into his cloak and withdrew the small leather pouch that contained the rings he'd shown Will right after their escape from Berkeley castle – the rings that had proven his identity to his son in Koblenz. "Take this, Will. I have no more need of them."

"Sir, I couldn't possibly . . ."

"I want you to have them. It would please me greatly to know you'll never have to fall into destitution." Will reluctantly held out his hand and Caernarfon pressed the pouch into it. By then, a monk had arrived and quietly opened the gate. "Be happy, Will. And remember me from time to time."

Will watched in silence, his heart overflowing, as Caernarfon guided his horse inside and the gate closed behind him.

CHAPTER THIRTY-FOUR

February 1339

Will was still in a sentimental frame of mind when the ship docked in Dover. The image of the abbey gate closing behind Caernarfon was emblazoned on his mind and showed no signs of fading. On the journey back through France, he'd contemplated remaining there, out of Guy's reach. But it wasn't practical. To begin with, he couldn't speak French, so how would he find work and make his way in the world. And at the end of the day, he was an Englishman at heart. With no one to keep him in France, the call of home was irresistible.

There was one more thing. Something Will felt honor-bound to do. Something that could only be done in England. So he'd sailed from Calais into a future that seemed even more unsettled than the past he was leaving behind.

He took his time on the journey to Westminster. The equinox was still almost two months away, so the days were still short and the nights were still cold once the sun went down. He was grateful for his fur-lined cloak during the day – even more so at night when it was far warmer than the thin blankets on the beds at the inns. Now and then, he'd catch himself looking over his shoulder for a sighting of Guy. In truth, he knew Guy couldn't possibly have discovered yet that he was back home, but the visceral memory of almost being caught outside Hastings and the race to set sail from Sandwich were the last associations he had with English soil. *Put it out of your mind*, he told himself. *You're not a fugitive now.* The admonishment almost worked. Almost.

Will had never been to London before. The sheer size of the city and all the hamlets outside its walls dwarfed even Paris, and the constant activity of so many people going about their business and the traffic in the streets and on the river were almost overwhelming. He had to ask directions several times before finding his way to Westminster. By the time he arrived, it was midafternoon, so he set about finding a good inn that also offered stabling for his horse. The prices astonished him. A whole shilling a day for a room, his meals, and his horse. "Would include your servant if you had one," the landlord told him.

"But as I don't have one, maybe you could reduce the price to ten pennies," Will tried to bargain, but the landlord was implacable.

"You want a nice room this close to the palace, a shilling's the price. There be plenty of other folk willing to pay if you're not." Which left Will with little choice. A nice room close to the palace was precisely what he wanted.

He took great care with his clothing and appearance as he dressed the next morning. This would be a momentous day if things went as he hoped they would. When the church bells started tolling midmorning, he made his way to the south entrance of the palace hoping his external appearance belied the frantic wing-flapping of the horde of butterflies resident in his stomach.

Two sentries stepped out of the warmth of an impressive gatehouse to stop him passing. "State your business," one ordered.

The butterflies kept flapping, but Will had practiced what he would say next. "William Makepeace, here at the invitation of the king."

The second sentry put a hand over his mouth, but not before Will caught a glimpse of the smirk on his face. The butterflies remained airborne, reminding Will of the first time he'd been invited into Caernarfon's chamber at Berkeley Castle. And that memory gave him the courage to quiet the fluttering. Things had gone well then; why shouldn't they go well now? The butterflies settled a bit, but Will knew from experience they were just biding their time.

"We don't have instructions to expect you today . . . what did you say your name was?" the first sentry spoke again.

"Makepeace. William Makepeace. And my invitation was not for this day specifically but for the next time I found myself near the court."

"And you expect us to believe you." Now, even the first sentry wore an expression of amused disbelief.

Will reached into his tunic and retrieved the precious letter. He'd hoped to be inside the palace, in the presence of some official of the court, before he had to use it, but it seemed that was not to be. "I expect you to believe me because I have the invitation here in my hand." Will held out the letter so the sentries could see the king's privy seal.

"And who'd you take *that* off of?" asked the other sentry, grinning.

"Don't get ahead of things, James," said the first one. "Look at him. Does he look like a common thief?" Then, turning back to Will, he added, "Let me have that." He reached out for the letter. "I'll go see if it's real."

Will knew the man's type. Officious, full of himself, drunk with what he thought of as his power to protect the king. Will could guess how things would likely play out. The sentry would open the letter as soon as he was out of sight. He'd find someone to show it to, of course, but he'd claim it was already open when the man at the gate gave it to him, so it was almost certainly stolen. And the official would keep the letter and order the sentry to send its bearer packing. Will stowed the letter back in his tunic. "Don't you get ahead of things either, my good man. Go find someone in authority and bring them back here. Tell them I have an important message for the king."

The sentry stared at Will, clearly surprised anyone outside the gate would dare to give him orders. Will returned his gaze and held it. Neither of them flinched. James watched, fascinated. Will knew he had the upper hand if he waited the sentry out.

Eventually, James couldn't contain himself. "Oh, for God's sake, Gil, just go fetch somebody. If you don't, I will."

That broke Gil's concentration, and he turned on his compatriot. "You don't give me orders, James. I'll go when I'm damn good and ready. *If* I'm damn good and ready." Then he turned back to Will, who was still staring.

But this time, Will said, "Well, *one* of you should go. *I'm* not going anywhere unless you do."

James turned and took a few steps toward the palace. "Oh, for God's sake, James." Gil sounded thoroughly exasperated. "You wouldn't know who to find or where to find them. Get back here and make sure this . . . this . . . what did you say your name was?"

"Makepeace."

"Get back here and make sure this Makepeace fellow keeps his promise not to go anywhere."

As James returned to the gate, Gil marched off in a huff. "Is he always so stubborn?" Will asked. James just grinned.

When Gil returned what must have been a full half hour later, he was accompanied by a richly dressed man wearing a chain of office draped over his shoulders and a velvet hat decorated with pheasant feathers. "There he is," Gil announced as they approached. "That Makepeace fellow I told you about."

"Very well," said the official. "Let him pass. I'll take responsibility for him."

Gil muttered something under his breath.

"You have something to say, Gil?" asked the official.

Motioning for James to step aside, Gil replied, "No, my lord. Not at all, my lord," as he bowed and took half a dozen steps backward to stand beside James.

"Come with me." The official gestured for Will to join him.

They walked in silence to the entrance door of the palace, which was opened as they approached by the guards stationed there. Still without speaking, the official led Will through a series of corridors until they reached a rather grand staircase where they stopped at the bottom. "Now," said the official, "Mr. Makepeace, I've been given to believe you have a letter from the king."

Will was still cautious. He knew he'd have to relinquish the letter at some point, but was disinclined to do so while the butterflies were still making their presence known. He withdrew the letter from his tunic and showed the seal to the man standing opposite him.

"That is indeed King Edward's privy seal." The official made no attempt to take the document from Will's hand. "May I ask where you got this letter?"

"Koblenz, my lord."

"And what was the occasion?"

"The official occasion? It was when our lord king was made a vicar of the Holy Roman Empire."

"And was there an unofficial occasion?"

The butterflies rose as Will realized he might have just made an irrevocable mistake. It might be that no one outside of those present on the occasion had any idea that father and son had met. He could think of only one way out of his predicament, so he extended the letter toward his inquisitor. "Perhaps, my lord, you should read this."

The official took the proffered missive, broke the seal, and read quickly. When he looked up from the page, there was a broad smile on his face. "It seems you are indeed the William Makepeace I was told to expect. I am Armand de la Roche, chamberlain to His Grace King Edward. Welcome to Westminster, Mr. Makepeace."

Will could finally breathe easily. He doffed his hat and offered a small bow. "My Lord Chamberlain."

"This staircase," de la Roche continued as he began to ascend, "leads to the royal apartments and reception rooms. His Grace is at present conferring with his Privy Council." Suddenly realizing that Will was not following, the chamberlain paused and turned. "Come. We shall settle you in a comfortable sitting room until His Grace is available to receive you."

Westminster Palace was far more luxurious than Berkeley or Kenilworth or even the Prince Elector's castle in Koblenz. The only place Will had seen such grandeur was at the papal residence in Avignon. As he followed the chamberlain, he had to remind himself not to gape.

In the midst of all the grandeur, the room where he sat waiting for King Edward was rather cozy – if one could call a room with an elaborately carved stone mantle, rich tapestries on the walls, an elegant sideboard, and soft cushions on all the chairs cozy. At what Will deemed to be approximately midday, a servant arrived with food and a pitcher of wine that he left on the sideboard. "With my lord chamberlain's compliments, sir," the servant said, offering Will a nod of the head as he exited the room.

Will surveyed the food. Pandemaine, roasted fowl of some sort, neeps, and lentils. Cheese and apples. Honeycakes. A glass pitcher filled with a wine almost golden in color that Will had learned came from Gascony. Not for the first time, Will wondered how a man from his humble roots could ever come to be among such richness.

Tempted to doze off after his rich meal, Will forced himself to stand and walk circuits of the room. It would never do for the king to find him napping. When he deemed himself sufficiently alert once again, he returned to his chair. The wait might have seemed interminable to some men, but Will was simply grateful that he was here and would, eventually, be received by the king.

When the door finally opened again, the chamberlain entered first then stepped aside for King Edward. "Mister William Makepeace, Your Grace," de la Roche announced. Will jumped to his feet, jerked off his hat, and bowed deeply.

"Indeed it is, Armand." Edward advanced toward Will with a broad smile on his face. "Please, Will, do be seated once again." Will put his hat back on and returned to his chair, taking care to note that the king was seated before his own buttocks came to rest. The chamberlain made his way to the sideboard and returned with two glasses of wine. Edward took a sip from his own glass. "What do you think of my Gascon wine, Will?"

"It's most pleasant, Sire." Now that he was finally in the king's presence, Will felt rather tongue-tied.

Edward continued with the pleasantries. "And how was your journey? Travel in winter can often be rather daunting."

"Not so distressing, Sire. Cold to be sure, but I was fortunate not to meet up with a winter storm."

"Travel any time of year is daunting when a man must take the entire court with him," Edward chuckled. "Not that I'm complaining, mind you. I'm fortunate to have Armand here to organize such things." He took another sip of his wine.

Will was growing anxious. How to begin the conversation he wanted – needed – to have? De la Roche remained at the sideboard, ostensibly to see to his master's needs but, Will thought, more likely as protection in case the king's guest should show any sign of being a threat. But his earlier realization that the chamberlain might not be privy to the meeting in Koblenz made things awkward.

Edward solved the problem for him. "I trust you have no other obligations and can join my family for our evening meal, Makepeace."

"It would be an honor, Sire."

The king turned to his chamberlain. "Perhaps you can see to those arrangements, Armand. And a room for our guest for tonight. There's no need for him to brave the cold night to return to his lodgings after we dine."

"As you wish, Your Grace." De la Roche bowed and left the room.

When his footsteps could no longer be heard in the corridor, the king quickly changed the subject. "The fact that you're here, Will, tells me my father is safe in his new home. How did he fare when you last saw him?"

"I think, Sire, he was content. Sad, perhaps, to know he'd seen you for the last time, but also proud, I think, of the man you've become." Will hesitated briefly but knew this was his chance. "Which brings me, Sire, to the reason I'm here." From a pocket in his tunic he retrieved a small leather pouch and held it out to the king. "These belong to you, sir, and I've come to return them. Your father entrusted them to me on the day he entered the monastery and sent me home."

Edward took the pouch, opened it, and poured the contents into his palm. "King Philip's rings." He studied the objects in his hand for a long moment. "Tell me, Will, what did my father say when he gave these to you?"

"He said he wanted me to have them so he would know I'd never fall into destitution. But, sir, they belong to your family, and it's only right that I return them to you."

"If only all men were so honest and honorable." He gazed at the rings one more time then put them back in the pouch and extended it to Will. "They might have been mine once, but now they belong to you. Kings – even deposed kings – have the rare privilege – responsibility, even – of rewarding those who serve them well. This was the only way my father had to thank you for what you gave up to protect his life. They are rightfully yours."

Will was at a loss. Touched, of course, but nothing in his life had prepared him to know what was the right thing to do. Would it be dishonorable – a sign of greed – to accept the gift? Or would it be rude to refuse his king's generosity?

Sensing Will's discomfort, Edward leaned over, took Will's hand, and pressed the pouch into it, much as his father had done. "Honor my father by accepting his gift, Will."

As Will wrapped his hand around the pouch and returned it to the safety of his tunic, Edward leaned back in his own chair and asked, "And where will you go now? How will you make your way in the world?"

"I haven't really worked that out, Sire, other than that I need to find work and get on with my life."

"Then perhaps I can help. This evening I intend to make you a knight. But I wanted you to know in advance so there'd be no awkwardness at the time."

"I'm sorry, Sire, I really don't deserve that. It's true I was a man-at-arms, but not the kind who fights in great battles or tilts in the lists. I don't have that kind of courage and don't deserve to be in the company of those who do."

The king smiled. "You have a different kind of courage, Will. The courage to do what's right when many another man would choose to avoid the risk to life and limb such a decision might entail."

"But, Sire, all the ceremony and all the attention . . . I don't think I'm cut out for that."

"In truth, Will, that suits me just fine. There's no reason to proclaim your feats to the world when that would just open old rivalries, old jealousies, old wounds better left healed. So it will be a private ceremony with only my family and the Countess of Salisbury as witnesses."

"The Countess of Salisbury, Your Grace?"

"This was something the Earl and I planned right after you left us in Koblenz. But as he's had to stay behind to keep our allies loyal while I make good on my promises to them, the Countess will take his place."

If he'd been tongue-tied earlier, Will was now at a complete loss for words. Which seemed to please the king enormously because he sported a broad grin as he rose from his seat. "Come with me, Will. My beautiful Philippa is eager to meet you."

***

At the end of the meal, the king called for his sword. Will knelt before him and pledged loyalty to Edward as his liege lord. Touching the sword to each of Will's shoulders in turn, Edward said, "Rise, Sir William Makepeace. I accept your pledge of loyalty and in return grant you the manor at Sandy, its market town and enterprises and incomes for the duration of your life. The manor has been vacant for nigh on two years now, so the income has reverted to the Crown." He held out his hand and the chamberlain rushed forward with a leather pouch. "You'll need something to start your new life," Edward handed Will the pouch, "so what say you to half of what the manor produced while it was vacant?"

Will was dumbstruck. "I . . . Your Grace . . . it's . . ."

Edward laughed aloud, breaking the solemn mood in the room. "A simple yes will do, Sir William. Do we have a bargain?"

"Yes, Sire. Indeed we do, Sire. Thank you, Your Grace."

"Good. And now to celebrate." He paused while the chamberlain poured an unfamiliar-to-Will brown liquid into small glasses. "Another specialty from our lands in Gascony – Armagnac. I propose we toast the future." Edward held up his glass and the others followed suit. "The future!"

When the royal family departed the room, Will was left alone with the Countess of Salisbury and his utter uncertainty about what he should say or do. *How's a knight supposed to act?* Before he could make up his mind, she surprised him by asking, "A word, Will, before you retire to your room? May I call you Will?"

"Of course, my lady. Whatever you wish."

She came to sit beside him. "There are some things you should know before you journey north to take up your new holdings. Things my own dear William wanted to tell you himself. But when he learned he'd be staying in the Low Countries for a time, he charged me with making sure you were fully informed in the event he wasn't back to do so himself."

"Of course, my lady." Will didn't know what else to say.

"They mostly concern Sir Guy Bickerstaffe."

Will fought to keep a grimace from his face. *Not this, not now. Not on a night I finally feel some freedom from his shadow.*

"What he did when he returned from France struck us all as passing strange," the countess continued. "My husband had arranged a new commission for Sir Guy and hinted at that in the message recalling him from Avignon. And yet Sir Guy never showed up to accept it. We learned later that he'd taken a girl from one of the Bankside bath houses, married her, and taken her north as his wife. Not at all what one would expect from a man of his rank.

"We also learned he had a brother who ran a mill at Blunham and a not-inconsequential sum of money left in his brother's care when he took the commission to guard Lord Caernarfon. He bought a house in Sandy and settled there with his wife. From time to time he would show up at a tournament and was still skilled enough to win some prizes. But he went out of his way to snub my William, who quickly gave up on the notion of supporting him in any way.

"Then, almost two years ago – it was the autumn of 1337 if memory serves – Edward grew increasingly concerned about French designs on the Duchy of Aquitaine and ordered a cadre of experienced knights to Gascony to protect our interests there. Sir Guy was one of those men. Several months later, Guy was one of half a dozen men riding as guards for a couple of wagons transporting weapons from Bordeaux to Aiguillon when they were ambushed by French renegades. He was killed protecting the wagons.

"My William wanted you to know, Will, that there's no longer anything for you to fear from that quarter. Sir Guy's widow still lives in Sandy, but neither of us has any idea what she's like or if Guy poisoned her mind against you. That's something you'll have to find out for yourself."

Will sat silent, overwhelmed by all he'd just learned – and by the Earl of Salisbury's concern that he should know these things. When he finally found his voice, he said, "Thank you, my lady. If your husband told you all this, then you must also suspect how heavily the prospect of encountering Guy has weighed on my thoughts about reclaiming my life in England."

"I can but imagine, Will. But there's one thing I know for certain. If you take as much care for the people of Sandy as you did for a king no one wanted, then they will be very fortunate indeed."

CHAPTER THIRTY-FIVE

Will stood outside the door of a quite respectable house in Sandy, girding his courage. *Is this really a good idea? God knows how she's going to receive me.*

The morning after he'd been given a new life, he'd retrieved his horse and his few belongings and started the journey north. There was nothing to keep him in London. Besides which, if he stayed there, he might wake up and discover it was no more than a dream. Two days later, he took up residence in the manor house and discovered the reality of his new circumstances.

Unoccupied for two years, the house had accumulated dust and dirt and cobwebs – and he didn't want to contemplate what else. He hired some women from the town to clean and as the grime disappeared, he began to see the numerous small repairs needed after so many months of neglect. Local tradesmen seemed eager for the work, though Will was certain that eagerness was spurred by curiosity about the new occupant. He didn't bargain but paid whatever they asked, even adding a bit extra if the work was particularly good or he thought the fee asked was too low. He didn't want to be known from the outset as the Miser of the Manor since his future prosperity would depend in large part on the goodwill of these people. And he was grateful every day for the king's generosity that allowed him to do right by them.

When the dust sheets were removed from the furniture, he found it quite to his liking. This could be a good life – and a comfortable one if he managed his assets properly. And if he didn't have a hard-bitten enemy in Sir Guy's widow.

He'd been able to avoid that confrontation while he was putting his new home in order, but he could postpone it no longer. And he thought he'd hit on a good pretext for calling on her.

Still wrestling with his anxiety, he realized people would soon begin to notice he was just standing there like a common vagrant, so he knocked on the door. Hurried footsteps heralded the arrival of a plump woman wearing an apron, clearly a servant, who stood in the open doorway and looked him up and down before asking, "Who might you be?"

"Sir William Makepeace. I'm looking for Mistress Bickerstaffe. Have I found the right place?"

The servant hesitated and from somewhere inside came another female voice. "Best let him in, Mary. We can't be rude to the new lord of the manor."

Mary stepped back to let him in then ushered him to a room that opened off the entry hall – a comfortably appointed sitting room with a small fire in the hearth to ward off the late winter chill. Beside the hearth sat one of the most beautiful women Will had ever seen. A woman so lovely that, in other circumstances, he'd have been inclined to make overtures. Instead, he bowed his head to her and said, "Far from a lord, ma'am. Just a simple knight."

"You? A knight?" her tone dripped sarcasm. This was going to be more difficult than Will had thought. "My husband said you weren't fit to clean his boots, but the king's made you a knight?"

Will was still standing, and Mary lurked behind him in the doorway. *Ready to throw me out if her mistress gives the order?* he wondered.

Then Guy's widow sat up straighter in her chair and appeared to shake off her mood. "We have a guest, Mary, and must be hospitable. Bring some wine, if you will, and then fetch me my sewing box."

Mary bobbed a little curtsey then scurried away, returning in short order with two glasses and a pitcher of wine. She filled their glasses then scurried away again, this time without the curtsey.

Through all this performance, no further words passed between hostess and guest, leaving Will rather puzzled. The woman took a sip of her wine then finally acknowledged him again. "I don't mean to be rude, sir. Please . . . take a seat." Will complied. "It's only that this has all been so sudden and so unexpected. I've only just adjusted to being a widow, and now my husband's nemesis appears on my doorstep – and not just on my doorstep but as my overlord – reminding me that *he's* survived and prospered while Guy lies in a grave in some faraway land, unmourned and unremembered."

Will sipped his wine. He hadn't expected this to be easy. Neither had he expected such vitriol. Perhaps if he made his request. "The reason for my visit today, madam, is that I'm now sufficiently settled in that I'm in need of a housekeeper, and—"

She bristled and slammed her glass down, sloshing most of the wine onto the table. "And you have the *audacity* to suggest that I might—" The color began rising from her neck to her face.

How does this keep going so wrong? "Please, madam," he interrupted her. "Please hear me out. What I was wondering is if you might advise me . . . if you know of someone in the town who would be suitable. Reliable, trustworthy . . . someone who knows how to run a household. It's not a talent I possess. I'm given to understand you've lived here for some number of years, so I thought only to ask for your help."

As the color began to recede from the woman's cheeks, Mary returned with the sewing box. "Just leave it on the table, Mary. And I've made rather a mess of things." She gestured to the spilled wine. "I'm sorry."

Mary lifted the corner of her apron and wiped away the mess before refilling her mistress's glass. "There be anything else, ma'am?"

"That's all for now."

"Ye just ring the bell if ye need anything, mistress." Mary bobbed another curtsey then scurried out once more. Will was beginning to think of her as a squirrel without a tail – or maybe the tail was hidden somewhere beneath her voluminous skirt.

It also seemed to Will as if that little interlude had broken the tension. Guy's widow lifted her glass, sipped her wine, then set the glass gently on the table. When she returned her gaze to him, the anger had been replaced by something a bit more pleasant. "I've made quite a mess of our first meeting as well, Sir William. And for that I must apologize."

"Perhaps I bear some of the blame. Perhaps I should have written to you first with my request."

"And perhaps we should deal with the past before we contemplate the future." She reached for the sewing box and rummaged among its contents to retrieve a folded page with a wax seal. "Guy always believed there'd eventually be a time when you'd have to come home – come to him with your tail between your legs looking for help – and he'd finally get his retribution. When he left for Gascony, he left this for you." She extended the letter and he took it, turning it over and over in his hands, thoughts turning over and over in his mind about what it might contain. After a long moment, he opened it.

> *Will,*
>
> *If you're reading this, it's because I've met my end without seeing you again. But don't think you haven't been on my mind every day since you disappeared from Berkeley and took my honor, my career as a knight, everything I valued in life with you.*
>
> *It also means you're almost certainly with Caitríona, my wife. I saved her from a life in the London Stews, and she mustn't ever return.*
>
> *You can never make amends for what you did to me. I'll go to my grave cursing your name to God, the devil, and anyone else who'll listen. So if you want to avoid those curses, take care of Caitríona. It's the last thing I'll ever ask of you. For her sake, don't refuse.*
>
> *Guy*

He folded the page and looked up at her. "Have you read this?"

"He showed it to me before he sealed it. He wanted me to know, if you ever came, what he'd asked of you."

"It's hard to imagine he hated me this much after all this time."

"Guy was . . ." She hesitated, contemplating her next words. ". . . a difficult man. When he returned from France and took me away from the bath house, he seemed much older than when he'd left – and quite world-weary. He found a priest who would marry us straightaway and brought me here. On the journey, he told me some of what had happened between you, but I always knew he held most of it back." She paused for a sip of wine before continuing. "I hoped he might become happier in time."

"When I knew Guy," Will said, "he never seemed to know *how* to be happy."

"That didn't change. If anything, he grew even more bitter. He felt he'd been betrayed by everyone – by Lord Berkeley, by you, by someone called Aldwin, and by Lord Montagu. But most of all, by you, Sir William."

"Call me Will."

She didn't acknowledge the invitation. "Guy won enough prizes in tournaments for us to live quite comfortably. But because he was so consumed by his resentments, we never had what I would call a happy life. Even so, he had rescued me from a life I loathed, and for that I was grateful."

"And you needn't fear ever having to return to that life."

"You fear Guy's curses that much?"

"Quite the contrary. It's simply the right thing to do."

"A truce then?" she asked.

"If that's what you want. But I'd prefer a friendship."

Finally, she smiled. "Then perhaps you should call me Caitrìona."

The Fieschi Letter

A translation from the original Latin. Images of the actual letter are available on Wikipedia, at the Auramala Project, and in Kathryn Warner's book *Long Live The King: The Mysterious Fate of Edward II*.

In the name of the Lord, Amen. Those things that I have heard from the confession of your father I have written with my own hand and afterwards I have taken care to be made known to your highness.

First he says that feeling England in subversion against him, afterwards on the admonition of your mother, he withdrew from his family in the castle of the Earl Marshal by the sea, which is called Chepstow. Afterwards, driven by fear, he took a barque with lords Hugh Despenser and the Earl of Arundel and several others and made his way by sea to Glamorgan, and there he was captured, together with the said Lord Hugh and Master Robert Baldock; and they were captured by Lord Henry of Lancaster, and they led him to the castle of Kenilworth, and others were [held] elsewhere at various places; and there he lost the crown at the insistence of many. Afterwards you were subsequently crowned on the feast of Candlemas next following. Finally they sent him to the castle of Berkeley.

Afterwards the servant who was keeping him, after some little time, said to your father:

Lord, Lord Thomas Gurney and Lord Simon Bereford, knights, have come with the purpose of killing you. If it pleases, I shall give you my clothes, that you may better be able to escape.

Then with the said clothes, at twilight, he went out of the prison; and when he had reached the last door without resistance, because he was not recognised, he found the porter sleeping, whom he quickly killed; and having got the keys of the door, he opened the door and went out, with his keeper who was keeping him. The said knights who had come to kill him, seeing that he had thus fled, fearing the indignation of the queen, even the danger to their persons, thought to put that aforesaid porter, his heart having been extracted, in a box, and maliciously presented to the queen the heart and body of the aforesaid porter as the body of your father, and as the body of the said king the said porter was buried in Gloucester.

And after he had gone out of the prisons of the aforesaid castle, he was received in the castle of Corfe with his companion who was keeping him in the prisons by Lord Thomas, castellan of the said castle, the lord being ignorant, Lord John Maltravers, lord of the said Thomas, in which castle he was secretly for a year and a half.

Afterwards, having heard that the Earl of Kent, because he said he was alive, had been beheaded, he took a ship with his said keeper and with the consent and counsel of the said Thomas, who had received him, crossed into Ireland, where he was for – nine months.

Afterwards, fearing lest he be recognised there, having taken the habit of a hermit, he came back to England and proceeded to the port of Sandwich, and in the same habit crossed the sea to – Sluys. Afterwards he turned his steps in Normandy and from Normandy as many do, going across through Languedoc, came to Avignon, where, having given a florin to the servant of the pope, sent by the said servant a document to Pope John, which pope had him called to him, and held him secretly and honourably more than fifteen days. Finally, after various discussions, all things having been considered, permission having been received, he went to Paris, and from Paris to Brabant, from Brabant to Cologne so that out of devotion he might see The Three Kings, and leaving Cologne he crossed over Germany, that is to say, he headed for Milan in Lombardy, and from Milan he entered a certain hermitage of the castle of Melazzo, in which hermitage he stayed for two years and a half; and because war overran the said castle, he changed himself to the castle of Cecima in another hermitage of the diocese of Pavia in Lombardy, and he was in this last hermitage for two years or thereabouts, always the recluse, doing penance and praying God for you and other sinners.

In testimony of which I have caused my seal to be affixed for the consideration of Your Highness. Your Manuele de Fieschi, notary the lord pope, your devoted servant.

Author's Notes

Historical Notes

When the facts of a time long past are in dispute, incomplete, or inconclusive, that's the space within which a novelist can weave a tale. And few events in history have as much potential uncertainty as the fate of Edward II of England.

It has been said that historical fiction is the small story told against the backdrop of the larger epic of history. That's precisely what I've tried to achieve in this novel. My tale of the conflict between Will Makepeace and his cousin, Sir Guy Bickerstaffe, takes place in the decade from 1327 to 1338 – a decade in which Edward II may have been murdered or may have survived to live out his days as described in the Fieschi letter. There is as yet no incontrovertible proof one way or the other.

Recent writers and historians (including Ian Mortimer, Kathryn Warner, and Alison Weir) have extensively examined primary sources and are inclined toward the view that Edward's survival is quite plausible and that there may even be stronger arguments for his survival than for his murder. Other historians are not yet swayed, and a couple even espouse the view that the Fieschi letter is no more than a blatant attempt to wring favors from Edward III. One thing everyone seems to agree on is that the lurid story that Edward II was murdered using a red-hot poker is purely a fabrication, written some fifty years after the fact by an individual intent on promoting Edward for sainthood.

Manuele Fieschi was a cleric in the papal administration, part of the legal branch and thus designated a "notary." At the time of this narrative, notaries were responsible for drawing up and certifying contracts, creating wills, ensuring proper bills of exchange for foreign transactions, recording important transactions and proceedings, and the like. In 1343, after leaving the papal service, Fieschi was made Bishop of Vercelli

I have mostly stayed true to the Fieschi letter, but have taken a couple of liberties for what I hope you'll agree are acceptable reasons. I've created a different scenario for Edward's escape on the night of the intended murder. First, it seems implausible that only a sleeping porter would stand between Edward and freedom. At a castle where such a valuable person was being detained, there would almost certainly have been sentries on duty around the clock. Second, the record is inconsistent on whether it was one, two, or six men in the murder party. And third, it seems implausible that, having been at Berkeley Castle for more than five months, Edward could move about and not be recognized. Please understand that I'm not making a judgment call on what Edward might have told Manuele Fieschi – merely taking a bit of artistic license for the benefit of the narrative.

The Fieschi letter also implies that Edward didn't leave Corfe Castle until after he learned of the execution of the Earl of Kent. I chose to have the catalyst for the departure be Kent's arrest as a way to set up the pursuit that follows. And the difference is only a matter of days.

One other bit of the timeline that I took some liberty with is the timing of William Shalford's letter to Roger Mortimer about a Welsh plot to free Edward. Having that letter arrive while Mortimer was still at Westminster allowed me to show Mortimer's increasing dominance of Isabella and to set up the young Edward III's growing awareness of the danger Mortimer posed. It was also a good way to introduce Edward III's special relationship with Lord Montagu, who would later be instrumental in the overthrow of Mortimer.

A few other items to note. John Maltravers was not actually made Baron Maltravers until 1329. Nor was he constable of Corfe Castle during the time of Edward's stay there – that was still Sir John Pecche. I've been unable to discover the surname of the "Lord Thomas" who was castellan at the time so have chosen one for him that is period-appropriate.

There is quite a bit of confusion around Lord Thomas Berkeley's role in the whole business. It's generally thought that Berkeley was away from home on the night of the supposed murder. Yet other bits of the record allege that it was Berkeley who dispatched Sir Thomas Gurney (who may also have been a member of the murder party) to inform Edward III of his father's death. And in the parliament of November 1330 Berkeley asserted that he had heard nothing about the death of Edward II until that very moment.

Some, including Ian Mortimer, speculate the whole thing might have been a huge conspiracy conducted by Berkeley and Maltravers – and possibly with Isabella's knowledge and support – to convey Edward II to a secret place and get him out of the minds of those who plotted to restore him to the throne by "conveniently" killing and burying him. Some even suggest the possibility that Edward III knew all that when he took control and started arresting Mortimer and his adherents and that putting Berkeley on trial was merely for show to be able to clear his name. While such a conspiracy might make for an interesting but different tale, I chose to adhere to the Fieschi letter.

Fieschi's short letter to Caernarfon is entirely my invention. It is not clear in the current debate how Caernarfon would have known where and when to meet with his son. I find it quite plausible that Fieschi might have engineered that meeting. As a notary in the papal court, he might very well have been aware of Emperor Ludwig's intent to make Edward III a vicar of the empire and realized this was an opportunity for father and son to meet. Unless he was acting on orders from the pope – which no one suggests – Fieschi would naturally have been very circumspect in his communications but could conceivably have moved the players into position.

I've used entirely secondary sources for the events and timeline in this novel. A good reference timeline appears at the beginning of Kathryn Warner's book *Long Live the King: The Mysterious Fate of Edward II*.

No one knows for certain when Edward of Caernarfon might have died if it wasn't in 1327, but there are clues it may have been in the autumn of 1341. Edward III did not make his heir Prince of Wales until 1343. There are many reasons why he might have chosen this time, but one possibility is that he waited until he knew his father, the first Prince of Wales, had died.

Niccolino Fieschi (a relative of Manuele) paid a visit to Edward III's court in November 1341. Might that have been to inform the king of his father's death?

The most convincing clue, though, comes from Isabella. In October 1341, she petitioned that two chaplains should say divine service in the chapel of Leeds Castle, praying for herself and her son, the king, and for their souls after death and also praying for the souls of Edward II and John of Eltham, Earl of Cornwall (the second son of Edward and Isabella who died in 1336). No record has yet been found of her ever having done something like this before. And she continued to do so regularly until her own death in 1358.

Place Names

Just as the English language has evolved over the centuries and spelling has become standardized, so have the names of some towns, villages, streets, and the like changed with the passage of time. Sometimes the reasons for the change are documented in the historical record; in other cases, we may not know why. All the towns, villages, streets, castles, monasteries, and churches mentioned are real places that existed at the time of the narrative. I've used the 14th-century names insofar as I've been able to determine them. Some are, in fact, unchanged from then until the present day. Here are those you might not recognize (given in alphabetical order rather than the order in which they appear in the story).

Bewsfield, in Kent, dates back to Roman times and also saw Saxon settlements there. Its church was originally 10th-century Saxon, with significant refurbishing done in Norman times. In the 17th century it became known as Whytefield, which eventually led to the current name of Whitfield. During the Black Death, the inhabitants relocated the village a bit to the west, presumably to get away from the perceived danger of living near the burial sites of plague victims. The location of Bewsfield in the 14th century is known today as Church Whitfield.

Bredeford, in Hampshire, first appeared in the records in 1281. It grew up around and took its name from Brydrs Ford on the River Blackwater. Today, the village is known as Blackwater.

Cambridge. Britain is an ancient land where, for millennia, those who lived in one part of the island had little or no congress with those in other parts. So it should be no surprise that multiple geographical features of the same name exist in disparate places. As an example, there are nine rivers on the island of Great Britain named Avon, an ancient Celtic word meaning "river." Likewise, there are two rivers named Cam. The most familiar flows through Bedfordshire and Cambridgeshire and is associated with the university city of Cambridge. There is, however, another River Cam located in Gloucestershire and a much smaller hamlet of Cambridge located on the main road between Gloucester and Bristol. This is the Cambridge that figures in this narrative.

Cheping Blandford is known today as Blandford Forum. It's a market town at what was originally a ford on the River Stour (cheping or chipping being derived from the Old English word *ceping*, which means market.) I've not found the exact date when the new name came into use, though that may have happened when the town was rebuilt after it was almost totally destroyed in the Great Fire of 1731.

New Street in Holborn is now known as Chancery Lane. When Henry II and Henry III banned the teaching of civil law within the city of London, the schools for and practitioners of civil law decamped to Holborn – outside the city walls – where the Inns of Court and Inns of Chancery remain to this day. Chancery Lane was still a new street in the 14th century – hence the name.

Sheen. The town of Richmond, in the London Borough of Richmond upon Thames, was originally called Shene (or Sceon or Sheen or Scheanes – that evolution of language and spelling thing at work). I've settled on Sheen, since it makes pronunciation obvious. The manor house at Sheen became a royal residence when Edward I took his court there in 1299. It was given by Edward III to his mother, Isabella, in 1327. Edward III eventually died there, and Richard II actually made Sheen his primary residence.

Sutton was the original name of what we now know as Plymouth. The name wasn't officially changed until a charter granted by Henry VI in 1440. The area known today as Sutton Harbor was originally called Sutton Pool.

Warre Wyke (in Gloucestershire) was recorded in the Domesday Book (1086) as "Wichen." The name changed when King John gifted the manor to the la Warre family. Over time, the name evolved to become the present-day Wickwar – not to be confused with Warwick, in Warwickshire.

Wykinglowe. In the 12th century, the Irish town of Wicklow was known as Wykinglo, and by the 14th century, the spelling had evolved to Wykinglowe. Though the town had an Irish (Gaelic) name – Cill Mhantáin – this book takes place after the Anglo-Norman invasion of Ireland, so I've chosen to use the Anglo-Norman name.

The Cinque Ports

The Confederation of the Cinque Ports was established by Edward the Confessor in the middle of the 11th century and still exists today, though changes in the coastline over the centuries mean that some of the towns are actually inland today. The main ports (hence the name Cinque – French for five) were, west to east, Hastings, New Romney, Hythe, Dover, and Sandwich. Other coastal towns were part of the confederation. The website Open Sandwich has a nice explanation and history of the Cinque Ports at http://www.open-sandwich.co.uk/town_history/cinqueports.htm. I also found a nice animated map https://www.tekportal.net/cinque-ports/ that shows what the coastline and the port towns would have been like in Edward's time and today.

Dates and Days of the Week

It should be noted that the modern Gregorian calendar did not come into effect until October 1582, much later than the events in this book. I found this site – https://www.dayoftheweek.org/ extremely useful to match dates in the historical record to day of the week. Admittedly, it's based on the Gregorian calendar, but the second paragraph in the entry for any given date provides the day of the week in the Julian calendar. And at the bottom of any individual date entry is a link to a full-year monthly calendar for the year in question. Just shift the first day of the week from Sunday to Monday and you've got the Julian version.

Language

One of the delights of writing historical fiction is exploring the language of the time. Sometimes it's easy to see the direct path from a medieval word or expression to the modern one, as in the case of "to have bees in one's head" leading to today's "to have a bee in one's bonnet." Now and then, I've come across a medieval word that's even more evocative than its modern counterpart. These days, we'd call someone who was making absolutely no contribution to the situation "a waste of space." In the 14th century, that person would be described as a cumberworld – not just a waste of the space they're occupying but an encumbrance on the entire world. Now, *that's* an insult.

In working on this book, I found a phrase that rocketed to the top of my favorites. You might not realize that "chasing one's tail" (to describe futile activity) is quite modern. Its first documented use is 1963. But humans have been describing the phenomenon for centuries. And in the 14th century, they would have said someone was "shoeing the goose." The modern cat/dog imagery is fun. But what an amazing picture shoeing a goose conjures up!

The Papal Palace (Palais des Papes) in Avignon

Pope John XXII resided in the Episcopal Palace in Avignon, which he had renovated and expanded to luxurious standards, beginning in 1316. This is the residence Edward II would have visited in 1331. The building we see today is an entirely different structure. It was conceived by John's successor,

Benedict XII, who envisioned a papal residence that was more austere and more resembled a fortress.

Construction on the new palace began during Benedict's pontificate and the old one was gradually demolished as space was needed for the new. Benedict's successor, Clement VI greatly expanded the new palace, essentially doubling its size, and enhanced the decoration. The palace we see today was finally completed during the pontificate of Innocent VI (1352-1362). Here and there in the palace we can now visit are bits of remains of John's original palace, though they were repurposed in the new construction. I've taken the liberty of appropriating a few descriptions of the current palace as stand-ins for John's lavish residence since its appearance in the novel is quite limited.

What is now a spacious plaza in front of the Palais des Papes was, at the time of this story, a crowded area of houses and their gardens, small orchards, and vegetable plots. *Champeaux* had the meaning "small fields."

Odds and Ends

Let's start with the obvious: how to pronounce Fieschi. So herewith, a mini-lesson on Italian pronunciation. The "ch" is pronounced exactly like the English letter "k." Each vowel is pronounced independently. In Italian, the letter "i" sounds a bit like the English "ee" while the Italian "e" is pronounced "eh." So, putting it all together, we get Fee-ESS-kee (emphasis on the ESS syllable).

I've had no luck finding information on tide times in the 14th century, though I admit my research was hardly exhaustive. As an approximation for the tides at Sandwich when Will and his companions set sail, I've used the tides for Dover on 15 December 2022. This is likely incorrect, but it's good enough for fiction.

The Florentine florin was something of a universal currency at the time, particularly for trade. In 1300, the florin was valued at 10 shillings so was equivalent to half a pound. By 1400, thanks to the impact of the Hundred Years War, the value of a florin had risen to 22 shillings. Since the Hundred

Years War didn't begin until 1337, I've assumed moderate inflation and valued a florin at 12 shillings in 1330.

Duifje is Dutch for dove. I loved the irony of an angry Bickerstaffe pursuing his quarry on a ship named for the bird of peace.

The Cologne Cathedral has the dubious distinction of the longest time from laying of the foundation stone to final completion of any cathedral in the world – 632 years. Begun in 1248, it wasn't finally completed until 1880. By the time of this story, the eastern arm was complete and in use, having been consecrated in 1322 and sealed off from the on-going construction by a temporary wall.

Acknowledgments

This is a work of fiction set against the backdrop of the mystery surrounding the fate of Edward II of England. For my research, I've relied on secondary sources, but have chosen sources that have comprehensive bibliographies that include primary sources as well as the writings of scholars who have delved into the period and the events. To develop the chronology of this story, I've relied on translations of the Fieschi letter available from numerous sources and on the following works:

Long Live The King: The Mysterious Fate of Edward II, Kathryn Warner, The History Press, 2017. This book has an excellent timeline at the very beginning that helped me stay on track with the known events that were happening in England during the years in which my story takes place.

Edward II: The Unconventional King, Kathryn Warner, Amberley Publishing, 2014.

Queen Isabella, Alison Weir, Ballantine Books, 2005.

Kathryn Warner's Blog "Edward II,"
http://edwardthesecond.blogspot.com/

"A note on the deaths of Edward II," Ian Mortimer
https://www.ianmortimer.com/EdwardII/death.htm

Weir's book – and her assertion that the evidence for a different understanding of Edward's fate bore marks of credibility – first planted the seed in my mind that there was a tale to be woven amid the gaps and questions raised by the Fieschi letter.

As with all my books set in the 14th century, I rely on a variety of sources, both online and in print. "List of price of medieval items," from Kenneth Hodges at the University of California Davis, was particularly helpful as it included not only a wide variety of items from household goods to cloth and clothing to tradesmen's tools to animals and armor and rents and wages along with a documented date for the price shown. And for a broad cross-section of daily life in those times, one can't go wrong with Ian Mortimer's *The Time Traveler's Guide to Medieval England*. Written in the style of a tourist guide (such as the Michelin or Fodor's guides or Rick Steves's guides and videos), it's a lot of fun as well as being quite well researched.

As always, I'm grateful to my editor, Linda Kirwin. We've worked together since my very first novel, and her insights always make my work better. I hope she's willing to keep editing as long as I continue writing.

Thanks also to my publisher, Black Rose Writing, not only for taking a chance on me in the first place but also for supporting me to take a step aside from my series (*The Second Son Chronicles*) to explore other facets of medieval and early Renaissance history.

ABOUT THE AUTHOR

Pamela Taylor brings her love of history to the art of storytelling. An avid reader of historical fact and fiction, she finds the past offers rich sources for character, ambiance, and plot that allow readers to escape into a world totally unlike their daily lives. She shares her home with two Pembroke Welsh Corgis who remind her frequently that a dog walk is the best way to find inspiration for that next chapter.

Other Titles by Pamela Taylor

The Second Son Chronicles

Second Son

My Father, My King

Pestilence

Upon This Throne

Shadows

The Weight of the Crown

Destiny

A Feeling in the Bones

The Burden of Choice

Note from Pamela Taylor

Word-of-mouth is crucial for any author to succeed. If you enjoyed *The Rest of His Days*, please leave a review online—anywhere you are able. Even if it's just a sentence or two. It would make all the difference and would be very much appreciated.

Thanks!
Pamela Taylor